The Field of GOLD

The Field of
GOLD

ROBERT BURTON

Contents

Part 1: The Present Time 9

   Chapter 1: In the Beginning 11

   Chapter 2: Help is at Hand..18

   Chapter 3: The Archaeology Begins 26

Part 2: The Conclusion of World War Two 35

   Chapter 1: Oxhill Gets a New Arrival 37

   Chapter 2: Discovering the Village 43

   Chapter 3: The Cousins 51

   Chapter 4: The Planning Starts 57

   Chapter 5: Night Flights 64

   Chapter 6: Back to the Drawing Board................................75

   Chapter 7: Second Lyon Trip 80

   Chapter 8: Lyon – Grusiner – Lyon 88

   Chapter 9: Oxhill Gold 97

   Chapter 10: The Present Time..106

Part 3: The Templars 1307 – 1308 109

   Chapter 1: Collecting the Rent 111

   Chapter 2: To London for Orders 118

   Chapter 3: Going for a Journey in Paris 124

   Chapter 4: 12th October 1307 132

   Chapter 5: Journey to Chartres 137

   Chapter 6: Chartres to Tours...145

   Chapter 7: Tours to La Rochelle 154

   Chapter 8: A Stormy Return...162

Chapter 9: The Last Leg...169

Chapter 10: 1308 and Finality.....................................173

Chapter 11: The Present Time....................................178

Part 4: Roman Britain Circa 230AD...........................181

Chapter 1: Fighting for My Life and Reputation.............183

Chapter 2: The Farewell Tour (5 Years Earlier) 190

Chapter 3: The Planning 197

Chapter 4: It's All Coming Together (One Year On)..........204

Chapter 5: Invaders (Another Year On) 208

Chapter 6: Squaring the Circle....................................217

Chapter 7: The Present Time.......................................223

Part 5: The First English Civil War, 1642....................227

Chapter 1: The Tower of London 229

Chapter 2: The Route to Oxford 235

Chapter 3: Powick Bridge 243

Chapter 4: Plans to Return to Oxhill 250

Chapter 5: Oxhill in October 1642 255

Chapter 6: The Battle of Edgehill................................262

Chapter 7: The Present Day...267

Part 6: Viking Times 269

Chapter 1: Life in Ribe 271

Chapter 2: Sailing Forth...276

Chapter 3: Battle of Ipswich.......................................284

Chapter 4: The Aftermath of Ipswich 292

Chapter 5: A New Learning Circle...............................298

Chapter 6: Winter in London 305

Chapter 7: A Visit from Birger 310

Chapter 8: Battle of Chippenham 314

Chapter 9: The Battle of Edington 322

Chapter 10: Helga Gets a Visit 328

Epilogue 333

The Present Time: Church Farm, Oxhill..............335

Main Characters...342

Present Time 342

World War II..345

The Templars 349

Roman Times 352

The English Civil War..354

The Vikings – Great Heathen Army 356

PART 1
THE PRESENT TIME

Chapter 1
In the Beginning

My Samsung watch buzzed at me, as it always does at six-thirty in the morning, seven days a week, three hundred and sixty-five days a year. Rolling over, I swiped north on its face, but it made no difference; it kept bleeping and vibrating, making sure that I was fully awake before conforming to my instructions.

I sat up on the edge of the bed, stretched, and looked at the curtained window, seeing a brightness that could only mean that the sun was shining. It shouldn't have been if I were to believe the weather forecast from the previous night; a low weather system was meant to be moving in from the west and should have arrived, bringing its westerly winds and an expected ten millimetres of rain. The ground certainly needed it, and I was hoping that it would have fallen during the night so there was time for it to seep into the ground before the sun started its evaporation process.

I am a farmer, so the weather is important to me. I could be the best or worst farmer in the country but, without the help of the elements, my efforts would be in vain. I know we have a reputation for blaming everything on the weather but to an extent it is true. I could prepare my land, plant and cultivate the seeds and look after the livestock to the best of my ability, but drought and flooding, heatwaves and gales will affect the yields. Unfortunately, yields affect my bank balance and my ability to look after my family.

With these dreary thoughts, I padded downstairs and put the kettle on the Aga before returning upstairs to shower, shave, and start the day. I wetted the tea and went through to the boot room to get my morning welcome from Asher and Mels, my two collie bitches - and companions - during my working day.

"Come on, girls, out you go before breakfast!" I said to them and watched them lope out of the back door into the yard beyond. I followed them out and walked across the yard and through the gate that took me onto the lawn that formed the majority of our garden. Looking up towards the west, I could see a grey line in the distance, a definite demarcation between the blue of the sky above and the approaching rain. *OK, weather forecasters, you got it right, just a little later than you predicted.*

I returned to the kitchen, poured myself a cup of tea and sat down at the large table that dominated the centre of the room. The kitchen, as in many farmhouses, is our nerve centre, the place where Sandy, my wife, and I plan our lives, make the decisions that affect our livelihood, and the room that we spend most of our time in. Yes, there are other rooms downstairs: a dining room that is generally only used of a Sunday when we have one of our sets of parents over for a family meal, a living room where we might retire after Sunday lunch and which we decorate for Christmas but was, at that time, in reality a playroom for Michael and Sean, our two boys, and their computer games. There used to be an office as well but when we moved in, nearly two years before this story begins, I had knocked down the partition wall that divided it from the kitchen so that, if I had to use the computer, I was still in the family hub. It works well with the amount of bureaucratic paperwork that goes with a modern farm and means that I can take advantage of the heat from the Aga and not heat another room.

Having checked the weather on my tablet and briefly looked at the news headlines while I had my tea, I got up and started to prepare breakfast for the family. The boys were easy; two bowls, two spoons, two glasses and boxes of cereal. For Sandy and me, it was toast and tea; not a gastronomic delight, but a working breakfast before we all started our separate days. I had just finished when I heard the sound of the morning race down the stairs - the winner wouldn't have to clear up the table and load the dishwasher.

"Morning, boys. What time does your cricket start, Micky?" Our eldest son had a cricket match against Bloxham that afternoon.

"I think it is a two o'clock start and just a forty-over match."

"I hope this weather front moves through before then, or you will be sitting in the pavilion all afternoon."

"I thought you said that it was coming in the night."

"It was meant to, but it must have missed the bus, which is what you two will do if you don't get a move on."

"Ah, Dad, we've got plenty of time, Robbie hasn't texted yet." They had somehow persuaded one of their friends who lived in the next village to text them when the school bus arrived there so that they knew when it was five minutes away.

"I'm not worried today," Sandy said, looking up from her telephone where she was typing something, "I've got to go to Kineton first before going to work, so I can drop them off."

"Thanks, Mum. Micky do you want a quick three-lap race?" Sean asked his brother.

"No way, boys. Just because your Mum is giving you a lift to school doesn't mean that you can boot up the PlayStation. Micky, is your kit all clean and ready? Sean, now you have got an extra five minutes can you fill up the dumper for Greg? I noticed it was getting a bit low yesterday." Sean, who was ten years old, had just grown tall enough to be able to drive the dumper truck around the farm. To him, it was a McLaren or Williams F1 car; it was the first thing that he had been allowed to drive, but it didn't do much more than ten miles an hour, and, once he had mastered the steering from the back wheels, he couldn't go too far wrong. It was his bit of direct involvement with the farm and whereas he loved it, Michael was totally different from him; hitting or kicking a ball was the most important thing, the farm was just somewhere he lived.

"Darling, I've left a pie in the fridge for you and Greg for lunch. It just needs to go into the Aga for twenty minutes. Right boys, are you ready?"

After everyone had left, I started to go across the farmyard when I saw Greg arrive in his black Citroen van. He was our only employee, and I had inherited him with the farm. In his fifties, six foot four and a former second row for the county, he had worked on the farm since he left school, knew every inch of the six hundred acres, what worked and what didn't. In my first year, I had come to respect his local knowledge of the farm, our neighbours, and the village. He might have been a terror on the rugby field in his youth, but I saw a mild-mannered man who cared deeply about the farm and its prosperity, was a superb stockman, and probably more loyal to the land than to me, the farmer.

"Morning, Greg, it looks like a wet one. When you have finished the pigs, can we go down to the bottom field on the Whatcote Road? I want to have a look at those patches below the copse that was almost barren last year."

"Those bits in Army Field, they have always been like that, Geoff, as long as I can remember."

"Well, I'm thinking of getting a survey done, just to see if there is anything odd that we can't see."

"OK, I should be done by about ten."

I left him and walked down to the new cattle shed to check on the heifers and to feed them. When I say new, to my knowledge it was built about twenty years ago, but everyone still called it "new."

We both got on with our normal morning routines: working separately, feeding, mucking out, inspecting, just doing our jobs until I went back to the house to put on the kettle to make tea for us both. It was a morning tradition that had gradually evolved - I would make the tea and put out a plate of biscuits for me and Greg to sit down to while we chatted, usually about sports or local news; it was good-natured, and friendly, giving us a chance to warm up in winter or cool down in summer.

"So, you think that there might be something down in Army Field?" he questioned when he had come in, removed his boots, and sat down at the table.

"I don't know. Can you remember when I took my metal detector down there last autumn? There was a reading, but it was very faint. I dug down about a foot and it was still there, but I didn't find anything."

"I remember the stories from when I was a kid that there was an army camp there during the war."

"What, the Second World War?"

"No, the Civil one, although I know the Americans did build a runway down there during the last one."

"A runway! I never knew that."

"It wasn't a proper runway, but a grass one. You can still see it where the earth is more compacted. They used to fly small, light aircraft from there. I remember my Mum saying it was used to fly people into France."

"Well, I can't see that affecting my yield, but you say that there was a Civil War camp there?"

"They say that's why it is called Army Field, but I imagine one side or the other probably camped in most fields around here at some stage."

"It makes sense."

"There were many a story about some of the land around here: Army Camps, Roman Villas, even a Cistercian Abbey in the village."

"You sound like the local history teacher this morning," I joked.

"Just look where we are! The Fosse Way is, what, five miles to the north, Edgehill is just over there… We're in the middle of the country, we've got Warwick, Stratford, and Leamington within a day's ride. I should think just about every army, every circus, and every religious group has passed through here at some stage, telling us what to do and what not to do."

"You have a point. You never know, we might have treasure buried in the field," I said, laughing.

"That's one bet I'm not going to waste my money on."

"Well, if we ever find an X marking a chest of gold in

that field, I promise I will send you to New Zealand, first class package, to see as much of the rugby World Cup as you want to see."

"Do you notice something? I'm not rushing to get my spade," he chuckled.

Half an hour later, I parked my truck in the gateway of the field on the Whatcote Road, opened the gate and followed one of the tracks made by the sprayer through the rape that was just beginning to come into flower. It was a new experiment for the farm to grow rape. For some reason, it had never been tried before. We both inspected the plants on either side of us, looking at the delicate yellow flower that would turn into long, black seed pods to be harvested.

The field was basically L-shaped, going around a copse that had been used in the past for breeding and cultivating pheasants. One side of the L ran alongside the road which we had driven down, then down a small hill to the gateway I had parked in. The other side of the L ran away from the road. Now that I stood there, I could see that it might have made a runway for a small, light aircraft; this side of the field ran roughly east-west, which made sense for the prevailing wind. As I entered the field, I looked back up the hill to my right, where I could see a good, even covering of green stalks and yellow flowers, and to my left, where I could clearly make out the edge of the field and the stream that marked it. We walked away from the road until we were in the shadow of the copse some twenty feet above us. Between where we stood and the bottom of the hill there were four large patches of bare earth where nothing grew in exactly the same place they had been the previous year.

"Greg, I didn't plot exactly where they were last year, but I reckon they are in the same place."

"Oh yes, they are there every year. Sam just accepted them, and I never thought too much about them." Sam McNally had been the previous farmer who had retired to a more peaceful life somewhere on the south coast.

We waded through to one of the patches, an area about the

size of two double beds and clearly defined. The soil looked the same as the rest of the field, slightly reddish brown in colour, and slightly wetter in texture, but that could be explained as it was at the bottom of the hill. I took out one of the containers I had brought with me and filled it with the soil, then I moved to an area where the crop was unaffected and did the same.

"I'll get these tested as a starter, but I think I know what the answer will be. There must be something down there that is causing this."

"Don't get me wrong, Geoff, but how much are you actually losing with these four patches?"

"I know, it's not going to make a difference in the grand scheme of things, but I guess I don't like things I don't understand."

When we got back to the farm, Greg went off to do some maintenance whilst I divided the two soil containers, kept half to do some tests on them myself, and packaged up the other half to send to Agricultural Supply Services in Gloucester for them to analyse.

Chapter 2
Help is at Hand

Although we had only come to the village just under two years before, we had been made very welcome when we'd moved in, and it certainly had helped to keep Greg on. Oxhill was, like many villages in the area, one that was in the middle of change. It was becoming more of a dormitory village where people lived but went to work in larger urban areas like Banbury to the south or travelled up the M40 to Birmingham and other large conurbations on its path. I made friends with both farming and non-farming families, I visited the Peacock, our local pub, and always found it to be a friendly, sociable pub. Our boys made friends at their school in Kineton, as children do, and in several cases, the parents of their friends became our friends.

Sandy probably knew more people in the village than I did, but this was because three or four other people at her work also lived here. It was a nice and easy introduction, but I found them to be slightly insular. Once they got home, they didn't really want to go out again, they didn't want to get involved in village life. Although it was before our time, there had once been two village shops, one with a post office, and another pub. Going further back, there had been a village fair once a year right opposite our driveway in one of our fields, known as The Green. This had been a great event where everyone who lived in the village got a day's holiday, much to the annoyance of those who worked in the village but lived in Tysoe, or Whatcote.

It wasn't dying, it was changing, and it was probably most noticeable in the pub. I remembered going to the Peacock when I worked on a farm on the other side of Kineton and it was a local in every sense of the word. Yes, it had a restaurant which served very good food, but in the main bar, either leaning against it or standing in front of the large open fire, everyone seemed to be included in the conversation. I agree that it now attracted more people from outside the village, but it had to, or it would have gone under; I preferred to have a village pub with people from outside visiting, than no pub.

I was thinking these thoughts as I walked down our back drive, passing the eastern end of St Lawrence's Church, and joined Main Street by The Old Rectory, on my way to the said pub.

"Hello, Geoff, what can I get you?"

"A pint of the usual, please, Kevin."

"Did I see you down at the Army Field this morning? I have to say, that rape looks good all coming along together."

"You're the second person to call that field the Army Field today. I never knew it had a name."

"I've always known it as that. I suppose Greg was the other person."

"Correct in one. What can you tell me about it?"

He placed the pint on the bar in front of me and said, "I don't know, I've always known it as that. I think that it goes back to the Civil War, probably just a story."

Kevin went off to serve someone else and left me thinking. *What were the chances of one of my fields having been used in both the Second World War and the Civil War?*

I was still thinking about this when The Major tapped me on the shoulder.

"A penny for them, Geoff." The Major, or, to give him his proper title, Major John Harker, lived in Oxhill Manor. He was in his eighties, I supposed, retired and a genial gentleman who supported most local activities as if he were some sort of titular village head.

"Nothing important, Major. I was just thinking about Army Field and its history."

"Now, if a field could speak, I bet that one would have a few stories to tell."

"Why do you say that?"

"We moved here just before the Second World War when I was 7 or 8. The village was a different place then. I remember them flattening out that field. Before, it had a curved base, like an elongated saucer, but they widened the area between the bottom of the hill and the stream. It was funny because they didn't build any structures; the comms tower was a trailer, and all they had was two other trailers or large caravans, really, to act as messes for the pilots and ground crew. When it wasn't being used, they towed the lot away and brought it back again for another mission."

"What did they use it for?"

"It was very "hush, hush" if you know what I mean. I never really knew, but it was said to be used to fly clandestine missions to Normandy; I supposed to drop off and pick up operatives, if you know what I mean."

"But that isn't why it's called Army Field?"

"Oh, no, I think that dates back to the Civil War when one side or the other camped there. I don't remember which side it was. I always get a bit confused about who was who. History is not my thing. What's made you all interested in this?"

"It's probably nothing, but last year I noticed some small areas that were barren just under the copse. I originally thought they had been missed by the seed drill, but Greg said they were always there and today I went down there, and they are barren again."

"If Greg says that they are barren every year then there must be another explanation. He will know."

"Anyway, I've taken some soil samples and have sent them off. I guess we see what happens."

I finished my pint, said my goodbyes, and walked home to where cricket matches, Banbury office gossip, and general family life took over. It wasn't for another two weeks that I thought about my barren patches in Army Field and that was when the soil report came back.

It came as no real surprise that they were as mystified as I was. There was a long list of what they had found in all the samples, but what they had found was that all the samples were exactly the same. They could not find out why I would get plant growth from one and not another.

Our second summer on the farm was now upon us with a vengeance, and it was all systems go on it. It had been our first year of lambing earlier in the season and now we had stock to take to Banbury market to supplement the income from the pigs, which were our staple income providers. The rape seed had been harvested. For this year's harvest, I had contracted Dom Trethewey whose farm was between Whatcote and Idlicote with a good acreage of rape. He had the machinery to harvest the crop and the silos to dry and store it before its sale. Dom had been the reason I had dipped my toe into this experiment; I could honestly say that without his help, his mentoring, and his hardware I would not have tried it.

So, the Army Field had been harvested and was laid bare, but it was still in my mind at odd moments. One such moment was at a wedding we all attended for an old colleague of mine from Cirencester. Andy Eames had been my best friend at college, was Best Man at my wedding and also accepted our invitation to become Michael's Godfather, but we had taken different paths after leaving college. He had continued his academic life by doing a BA (Hons) degree at Oxford studying Archaeology and carried on in this line, working for various universities on various projects. Over the years we had probably only talked on the telephone three or four times a year, on birthdays and at Christmas, and only seen each other on occasions like this wedding. However, whenever we met or spoke it was as if it had only been a couple of days since the last time.

We were standing in the marquee at the beginning of the reception, both of us with a pint of bitter in our hand, discussing the service and the hotel where we were staying.

"So, how's the farm, now you're in your second year?"

"I'm not regretting it at all. We're certainly going to have to keep a hold on the purse strings for some years, but we knew that was going to be the case."

"What's the land like there? It's in the Vale of the Red Horse, isn't it?"

"Yes. Don't tell me you are planning a dig in the area."

"The plans aren't quite that far advanced yet, but I've been asked to do some preliminary work regarding Saxon Gods. One of them is "Tiw" or "Tiwaz" their horse God, and Tysoe was mentioned. I was going to ring you earlier this week but thought I would wait until I saw you here."

"That sounds interesting. If you are going to visit Tysoe and don't plan to come and see us, you can expect to see my truck coming to look for you! Tysoe isn't that large."

"Don't worry, if I'm in the area I will be packing an overnight bag and a bottle of whiskey."

"That sounds more like it. Actually, if you do come, I've got something to show you which has been in the back of my mind. I have a field called Army Field where there are four barren patches. Apparently, they have been there for as long as anyone can remember."

"Army Field, you say? Why's it called that?"

"I suspect the reason is lost in the mists of time, but some locals say that it was used as an army camp in the Civil War."

"Have you done any tests or anything?"

"Just some soil tests, but they are inconclusive."

"Sounds interesting, a second excuse to come for a visit."

We carried on chatting until Sandy dragged me off to meet some of her friends and, although we spent more time together later on that day, the subject hadn't been revisited. The next day, we were off early as I wanted to get back to the farm and Micky had a cricket match, so we left without seeing Andy, who was obviously sleeping off the effects of the night before.

The summer wore on and I had almost forgotten my conversation with him or that he might be coming to the area when he suddenly called one evening while I was trying to finish off combining one of the fields. I must admit, I wasn't really paying too much attention to what he was saying until he said, "Are you listening to me? All I seem to get is umms and ahhs. I said, is it all right if I come and stay for a couple of nights next week?"

"Sorry, mate, I'm in the combine just trying to finish this field before it starts to rain. Yes, next week will be great, what nights did you say?"

"Wednesday and Thursday. Don't worry about entertaining me during the day. I will be busy."

"OK, sorry about my lack of attention. I'll see you next week."

Andy telephoned again the following Monday, but this time he spoke to Sandy and confirmed he would be coming to stay on Wednesday night and return to London on Friday afternoon. I was still working when he arrived. The first time I saw him was when my truck came bouncing over the field towards me; I could tell it wasn't Sandy driving as she would have been more circumspect.

"Geoff, great to see you!" he said to my back as I climbed down the ladder from the combine harvester. "I arrived about an hour ago and couldn't wait any longer."

"Great to see you too, I've nearly finished up here, I'm just waiting for Greg to come back up with the trailer. How was your meeting in Tysoe?"

"Good, thank you, they want me to do an exploratory dig with a small team as soon as I can, so I guess you will be seeing me a lot more over the next month."

"All good. Look, here's Greg. Let's get the grain into the trailer, then I will show you around."

I sent Greg back to unload and parked the combine up in the corner of the field before getting behind the wheel of my truck.

"So, this is Kineton Road," I said turning left out of the field. "I don't actually own this field, but I've rented it for five years and the yields have been good, so far." We dropped down a small hill and entered the village, but instead of turning left to into the main village, I stayed on the same road heading towards Whatcote.

"I thought I'd show you the Army Field that we talked about at the wedding."

"Oh, yes, I remember that."

When we had got about halfway to Whatcote, I turned right off the road and drove into the field before I stopped.

"As far as I can make out, the flat area in front of us was a grass runway during World War Two and that wood up there on the right is where they used to breed the pheasants. It's the patches just below the wood, on that bank, which interest me. Shall we walk over to them?"

"So, tell me, what have you done with them?"

"Nothing, really. Last summer, I ran a metal detector over the largest without any really positive results and earlier this summer I sent off some soil samples which I can show you when we get back to the farm."

"Have you dug down at all?"

"No. Obviously, it has been ploughed most years, but as far as I know nothing has come up."

We arrived at the first of the patches and Andy got down on his haunches, rubbing his hands over the soil on top before sniffing his fingers. He then picked up a clod of earth, breaking it in his right hand. He then stood up and looked around, pointing to a large oak tree in the copse before turning round and looking towards the village of Whatcote.

"That's interesting, it might mean nothing, but it's interesting. Come and stand here. Now look at that tree, now turn round and what's directly in front of you?"

"Nothing, really."

"Now look again." He took my arm pointing towards the village in the near distance. "What do you see?"

"Whatcote."

"Yes, but what in particular?"

"I'm not with you."

"The church, you idiot. This spot is in a direct line between that tree and the church tower. It might be a coincidence, so now let's see if we can spot another two points to cross-reference." He looked around to see if he could find another two reference points. There were some grunts, some groans, and, finally, stillness before he did another two one hundred and eighty-degree turns.

"If you were to stand on the top of that hill, could you see Oxhill church?"

"I don't know, I've never been up there. Why?"

"If you had two people, one up there on the hill and the other down here. and the person down here lined himself up on the axis between the tree and Whatcote church, the other could then tell him where his axis crossed the axis between him and Oxhill church. Bingo, X marks the spot!"

"I don't know. We don't know if one can see Oxhill from up there, it's all a bit theoretical."

"Of course, it's theoretical. We don't know if anything is down there, but I'm just looking at a patch in the ground that is unusual and saying that it could be located again."

"I understand the triangulation but what are the odds?"

"I don't do odds, but what I would say is that I've signed off a dig on less evidence."

We walked back to the truck, both of us deep in thought. I was wondering why I hadn't seen what Andy had seen in five minutes, God knows what Andy was thinking.

That evening we didn't speak of the Army Field again. Sandy had prepared a great meal of gammon, new potatoes, and broad beans, all of which had been raised or grown on the farm. We talked about ancient gods, making TV programmes, farming, our son, and his godson. We caught up, we relaxed and we, probably, had too much to drink.

Chapter 3
The Archaeology Begins

I always find it a relief when the main harvest is over and the grain was in the barn, but it also begs the age-old question: sell or store? That year, I was going to have to do a bit of both as the yield meant that I couldn't store all of it safely, but the price at the time meant that I risked not getting the maximum return. It is always a juggling match and Sandy and I were going to have to sit down and bang our heads together over it. This is where I rely on her superior Excel skills as well as her financial management skills.

I had asked Brian Mansfield to come over to see us the next day and wanted to be ready for his visit. Brian worked for Midland Grain Merchants and, although I had known him for quite a few years from when I had worked on other farms, this was only the second year that making the final decision was up to me. We sat down after dinner to prepare for the meeting, both of us with laptops, and started by reviewing what we had done the year before. Sandy had been critical of my gung-ho attitude to the negotiations on my first attempt and had built a financial model so we could enter various parameters to see what the best result would be. Some of these variables were exactly that, variable. I would not know what the price would be in six months, or the cost of storing the grain, but we could play a game of "what if" until we were satisfied with the outcome.

Sandy had taken the day off for our meeting with Brian and we were both ready for him when he arrived, coffee made, laptops powered up, and hopefully brains in gear.

"Good morning, Geoff," he said, getting out of his car. "How's your second harvest gone?"

"Good morning, Brian. It will depend on whether you have brought your chequebook or not," I joked. "Where do you want to start?"

"Have you got it in all the usual places?" Brian was the grain merchant that Sam had used before I took over.

"Yes, but I am thinking of building a new silo for next year. I would like to talk to you about it at some stage."

"No problem," he said as we walked over to the main storage barn. "What sort of size are you thinking of?"

"I was thinking about four hundred tonnes."

We carried on talking as he inspected the wheat in the main barn, measured the moisture content, and tasted a few grains before he made some notes and pronounced his satisfaction.

We went inside and sat down at the kitchen table to start the real reason for his visit.

"Well, Geoff, we have got a few things we can do for you, but first, what kind of broad yields are we talking about?"

"I have taken Sandy's advice this year and have been more organised, but I reckon that we are talking between eight hundred and thirty to eight fifty tonnes in total."

"OK, for all of us, let's say eight fifty, it makes all the calculations easier. At the moment, we are seeing a bit of a spike in the price, it often happens at this time of year. Yesterday the price was two hundred and fifteen per tonne. We are expecting it to peak at about two twenty before dropping back."

The negotiations had started and went on for over an hour; how much we wanted to sell now, what price we would get for it, what would the future price look like and the cost of storage. As soon as Brian gave us a fact, Sandy entered it into the model, saving multiple scenarios to be discussed at a later date. We, and Brian, knew that we weren't going to conclude today. A pound either way on the price of wheat could mean about a thousand pounds in the bank, but he had given us options, and that was all I was asking for at that stage.

He left just before lunch and my head was just about to explode with all the information, not helped when Greg came in.

"I see Brian has gone, down the Plough I expect. It will be red wine if he thinks he has had one over you, or bitter if he thinks you have won."

"No decision, I'm afraid, but he came up with a few ideas. Was it always a "slam dunk" with Sam?"

"Well, Sam was a bit old-fashioned; he'd call Brian in after tea and set up the table with a pot of tea and a bottle of whiskey. More than likely, I'd be doing the stock on my own the next morning. Never take Brian on at poker or believe his handicap at golf: one is steadfast, and the other is fluid."

"He seems fair enough."

"Oh, he's fair enough as long as he ends up ahead."

"I take it that you have lost at both poker and on the course with him."

"No, I wouldn't say that, but the first time I played golf with him was at a charity event at Tadmarton. Having told us he played off twenty-four, he smoked one two hundred and fifty yards up the centre of the first. Forty-six points he ended up with. Bandit."

"Well, I'm not going to base my judgment on that; he isn't the first, and he certainly won't be the last to do it. Do you think Sam trusted him?"

"Oh, yes, I'm sure he did. He didn't always agree with him, but he carried on using him till the end."

My thoughts on Brian Mansfield and his trustfulness were interrupted by my mobile buzzing in my back pocket; Andy Eames was ringing.

"Andy, how goes it?"

"Well, thanks. I was just giving you a ring as I am going to have a team up in Oxhill next week and, having spoken to them, they are as intrigued as I am. They would love to come and have a look when we have finished in Tysoe."

"That would be great, when are you thinking of?"

"We are due to start next Monday, so the weekend after;

don't worry, you won't have to house them, they are quite happy to camp in the field."

"How many are there going to be?"

"Don't know exactly at the moment, but I would say about six plus myself."

"That sounds great. I hate to ask, but how much is this going to cost me?"

"Don't worry, you have got the Nerds team. They are quite happy to explore and dig anywhere that has never been dug before. A few beers and a barbecue on Saturday night and you will have very happy campers."

"Even better, I will sort something out with the Peacock. Are you staying with us for the week?"

"If you will have me."

"Of course, we would be delighted."

It turned out that the team of archaeologists thought that moving camp a couple of miles away after they had completed the work in Tysoe would be a waste of time. That Sunday night, two Ford Transits, a Ford truck and a camper van turned up at the farm. Andy jumped out of the truck and was greeted by Asher and Mels jumping up at him and trying to lick his face. The rest of the team was a total mixture: a university lecturer, his sidekick, and the sidekick's girlfriend, two students and, lastly, a professional archaeologist who specialised in interpreting soil. Later on that evening, Sandy christened them The Motley Crew.

I led this convoy up Green Lane and onto Whatcote Road to get to the field where they all parked up.

"Can we see the patches?" asked Professor Paul Gil whom I assumed to be the leader of the team.

We were standing on the flat piece of land below the copse where they had decided to camp and looking back at the hill. "Yes, you can make them out from here. You see those four patches where the soil is prominent and hasn't been grown over?"

"Oh, yes, I see them. And you say they are always like that?"

"Well, I've only been farming here for a couple of years and the first time I thought I might have been a bit lapse with the seed drill, but Greg, who works for me and has worked on the farm since leaving school, said that they were always like that. They were just accepted without question."

"They are pretty random," said Dave Fallon, the soil expert, "I would expect them to be more uniform if they are archaeological. You said you had a soil survey done on them; could I see it at some stage?"

"Of course, Dave, I'll drop it up later, or if you are going down to The Peacock, I could drop it down there."

"That sounds like my sort of excuse to go for a pint," he replied with a chuckle in his Gloucestershire accent.

I left them to set up camp and went back to the house with Andy who had intimated that they would probably have an early start the next morning.

So, the week carried on and I didn't really see much of The Motley Crew apart from on that Thursday evening when Andy and I walked down to the pub for a pint after dinner. They were all in residence, sat around two tables with the evidence of dinner still on them and a collection of different glasses suggesting that the drinks orders had been split between the sexes with beers for the men and wine for the women.

This was confirmed when I offered them a round and we joined them with ours.

"Geoff, I'm glad you dropped in," Dave started. "You know those soil samples; did you get them done for all the patches? It's just that I have done my own and they show different results in some of the constituents in the soil."

"No, I didn't. I thought they would all be the same. What sort of differences are you seeing?"

"I admit that the tests I did were probably more specific than the ones you had done. I had the advantage of knowing what I was looking for. That's not necessarily the best approach, bearing in mind the need to avoid subjectivity and all of that, but it does save time. Anyway, there were different traces of copper and lead in all the samples, which could suggest different time scales."

"What are you saying? That there could be some things

down there from different points in history?"

"No, I'm not saying anything of the sort. I can't say for sure that there's anything down there at all, but it is a bit odd. Don't worry, we will get to the bottom of it, if you'll excuse the pun."

"Geoff, what did you have in that field this year?" Max asked.

"Rape Seed. It was the first time I've tried it. Why?"

"That explains it; Even through the ground sheet I could smell something I wasn't expecting, and Rape Seed would explain it."

I bought another round before we walked home and didn't see The Motley Crew until that Saturday. I suggested that we all went down to see how they were getting on after the animals had been tended to and was surprised when even Micky agreed without even asking if he could take a ball down there. There seemed to be a hive of activity with Charlotte, Ariana, Dave, and Jonathan in a line like four slips in cricket, except they were walking slowly down the field between two pieces of red rope laid on the ground. Even as we watched them, one would stop and bring the line to a halt whilst they studied something on the ground, stored it in a bag and noted it on a clipboard. With the admin done, the line moved on. Max was also walking in straight lines, carrying a backpack and holding some sort of probe which he planted into the ground with every step. The sound of our car brought Paul out of the back of one of the Transits. Seeing us, he waved for us to come over.

"Morning, Geoff, Sandy, and boys," he said as we got out of the car, "you couldn't have come at a better time. We're just processing the results of the first tranche of geophysics that Max did earlier. Come and have a look."

The back of the Transit had been turned into part office and part computer room, with a small desk in the middle on the left and various boxes of computer processors stacked up on the far wall. Paul climbed up the steps and invited us to follow him. When he was seated behind the desk, we crowded around him.

"Now, you see these darker areas," he said pointing at what looked like grey puddles on a white background, "these show the areas of greater resistance and are generally where we would concentrate our search. Now they may be anything, or nothing, a bonfire two hundred years ago, a pot or something dropped on the ground and covered with earth. In the evenings this week, Max has been using his cartography skills and has drawn a computerised map of the field. If I overlay the map, you'll see where these areas are. This one here corresponds with that patch there, but this one doesn't, it's in an ordinary part of the field. I can't stress enough the Geophysics that we are using here should only be used as a guide; it gives us 'areas of interest,' not a lot more."

"That's fascinating. So, you have got some 'areas of interest.' I'm glad about that. Any news from the field walkers?"

"Not yet, let me have a look," he got up and poked his head out of the back of the van. "They should be finished in about fifteen minutes and then we will see."

"Paul, have you and the team got any plans for this evening? It's just that we were thinking of having a barbecue either down here or up at the farm," Sandy said.

"That's very kind of you. No, I don't think we have any plans other than a couple of pints in The Peacock."

"That's great. I'll get Geoff to bring all the kit up here. No dietary issues, are there?"

"No, the only dietary issue is normally not enough food. This lot eats like an army."

Rather than get under their feet, we drove back across the top of the village and out to Kineton. Sandy to go to the butchers and me to the off-licence. If they ate like an army, I was sure they would drink like one.

I filled the back of the truck later that afternoon and transported everything I needed to wine and dine them except for the actual wine and dine. They were all heavily involved in doing whatever they were meant to be doing, so I left them to it, but I did notice that one hole was in the process of being dug.

I have to admit that the next morning I was not feeling my best or sharpest. My suspicion about hollow legs had been correct and, although it had got quite cold, the fire pit I had taken up there had worked a treat, along with the whiskey that was consumed after the beer ran out.

It was after lunch that I got a call from Andy.

"I think you had better come up here," he said, with more than a hint of excitement in his voice.

We all packed ourselves into the car and drove up there to find a group of people standing around a hole in the ground.

"What have you found?"

PART 2

THE CONCLUSION OF WORLD WAR TWO

Chapter 1
Oxhill Gets a New Arrival

Major Pete Caruso arrived in Oxhill on a chilly November afternoon, making the most of the last of the daylight as he banked his Fairchild 24 four-seater single-engine monoplane, now known as the UC-61, over the church tower of St Lawrence in Oxhill. He looked out of his right-hand window down over the sleepy village before heading southwest towards Whatcote. He had been told the new runway was in a field between the two villages.

He saw a string of runway lights and circled the field to get his bearings, but his thoughts were interrupted by his radio.

"Oxhill Base to Caruso, do you read me?"

"Caruso to Oxhill Base, receiving you loud and clear. What's it like down there?"

"A gentle breeze from the west at 5mph, runway soft and bumpy. Look out for the wood on the right-hand side as you approach; it is on a hill above the runway."

"Roger, and out."

He circled again at a lower level before lining up and carefully dropping the plane on the grass strip. Turning at the end of the runway, he bumped his way across to the mobile control tower and was directed to park in front of it. He shut the engine and went through the normal procedures of closing down the plane before reaching behind the seat to pull out his travel bag and open the door to climb down.

"Good afternoon, sir, did you have a good flight?" Tommy Hughes, a mechanic and flight attendant he knew from Barford

St. John, the USAAF base that he had just flown from and where he used to be based.

"Tommy, don't insult me, a twenty-minute hop can hardly be called a flight."

"You took off, you flew, you landed; that's a flight in my eyes."

"Who is it in the tower?"

"Technical Sergeant Frost."

"Teddy Frost! Wow, we must be important for him to call me in. Who else is here?"

"That's it at this stage, but I guess when we go operational, they will ship a couple more over to look after you."

"So, do you stay here?"

"No, we're out of here as soon as I have put your baby to bed."

"Wow, what a life! Well, I'd better go and see old Teddy."

He walked over to the control tower and opened the door to find Technical Sergeant Teddy Frost, a man older than himself - Pete supposed he must have been in his early thirties - but he was not one to take care of himself; 230 pounds and only five foot nothing meant that he ate more than he exercised. The look was amplified by a balding head and bad skin. Not a good sight, but Pete knew that, as a flight controller, there was not a better man.

"Teddy, my old friend, so what are my orders? I was told you would have them ready for me?"

"Major, it looks like you have hit the jackpot again. This is your airfield, your fiefdom, your ticket to a quiet time. We will be leaving you a Jeep. This is your billet," he said, handing over a piece of paper, "and you are to stay here until we get in contact with you. As far as I know, you will be used to flying agents across the sea and behind enemy lines. Why the secrecy? That must be above my paygrade."

"How the hell are they going to get hold of me?"

"They have installed a separate line in the house you are billeted in just for you. Mind you, you're not allowed to use it, not to answer it or make calls from it. The only person to touch that telephone is Mrs Holland."

"Mrs Holland, eh? Now you are going to tell me she is twenty-three, good-looking, voluptuous, and hasn't seen her husband since she waved him away in thirty-nine expecting him back for Christmas."

"Knowing your luck, that's probably right."

"So, I just sit here waiting for the telephone to ring, like a goddam cabbie?"

"I'm told there is a very good pub in the village, and the countryside round here is good for walks."

"Walks! What would you know about walks? The furthest you've walked is to the pantry to get another pie"

"Now, now. You could always brush up on your Shakespeare. After all, Stratford is only 10 miles away."

"What, you first tell me there are nice walks and then to brush up on my Shakespeare; what do you think I am? I couldn't understand him at school, he doesn't write in English. I will be bored stupid in a week, bored to death in two if that telephone doesn't ring before then. Then you can come and find me in that churchyard I flew over."

"You never know, Mrs Holland might be as you described her."

"Pigs might fly. Ahhhh, where's this Jeep? I might as well start my sentence in hell before it gets dark. One thing before I go, you had better get your arse in gear when that telephone rings and get yourself over from Barford in double quick time."

He went out, slamming the door behind himself, found the Jeep and chucked his bag in the back, fired it up and drove down the field as if he were competing in the Indy500 at the 'Brickyard'. At the gate, he sped out onto the road, turned left without looking and accelerated up the hill. His mood was so black, he missed the right turn he was meant to take to go down Green Lane and nearly crashed the Jeep into the front of an oncoming car as he sped on.

"Goddam Limeys, why can't you drive on the right side of

the road?" he shouted at the car whilst swerving left and going round it. He continued down the hill but at a greatly reduced speed as his anger fled his mind and turned right at the bottom to drive through the village, a very dull-looking village in the last of the daylight, all the windows covered with blackouts, all the inhabitants safely tucked behind them. He noted the pub as he passed it and carried on until he came to the church and then turned the Jeep around, stopped, and looked at the notes he had been given. "The Old Rectory will be the first house after the church on the right," the note said. *OK, that's you over there,* he thought, looking at a solid house built from the red local stone that was prevalent in the area. He parked on the side of the road and, pulling his sack from the back of the Jeep, went up and knocked on the front door. He heard a curtain being drawn behind the door such was the silence and then he heard the lock being drawn back before the door opened.

"Hello, I'm Major Pete Caruso, I hope you are Mrs Holland, or I'm at the wrong address."

"No, Major Caruso, you're at the right house. Now come on in before the warden spots any light getting out."

She was a tall, slim woman with a slightly gaunt expression on her face, her hair beginning to show the first signs of grey, although her eyes were bright and skin almost translucent in the dim hallway light. It was her nose that made her look gaunt, he decided. Long and straight, slightly too long for her face, a Napoleon nose.

"Come through to the kitchen and I will make you a cup of tea - unless you would like something stronger?"

"A cup of tea would be great, Mrs Holland."

"You can cut the Mrs Holland; my name is Charlotte. If we are going to be living in the same house, we might as well use our Christian names. Leave your bag there, I'll show you to your room later."

He followed her along the hall, past various paintings of hunting scenes and through an open door into the kitchen. It was a large, airy room, dominated by a pine table in the middle which was placed on a rug where the rest of the floor was made up of red floor tiles. A range was situated on the back wall recessed into the old chimney with various cooking utensils and pots hanging on either side. There was a large stone basin with a window above it, but the view was blocked out by blackout curtains. There were signs of a recent meal; the washing up was draining on the sideboard.

"Sit down," she directed him and took the kettle over to the sink to fill it. "I should tell you that I have seen your Air Force records, quite impressive, I must say. I hope you won't find life in Oxhill too dull while you wait for the call to come. You are free to come and go as much as you like and, as any flying you will be doing will be at night, all I would ask is that you are back here by four o'clock each day."

"Mrs. Ho-, I mean, Charlotte, can I ask something?"

"Of course."

"All I know about this assignment is that I am going to be used to fly operatives behind enemy lines and that this cannot be done from a regular base, hence Oxhill. What is your involvement? I feel that it is far more than providing a roof over my head."

"I can't tell you everything except to say that, since I heard of my husband's demise on the beaches of Dunkirk, I have worked for the War Office and have spent some time with the French Resistance setting up escape routes."

"What?! You have actually been in France?"

"Oh yes, I have been in and out three times now, but I won't be going again until after the war."

She poured the boiling water into the teapot and brought it over to the table, setting it on a mat before going back to bring a jug of milk from the pantry and two cups. She sat down at the head of the table.

"I'm impressed," Pete said. "I would like to read your military records at some stage, it sounds like they would make interesting reading."

"No, they wouldn't, they would be dull and factual. I saw

heart and soul in France, the naked courage it takes having to live in occupied territory, the terror, the heartache, the hardship that so many are going through. Never make the mistake of glorifying war. It is horrid."

"What do you do now?"

"I am still involved, but not in the field, and I help out at Church Farm just behind the church here."

"There is no chance of you getting bored by the sounds of it."

"Luckily, it looks as if the war is turning now that we have a foothold in Europe. When it's over, I will go back to my riding, hunting, and enjoying life. What about you, Pete? What will you do when you get home?"

"I haven't decided yet. Technically, I'll have to go wherever the USAAF send me. I'm a commissioned officer who joined up way before this war started."

"You wouldn't give up your commission?"

"What would I do? I left New York when I was eighteen to join the USAAF and have hardly been back. I can't see myself working in my parents' ice cream parlour. Flying is all I know, but I don't want to go crop spraying, no, too dangerous."

"You have a brother, don't you?"

"Yes, Antonio. He's in the army, he was in the second wave that landed in Normandy and is somewhere in France."

"You don't know where?"

"He's a Captain in the Transport Corp and I haven't heard from him in a while."

"What do you do when you're not flying?"

"Jazz, I love my jazz. Listening and tickling the ivories."

"Oh, you'll have to show me. We have a piano in the drawing room."

"Really, do you play?"

"No, my husband did, and I don't know why I've kept it, really. I suppose I don't know what I would put in its place."

"Would you mind if I gave it a whirl?"

"No, I'd be delighted. Now, let me show you your room and give you a tour of the house."

Chapter 2
Discovering the Village

Pete woke up the next morning to the sound of Charlotte going to the bathroom. He turned over and looked at his watch. Six-thirty. *Boy, she doesn't believe in a lie-in*, he thought. He sat up in the bed, a very soft, feathery double bed, and looked around the room. In front of the bed was a double bay window with a radiator in the middle section and a window seat going all the way around. Curtains blocked his view into the outside world. To his left, a big brown wardrobe dominated the wall and to his right, a rather female dressing table with mirror that looked small against the long wall. The only other piece of furniture was a chair in the corner. If this was going to be his digs, he had had far worse, that was for sure.

He slowly got out of bed, stretched, and went over to draw the curtains. His bedroom was at the back of the house, so his view out of the window was over the garden, a garden mainly laid to grass with five or six apple trees dotted around. Further down, he could see what looked like a vegetable garden, now bare earth for the most part. He stood there, taking in the beauty, and thinking how different it was to the view out of his old bedroom in his parent's apartment in the Lower Manhattan district of Little Italy.

"I will appreciate the extra food allowance that I am now getting, especially as the extra food is coming from your NAAFI: extra chocolate, extra eggs, and even extra bacon. I'm also glad they are delivering it; I can't see Kathy at the village shop giving me extra provisions just because you are staying," Charlotte said as she put two large rashers of bacon into a pan on the range. "What are your plans for today?"

"I thought I would start by taking a walk around the village, introduce myself to the shop, and maybe go for a pint in the pub I passed coming through the village last night."

"The Peacock? They won't be open until eleven thirty. Kevin and Debby Hare own it, but Kevin is on active duty with the Army and Debby's brother has moved in. I haven't met him, but I gather he was in the Merchant Navy. He was torpedoed in the Atlantic and has been invalided out. The word around the village is that he is not very pleasant. I gather he thinks the world owes him something."

"I've seen that attitude before," he said as she placed a plate of fried eggs and bacon in front of him. "This looks and smells delicious." He was silent as he set about the plate of food with gusto.

"I could introduce you to Tom and Cathy McNally over at Church Farm if you want. I know they could always do with some help if you get bored."

"I've never done any farmwork in my life, what would I be doing?"

"I don't know, but if I introduce you and you want to give it a try, you might enjoy it. Well, when you come back from your walk we'll go over there."

"Sure, sounds like a plan."

Soon after breakfast, he put on his flying jacket, walked out of the front door, and stood in the middle of the road outside. *Which way should I go?* he thought before turning to his left and walking towards St Lawrence's Church. Stopping outside it, he stood and studied the building. What he saw was a twelfth-century church that had gone through several updates and restorations in the nineteenth century. Looking at it, he now knew his orientation. He was standing to the north, since the tower had to be to the west, and the newer extension had to be where the alter was, to the east. As a pilot, he always wanted to know his orientation; it was his lifeline without which he couldn't navigate his plane. Yes, he had a compass on the dashboard of it, but he always wanted to see it on the ground.

He carried on past the church and turned right up Green Lane, which he would have come down the day before, but for his enraged driving. He carried on up the lane, fields on either side of him, those on the right allowing him to see into the village. At the top, he turned right and walked down the road he had driven down but went past the turning to the main village. He walked on until he got to Brooklands Farm and saw men working in the orchard at the back of the farmhouse, picking the last of the apples. There was a lot of chat between the workers which made him look up. He could see they were wearing military uniforms, but what had caught his attention was that they were speaking Italian.

"Ciao," he called over. The chat suddenly stopped.

"Chi sei?"

His parents had always spoken Italian in the house, it was their first language and he had never spoken anything else until he went to school.

"Just an American who speaks Italian," he continued in Italian.

"What are you doing here?"

"What are *you* doing here? How are Italian servicemen working on a farm in the middle of England?"

"We work here."

"Are you POWs?"

"Yes, but we are called 'Co-operatives' which means that we get paid wages for work. So, what's your name?"

"Pete Caruso."

"We have a Caruso here. Lads, where is Marco?"

"He's down by the stream," one of them replied.

"Get him up here. There is another Caruso here."

"What's your name?" Pete asked the Italian who had done all the talking.

"Mario Bonetti."

"Mario, what are POWs doing working here? There are no

guards, no fences, why don't you run away?"

"Where would we go? Italy is a long journey, and we are being looked after well here, we are paid, we're in Ettington camp and we are not treated like criminals. Ah, here comes Marco. Marco, there's a Guido here with the same name as you."

"So? It's a common name."

"Ah, come on, Marco, the least you can do is say hello."

"Hi, Marco," Pete started. "Where do you come from?"

"You won't have heard of it, a small village called Diodato near Cosenza in Calabria."

"Diodato? Near Cosenza? No! Not only have I've heard of it, but my father is from there! He immigrated to New York in nineteen-ten. All of our family are still there. I'm named after his brother, Pietro."

"That's my father's name, what's your father called?"

"Mario."

"That's my father's brother's name and he went to New York." Marco was starting to warm to the subject while the other Italians had drawn closer and were discussing the amazing coincidence among themselves with great excitement.

"Marco, hey, do you realise we could be cousins? You know what, I think we look alike. See? What do you guys think?" They stood side by side, gesturing to the other Italians to take a look.

"Oi, what's going on here? Back to work! And who are you?" A gruff figure came striding across the orchard, shouting as he came. The group broke up quickly, every man hurriedly trying to look as if he'd been working all along.

"Hello, sir, my name is Major Pete Caruso, USAAF, I've just been billeted in the village."

"Well, what are you doing talking to these men? They are meant to be picking apples, not talking to American flyboys."

"I was just walking by and heard them speaking Italian and got talking to them."

"I don't pay them to talk to the likes of you."

"I'm sorry, sir," Pete said, beginning to get angry. "What do you mean by 'the likes of you'?"

"You flyboys, always think you are better than everybody else."

"Oh, we do, do we? What makes you say that?"

"I haven't got the time to debate with you, now be off with you!"

"Marco, I'll see you tomorrow," Pete called out to his newfound cousin.

"No, you won't, I don't want to see you around here again."

Pete turned around and went back towards the T-junction where he could go up Main Street, fuming. He was just passing the village shop when he noticed a man slowly going down a row of vegetables, examining them. *That must be Bill Ward*, he thought when the man stood up and looked over at him.

"Morning," the man said in a strong south Warwickshire accent. "Cans I help thou?"

"Morning, I've just moved into Mrs Holland's house and was taking a look around the village. You must be Bill Ward, sir; Mrs Holland said I should come to introduce myself to you."

"That's me. Heard she was having a Yank come to stay."

"Well, I'm that Yank, otherwise known as Major Pete Caruso," he said, going over and offering his hand.

Bill stood up and walked to the end of the row whilst wiping the soil from his hands on his trousers.

"Nice to meet you," he said as they shook hands, "The wife is in the shop if you'd like to introduce yourself."

"I will do, but I don't know if I can buy anything as I don't have a ration book."

He walked further up the supply road towards the low building. There was a post box attached to the wall beside a low door. A bell rang as he opened the door and a small woman in a house coat with greying hair and a warm smile came out from the back of the shop.

"Morning there, you must be the American staying with Mrs Holland," Kathy said.

"Yes, Major Pete Caruso, at your service, ma'am."

"You can cut out that attitude, now what can I get you?" Still smiling.

"I wasn't planning on buying anything, I was just dropping by to introduce myself, but as I'm here I might as well take a newspaper."

He bought a Daily Express and was walking up the road when he noticed a small boy watching him.

"Sir, are you American?"

"Sure am, and who might you be, son?"

"John Harker, sir, and I'm nine."

"Nine, that's a good age. So, what do you do, John Harker?"

"I'm at school. Do you fly planes?"

"I certainly do."

"Have you shot down any Jerries?"

"I have, but I can't tell you how many."

"Why not?"

"It's secret. We are not allowed to say."

"Oh, OK, well, bye-bye."

Pete carried on up the road, chuckling at the innocence of youth and feeling better about himself now the anger from the encounter with the farmer had subsided. Passing The Peacock, he noticed that the front door was open and entered the small lobby. Left to the public bar or right to the snug. Left it was. He entered the bar and the first thing he noticed was the large inglenook fireplace dominating the wall opposite the door, with wooden seats with cushions going back into the fireplace and a warm and welcoming log fire burning in the hearth. The bar ran across the room on the right, with three large beer taps and a row of optics behind it. There were three tables spread around the room that would seat twelve or thirteen people, he reasoned. The bar was empty.

"Hello!" he called, with both hands on the bar top, looking both left and right, wondering where someone was going to come from.

"Yes, be with you in a minute," a man from the left replied, followed by a large Labrador who padded into the area behind the bar and put his paws up on it.

"Hello, boy," Pete said. "Now I guess you aren't the staff

and can't pour me a pint." He patted the dog on the head to an affectionate response.

"I'm sorry, we aren't really open. But since you are in and have been accepted by Bruny, what can I get you?"

"A pint of your best, please. I'm Major Pete Caruso, I'm staying with Mrs Holland."

"Oh, yes, we heard that a Yank was going to be staying with her. You're air force, aren't you? Oh, by the way, I'm Frank, I'm helping my sister out here whilst her husband is away with the army."

"Well, I'm glad I'm not on a secret mission as everyone seems to know that I'm expected."

"It's a small village, I'm afraid. Everyone knows what everyone else is doing," Frank said as he placed the pint in front of Pete. "Me and the sister were born here, but I couldn't stand it and went to Birmingham as soon as I could."

"What did you do there?"

"A bit of this and a bit of that, you know, kept myself busy. And then in thirty-four, I joined the Merchant Navy. Best move I ever made, can't say I saw the world, but I went to Australia and New Zealand with stopovers at Cape Town. You, have you been abroad, apart from here?"

"Yes, I joined up in thirty-five and was in Pearl Harbour when it all kicked off for us."

They carried on swapping war stories, or stories of their lives, whilst Pete finished his first pint and ordered another; during that whole time no one else came into the pub, but it was during this time that Pete felt comfortable in the atmosphere. He had begun to like The Peacock.

After he had finished his second pint, he walked up through the village back to his billet to find that Charlotte had spent the morning baking bread and making tomato soup for their lunch. They sat down at the kitchen table and discussed this varied morning. Charlotte informed him that he had had the pleasure of meeting David Hatch, a man who was not liked in the village because of his unpleasant views and general cussedness, which prevented him from joining in with village life.

When they had finished the meal, he cleared the table and, much to her irritation, started to do the washing up. When it was all cleared away, they walked over to Church Farm, situated on the other side of the church, where she introduced him to Tom and Clare McNally.

"What are you going to do all day?" Tom asked him.

"I'm not sure, I guess I'll just wait for the telephone to ring and get frustrated when it doesn't. Tell me something: I was walking past Brooklands Farm this morning and there was a team of Italian POWs working down there. How does that work?"

"They are treated like any other worker. They are paid the same rate, they are allowed around the village and go back to Ettington in the evening. I think most of us were surprised that David took them on. It would have been understandable had they been cheaper."

"It was a total coincidence, but one of them might be my first cousin."

"You're joking! How?"

Pete went through the circumstances and stressed that, if it was true, he would like to find out how he could help him.

"It's so strange, this war; two cousins on different sides brought together in a tiny village in the middle of England," Clare said, shaking her head in amazement.

"Tom, Charlotte said you might need some help here, not that I have ever worked on a farm, but I would be interested just to keep myself out of trouble."

"Typical of you Yanks," he said with a laugh. "As soon as the hard work is done, you come along and offer help."

"Yeah, yeah, I know what you mean. We can take it. I'm not offering to buy your farm, just to stop boredom from setting in."

"Let me see what I can find."

Chapter 3
The Cousins

Pete spent the evening wondering and fretting about his meeting with Marco. Surely it was too much of a coincidence for it not to be true that they were cousins. He was determined to speak to him again, there was so much he wanted to ask, but that would mean eating a whole heap of humble pie. He would have to go and talk to David Hatch, appeal to his better nature.

After breakfast the next day, he walked down through the village and knocked on David Hatch's front door.

"Yes, what do you want?"

"Mr Hatch, I apologise for my actions yesterday, and I'm sorry if we didn't get off on the correct footing."

"I don't know about any footing, all I know is that I am paying for those Eyeties to pick my apples, not to help you practise your Italian."

"I appreciate that, it is just that I think one of them might be my cousin, a cousin I did not know I had. I was just trying to find out if it was true."

"How could you have a cousin who is an Eyetie POW?"

"Our fathers both come from the same town. I know that my father's brother has the same name as his father and vice versa."

"So, you are cousins, it's no big deal. I've probably got cousins in Whatcote that I don't know about."

"I would just like to talk to him, get to know him. If it's about the money, how about I pay you for an hour of his time?"

"Bloody typical of you Yanks! It's not all about money, you

know. You think you can buy me? Bloody typical. Even if I took your money, who's going to pick the apples?"

"Mr Hatch, I'm not trying to buy you, and I have tried to be as reasonable as I can. All I want is to speak to my cousin."

"Well, you can't."

"OK, if you are going to play it that way, I'll speak to him during his lunch break."

"No, you won't, they are not allowed to leave my farm, whatever the government says, and you're not allowed onto it. If I see you on my land, I will have you for trespassing."

"Play it your own way, but you haven't heard the last of this."

"Get off my land now before I call the police."

Pete retreated with the old adage ringing in his head: he might have lost a battle, but he hadn't lost the war. He marched back up the village and into the house.

"That man! I'm raging. Who does he think he is?"

"I'm guessing having a polite word didn't work. What did he say?"

"I'm not allowed to speak to him, I'm not allowed to buy an hour of his time, I can't speak to him at lunch, he is not allowed off the farm, and I'm not allowed on it."

"You said he's not allowed off the farm?"

"That's what Hatch said."

"Well, that's not right. The Co-operatives are allowed free access into the village, but, obviously, not to the pub. They can visit the shop and buy things and they can visit people in their homes. They are brought to the village in the morning and collected in the evening; between those hours when they aren't working, they are pretty much allowed to do what they want."

"How does the theory of the law help me? I can't go to him, and he's not allowed to come to me."

"Come on, we haven't finished yet. I might be able to speak to someone at Ettington. If I haven't got enough authority, I'll find someone who does."

"Oh, shit. I'm sorry, I shouldn't have sworn, but it is so frustrating."

"Don't worry, I've heard far worse for smaller reasons. Now, you go and try out the piano and I'll hit the telephone."

"Thank you, Charlotte."

Pete went into the drawing room, a room he had only looked into before. It was a formal room, a room where one felt one had to behave, a room where one expected one's grandparents to tell one off. Formally decorated with two-seater sofas, side tables, single armchairs all arranged around the room, with the fireplace being the focal point. The piano was almost hidden at the far end of the room near the double doors that led to the garden. He went over to it, lifted the lid and, standing up, played a few notes. Unexpectedly, it was in tune. Sitting down on the stool, he warmed up his fingers, did his scales and tuned up. He didn't know what to play, so he sat back on the stool and thought. *What should I play?* Then he just closed his eyes and played; C Jam Blues came out, written by his hero Duke Ellington. He had been playing for about fifteen minutes when he sensed that he was not alone and turning around he saw Charlotte leaning against the doorframe.

"That was beautiful, what was it?"

"A very bad rendition of a song I learnt to play when recovering after Pearl Harbour. I was in hospital for three months and I think I must have driven the others in the ward mad playing the piano. I would get the nurses to wheel me over to it and play requests for hours and, when they ran out, I would just play jazz."

"That's a ward that I would have liked to have been on. I made a couple of calls, and you can go over to Ettington this evening at six and they will arrange for you to be able to talk with your cousin."

"That's amazing, how did you manage it?"

"It was easier than I imagined. I rang them up, spoke to Lieutenant Colonel Michael Craven, and he said yes. It probably helps that we both hunt with the Warwickshire, and I see him most weeks out hunting."

Pete burst out laughing. "I never thought that 'old boys'

club'," he said, mocking an English accent, "would do me a favour."

"Don't knock it. I know you Americans think it is stupid, but it works sometimes."

At five-thirty that evening, he climbed into the Jeep for the ten-minute drive to Ettington and arrived at the guard house at the head of the drive to find that he was expected. Captain Morrissey was waiting to escort him to the administration hut in the compound where the eight hundred or so Italians were kept.

The captain showed him to an office. "You can use my office, it will be a bit more comfortable, and definitely warmer than the interview room. I'll go and get Major Caruso."

It was a very utilitarian office. Three filing cabinets - a picture of the King above one of them - and a coat and hat stand behind the door were the only furniture apart from the three chairs in front of the desk and one behind it. There was no carpet on the floor and no pictures on the walls except for a map of Ettington Park. Pete sat down in front of the grey metal desk.

The door opened and Marco entered.

"Marco, I had to see you again," he said, embracing his cousin. "That bastard you work for won't let me talk to you."

"How did you manage to see me here?"

"The woman who is giving me digs hunts with the commanding officer here. They call it the 'old boys' club'."

"I can't believe this; how did we manage to bump into each other?"

"I know, what are the chances? If your friends had not been speaking Italian, I wouldn't have stopped. It made me feel at home hearing the language again."

"Bring me up to date, what's happened to my uncle Mario since he went to America?"

"He came over in nineteen-ten and hasn't moved more than three miles from where he landed. He started off working in an ice cream parlour, fell in love with the owner's daughter and married her. My younger brother and me are the result. It is a story that has been told and lived out a million times in the ghettos in every city in America. How did you come to be here?"

"I was captured during what they call the Battle of Alamein in nineteen forty-two. My unit got detached from the main force when we were retreating, we got surrounded and had run out of ammunition; what could we do but surrender? Anyway, after being held in North Africa, I was shipped to England in nineteen forty-three and landed here. Or, rather, in Camp 31, Ettington Park. They just bring us here to work. To be fair they have been very reasonable to us. We have always had food - sometimes more than the locals, I think - and they pay us for doing the work."

"Is this why you don't try to escape?"

"And go where? Italy is a long way away."

"I understand."

"You don't agree, you see escape as a prerequisite for a captured officer. A matter of honour." Marco stiffened.

Pete held up his hand to reassure him. He said, "No, I wasn't thinking that; I don't know how I would feel if I were in your shoes."

"Well, I can tell you, it's shit. It's boring, it's depressing, and I can also tell you, as much as I hate Hatch, life working for him is better than whittling wood here. Anyway, I have a suspicion, from the latest news reports, that this war is going to be over soon."

"Spit three times for good luck!" said Pete. "That's one thing I know from the old country."

Both men laughed. "A gift from home!" said Marco. "Here in an English orchard!"

"See, we aren't so different!" said Pete. "And you are a Major as well. Two Major Carusos in the same room, who would have thought it? What about your family in Calabria, what does Pietro do?"

"My Dad like everyone in our village, is an olive farmer and keeps pigs. Among other *things*." Marco stared at Pete intently, as if willing him to read his meaning. There was a long silence.

"Among other *things*?" Pete repeated carefully. "Do you mean 'our things'?"

Marco nodded. "I tried to get him out of it, but he would always ask where the money would come from if he wasn't 'connected'."

"Wow!" Pete was startled. He hadn't expected this reunion to take such a turn. "Luckily, we have always stayed away from them - as far as I know."

"Me too. Joining the army was my escape."

The cousins' eyes met properly for the first time, and Pete felt he had found a kindred spirit in the most unlikely of places, although their circumstances could not have been more different.

"What do you need here - money, cigarettes, food?" he asked, eager to make his cousin's stay more comfortable.

"Not money, but cigarettes are always good."

"I will see what I can do. I can usually pick some up from the base, but I can't make any promises. And how am I going to deliver? I can't get onto the farm, and I don't think I will be allowed here again for a while."

"There is a stream at the bottom of the orchard by the barn. Let's try to meet there. Come at 6 o'clock when I've finished work. They don't pick us up to take us back to Ettington until 7 o'clock. We can find a place where you can leave stuff too and I can always get over the stream. If I'm not there tomorrow, try again the next day and the next until I am."

Their time was up. Pete went out of the office to find Captain Morrissey in the larger outer office reading a paper. He thanked him, walked out, and drove back to Oxhill.

Chapter 4
The Planning Starts

But by the end of his third week, Pete was getting restless again. It was all well and good sitting around in the village doing nothing, waiting for the telephone to ring, but he wanted to do something now. He had checked the plane every day and turned the engine over but hadn't taken her up. He had fallen into the habit of going down to the stream at 6 every day and had spoken to Marco most evenings, but he had nearly been caught on a couple of occasions. He had walked around the village and chatted to the locals, but he wanted more.

He drove over to Barford St. John and walked into the mess but there was no one around. He walked down the corridor and knocked on the door of his commanding officer, Colonel John Polman.

"Come." he heard his friend call out, as he turned the door handle and opened the door.

"Colonel, I thought I'd better check in with you."

"Pete, what the hell are you doing here? I thought you were meant to stay in Oxhill. There's no point in our leaving you there only for you to come here every day."

"John, you know me, I can't just sit there, walking around the village and playing the piano."

"That's exactly what I want you to do: nothing. Shit, the reason you're there is so that you're not seen here."

"Well, I needed some cigarettes and other things. And I'd like to know when I am going to fly again."

"You'll fly again when I get orders for you to fly again. So, what's Oxhill like?"

"It's OK." He was debating with himself whether to tell him about Marco, but decided not to, "the pub is quiet, everyone knows what everyone else is doing. One guy was trying to make me help out on his farm. Can you imagine city boy me working on a farm?"

"That's something I can't imagine. Now, it is quiet around here this afternoon, so do me a favour and get the hell back to Oxhill before anyone sees you. By the way, if you do need anything, get Mrs Holland to ring it through with the food order. What's she like? She seems to be fairly well respected."

"I'm not surprised. She's been behind enemy lines. She lost her husband at Dunkirk, and she's worked for intelligence; how can one not respect her? What's more, her cooking is only just behind my mother's. I was told British cooking was dull and boring, boy did they get that wrong!"

"Now, get your arse out of here before someone sees you."

The next morning, he walked down past Brooklands Farm towards the stream, looking out for David Hatch as he went, just as he had done every evening. When he spotted – or heard– him, Pete had just had to carry on up the road without stopping. But this morning there was no sign of Hatch. Having walked over the bridge, he entered the field through the gate, walking a parallel line to the road, but looking out for both the farmer or his brother. Seeing neither, he walked across to the stream and looked closely at the willow trees that sporadically lined the stream until he found what he was looking for; a slightly rotten one. He took his knife out and started gouging out the slightly rotten wood to create a cavity where he could hide contraband for Marco. He was concentrating so hard that he didn't hear the chatting Italians walking towards him down through the orchard.

"Hey, you want Marco?"

"Is Hatch around?"

"No, that's why we took a break."

"Then, yes, if he is around."

"Marco," one of the Italians called out and followed it with a whistle.

Pete went back behind the tree in case someone else who would object to him speaking to the POWs would see him.

"Pete, are you there?"

"Marco, where's Hatch? It's unlike him to leave you unattended during the day."

"He has a habit of turning up when least expected or wanted."

"Marco, I have picked this tree as it is a bit rotten and carved out a bit at the back."

"Why did you pick there, it is the deepest part of the river, you idiot."

"Shit, I didn't think of that, where can you get across?"

"I'll show you."

They walked on either side of the stream following its meandering route around the orchard until they reached a spot behind the barn that almost ran down to it. Marco stopped and looked around, looked over the bank to visually measure the depth and on the inside of a bend, he knew he could easily wade across.

"Here, it is shallow on this side, and I can use those boulders on your side to get across."

"OK." Pete started to look at the nearby trees but found nothing that he liked; he then started looking at the ground but quickly discounted that route: if the river was going to flood it would flood on the outside, where he stood. He looked again and found another tree that had a dip between the first branch and the trunk.

"What about this," he pointed out the tree to Marco, "I can leave stuff here."

"Yes, that works. You'll have to wrap everything in hessian so that it won't be seen. And thank you!"

Over the following days, Pete and Marco established a system for leaving messages too, and they met by the tree frequently as they got along better and better, finding they had a great deal more in common than they had first realised. Marco loved Jazz nearly as much as Pete did and played the trombone.

They talked about jamming together one day. Both had brothers they missed. Marco's brother, Luciano, had joined the resistance when the war began. He was only fifteen and loved by everyone in the village for his cheerful kindness. Marco knew he was hiding out in the hills, but he had no idea where. Pete's brother, Antonio, was somewhere in France but he too had no idea where. For all they knew, both their brothers were already dead, and they took comfort in having found each other. For Pete, these meetings were especially welcome as the time dragged by with still no orders for any missions.

One lazy evening as they lay in the long grass by the stream, idly chatting and smoking the cigarettes Pete had managed to scrounge from the base, Marco turned to him and said, in a speculative tone of voice, "You know, I've been hearing some interesting stories, even here."

"Stories? What kind of stories? From Italy or from here?" At first, Pete didn't understand what Marco meant.

"Both, in a way," his cousin replied, smiling. "You really don't get this, do you? If I say I've heard a '*story*', it means a '*story*'." He put a lot of emphasis on the word. "A *story* story. About *things*."

Pete laughed. "Sorry, I was being a bit slow there. Tell me!"

"Stories about mafia gold, boxes of it, being transported to the north in secret and hidden to avoid it being captured by either the Germans or the British."

"Now I'm interested! Where do you mean by 'the north'? What do you know?"

"I don't know anything concrete. I've just heard things here and there. There are people with connections here, people who were conscripted into the army, even people who know my father. It's weird. I thought he just, you know, took messages sometimes, or sorted out small problems. I think I may have underestimated him. Anyway, the gist of the story goes that last summer some 'unofficial' gold from Calabria was moved across Italy in secret and hidden in a cave in the mountains above a hamlet called Grusiner in Piemonte."

"Gold! Like bullion bars? This is crazy! How much gold?"

"I don't know. I don't know anything in detail, but boxes are mentioned. And when they say the word 'box', the way they say it makes them sound big!" He held his arms out wide in illustration.

"Hey, buddy, this could be our transport to a better world. We could swoop in there and grab the gold and run away to, I don't know, somewhere with palm trees and pretty girls," Pete said in jest.

"And no war," Marco added. "No cold mornings with Hatch making us wash under the pump before running round the yard, no cold porridge, no rules…"

Pete sat up. He could feel his heart pumping. "Try and find out more. Who took the gold, and how much of it is there? Is there really no one left who knows where it is? I'm starting to think there might be something in this. For real."

"But even if I find out more, how would we get it out of there? We are in England and it's in northern Italy." Now Marco was starting to take it seriously too.

"I don't know, but my brain is buzzing with ideas. I have a plane in Oxhill. I have papers that allow me to fly anywhere. I know it sounds crazy, but I could fly it to Oxhill! It's no crazier than half the things that have happened in this war…"

"That would be great for you, but what about me?"

"First, we'd have to get you out of Hatch's clutches. We'll need at least three of us to make it work so we need someone else we can truly trust. I'd better start looking for that brother of mine. But let's not get ahead of ourselves; we are working on rumours. What we need is precise information. You get the information, and I'll make a plan that will ensure you get your share."

"While I try to verify the stories and find out more details, I'll need more cigarettes and some food if I'm going to get anyone talking. Leave them in the hollow, as usual, by tonight. See you here tomorrow!"

The following day when they met again, Pete asked, "Have you heard anything?"

"Yes! I will come across and I will tell you."

Pete watched his cousin step down onto a small beach created under the bank before he started to wade across. When he got to the middle he stopped, looking into the stream, trying to find the shallowest route, before standing up and nodding his head. One leap and he was on a boulder, and another he was in the shallows of the opposite bank and clambering up. The cousins embraced.

"I've spoken to The Club, as we call them, and they are very worried about the lost gold. There may be hundreds of caves up there, it might be like searching for the Grail."

"No, no, no. We are searching for something physical, the Grail is based on rhetoric, ancient history. There must be something else."

"I will keep asking around to see if anyone knows anything more, but I don't want to seem too keen to know the details."

"I know, I know, but see what you can do. Look, I'd better go before Hatch comes looking for you."

As Pete walked back through the village, he couldn't think about anything else. The thought of gold had got to him, it was invading his mind, and it would be his escape after this war was over. He could see it, it was there in front of him, yes there was more information needed, but it was becoming real. He needed to get hold of his brother.

When he returned to The Old Rectory, Charlotte wasn't there, but she had left lunch out for him on the kitchen table, a chicken sandwich, a note, and a letter addressed to him. He sat down and opened the envelope only to find another envelope inside; this one was addressed to him at Barford St. John, and he recognised the writing, his brother's. It felt like fate was on his side. Ripping it open, he pulled out a single sheet of paper and, picking up the sandwich, started reading.

> *Dear Bro,*
>   *I hope this finds you at some stage.*
>   *I managed to get through the Normandy landings*
> *OK, with a few scrapes, a few near misses and a few*

bullets that came far too close. I can't tell you how bad it was. I was scared, I'll admit that, but whatever anyone says, everyone was. The first few days were a complete mess, no one knew where we were meant to go, and no one knew what we were meant to be transporting; we would take a load of food to a location only to find that it was back in Jerry hands. Another time we would try and supply a forward base only to find they had had a delivery the day before.

Anyway, I made it to Paris. Oh, how you would have loved it; jazz playing, wine on tap, and the women, oh, the women. It was two weeks in heaven.

I have now been moved down south to Lyon and am out of the firing zone, thank God, just letting the boys go out whilst I sit in our camp and tell them where to go. I hope, above all hope, that my war is over and that I can sit here to see it out.

How goes it with you? I hope that you have flown enough for this war and can now sit behind a desk and send others out. I know that will never happen, you will always put yourself forward if there is a fight, and you will always be in the middle of it. Do you remember the time when I was being bullied at baseball? You came and put yourself in the firing line to sort them out. It cost you a black eye, but I was never bullied again.

If you get this, write to me at the address above, mail seems to be getting through. Bro, I would love to hear from you, just to know you have got through this shit.

All my love,
Antonio

Chapter 5
Night Flights

Charlotte and Pete had fallen into a routine for their mornings, Pete would be the first to rise and would go down to put the kettle on the range, and then go through the bathroom. Charlotte would go down whilst he was doing this to start breakfast and lay the table. He would then finish off downstairs whilst she got dressed. To many, this might seem over-complicated, but it seemed to work for them. Today it was just porridge (hot!) and tea to start them off on their day, along with the paper that had been delivered.

In normal times, he would not be a regular reader of the paper, but now that he didn't see anyone from the Mess, his normal method of finding out what was going on in the war, he had to read it. He found the press, and the language they used, difficult to read; they were not as gung-ho as the American press, facts were more important than rhetoric, along with the censorship, which was far more rigorous than in the States. He read through the reports, looked at the maps, and tried to imagine what it would be like at the front.

He put the paper down with a large sigh and went through to the drawing room to play the piano. He had just sat down and was warming up when he heard the telephone ring in the kitchen. His telephone. He rushed in to see Charlotte holding the telephone to her ear and writing something on a pad.

"Well?" he asked.

"You're to be at the field at three o'clock to prepare for a flight tonight."

"Is that all they said?"

"Yes, what did you expect?"

"I don't know, but something."

"Patience, you know the saying 'never found in men.' Now I've got things to do this morning. I'll do lunch for one o'clock, full-scale fry-up as I don't know when you will be eating again."

That morning was hell for him. Charlotte had been right when she spoke about patience, it was something that he was not very good at. First, he walked around the village, but just when he wanted to bump into someone to make the time go faster, he met no one. He returned and played the piano and then went upstairs to make sure his flying gear was in order, anything to pass the time. At long last, he heard Charlotte coming in through the back door and the sound of lunch being prepared which was soon followed by its smell. He got into his flying gear and went down to find the table laid for one and a growing mound of food being placed on the serving plate that now dominated the centre of the table.

"Right, sit yourself down, and tuck in. Don't worry about me, if I ate any of that now I would be asleep all afternoon."

"I wish that telephone would ring a bit more often if this is the lunch I get. Are you sure you don't want any?"

He started filling his plate and was silent throughout the meal, mainly because he was enjoying it so much, but also because he was thinking ahead to what he might be asked to do later.

At three o'clock exactly he turned into the field to see that it changed back to how he had seen it the first time he had landed. The two mobile trailers were placed as before but now there were a few more people evident, a fuel wagon was parked by his plane and was filling it up and a tractor was pulling a mower over the runway. He parked by the mobile control tower and got out, climbing up the steps to enter it.

"Good afternoon, Pete," his Commanding Officer, Colonel John Polman, greeted him.

"Good afternoon, sir, I wasn't expecting to see you here."

"I'm only here to brief you and see you on your way. Now come over here to the desk. This jaunt is not strictly what you are here for, and I'm not happy you are being used, but I got over-ruled from a great height. Very soon three people will arrive in two cars with police escorts. You will definitely recognise them and, quite frankly, they are using you as a cabby. From here you will fly to Fécamp on the Normandy coast, where you will land at an army base. You will be instructed to park away from the main base, but you will be refuelled and probably provisions will be brought out to you. When you have been serviced, you will fly down to Lyon Bron Airfield which currently is the base for the 50th Fighter Group and their P-47 Thunderbolts, but again you are to keep well clear of them. You will park up the plane and you will be given a lift to your hotel along with your three passengers. Now, I know that your brother is posted in the area and, because I also know you, I know you will try and find him, so I've arranged for him to be brought to the hotel tomorrow to meet with you. When your passengers have finished their business, you will fly them back here using the same route. Is that clear?"

"Clear. I can think of any number of questions, but I can't see you answering them. Let's start with: Why me? And then go to: Will we have any cover, what's the airfield like at Fécamp? Lyon will be OK if they are flying P-47s out of there, so how long will I be in Lyon? Lastly, to start off with, can any of these VIPs navigate a plane?"

"I wouldn't be surprised if they could, but I doubt they will offer to read your maps for you."

"I assume that I am in radio silence for the entire journey."

"You will be called up from both bases and will identify yourself as 'Captain Bosanquet'. You will also have an escort of six Spitfires flying in formation around you."

"Boy, who are these guys, and why the secrecy?"

"I am not allowed to tell you in case there are any last-minute changes. Now get a good look at these maps. Your route has been marked up and will bypass any bases on the way."

"Yes, sir."

Pete sat down at the desk and opened a series of maps to study the planned route. The first part of the journey to France was a complicated, snake-like route, circumnavigating the many airfields in Southern England, which made it look as if a spider had walked over the map. Once they crossed the coast, they headed in a straight line to their destination. The journey from there to Lyon was much simpler, keeping to the west of Paris and then straight down. He worked out that the flight to France was just over 200 miles, well within the range of the Fairchild, and calculated that - with the current weather conditions - it would take him an hour and three-quarters. He chuckled as he thought of the Spitfires flying at that speed; their pilots would think they were crawling.

When he had finished all of his planning, he went and did a thorough check of the plane, walking around it, prodding bits, and generally making sure it was in the same condition as when he had last flown it. He was halfway around when Tommy Hughes came over.

"I gave her a good going over this morning, everything checked out OK. She is brimmed full of fuel and ready to go. You must have turned her over every day by the way she fired up the first time and ran so smoothly."

"Yup, I've been up here every day, warming her up for twenty minutes and shutting her down again."

"Well, she's ticked all the boxes and is ready to go to wherever you're going."

"If I told you that, I'd have to shoot you. This is so deep undercover I'm going to have a cage of canaries with me, or whatever birds they take down mines."

"I know. We have all got to be off the field before whoever turns up, just Teddy and Colonel Polman are allowed to stay to see you off."

"Is that so, well I hope we don't have a problem on take-off."

"Nah, you're a pro, could take off anywhere. A nice, quiet day like today is like taking candy from babies. Right, I must be going, good luck."

Pete had just finished his inspection when he heard a honk from the transport lorry that was taking the unneeded personnel back to Barford; he waved them off and walked back over to the control wagon.

"Do you know what time they are turning up? 'Cos it is an hour and three-quarters to get to France."

"If they come, you will be taking off at six o'clock. If they are not here by six fifteen, I've been told to abort."

"OK," Pete said looking at his watch. "So, about half an hour."

He walked out and went to the end of the marked-out runway to walk down it to check its condition. Now that the grass had been cut and rolled, it was as good as he was ever going to get. It would still be a bit bumpy, but it was definitely better than when he first arrived. He had just started to walk back towards the control wagon when two police motorcycles, followed by two large black cars, rolled onto the airfield, and parked up. He observed John going over to the first car and speaking to the driver as he continued to walk towards them, with more vigour than before, but no one got out of the cars.

"Major, your passengers are keen to get going, when will you be ready?" His commanding officer asked.

"As soon as they are loaded aboard, sir," Pete replied. "Whilst they are doing that, I will take one last look around the bird."

As he spoke, the rear door of the second car opened and to his surprise the most recognised man in the world climbed out, preceded by a massive cloud of cigar smoke, Sir Winston Churchill. He straightened, stretched his shoulders back and looked around before settling his vision on the two Americans who suddenly came to attention.

"Young man, I assume you are the one who is going to fly us this evening."

"Yes, sir," Pete replied very formally.

"Good. Although I am keen to get going, I want to finish my cigar before we take off."

"Yes, sir." Pete was just getting over the shock of what he

had just seen when the other back door opened, and General Eisenhower climbed out.

"Winston, surely you don't need any more of that confounded thing. You've been fogging up the car for the last twenty minutes with it."

The third gentleman now got out of the first car and walked round to its boot which the driver had opened. He took out a briefcase and joined the other two. Pete went over to the plane to supervise the loading of the three small suitcases whilst John invited the three to climb up the ladders at the plane's side and take their seats.

Five minutes later, Pete taxied the plane to the end of the runway.

"Sirs, I'm afraid the take-off is going to be a bit bumpy but, as soon as we get airborne, it should become more comfortable. We will be heading south from here where we are to meet up with our escort for the hour and three-quarters flight to Fécamp, where we will have to refuel."

He took off and climbed to the arranged height of seven thousand feet where the Spitfires came down to surround him so that he became the hub of a very large wheel. In this formation, they weaved their way south and out over the channel and then flew in a straight line to their destination. Pete dropped out of the formation when they were above the airfield, circled it once, and was called into land. He touched down lightly and taxied towards the tower. A jeep approached him, directing him to a quiet spot where he parked and deposited his three charges into a limousine. He oversaw the refuelling before his passengers returned and continued his journey south with his trusty escort.

The flight to Bron Airport, just to the south-east of the centre of Lyon, was straightforward and he landed on the runway, followed down by his escorting Spitfires. Being a former international airport, it had the facilities to handle passengers. However, the terminal appeared to have seen better days having been used by the Vichy Airforce before being taken over by the Luftwaffe in 1943. He taxied directly to the terminal, coming to a stop as close as he could. As soon as he did, a convoy of American jeeps and one large limousine halted to the left of the plane. An aircraft stepladder was rolled up to the door, but it had been designed for a much larger plane and was never going to be fit for purpose, a fact that his three passengers were not amused about. Eventually, they disembarked and were ushered into the limousine.

Pete was left to supervise refuelling the aircraft before taxiing it over to a hangar where it would be parked up until their return journey. He was just walking out of the hangar when a jeep pulled up and he heard the unmistakable accent of his brother.

"Hey, Bro, I thought it only fair if I gave you a lift to your hotel."

"Antonio, what the heck are you doing here? I thought this mission was meant to be secret."

"It is secret, but everyone needs transport; how do you think those bigwigs were going to get from here to their hotel? Anyway, where's my welcome, aren't you pleased to see me?"

"Jeez, yeh, I'm just kind of shocked. I was planning to come and find you tomorrow. Now, come here, Bro, and give me a New York hug."

It had been over two years since they had seen each other, and the two brothers were not going to waste these precious moments.

"So, which flophouse have they put me in? Not that I would know any different."

"No flophouse for you, Bro, they have put you into the same hotel as your passengers; only the best for you. The Fourvière. The smartest hotel in Lyon. Even the Nazis didn't mess it up 'cos their high-ranking officers all lived there and barred anyone else from entering. Smart place. I've only been in it once, and that was only to the reception. It's supposed to be an old convent or something. Anyway, it looks religious, and I checked it out, it's got a bar, so you can buy your taxi driver a drink."

They began the catch-up on their six-mile journey into

Lyon, stories about how their wars had gone, scrapes that they had had, people they had met; a general catch-up. When they got to the hotel, Antonio parked up and Pete stood outside with his small bag, looking up at the outside of it. He could only see one side but, oddly, the entrance hall was on the left, a huge gothic door frame with a carved cross at the apex topped by a gothic window separated by five columns. He walked in to find that the gothic theme had been carried on through the reception area. Cold stone walls gave it the look of a church, the biblical wall painting emphasizing the feeling and acting as a reminder of its original use. He went over to the desk to inform them of his arrival and to ask them to take his bag to his room, then walked further into the hotel. He came to a glass door and looked out at an enormous courtyard and cloister running around it. He was at one corner and the entire cloister was illuminated by spotlights set on the floor, pointing up.

He took in the view and headed for the bar. Antonio was about the only person there, standing against it with an open bottle of wine and two glasses beside it.

"Some place this, have you seen the courtyard?" Pete asked his brother.

"Kind of creepy."

"Yeah, I've seen places like this back in England, some places built back in twelve or thirteen hundred, can you imagine that?"

"Except I was told this is all fake, built in eighteen sixty apparently."

"No way, who told you that?"

"My CO, he's into all that, you know, the architecture. Every time we go into a village here, he has to go and look at the local church, or castle, can't get enough of it, and even goes and looks at the local houses, or chateaus as they call them."

"Oh, chateaus, is it? Are you learning the local lingo or something?"

"No, it's just that I have heard him talking about them so often. We're not really meant to have any contact with the locals, but it's hard not to."

They took their drinks over to a quiet table and as soon as they had sat down, Pete leaned in to ask, "How much freedom do you get, freedom to go out and about?"

"Why the whisper?" his brother replied.

"I might have come across a plan that would mean we wouldn't have to work ever again."

"Not another one of your plans; I thought I'd heard them all."

"Just hear me out and then decide. You see, I was just walking around the place where I'm billeted when I came across a bunch of Italian POWs working on a farm, and I got talking to them. It turned out that one of them was the son of Pietro, you know Dad's brother in Italy."

"You're kidding! Are you trying to tell me that in the middle of England, in the middle of a war, you come across an Eyetie who is our cousin? What do you think I am? Mad?"

"No, I swear it. We swapped names and information. He's Marco, it must be correct, it all checks out. I've spoken to him a few times and I'm sure."

"OK, so what story has this Marco been telling you?"

"Pietro is involved with the Mafia in some way, possibly more than Marco realised. Early in the war, they were worried about Italy's involvement and were worried about getting invaded. Apparently, they took all of their gold, or at least some of it, up to northern Italy and hid it in some caves above a village called Grusiner. I've looked at the maps and, considering everything, I reckon you could be there in two days, say three days to find the exact cave and two to get back. A week. I can then make an excuse to fly down here and take it back to England."

"OK, let's put some realism into all of this. Neither you or Marco know if this is true. You don't know how much gold there is, you don't know where it is, and - most importantly - even if you somehow got the gold to England, how the fuck are you going to get it to the USA?"

"Bro, details. I haven't got all the details, but I'm working on it. Marco is working on it. I'm not going to ask you to go on a wild goose chase."

"Wild goose chase? It's madness, it's complete and utter madness. I can't believe you ever thought it was anything else."

"Antonio, I know I have come up with some mad ideas before, but this is not one of them, I know it isn't. It's not an idea, it's destiny, it's for all the Hail Marys we said in the past, it's our route out. Let me get all of the details and then let's see if I can persuade you."

"Well, I can't stop you from doing that, but you are going to have to come up with much more than hearsay."

"OK, now are you staying to finish this wine?"

"It would be rude not to. What are your plans for tomorrow?"

"I don't really know. I don't know how long these talks are going to take, but I would guess they would want to be back in England sometime tomorrow. What are your plans?"

"I've got to take a convoy to Turin."

"Turin! That's near where the gold is hidden, I don't know what the roads are like, but from the maps I have looked at, it should be about a two-hour drive north from Turin, if that."

"Look, I'll take a look around to see what gives. I haven't been to that area before. Right, I had better be going, Bro. How are we going to keep in contact?"

"Can I contact you at your base?"

"You should be able to. I know there are lines to England, but I don't know how secure they are."

"Hopefully, I will get to do this trip again. I can't believe they would invest all the time and money for just one trip."

"You wouldn't have thought so. Look, Bro, keep safe, don't do anything stupid, and please, please don't put too much faith in this gold business."

"Don't worry, I'll not do anything stupid. You, you stay safe, you are closer to the action than I am."

They held each other in the kind of brotherly embrace that they hadn't been able to have since before the war started. Pete didn't follow his brother out of the bar, but sat down, his head in his hands. Tears were welling up in his eyes, his brain was moving at sixteen to a dozen. He wasn't cross at his brother's rejection of his plan, he almost expected it, but he was determined to give him the facts that would change his mind.

The next morning, he made the most of the fact there were important guests in the hotel, which meant that there were ample eggs, coffee, and bread for breakfast and then, because he didn't know what to do, he made his way back to Bron. Firstly, he went to the control tower to see if they had any information; he reckoned that they might have been told when the Spitfires were going to return, but no. Next, he went to the Mess. He had flown with some airmen who were now with the 50th Fighter Group and wondered if any were around.

"Petrol Pete, what are you doing here? Don't say you are joining the real flyboys!"

"Brian, no, don't worry, I'm just here for the day."

"Did you bring down the hotshots? 'Cos if you did, we've got to escort you back to the coast."

"It will be a privilege for you to fly with me again, although you might have to remember I won't be going as high as you normally do."

"Don't worry, we can go low when we need to. Now, come on in and I will introduce you to some of the others."

They walked into the Mess together and Pete realised what he had been missing whilst he had been in Oxhill; the good old male American company that flew planes. Before he knew it, lunch was being served. Halfway through it, the telephone rang to inform him that he was required in the control tower. His passengers were wrapping up their meeting and wouldn't be staying for lunch, they would like to start their journey home as soon as possible.

Chapter 6
Back to the Drawing Board

Pete sat at the kitchen table, the house to himself, opened his notebook, picked up his pencil and put his brain in gear. He was the kind of person who liked to think with a pencil in his hand, jotting things down, striking out words, and doodling. Today he was thinking about what he had to ask Marco when he saw him later. Messages had been passed between them using the tree beside the river as a post box; the last of these had informed him that David Hatch was going to Banbury market that Tuesday.

He started off with some bullet points: need more detail re. cave location; how much gold; is it buried or stored; how far from the road. The list was beginning to take shape when he heard the front door open, and Charlotte came into the kitchen.

"Hello. Writing?" she asked, "I don't think I have ever seen you hold a pencil before."

"Very droll. I got my School Cert exams, you know. In fact, I was quite a student."

"I'm sure you were. Don't worry, I was only joking."

"I was actually writing to my parents telling them who I had in my taxi the other day."

"Who will they be more impressed by, Churchill or Eisenhower?"

"Churchill, I would think; he's the real deal. He even thanked me when we returned and said he thought we would see each other again. I'm now waiting for my invite to tea at Number 10. I could discuss many things with Clemmie."

"Now you are getting ahead of yourself," she smiled. "Why

would our esteemed Prime Minister ask you to tea? Not to discuss painting, I would suggest."

"Well, I can't sit here and discuss my painting acumen, I've got things to do."

They had developed a good camaraderie over the weeks that he had been billeted with her, a banter that she had missed since her husband had gone to war. She liked his humour, enjoyed his piano playing, and appreciated having a man about the house again.

Pete went up to his room to return his notebook and collect a coat before heading out to meet with Marco. He walked down the main street of the village, acknowledging greetings from some of the villagers, but not stopping for a chat which he sometimes did. He walked past Brooklands Farm and over the bridge before entering the field, crossing it to the bank of the river where Marco was sitting, leaning back against the tree.

"Hi, Pete, how's the good life?" Marco greeted him, getting to his feet and embracing him.

"Not so bad. I had to go over to Lyon last week and met up with Antonio. Unfortunately, he is not as keen as I thought he might have been. He is cautious by nature, and he wants more information."

"What you mean is that you couldn't sell it to him. Luckily, I might be able to help you out. I met up with a captain in the camp whose brother was part of the group that took the gold up there. They come from Grusiner, which is why it was chosen as the hiding place. He said that there were four boxes, ammunition boxes, filled with gold bars, and the boxes are hidden under camouflage netting at the back of the cave."

"That sounds encouraging. Now, this cave, did your captain's brother tell him exactly where it is?"

"He did better than that, he gave me a map."

"Marco, a four-year-old could draw a better map than that."

"No, no, no, let me explain. Grusiner has only 37 houses, it is very small. This shaded area is where the valley side is. It is very steep, going into the Alps. Above the cave, the land flattens, that is where the locals graze their sheep in the summer. The track is where the locals herd their sheep up to the grazing ground and goes past the cave. Everyone in the village knows this cave but not what is in it. It is about thirty meters deep, and the gold is at the end," said Marco, tracing each element of the map with his finger as he explained it.

"How much faith do you put into this map?"

"Total, we do not lie in the brotherhood."

"But you are prepared to steal from them?"

"It is not stealing when the goods are already stolen. They have just misinterpreted my interest. I ask questions, they give answers, what am I supposed to do?"

"I think you are pushing the boundaries with that statement, but who am I to judge?"

"I know these men, let me play it my way. Now the split. I suggest that we go fifty: fifty, two boxes each."

"No, Marco, seventy-five: twenty-five. My brother and I are

taking all the risks to get it out and will have more men to pay at the end. Don't forget, Antonio will have to split it with his team, he can't possibly lug all those boxes down the mountain on his own."

"But without my knowledge, you wouldn't even know about the gold."

"That's why you are getting twenty-five per cent. You are taking no risk, you will be able to sit here and see the war out and, when the time comes, walk out of here with a box of goodies."

"But how can I trust you, and where are you planning to hide my half?"

"Your quarter. I'll bury it in the airfield. As for trust, we're cousins. I'm not going to cheat you, am I?"

"We may be cousins, but until a few weeks ago I didn't know you and I don't really know you now."

"Marco, let's not fall out over this. Firstly, we haven't got anything yet, and secondly, if we have something it is still in Italy. Let's see how much we get out and then settle it once and for all."

"Pete, you're right, I'm sorry for doubting you, it's just that I can nearly touch the gold, I'm getting nervous."

"Don't worry, I know how you feel. I must be getting going or Farmer Hatch will come back from Banbury and catch us."

He walked back up the village with more purpose, knowing that he had won the battle with Marco about the share. At the end of the day, Marco wouldn't have a say in the matter and Pete thought he realised that. One box was better than none and that's what he would get if he pissed off the Caruso brothers, cousins or not.

He still had the problem of remaining in contact with his brother in Lyon and it was a problem that was becoming more acute. He didn't want to use the secure telephone in Charlotte's house for the obvious reason that he didn't know whether it would ring any proverbial bells if he used it; he thought probably not but couldn't be sure. Eventually, he decided that deception was the best course of action. He rang Colonel John Polman on the telephone to request that he could call Antonio as he had heard some bad news from home and needed to tell him. No, no way that line still went through a British switchboard and was not secure, but he could do better by using the powers that be. From the very top they had been very impressed by his flying, and they wanted to open a face-to-face channel of communications with the new Government of the French Republic away from the public eye. That meant Paris. He would be transporting high-level civil servants there and back on a weekly basis. The first trip would be tomorrow.

Chapter 7
Second Lyon Trip

Pete was better prepared for the second trip to Lyon. Not only did he know what was expected of him, but he had flown the route before, knew both airfields, and, more importantly, he wouldn't be overawed by the people he was flying. That still didn't make him any less thorough in his pre-flight checks. Tommy Hughes had met him when he had arrived and assured him that the plane was as good as he could make it. As before, he walked the runway to make sure that there were no mole runs that would make the aircraft unstable on take-off.

He could tell there was a more relaxed atmosphere among the ground staff. There was no sign of Colonel John Polman, Pete's commanding officer. This absence was reinforced by the convoy that arrived, if one could call it that, with just one police outrider and one staff car. Pete walked over to where it was parked, wondering what was ahead.

The back door of the car opened, and a tall thin man got out, looked around, and stretched before putting his head back into the car and finally emerging with a document holder. Whilst this was going on, the door on the other side had opened but no one had emerged. Then, a large, bespectacled man eased himself out of the car slowly, again with a document holder, and went to the rear of the car, waiting for someone to open the boot. There was no movement from the front of the car although Pete could see that his third passenger was sitting there. It appeared that he was talking to the driver. Just before he arrived, the front door opened, and a diminutive man got out while still talking to the driver. All three, even with their different builds, were dressed exactly the same in formal three-piece morning suits with three-quarter jackets, striped trousers, and white dress shirts. The only difference between them was their ties, each from a different cricket club. By the time he arrived at the car, all three were standing behind it with their luggage on the ground in front of them, looking apprehensive.

"Good afternoon, gentleman. I'm Major Pete Caruso and I'll be flying you this afternoon down to Lyon. Now as we are flying a four-seater plane I'm going to have to place you in specific seats to balance it. I'm sorry, sirs, but I don't know any of your names, and it may be that I shouldn't know your real names, I don't know, but I need to call you something."

"As civil servants, I don't think we need to go to all that subterfuge. I'm Adrian Steel, from the War Office," the tall thin man said. "My colleagues are Dermot Dunne and Frederic Marland, both from the Foreign Office," he said pointing to, first, the large bespectacled man and then the person who had been sitting in the front of the car.

"Thank you. In order the even up the weight, I think you, Mr Steel, should sit up front with me, and the other two in the rear seats. Now, if we can get your luggage loaded and yourselves seated, we will be away."

When they were all aboard, and he was taxiing to the end of the runway, he told them that if they put on the headphones, not only could they hear his conversations, but they could also talk to him.

After they had taken off, he rose to seven thousand feet, and he headed south. He went on the internal channel and spoke to his travellers.

"We have now reached our cruising height and are heading in a southerly direction. Unfortunately, we will not be able to fly in a straight line to Fécamp, as we have to snake our way around certain airfields, but when we have crossed the coast, we will take a more direct route."

For this trip, the powers that be had decided that an escort of Spitfires was not required which meant that, apart from navigating their route, Pete also had to keep a lookout for any marauding German airmen that might be looking to be a hero towards the end of the war. He had just crossed the coast and set his route for the French coast when his radio lit up.

"Calling American Fairchild, heading one-seven-six degrees at seven thousand feet, are you call sign Captain Bosanquet? This is a patrol of Spitfires above you at nine o'clock. Do you have a visual?"

"Mr Steel, could you look out of your window and up? Can you see a flight of aircraft?"

"Um, what exactly am I looking for?"

"Aircraft, Spitfires, not that you would be able to recognise them as that."

"Yes, yes, I see them."

"We have a visual."

"Remain on your current course but be aware we have had notice that there are bandits around. We are currently looking for them, we think they are to your west at height."

"Roger. Can you provide cover? You know my circumstances."

"Negative, I need all of my hunters. I would advise dropping down to skim the waves."

"Roger, I'll keep this channel open."

"I take it you were talking to those Spitfires," Adrian Steel said.

"Yes, I'm taking us down to base level as they have reported some enemy activity in our area. Can you all keep a good lookout for any activity."

He took the aircraft down until he seemed to be flying on top of the waves. It required all of his attention not to ditch it in the sea.

"Captain Bosanquet, you have two Messerschmitt 109s on your tail. We are diving to intercept. Gain altitude, you might need it."

Pete came up to two hundred feet and turned to port, trying

to increase his speed. As he turned, he took the chance to try and find his pursuers, Jeez, he thought, seeing the two aircraft diving towards him, and then seeing fire erupt from the wings of the front plane. He immediately turned to starboard, trying to make his plane as small as possible. The next thing he knew was the sound of the two planes passing above him as they climbed for another attack; he kept them in view for as long as possible but lost them. *Where were they, where were the Spitfires?* He kept his zig-zag course, varying the turns so as not to be predictable. He now had a target; he could see the coast of France and the safety it would bring.

"Captain Bosanquet, we have engaged the Messerschmitt's and are keeping them entertained. They shouldn't be worrying you again. Head for the coast at full speed and I liked that move."

"Pearl Harbour, the last time I felt like a sitting duck, until today."

"Pearl Harbour, impressive. I'd like to discuss that with you when you get back. Where are you based?"

"Out of Barford, but on my own at the moment. Can I say thank you for the support, never nice being unarmed against those bastards."

"Agree, over and out. Have a happy journey."

Five minutes later, he was crossing the French coast, circling the Fécamp airfield before landing lightly and taxiing to the same spot he had used before. He let out a massive sigh as the plane came to a halt; it certainly hadn't been the flight he was expecting, and it was his first encounter with the enemy for some months. He took off his headphones and motioned to the other three to do the same.

"I'm sorry about that, are all of you alright?"

"Yes, I think it is a good thing that we see the pressures that you put yourself through first-hand; we can often think it is easy at the front, but I think I can say for all of us, we have had an education today. Thank you."

"Look, I've got to get this thing refuelled, and I would like to get going again as we've still got a fair way to go. Here comes some transport and I hear that the food is quite good here, at least that's what your Prime Minister said last week." He sent them on their way, thinking that having two 109s on your tail was not an education, it was fucking frightening.

Their trip down to Bron was, thankfully, uneventful and he was able to dispatch the three Civil Servants to their hotel and put his plane in the hangar without any hassle. He was just thinking about how to get to the hotel when he heard familiar words shouted from a Jeep as it screamed to a halt.

"Hey, Bro, want a lift?"

"Hey, there is a bottle of Whiskey in it for you if you get me there double quick. I have just had a life-changing experience and I need a drink."

"Jump in."

Their journey to the hotel was a quiet one. Pete didn't feel like talking and Antonio sensed the vibe and didn't ask any questions. He checked in as before and went straight to the bar; a bottle of Whiskey and two glasses were standing in front of his brother. Pete poured himself a large one.

"Let's take a seat," he said. "For some god-forsaken reason they thought that I didn't need an escort today and I came across the only flight of 109s left flying. Two were up my ass and firing at my sweet, unarmed, totally defenceless piece of flying shit. I thought I was past this. I thought dog fights were behind me, at least I thought they might give me some protection, and to make it worse one of the "up his arse" civil servants then thanked me for the education. Jeez, how can a country be run successfully and deserve to win a war when it is run by idiots like that?" He finished his tirade and noticed that his brother was laughing behind his whiskey. "What's up with you?" he asked.

"I take it that those three sitting over there and trying to listen to what you are saying were your passengers."

"Shit, what did I call them? Do I need to go over and apologise?"

"I wouldn't worry, you can't take back what you have said, and I don't know if they heard you anyway. Oh, the tall one has got up and it looks as if he is coming over."

"Mr Steel," he said to the approaching Civil Servant, "I didn't mean all that I said then, it is just me blowing off steam. It was not the flight I expected."

"Major, there is no need to apologise. If it wasn't for you, we would have been going for a swim, at the best, tonight. Sometimes between American and British people, the words we use, make the joint language we speak a travesty, a travesty that needs a translator. I apologise for what the "up your arse" person said. Now will you introduce me to your brother as Adrian, not Mr Steel and can I join you for a nightcap?"

"Adrian, you are correct, this is my brother, Antonio. He seems to run the transport here in Lyon. How did you know he was my brother?"

"The PM said that your brother picked you up last week and I made the assumption that he would pick you up again."

"That gets you a whiskey, if that's what you want."

"Ice and water, please. I heard you mention Pearl Harbour when you were speaking to the Spitfire flight, were you there?"

"Yes, it was not one of the best times, for America or for me."

"Do you mind talking about it?"

"Yes, and no; I don't mind talking about how America was caught with their knickers down. I don't like talking about my personal involvement, it is still too raw."

"I can understand that. You see, I have seen action. I spent three days on the beaches of Dunkirk before I was repatriated, I can't talk about that, but I can talk about the administrative cockups that brought that whole episode to bear."

"I read about that, a kind of victory in the middle of a defeat."

"I think the least said the better. Now I must be going. I have got a long day ahead of me, especially as I will have to be speaking French for most of it. Good night to you both."

"Good night, Adrian."

When he had departed, the two brothers filled up their

glasses and pulled their chairs closer together so they could easily talk and not be overheard.

"Have you got any more information?" Antonio asked.

"Yes, there are four boxes, ammunition boxes, full of gold…" Pete continued to tell his brother all the information that Marco had passed on to him before he showed him the map. Antonio studied it before he sat back in his chair and was clearly thinking.

"You know something, I think this map is quite accurate. I haven't told you, but I have been down this road since you were here last. I made an excuse to go this way to Turin and was looking out for the village. It is just as Marco described and the map outlines. It is very steep up the side of the valley and I remember seeing a track going up there. If there is anything up there it is not going to be easy to get it down."

"Bro, you seem to be a man who has changed his mind."

"I think it all sounds too good to be true, but it just could… could be true. Now let's say that I do find it and can get it here, how do you plan to get it away?"

"It looks as if I will be doing this trip every week, but I won't be able to take more than one box at a time. It will be easy enough to load a box here and at the other end, the plane is sat in the field until she is needed. I was planning to bury it in the field. It is how to get it back to the good old US of A that I'm worried about."

"What is the split you have agreed with Marco?"

"Three boxes for us, one for him. Now I assume you will have to pay off some of your guys, what do you think?"

"There will have to be eight people plus myself to carry the gold down the hillside; I was thinking that two bars each should be enough."

"OK, if my calculations are correct, there should be as many as one hundred and eight bars in each case if they are packed in tight. If you are pushed, you could go three each; for the sake of eight bars, I would hate to lose the lot."

"I agree. What is Marco doing with his box?"

"At some stage, he will be released and go back to Italy. I will bury his box separately and let him sort out how to get it home."

"Why don't we leave him one box in the cave? He can then transport it when he is released."

"I'd thought of that, but he is worried that someone will come and reclaim it before he gets a chance to and then find only one box. Why would someone steal three boxes and leave one; he thinks that all hell would be released in the South and that someone would talk. If there are no boxes there, they would be cross and ask questions but might conclude that someone just found them. I don't go with that, but it is his shout."

"OK, I'll see if I can get a trip lined up and let's see what is in the cave. I'll try and come and see you in the morning."

"Bro, I'll see you tomorrow and I hope I have a better flight back. I am, as the Brits like to say, bushed"

Chapter 8
Lyon – Grusiner – Lyon

Antonio was sitting in his office, a hole at the back of a large warehouse. Boxes took up most of the available floor space, the cheapest desk imaginable was against the far wall and he was sitting behind it. The walls were covered with maps, except in one area, and that was because the map that should have hung there was on his desk. He was studying it again, as he had yesterday, but today he had a mathematical compass to measure the mileage between certain points. He was measuring all points to Grusiner and onwards to Turin.

Although he had been there the week before, he had not meant to; it had been a late change of plan, a diversion off the route he had chosen, a decision made in respect of his brother, but also a change of plan brought about by the images of gold. Now he had his logistical head on; what was the best way to get there? The bloody Alps, they were the bane of his life. Every time he looked at a straight line between two places, the bloody mountains got in the way. His original plan had been to go to Grusiner before heading into Turin, but the more he looked at it this was not going to work; no, he was going to have to change it around and his justification to himself was that it was better to be lighter than to try to add the gold to their load of medical supplies.

He now turned to personnel and who to take. The convoy would be made up of three Jimmies, or to give them their full title GMC CCKW, a six-wheel drive cargo carrier that was the commonest in the American Army, along with a Willys MB, that he would use with a driver. He knew he would need eight men to carry the boxes down from the cave. Who could he trust? He pulled his pad of paper closer and picked up a pencil and unceremoniously placed it between his teeth. His first choice was to pick the three drivers, and this was quite easy: Funny Boy (Alun Witty), Jules (Julian McLeary), and McD (Donald Murdoch). Rog (Roger Anderson) would drive the Jeep and Money (Richard Cashmore), their medic, would also go in it. From the start he had decided not to take anyone of Italian extraction, which cut down his options, so next he wrote down Jake (James Bohan), Pro (Steve Prosser) and Pete (Peter Clugston). He looked at the list. Can I trust them, are they going to try and steal the lot? He had landed on the beaches of Normandy with most of these boys and they had gone through a lot. OK, none of them had a halo floating over their heads but he thought he could trust them. Pro was the only one that was new to the team. He had only joined them when they had got to Paris. He was like all of them, scared, mouthy and full of himself, a typical GI but Antonio had noticed over the last few months that he had settled and matured. Yes, he would be OK.

Antonio was well aware that many things could go wrong, the main one being that they would find the cave empty, but at this stage he could only plan for what he could control. He decided that he would brief his men that evening before they set off the next day with three trucks of medical supplies for Turin.

When they were all seated in his office, sitting on boxes, crates and whatever else they could find, he closed the door and stood behind his desk.

"Right, lads," he started, "tomorrow we will be taking three Jimmies with medical supplies to the hospital at Turin and I will be in the Jeep with Rog and Money. It will be the same procedure as before: we drive down there, unload, and come home with three empties. No hassle, no dramas, the war is over in this part, our only problem will be the road surface. On the way back, I want to make a small diversion to a village called Grusiner."

He stopped at this point, from here on in he was putting his whole trust in this team. He looked around the room at the seven men who were looking bored, wondering why they were having a briefing for such a mundane operation.

"Sir," said Funny Boy, "isn't that the village we drove through last week? A shithole of a place with the river running through it; looked as if it was stuck in the last century."

"Full marks, Funny Boy. Let me tell you all a story. Back in '42, the Mafia in Southern Italy became concerned that Italy could be invaded by the Allies, and they reckoned that the invasion was probably going to happen in Sicily. They knew that the Italian forces couldn't keep out the invaders and that an enduring fight was forthcoming as the German army would try and defend Italy. That ends my history lesson. Guys, we have all heard rumours about Mafia gold being taken north and hidden. Well, I think I might have found some. It is no guarantee, but I think it is worth a look. What I have been told is that there is a cave in the hills above the village and in that cave there are four boxes of gold."

"Boss, we've all heard these stories - gold in caves, painting masterpieces in chateaux, God knows how much jewellery hidden in drawers. At my estimation, one in a hundred of these stories are true. What makes you think this one is?" asked Funny Boy.

"I don't know. When I first heard the story, I laughed in my beer. It was my brother telling it, having just flown three VIPs from England to Lyon. I thought the same as you until we went through the village and I saw it could be true. What swayed me was a map. You see, this information has come from England, from an Italian POW, an Italian POW talking to an American pilot who are cousins. The map came from inside the POW camp, from members of the Mafia who feel let down from the lack of support they have received. Look, I don't know how good this information is, but it is worth a look."

"Boss, what's it worth?" McD asked.

"I don't know because I don't know how pure it is, but if it is pure gold and the ingots are the same size as an American one, an ingot is worth about fifty thousand dollars. That's one ingot and we may have four hundred."

There was utter silence as various calculations were done in the minds of his team.

"That's twenty million dollars!" McD exclaimed.

"Yes," Antonio replied, aware that he had now got their full attention, "but, and it is a big but, at the moment we have got nothing, and we don't know if there is anything there. In my opinion, I think that it is worth a look. At this stage, I am not going to discuss how the gold is going to be split because we don't know how much there is, but don't forget there are people not in this room who are due a large slice of the cake."

"Boss, let's say we find some of this gold, how do we get it out? Gold is of no value to me in France or Italy."

"A very good point, Jules. I am afraid I have a plan for mine, I suggest that you all make one for yours."

"Can you tell us what your plan is, Boss?"

"Yes, you can. I'm going to fly it to England."

"Well, it's all right for you, but what about the rest of us?"

"Funny Boy let's not get beyond ourselves. At the moment, we have nothing, and in my opinion there is probably less than a fifty per cent chance that we will find anything. Now, let's get ready for tomorrow, all the normal things, nothing out of the ordinary, and we will leave after we have loaded the lorries in the morning."

They pulled out the next morning with the Jeep in the front of the three lorries loaded up with medical supplies. The weather was not playing its part. It was dull, rain kept sweeping over the concourse currently filled with the various vehicles that made up the transport division. It was not going to help them, it would slow them down, and the roads were not great at the best of times. They crossed the border in the early afternoon, having encountered no traffic, not that they were expecting any, and, as dusk approached, they were pulling into the depot at Turin. As it was their second time doing this run, they knew where to go, what had to happen and who to speak to, which made the whole process faster; by five o'clock they had unloaded everything, obtained the correct signatures and were back on the road, as far as everyone knew, to the barracks for their overnight stay.

The next morning, he led them north out of the city as if he was going to Geneva before turning northwest on a secondary road that would take them to the village of Grusiner. The actual village lay to the right of the road they were driving down, with the river on their left. Turning right off the road, they drove through the village until they ran out of road and had to park up under some trees that provided cover for the lorries. Marching back down the road, they passed two houses that seemed derelict. One had slates missing from its roof and the other, although probably waterproof, was dark and unwelcoming with its front door ajar and shattered glass on the ground in front of the window.

Further down the road, there was a break in the hedge where the map showed there should be a path. Forming up as if they were on a patrol with Pro and Duke on point and the others following behind in formation, with weapons drawn they made their way across the field, each man looking left and right, slowly, carefully until they reached the treeline and the path became more obvious. As they hit the treeline, the slope began to get steeper and twisted amongst the rocks, making Antonio think that carrying the boxes down was going to be a problem. The trees were so dense that it came as a surprise when they came out of the other side and were faced by the solid rock face towering above them. A track about three feet wide had been cut into the rock face. There was solid stone on one side, with a vertical drop on the other.

"Jeez, we're not going up there, are we?" Pro asked.

"I guess so," Antonio replied. "I'm just a bit worried that we will not have any cover. We will stick out like a hooker on Broadway."

"I reckon if we went up one at a time it would only take fifteen minutes and if anyone did see us, they wouldn't think anything of it," Pro said.

"It's not the going up that I'm thinking of, it's the coming down carrying the boxes. I had hoped that we could do the descent when it was dark, or near as, but there is no way we would make it. Have we got any rope in the trucks?"

"Yes," McD replied, "but if you are thinking what I'm thinking, I doubt there is enough of it."

"What are you thinking?"

"Lowering the boxes over the edge."

"The same. Well, we're not going to get them down tonight so we either camp down here, or we climb up there," he said pointing to the rockface, "and see if we can find this cave. At least we will have some shelter then."

Pro, being their best point-man, volunteered to go first and confidently started the climb, going up the track until it doubled back on itself.

"It's pretty easy-going," he called down to the eight sets of eyes following his every move. "It's solid rock, no shale, might be different if it was raining, it would be as slippery as shit. I can see the road from here. Why doesn't someone come up here and watch out whilst I do the next section?"

"Good idea," Antonio called up. "Jake, you go up next, stop where Pro is, and keep watch. When he gets to the next turn, I'll send Pete up to join you, and you send him up to Pro. That way we can get up there quicker."

Using this relay, they all got up to the top of the cliff face and were greeted by a gentle slope across lush grassland until the next cliff face. At the base of it, they could all see the gaping hole that was a cave. Hopefully, *the* cave. Now that they were above the first cliff face, they couldn't be seen from the road or the village, so they almost ran to the opening of it.

It looked like a fissure in the rock, about five feet wide. and it seemed to go straight back into the mountain. The front was the similar size to a large front door but set at a twenty-degree angle. Antonio switched on his torch, shining it into the cave.

"What can you see?" Money asked.

"Nothing, I'm going to go further in. It seems wider at the back."

The floor was sandy, and he could see animal prints, he supposed sheep looking for shelter. The sides shone with water running down them, the ceiling was about three feet above his head. As he entered further into the cave it got wider and he noticed a couple of patches of darker earth or ash where fires had been lit, giving him renewed hope; at least it meant that people had been here before. Suddenly his torch light caught an object, and he could see the back of the cave. On the floor, he could see a tarpaulin covering something. Rushing forward he stopped and carefully looked around the tarpaulin looking for a concealed trap.

"Hey, guys," he called out, "can someone bring a bayonet forward."

The rest of the men came forward and now there were four torches aimed at the lump under the tarpaulin.

"Don't look like four ammo boxes to me," McD stated.

"No," agreed Antonio, "That's why I'm trying to be cautious in case someone has left us a surprise."

Kneeling down, he carefully lifted the tarpaulin with the bayonet and shone his torch underneath. He could see an ammo box. He did the same at either end, trying to see down the back of the box, but couldn't see anything unusual. Slowly he started to lift the tarpaulin, feeling for any resistance, but he couldn't feel any. Eventually, it came away, revealing an object that they had all come to know only too well: an ammo box that would have held standard 303 bullets. It was about a foot and a half long by six inches and nearly a foot tall, the lid secured by two clips and a padlock.

"I thought you said there were four boxes," one of the soldiers said. Antonio wasn't sure who.

"I did," he said with his back still turned towards them. "That's what we were told, now I don't know if that information was wrong, or if there are three more boxes somewhere in here, or someone has come before us and taken three, and this is the last. Let's get this opened and see what we have."

"I think these will help," McD said pulling out a key ring with several keys attached. He went forward. Kneeling in front of the box, he started to try his picklock on the padlock. After a few tries and some huffing and puffing, there was a satisfying click and he was in. He opened the lid and removed the cloth that was covering its contents. The four torches shone down on what looked like a flat surface of gold which seemed to reflect the light back up and fill the cave. No one moved, they all stood there staring and not really believing. Antonio bent down and touched the surface, before running his fingers around one of the ingots tightly packed on the top layer. He prised one free, shocked by its weight, and held it up.

"Twenty-eight per layer and there should be four layers. That makes one hundred and twelve golden beauties, each worth fifty thousand dollars. Do the maths, boys, that's over five and a half million dollars." He turned to look at their faces for the first time. All he saw were eight pairs of eyes staring at the box and eight incredulous expressions.

"Well come on, boys, there might be three more of these here. Now, let's cover every last inch of this cave."

He closed the lid to the box, knowing that nothing would get done if they could still see the gold, and then sat on the box to protect it. At first, there was a charge, like children starting an Easter Egg Hunt, running around with no rhyme or reason. Then the second wave started. They all lined up on their knees with bayonets and started to stab the sand around them before all moving on and stabbing the next area. This carried on until they had covered the entire cave with no results.

"OK, I think we can discount the idea that there might be another three boxes hidden here. Let's be thankful we have found one. It is too late to make it down to the trucks, so we will stay here for the night. I want two on guard at the entrance on a rolling basis, but the last two shifts must be taken by non-drivers. Money, can you sort that out."

They had a quiet night. Since the Normandy landings they

had all become used to sleeping rough with only basic rations. Antonio didn't sleep, he sat with his back against the ammo box and thought. He thought about how to get the box down the mountain, thought that it would be easier now there was only one to transport, thought about how many of the bars he was going to have to give away to his troop, thought about how he was going to stay alive now that they had seen the gold and the fever had set in. He thought and thought, but he didn't come up with many solutions. He knew that his brother would believe him that there was only one box but would Marco? That would be his brother's problem.

His troop started to move at sunrise, some just waking up, others leaving the cave for calls of nature. Slowly the cave gained some light as the sun shone in through the opening and he was able to see more of it as a whole rather than lit by the four spotlights from the torches. Jake came in through the entrance with an armful of dried sticks and started to make a fire where others had made them. Soon he had a base and went out to collect more wood. With the fire started, the cave began to warm up and it wasn't long before the kettle was boiling and coffee drunk.

Pete and Jules carried the box out of the cave and started the march back towards the cliff edge. When they were twenty yards from it, Pro motioned that they should all go to ground, and he slunk up to the edge. Looking over, he had a clear view down over the trees to Grusiner. He searched the area for any movement but couldn't see any. Calling the troop forward, they reversed the descent, zig-zagging their way down, changing the duty of carrying the box at every change of direction. They were all glad when they got to the bottom and, although the conditions underfoot were not ideal, they took it slowly and carefully until they got to the road and the box was loaded into one of the lorries.

Chapter 9
Oxhill Gold

Pete was sitting at the table in the kitchen eating his breakfast and thinking that it couldn't be too long before this whole saga would come to an end, and he would be repatriated to the US of A. The telephone in Charlotte's house had not rung for nearly three weeks, it was as if he had been forgotten.

"That's the longest face I've seen on you for a long time, what's the matter?" Charlotte said as she entered the kitchen and put the kettle on the hob.

"I was just thinking that the telephone hasn't rung for a long time, the war is over, and that it is not too farfetched to think that I have been forgotten."

"Major Pete Caruso forgotten? No, I don't think so, Pete. How many GIs are there over in Europe at the moment? Two million, three million? You can't just expect them to transport you all home at once, it's going to take some time."

"I guess, it's just my impatience showing through."

"If I were you, I would go and make sure that plane of yours is airworthy and also see your cousin."

"You know something, don't you?"

"No, I promise I don't, but my food box from your NAFFI is definitely smaller - fewer eggs, less bacon and, more importantly, less coffee."

"You shrewd old thing. So, you think that they are going to call me back?"

"Yes, and less of the old, if you don't mind," she said with mock sternness.

"You know what, I'm going to make you a special cup of coffee, a Pete Special, for cheering me up."

"What, may I ask, is a Pete Special?"

"A Pete Special. Don't you Limeys know anything? It's a coffee that's special because it's made by Pete."

"Oh, *that* Pete Special," she said, laughing, and sat down at the table. "Well, I can't refuse one of those."

An hour later it was an invigorated Major Pete Caruso that walked up Green Lane towards the field, enjoying the early spring sunshine. When he got there, he uncovered the plane, unlocked it, and fired it up, then climbed down and completed his normal checks. He walked down the runway, thinking that he would need to get the grass cut soon but he noticed that the fine weather of late had firmed it up. Lastly, he went up the hill to the two spots where the gold was hidden. He saw that the turf had now knitted in, and no one would notice where he had dug the two holes. He stood there thinking back to the two journeys that he had made from Lyon where he was overloaded with three passengers and half of the gold. How sluggish the plane had felt, slow in responding to his wishes, and how nearly he hadn't been able to stop at the end of the runway! It seemed to be so long ago since the disappointment when Antonio had told him that there had only been one box, the initial mistrust. No, his brother wouldn't try to have one over him. The acceptance, and then the same argument, in reverse, with Marco who naturally thought he had been swindled. He chuckled as he remembered that conversation and how he was in fear for his life.

"Hi, Marco, I've got some good news for you," he'd said as they had met up in their usual place across the stream at the back of Brooklands Farm, a meeting that could only take place on a Tuesday when David Hatch was at Banbury market.

"What, my friend, don't tell me you have got the gold."

"Yes, I flew the first consignment up last week and have buried it in the field."

"You got two whole boxes up in one flight?"

"No, I'm afraid there weren't four boxes in the cave, only one."

"No, there were four, there were four. You, you are trying to cheat me. I know there were four."

"Marco, I'm not trying to cheat you and I'm as disappointed as you, but when Antonio got up there, there was only one box hidden under the tarpaulin."

"It is your brother, then. He has cheated us both, there were four boxes up there, I know. You'd better fly back to Lyon and tell him that I know there were four boxes, and I want my share, or else he'll have me to deal with, and my influence stretches a long way."

It had gone on for another fifteen minutes, Marco insisting on his life there were four boxes and threatening all kinds of retribution. Suddenly, and Pete to this day didn't know what changed in Marco's mind, he accepted that his cousin was not trying to cheat him. Perhaps it was the thought of twenty-eight gold ingots worth nearly one and a half million dollars.

Pete could laugh at it now, but at the time it was not so funny until Marco changed, like turning on a light bulb. He walked down the hill, checked the plane again, checking that the engine had warmed up and was running smoothly before he shut her down and covered her up. He left the field, making sure to shut the gate, he never knew why, but he had always been told to, and started the walk back towards Oxhill.

He walked past Green Lane, carrying on down the Whatcote Road. As he walked, he found himself remembering the first night he had driven down there too fast and on the wrong side of the road, nearly taking out Doctor Gilroy who had been rushing towards Whatcote to help in the delivery of Paula Howarth's first child. Names of villages, names of inhabitants were just names then but over the six months he had been living in Oxhill they had become more than that.

He walked on down the hill to the T-junction with the imposing Oxhill House on the right and then continued on the familiar walk down to Brooklands. He approached the house and knocked on the door. The sound of dogs barking inside assured him that David Hatch was in. He heard the sound of Hatch shouting for the dogs to stop their "infernal din" before the door opened.

"You, what do you want?" This was Hatch's idea of a welcome.

"Mr Hatch, I know we have had our issues, but I think I will be leaving the village any day now to go back to the States and I wondered if I could have a couple of minutes with Marco to say goodbye."

"You're leaving, then. Going to bugger off and leave us to clear up the mess you have left. Typical."

"Mr Hatch, I promise you that I have not come here to have an argument with you. I just wanted to say goodbye to Marco."

"Well, as you are leaving, I suppose so, but don't take too long, he's got a lot to do today."

"Thank you."

He turned round to go through the gate in the hedge that took him onto the farm lane from where he could access the main yard. Calling out Marco's name, he was answered by the squeal of a pig in the shed opposite and his cousin's shout. He went over and entered the shed which held six sows with their litters.

"Marco, don't worry, I have spoken to Hatch. I think I may be leaving very soon and just wanted to say goodbye to you."

"My cousin, you are leaving so early, but why, you don't like our company?"

"Oh Marco, I'm going to miss your humour. I haven't been told yet, but Charlotte said something this morning that made me think she knows. She's usually right and Magic Carpet seems to be in full swing now."

"So, this is it? We go our separate ways and never see one another again?"

"No, I don't think so. I think that travel will become so much easier in the next few years, planes will fly between New York and Rome. I know we will see each other again."

"Oh, you may well be right. Arrivederci, my friend, let's not make this harder than it already is."

"Arrivederci, until next time."

They embraced and Pete turned to leave.

He was walking back through the village when he heard the sound of horse's hooves trotting up the road behind him. Turning round, he saw it was Charlotte who waved at him to get his attention.

"Pete, I seemed to have been chasing you all over the country," she said. "Colonel Polman wants to see you this afternoon. The telephone rang soon after you had left."

"OK, did he give a time? What I mean is can I have some lunch before driving over?"

"No, you don't understand, he wants you to fly over there."

"Fly, no, I can't." He was now thinking on his feet. He couldn't just fly out of here, impossible.

"Why not?" she asked.

"'Cos…The grass is too long; it has really grown over the last couple of weeks."

"Well, you will have to tell him then, but those were your orders."

"You mean I can actually talk to him on the telephone?"

"Yes," she laughed.

He got back to the house before Charlotte and telephoned his commanding officer. He got through immediately. "John, it's Pete."

Although there had to be a level of respect when they met on the base in front of other officers, Pete had known John Polman for a number of years, and they had gone through some tough times together.

"Pete, good news, I've got you a berth on the USS Washington along with your little bird. You set sail in two days' time, so you had better get your arse back over here."

"Yezz, thank you, I'm getting out of here!"

"On the points system, your time is up. Now, how quickly can you get here?"

"Well, that's the problem; I will need to get the runway mown."

"Mown? What do you mean?"

"The grass, it needs to be cut. I could get the local farmer to do it this afternoon or tomorrow morning and be back there for lunch tomorrow."

"Now, Pete, if I didn't know you better, I would think you were running a ruse. I wanted you back this evening so we could get roaring drunk in the mess."

"Shit, I wish I could. Can't we do that tomorrow?"

"Suppose we will have to. Well, you go and get your bloody grass cut and I will see you in the morning. Make sure you say a nice goodbye to that Mrs Holland, by all accounts she is one hell of a woman. Grass cut, my arse, have a good last night with her."

"Yes, sir." He rung off and was just going upstairs when Charlotte returned from the farm.

"So, what's news?" she asked.

"I'm going home. My name has made it to the top of the points system, and I sail on the USS Washington in two days' time. Do you think I can get Tom to run the hay mower over the runway?"

"Yes, I should think so, when do you need it done by?"

"John wants me back there by lunchtime tomorrow, so sometime in the morning."

"So, tonight is going to be our last night. I don't know what I am going to do without you, I'll miss you."

"And I'll miss you," he said, putting his arms around her, and he thought he would; he hadn't realised it but the two of them had grown close over the six months that he had been staying. It turned out to be a rather sombre lunch, neither of them knew what to say, both of their emotions running high. His thoughts were spread between what he would be leaving behind and how he was going to get the gold out of the ground and into the plane; her thoughts were unidirectional, she was going to miss this great big bear who had come to live in her house, play her piano, and invade part of her heart.

After they had cleared up the meal, he went round to see Tom and arranged that he would cut a slim strip first thing in the morning. Then he drove up to the field, retrieved the spade that he had hidden in the wood, and carefully started to peel back the grass before clearing the soil from the top of the box to give access to the gold. He had parked the Jeep beside the hole to give him some cover in case anyone came down the road. He deliberately hadn't buried the box very deeply as he had anticipated a quick departure. He had also been busy at the farm making two bespoke boxes which he had already fitted into the hold of the plane. He loaded the sixty ingots into the back of the Jeep and drove them down to the plane and then reversed the process of loading them into the boxes. He had just finished and was back up the hill, filling in the soil and grass, when he heard horse's hooves a moment before Charlotte's head appeared over the brow of the hill. He dusted himself down and walked down the field to meet her at the gate.

"You look as if you have had a busy afternoon," she said. "I have been down to the Peacock and persuaded Deborah to sell me two bottles of her best red wine. Luckily, there were two steaks in your food box this week. So, you had better finish up here and get yourself into a bath, because you look as if you need one and I'm not eating with a grubby, sweaty oik having spent time and money putting on a feast."

"Madame, I will be finished shortly and your oik will turn himself into an American gentleman. I'm not sure what an oik is, but it doesn't sound like a compliment, and I'm not sure there is such a thing as an American gentleman, but I'll do my best to entertain you."

"Your best is all I ask. I want a glass of wine in the drawing room as I listen to you play the piano, a second glass whilst I'm putting the finishing touches to our feast… And that is as far as I have got."

"Your wish is my command," he retorted, with a mock bow the like of which David Niven would have been proud of.

The next morning, Pete woke up aware that he had had too much wine the night before. He rolled over in his bed and very slowly put his feet on the floor before righting his body. His head felt fuzzy, a sensation he hadn't felt for some time. Rubbing the stubble on his chin, he slowly got up, went to the bathroom, washed, and shaved. Feeling slightly better, he returned to his bedroom and took his uniform out of the wardrobe and got dressed.

The aromas coming from the kitchen made him realise how hungry he was: bacon, toast, and fresh coffee. Charlotte had her back to him as she stood in front of the range, the sizzle emanating from various pans had her full attention and she almost jumped as he wished her good morning.

"I didn't hear you come downstairs," she said. "I know that you haven't got far to go today, but I thought you needed a hearty breakfast as an Oxhill send-off."

"I doubt it will be my last meal in the village. I said yesterday to Marco that the biggest growth area is going to be aviation when all of this settles down. Planes are now flying further, faster, and getting bigger, and I can see transatlantic flights becoming the norm very soon."

"You really think people will be able to afford to fly over here from America?"

"I think that people will weigh up a week on a boat against half a day on a plane, and the plane will win."

"I can't quite see that; I like the idea, but I'm not sure."

"Mark my words, within five years there will be daily flights between London and New York, and then another flight from there to the West Coast. England is in an ideal position; what else are you going to do with all the airfields?"

"We can't use them all," she said bringing his plate over to the table, "but I see what you mean. Perhaps I could come and see you in New York - imagine that! - to see all the sights."

"It would be a pleasure to show you around. It's the greatest city on earth, you know. When things start picking up again, I'll take you to a Broadway show after cocktails in the Rainbow Room, and to eat in a real New York diner – although you give even our diners a run for their money with breakfasts like this!

"What do you think you will do when you get home?"

"I don't know. I am a commissioned officer in the US Airforce and I haven't thought about resigning that, so I guess it depends where I am posted. I guess I'll get a few weeks' leave to see my parents again."

"You must be looking forward to that."

It came to the moment of saying goodbye as Pete threw his kitbag into the back of the Jeep and turned round. They embraced before he climbed behind the steering wheel, started the engine, and reversed out of the drive. No words were spoken, no words were needed.

He drove to the field to find that Tom had finished cutting a strip down the runway and that one support truck was parked in its normal position. Airman Tommy Hughes was sitting on its wooden steps.

"I've given her a once over, but I haven't put any fuel in as you seem to have enough," he said as they walked over to the plane. "What are those two boxes bolted into the hold?"

"I've got some personal stuff that I have been collecting in them."

"You shouldn't have done that. Technically, I should take them out, sir."

"Come on, Tommy, I'm not going on any more operations. It's just a way of getting my stuff home."

"Well, I don't know, but I suppose you're flying out tomorrow so I'll turn a blind eye."

"Thanks, mate. Now, I'll be getting going, Colonel Polman wants me back for lunch."

"Right, you are, sir."

The flight back to Barford St. John was uneventful after he had taken off from the field. When he was halfway down the runway, for one heart-stopping moment he'd thought he'd have trouble taking off but eventually, the tail came up and the plane lifted off, skimmed over the hedge, gained height, and was away.

Chapter 10
The Present Time

I was standing in the field that evening at the end of a hot, sunny summer day, with Andy, both of us holding a bottle of cold beer that I had just brought up from the house. I knew that Professor Paul Gil and Max Nokes were finishing off the analysis of the day's geophysics as I had already delivered beers to them.

"It really is quite an interesting field. The more we look at it, the more we want to dig it up," Andy said.

"I would really not like you to do that. After all, it may be archaeology to you, but it is having bread and butter on our family table to me."

"I know, I know, but depending on what the geophysics shows today – and maybe a test pit - the County Archaeologist will have to be informed. Both Paul and I know Michael Bain very well, he's very reasonable and will respect your wishes as well as his job."

We were just finishing off our beers when Paul Gil called us over. He had a massive smile on his face.

"Come and look at this," he said excitably, holding out a printout. "You see these shadows here and here? They are indicative of a building. These lighter bits could well be internal walls. This whole area looks as if it may be a large peristyle with rooms off it, and this here looks like an atrium, again with rooms leading off it. To me, if I was giving a lecture on how a large first-century Roman villa would look on a geophysical analysis, this would be it. This is something big."

"I would suggest we dig two test holes over this supposed

wall and here too, in what may be a room. We should be able to do that tomorrow, assuming you don't give us too much wine tonight."

"OK, that sounds sensible. Burgers on the barbecue, all right for everyone tonight. Shall we say about eight-thirty? That should give you all time for a pint down at the Peacock."

"Sounds good," Andy replied.

I was giving Micky some throwdowns on the back lawn to get his eye in before a cricket match later that afternoon when Andy turned into the driveway and honked his horn.

"You had better come up and see this. It is pretty amazing, far more than an empty World War Two ammo box."

PART 3

THE TEMPLARS
1307 – 1308

Chapter 1
Collecting the Rent

The Preceptory in Oxhill was situated on the stream flowing through the village. It was not a grand building, but it was solidly built using the local reddish sandstone found in the hills above Tysoe in the Vale of the Red Horse. It was a building that suited the knights' needs, a main room dominated by a table where the four knights ate their meals and entertained any travelling guests, a large open fire at one end and a door to the kitchen at the other. Another door in the middle of the room led to the sleeping quarters to form a T-shaped building.

Currently, the Preceptory had four knights in residence and two Sergeants along with the accompanying staff to cook for them and look after the limited livestock held in pens behind the stables. Sir Guillaume de Stowe was the Templar Commander. Now in his sixties, he had fought alongside Jacques de Molay at the Fall of Acre in 1291, the last time The Templars would fight in Palestine, and was with him on the retreat to Cyprus. A veteran of the Templar Order, he spent most of his time in prayer at the Cistercian church within the property given to the order in 1241 by John de Wauton. Sir Robert le Jay, younger brother of Sir Brian, who had been the Templar Grand Master of England until he was slain at the Battle of Falkirk, was the senior knight. He had never gotten over the death of his brother in what he considered a political adventure at the behest of King Edward the First to align the Knight Templars in England to the Crown.

Two younger knights made up the quartet: Sir Alain Heath and Sir Gui de la Granville. Both had been on the excursion to

Scotland, and both had been knighted by the king before the Battle of Falkirk. In their late twenties, they saw themselves as the future of the Order. A future that didn't include its original purpose, whereby they were the protectors of pilgrims to Jerusalem, but a more political and financial order that would stabilise the power struggles within European kingdoms and would return the Papal administration to Rome.

On this fresh spring morning, the two younger knights were on a mission to visit all of their properties in the triangle between Oxhill, Shipston, and Tysoe. The visits were twofold: firstly, to inspect the property's condition to ensure that the tenant was maintaining it, and secondly, to collect their rent. The Templars were seen to be preferable as landlords due to their altruistic ways; they were seen to charge a fair rent and took an interest in their land.

They weren't dressed in their full armour, nor were they riding their destriers but rouncies, an everyday horse rather than a war horse. Both were very proficient riders, used to riding the destriers in battle and in Tournaments. They were not easy horses to ride, especially in full armour, with limited movement possible and a good sense of balance an essential if you weren't to tumble off. Today they were dressed in linen shirts with leather sleeveless jerkins and their traditional three-quarter length white surcoat with the red cross over the top. They were accompanied by Sergeant Simon Amblard dressed in his brown Sergeant uniform. He was driving a six-wheel cart pulled by two horses with a strongbox in the back. The small party left the village with the two knights leading the way up the track to Whatcote, their speed regulated by the rut holes in the road which were a real problem at this stage of the year when there hadn't been time to fill them in after the hard winter that hopefully was behind them. Alain and Gui were in good spirits. It had been a long winter where they had not left the village and it was now a relief to see the countryside, hear the bird calls, and the early spring flowers at the side of the track.

"How much longer do you think we will be needed?" Alain

asked his friend.

"Needed? I would say that we will always be needed. Maybe not in our original role, I think that will change, I think we will take on a more diplomatic role as Papal envoys and bankers."

"You don't think that Grand Master Jacques will get his crusade?"

"He wants it, but I don't think he will get it unless we finance it, and I can't see that happening. King Phillip won't help. Anyway, he owes the Brotherhood too much money."

"What about Edward Longshanks?"

"Our Great King? I think he has burnt his boats with the Templars after Falkirk. Our Robert wouldn't march again with him, of that I'm sure."

"I worry about King Phillip and that snake Guillaume de Nogaret. He was behind the expulsion of the Jews last year and the "transfer" of their wealth, or should I say he stole their wealth for the French chancellery? I worry that it was not enough."

"Alain, you might be right, but we are aligned to the Pope and have free access to go where we want. We are tax-free, we lend money, no monarch can touch us, we will survive."

"I wish I had your confidence. I would still like another crack at Palestine and kick the Mamluks out of there."

"You'd better pray De Molay has learnt some persuasion and diplomacy skills to go with his warrior ones."

"That's the frustration, the not knowing; when we were in Paris, we heard what was going on, but stuck in Oxhill, I doubt they have even remembered we are here."

"Don't worry, we haven't been forgotten. If we didn't pay in the rent money we are collecting, someone would be asking questions."

"I suppose you are right about that. I suppose we had better start here. What is the tenant's name?"

"Cyrus Albery, can't you remember anything?"

"Oh, you know me, I'm able to pick a horse out of a field but remember the name of the last person I met? No, I haven't a clue. What should we be looking for here?"

"Let me do the talking. Last year they had a problem with the roof on their main barn. They had tried to fix it, but we had to step in and help them out; we need to inspect how it looks now. Also, they had not been following our farming acumen regarding keeping their livestock."

"What am I meant to know about the acumen of keeping livestock? I am a warrior, not a farmer!"

"Well, for the next two days, you will keep quiet and learn."

They rode up the lane towards the house, a single-story one made from wattle and daub, with a whitewash finish. A low wooden door was in the centre of the whitewash with one small window on either side with shutters to stop any inclement weather. The roof was thatched, thatched last summer, and still showing a glow in the spring sunshine; only one winter old, it had not yet lost its original colour. A livestock barn, the same size as the house, was attached to the dwelling. It had not been whitewashed and had no windows, but a double-sized door was in the middle.

The two Templars stopped and looked at the scene in front of them. Simon stopped behind them. The door of the house opened, and Cyrus and Sarah Albery came out with their three children clinging to their clothing. For the Albery family this was a big day in their lives; not only did they have to pay the Templars to carry on living and working in Whatcote, but they also had to show they had learnt lessons.

"Sirs, welcome, would you both like a beverage before we start?" Cyrus asked.

"Thank you, but no, Cyrus, I fear if we had a beverage at every farm we have to visit today, we would be asleep in the cart before we ended, and poor Simon would be looking after double the horses that he is now."

"My wife has prepared some honey cakes, perhaps you would like some now or later."

"Later, I think, Cyrus. How has the new thatch worked over the winter? I must say, it is looking good."

"It has worked perfectly; I think that putting that extra layer on made all the difference."

"Good, I am glad you have also whitewashed the walls. Have you finished sowing the spring wheat and barley?"

"Almost, with the good weather the last week I have caught up and was hoping to have finished before you came today, but I will probably finish tomorrow."

"That's good. Let's hope we have a good summer and that the harvest is better than last year. Now I want to inspect the barns. I remember that last year there was an issue with the livestock husbandry."

"Yes. Sergeant Peter, has helped us over the winter; we mucked out the barn in January, which we have never done before, and they have come out of the winter better than before."

"Good, let's go and have a look."

The two knights and Cyrus walked over to the main livestock barn. The farmer opened one of the main doors and walked in. The barn was separated into twelve separate pens with hurdles separating them. At the far end there was a larger area where the cattle were housed. It had been this area that had caused the issues before. Even though it had been cleared during the winter, the straw was wet and when stood on brought up water.

"Did you put the drainage holes in the back wall as was suggested?"

"Yes, you can see from the other side that it is draining, but not fast enough."

"I would suggest you go down another foot and then dig a ditch to let it run away."

"Yes, sir."

"Well, I think that probably covers all of the checks that we have to do; now is that offer of honey cakes still on the table?"

The questions had been answered, the money counted and loaded into the strong box in the waggon and goodbyes said. This would be the same procedure at all the farms they visited that day and they arrived at the inn in Shipston that evening in a relaxed condition. They had collected the rent, they had seen the improvements to the farms and, with this improvement, they could charge increases for the next year.

The two knights were sat at a table next to the fire in the inn. They were privileged seats. Both had jugs of ale and bowls of potage in front of them and were discussing the various farms they had visited that day. For Alain it hadn't been an interesting one. He knew that armies cost money, but he didn't see why he had to go around farms discussing thatched roofs or drainage. He was discussing this with Gui when the door of the inn opened and their other Sergeant, Peter Ryckman, came in, looked around and came over to their table.

"Sirs, I'm sorry to interrupt you but a messenger has arrived from London and Sir Guillaume requires you both back at the preceptory as soon as you can. I would suggest that we leave now."

"We will go and get our horses ready and be ready to leave in ten minutes. Sergeant Simon can stay here tonight and come back in the morning," Gui said.

"I saw Simon in the stables when I arrived. He has already started to tack them up."

"Good, let's be on our way, then."

The return journey to Oxhill was much quicker without having to go at a snail's pace with the cart but they still had to be careful in the dying light not to break one of the horses' legs in a pothole. When they arrived at the Preceptory, Sergeant Peter took control of the horses, and the knights strode through the front door to find Sir Guillaume standing with his back to the burning fire and Sir Robert sitting at the table finishing off his dinner; another knight was sitting there who neither of them knew.

"Sir Gui and Sir Alain, may I introduce you to Sir Henry de Faverham who is attached to the London Preceptory? He has brought a message from Sir Guillaume de la More that the three of you are to make haste to London in the morning and be prepared to travel onwards from there. The Grand Master will relay to you your next destination. I suggest you all get some supper and be ready to leave after Prime. You are to take your destriers and packhorses with you. Now I think that we should all go to Vespers and pray for your future journey, wherever it may take you.

Chapter 2
To London for Orders

The next morning the preceptory was abuzz with activity. The sergeants and grooms were preparing the three destriers and three packhorses that the Oxhill knights would take; they had to be fed, groomed, transport boxes strapped to their backs. Armour and weapons had to be loaded for the first part of their journey to Temple Cowley where they planned to spend the night. The knights had started their day at Prime around dawn in the Cistercian church, followed by breakfast, before seeing that the servants had packed their personal items into bags that they would carry.

They all wore light garments under the chain mail and their white surcoat, all had their swords attached and their horses wore the cloth breastplate, again in white with the red cross. They were dressed for a journey, not for battle.

Sir Guillaume de Stowe came out of the preceptory building into the courtyard as the four knights were mounting their destriers and getting ready to depart.

"Sirs," he addressed them, "I wish you haste in your journey. I know not where it will take you, but I trust that wherever you go, you will bring honour to our brotherhood, will follow our decrees, and succeed in whatever you are ordered to do."

They all saluted him, took hold of their packhorse, and rode out of the yard, heading first for Banbury about twelve miles away. They rode two-by-two with Sir Robert and Sir Henry at the front and Sir Alain and Sir Gui behind, The pace was dictated by the standard of the road; sometimes they were able to trot for a period, but at other times they had to walk, especially when they came to the escarpment of Edge Hill. The day was sunny and quite warm. They passed fields with sheep and their lambs grazing totally unconcerned by the warrior knights passing and other fields where the autumn wheat had been sown and was now poking its head up above the soil.

"Sir Henry, what is your history with the brotherhood?" Robert asked his riding companion. As he was the younger brother of the past Grand Master of England, he thought that he would have heard of his riding partner.

"I knew your brother; he was a great man. Although I wasn't at Falkirk, he communicated back to the Temple that he was not an advocate of King Edward's battle plans and nearly brought the Templar knights away from the field. I only wish he had."

"I was there, as were Alain and Gui. In fact, they were both knighted there. It was not a good time, historians will all say that the king won but William Wallace was not a bad man, and I think he was dealt with badly, although it was inevitable."

"I'm afraid that losing a battle, especially when one is fighting for one's country's independence, is not good news if one wants to keep one's head attached to one's neck. It is different when two kings have a disagreement; one may get killed in the battle, but the divine right of kings means that, even if one was captured, they would be ransomed, not executed."

"That's very insightful. We, of course, sit in the middle, aligned to no King or country but the Pope. We pay no taxes; we can go where we like and will not be questioned. Our land has been given to us, and kingdoms, kingdoms not people, owe us money. We could become the greatest peacekeeping brotherhood, stopping wars, and making Kings talk rather than fight."

"Sir Robert, I admire your hope and faith in where we could go, but I fear that in Oxhill you have not been kept in touch with current news."

"What news?"

"Two main things: the Pope would like us to join with the Hospitallers and has asked Sir Jacques de Molay along with

Foulques de Villaret to meet him in Avignon to discuss it. Secondly, we have been accused of various heretical crimes, with no basis, by King Philip IV and the Pope would like to discuss this with Sir Jacques."

"This is news to me, why would he want the two orders to join together?"

"He feels that having two papal orders dilutes the authority of both."

"But we are different, we have different agendas, we do different jobs."

"I agree, but Pope Clement thinks that we would be stronger as a combined unit."

"But that is stupid. Any revenue that we accrue would be given away by them, we need that revenue to recapture Palestine and kick the Mamluks out."

"My heart agrees, but my brain says otherwise, I don't see the appetite for another Crusade. Edward has Scotland to worry about, Philip always seems to have three or four wars to fight at the same time and can't afford it. The Pope would obviously like Jerusalem to be returned to Christian rule, but he is under Philip's control."

"I have to say, Sir Henry, you don't paint a pretty picture, so why do you think that we are being called to London?"

"I couldn't say even if I knew."

They rode into Abbington and took the road to the Cowley Temple. It had been a long day and, once they had come up the escarpment at Edge Hill, the ride had been fairly flat. They were expected at the preceptory, as Sir Henry had advised them that he would be returning with three other knights on his outward journey. The Templar complex was a lot larger than the one at Oxhill. Four grooms helped the knights to un-mount their destriers and then the grooms took the packhorses away to off-load them, rub them down, feed them and stable them. The knights were welcomed, wine was brought from the cellar, introductions were made, and old friendships renewed.

The next morning the four knights rode north to begin

with and then down the Thames. It was an equally long ride but an easier one. They lunched at Maidenhead, followed the river towards London, going through Windsor and passing the castle without stopping, heading towards Putney and the village of Kensington. From there they still followed the river to the London Temple.

The London Temple hadn't changed since the knights from Oxhill had last visited it after their Scottish adventure. Although it had many buildings - kitchens, stores, stables, sleeping quarters - the church was the central building. For Sir Robert, it had the sense of coming home, a majority of the years that he had been in England had been spent in these halls and yards; he was welcomed by the groom who had looked after his horses in London, Cyprus, and Palestine. When he had dismounted and embraced the groom, he turned to see a sergeant hurrying towards him.

"Sir, the Grand Master is waiting for you."

Grand Master Guilliam de la More had been elected to lead the English Templars after his predecessor had been killed at the Battle of Falkirk; he now sat at the refectory table waiting to greet the three knights from Oxhill.

"Sir Robert, it is good to see you again, I trust you are well?"

"Grand Master, it is always an honour to see you and yes, I am well, thank you. May I present Sir Alain Heath and Sir Gui de la Granville."

"Sirs, it is good to make your acquaintance. I don't know how up to date you are with the current situation, so I will tell you everything that I know. Pope Clement, we think, under pressure from King Philip, is of the opinion that we should join with the Hospitallers and has invited our Grand Master and Sir Philip de Thame to meet him in Avignon. As far as we know Sir Philip hasn't turned up yet. That is probably the least of our problems. King Philip, or more particularly, Guillaume de Nogaret have been filling Pope Clement's brain with ideas that we are a heretical brotherhood, that we should be disbanded and that all our property in France should be given to the King. We would not exist and the debt that King Philip has with us would be eradicated and he would steal all our property.

"Grand Master, what are these heretical accusations?"

"Apparently, they have to do with initiation rights. I am not sure of the details, but it has been reported to me that the Pope is sceptical."

"If that is the case, surely he will back us?"

"Maybe, maybe, but what if King Philip acts independently? What if that worm de Nogaret gets his way - he definitely has the King's ear - and decides to capture and imprison Templars in Paris?"

"But we are protected by the Pope, he couldn't do that!"

"He shouldn't, but he could. He could justify it by saying he is doing it for the Pope."

"But who would believe him?"

"It wouldn't matter, within days he would have confessions to whatever he wanted a Templar to say."

"Grand Master, you paint a very bleak picture. You have not called us down just to tell us this news, what are your orders for us?"

"Robert, I don't know the details, I don't know the exact orders you will be given, but I have been asked to find a preceptory that is not well known, that has a small number of "blooded" knights that could travel to France to help Sir Gerard de Villiers in a plan. I confess I do not know what that plan is."

"What exactly are our orders?"

"You are to travel to Paris and receive further orders there; you are not to travel as Templars, you are to travel as gentlemen, you are basically to travel undercover. We will provide each of you with a groom, and a valet, plus you will have a wagon with a driver and two horses. So, no Templar surcoats, no swords; you are going on a journey to Paris and, if asked, and you will be, you will say that you are going to visit Sir Gui's ancestral home in Chantilly."

"I'm sorry, sir, but I don't have a home there."

"Sir Gui, you do now. What is more, you will be leading your troop, you will be the one who speaks when questioned, these are your friends whom you are taking back to France to show them your estate. That is all I can tell you because it is all I know; however, I would say these orders have all of the hallmarks of our Grand Master Jacques de Molay.

Chapter 3
Going for a Journey in Paris

The three Oxhill Templars had spent all of the summer in London, mainly confined to the Temple boundary for security purposes; if they were to go to Paris under cover, then it was imperative that they weren't seen. This had had certain consequences for all of them; their horses had been exercised mainly by the grooms, their own fitness, which they had never worried about before, had been kept up by doing laps around the walls of the Temple. Once a month the three of them went on a trip out of London with their grooms to build a strong relationship, that lasted over a week. They had all shaven off their traditional beards to help their disguises and, over time, the colour of their facial skin had darkened.

The two younger knights had used the time to increase their sword skills and had made use of the armourer in the Temple to advise them on their techniques. Sir Robert spent most of his time with the Grand Master discussing the issues of the moment or in prayer. The Grand Master was very worried about the political situation that was happening in France; King Philip's power over Papal matters, especially how he was able to convince the Papal Conclave to vote for Pope Clement V and then move the Papacy from Rome to Avignon. He was of the opinion that the French King had gained too much power over the Pope and that it was going to be detrimental to the Order. He knew that Grand Master Jacques de Molay had answered the Pope's invitation to discuss the merging of the Templars with the Hospitallers, and that neither of them was keen on this plan.

His latest news was that Foulques de Villaret was yet to arrive. Whilst he did not know the final orders for the three Oxhill knights, he was certain that they would be instrumental in the continuation of the Order.

In the first week of September, orders arrived that the three knights were to embark on their journey to Paris. It was that time of year when it became noticeable that the days were just beginning to become shorter, and it was in the half-light that the three knights, along with their three grooms and one waggon driver, rode out of the Temple compound and headed south to cross the River Thames on London Bridge. They were dressed in fashionable travelling clothes, a party of three gentlemen going on a small tour of the continent. As they cleared the sprawling villages that made up the southern part of London, the sun burned off the dew on the fields and gained some heat. They made good time going south-east through Blackheath, heading to Maidstone where they intended to spend the night. They were not in a particular hurry and did not want to tire the horses too much so early in their journey. They lunched at Dartford, and in the afternoon bypassed Chatham, heading south to Maidstone. When they stopped, they were asked who they were and where they were going, Sir Gui spoke out, using all their Christian names but changing around their surnames. None of them had spent any time in this area of Kent and it was very unlikely that they would be recognised.

Luckily, they found Maidstone quite quiet. There were few religious pilgrims on their way to Canterbury at this time of year and they were able to get three separate rooms, a luxury. The next morning, they went to the Prime service in the town church, breakfasted, and left for their final destination in England: Sandwich.

It was another warm day, and they were heading generally east, so the sun was on their backs as they crossed the Kentish Weald towards Faversham and onwards to Canterbury.

"I think we should take Nones there," Sir Robert proclaimed. "It may be the first and last time I will have a chance to pray at the shrine of Saint Thomas, and I'm not going to miss the opportunity."

"Sir Robert, I think that would be a good idea before we sail," Sir Gui proclaimed.

When they got to Canterbury, they made straight for the Cathedral. Leaving their horses outside with the grooms, they walked in and immediately stopped to take in the vastness of the building. They had some time before the service was due to start and spent the time walking around the cloisters, admiring the decorative stonework on the arches, going down to the crypt, and marvelling at the stained-glass windows telling the story of Christ.

The service was in essence the same service that they had attended any number of times, but the surroundings, the magnitude of the occasion and being totally in the dark about what they were heading into, made it all the more solemn and personal. Behind their screen, the choir was far more musical than anything they had heard before. The Dean, who conducted the service, spoke and chanted in a deep bass that carried and reverberated around the cathedral, filling them with hope. At the end of the service, they stood looking at each other.

"That was a very moving experience," Sir Robert said.

"Uplifting," Sir Gui added.

When they left the cathedral, they were about to head towards the Canterbury Preceptory until they remembered that this would not be sensible and instead found an inn near the centre of the city that looked to be in keeping with their disguise. The grooms took care of the horses and would sleep in the stables whilst they spent the evening sitting at a table in the front room of the inn. They discussed their journey so far, what they would like to see in Paris, basically anything that was not Templar related whilst eating bowls of potage, which they all agreed was better than average, and drinking ale brewed by the landlord from local hops. They were abstemious compared to others in the inn and retired fairly early, aware that they would be sailing from Sandwich to Honfleur the next day.

The next morning the three knights all attended Prime at the cathedral before returning to the inn for more potage and ale whilst the grooms prepared the horses for the short journey to Sandwich. It was only thirteen miles due East to the port over flat farmland with sheep grazing in fields, in others barley was being harvested and their small group was waved at and warmly welcomed by those that they met on the road.

Sandwich was different, it was a busy port dealing with all the other ports along the northern French coast, goods coming and going, boats loading their holds with wool or cereals, and others unloading wine and textiles. Sir Gui was afforded the job of finding a boat that would take them all across the Channel. Captain Dyke came to their rescue; he had been let down by a trader and wanted to sail on the early afternoon tide. He could accommodate their waggon, the four horses and the nine men. Hopefully, he would be across the Channel and sailing down the north coast of France that afternoon. If they didn't reach Honfleur, they could easily overnight at Dieppe.

They set sail on the tide and made their way across the Channel. As they got into the middle, the seas became rougher and the boat, with quite a shallow draft, wallowed in the choppy sea. The knights, having sailed before along with two of the grooms, were accustomed to the movement, as were the horses but for the valets, who had never left London, and one of the grooms, it was a journey from hell. Richard, one of the valets, was hanging over the side of the boat emptying his stomach before they even left the port. It was a very long journey for him.

"Tell me, what are three gentlemen travelling to France for? I wouldn't have thought it was very safe, given the current situation." Captain Dyke had come down from his bridge and was standing beside them looking out over the sea to France.

"We are going to the wedding of my cousin in Chantilly," Sir Gui replied.

"Are you, now? Mighty fine horses you are riding, they look more like war horses. Now why would three knights be riding destriers heading towards Paris?"

"Captain Dyke, I don't know what you are implying, but I don't appreciate your line of questions. I have told you where we are going, which is more information than I needed to give."

"Well, it is like this: to transport groups of people to France we are meant to question their intent, that's all I'm doing."

"I would suggest that you should have done that before taking us onboard and before taking our money."

"Now where's the profit in that? If you are not telling the truth, I can't take you. This way, I take you, you pay me, and I tell the authorities what you have told me. Everyone's happy. Now I must be getting back to sailing you across the Narrows."

He left them and they huddled together to discuss all of these questions. They were all used to travelling as an army and it was strange for them to be such a small group. They decided that Captain Dyke was on a mission to get more money, not more information.

They crossed the Narrows and sailed down the north coast of France. The view from the ship gave them a clear look at the coast, the fishing villages and larger ports as they sailed down to Honfleur. They had made sure that the grooms and valets were prepared to disembark as soon as they docked, and they were the first to reach shore; the conversation with Captain Dyke was still worrying them and they wanted to get away from the port as soon as they could. It had been their intention to stay overnight there but now they made their way up the Seine to Caudebec-en-Caux, where they found an inn for the night. They had discussed going on to Rouen but had decided to stay in the smaller town where fewer people might be looking for them.

The next morning, they set off early and bypassed Rouen, afraid of being questioned. They arrived on the outskirts of Paris and, if they had looked up, they would have seen a heavy grey sky, the heavens opened, soaking the little troupe, but more importantly, making the roads a muddy mess the further they went into the city. Mud, dirt, and sewerage made the horses walk almost hock deep in a squelching mire that earlier in the day was probably passable. The two horses pulling the cart were finding it difficult to keep it moving forward and the grooms were kept busy by manually pushing the wheels around to keep them from getting stuck. Eventually, they arrived at the gates of the Paris Preceptory, a building, or compound, surrounded by fortified walls with the only entrance being through a guarded gate.

In a place where they should have felt at home, they all seemed to stick out; it was the first time that any of them had ever been in a preceptory of this significance clean-shaven. It didn't help when a man came out of the Chapter House, saw the three knights standing in the courtyard and burst into laughter.

"Sir Robert," he said, "I have seen some sights in my time, but you without a beard is probably the scariest. My friend, I'm glad to see you, and your companions."

"Visitor, it is good to see you, although I admit to feeling naked," he said to the advancing Visitor of the Order, Sir Hugues de Pairaud, whom he had last seen in Cyprus after their retreat from Acre.

"Thank you for coming, now it is time you introduced me to your young companions."

"Sir Alain Heath and Sir Gui de la Granville."

"It is an honour to make your acquaintance, sirs. You come highly recommended to Paris having been mentioned for the part you played at the Battle of Falkirk. Now, let's get you all inside; you all look as if you have swum up the Seine to get here."

They all followed him into the Chapter House where he sat them in front of a roaring fire, not only to warm them but to dry them out. By the time he was ready to talk to them, their clothes were almost steaming from the heat.

"You must be wondering why you have been ordered to Paris under clandestine circumstances. I was hoping Sir Gerard de Villiers, our Preceptor, would be here this evening, but we didn't know what your timetable was going to be. I don't think it is unreasonable to say, but the Order is currently under more pressure than it has ever been. Not military pressure, but political and social. This is brought about by King Philip IV, who has decided that the Order has become too powerful in areas where he wanted power, which it is not needed in this modern world, and that we should be made illegal. He obviously has the Pope's ear, as he was implicit in the persuasion of the voting of The College of Cardinals. We believe he has, through Guillaume de Nogaret, sent orders to all the mayors, where we have preceptories, to arrest all Templars and bring them to Paris for interrogation. Technically, he cannot do this, but he will say that he is doing the Pope's work and will get away with it."

"Visitor," Sir Robert said, "from what you have said, you must think he will get away with it. These charges, I heard that they were of heresy, something to do with an initiation ceremony. These are surely just made up."

"Of course, they are. But they will bring in the Inquisitors, and when they get you on a table or rack, you will say what they want you to say. We know what they did to the Cathars in Carcassonne."

"Yes, but we should be stronger and able to resist."

"I fear not. In fact, I would say that no one would be able to hold out."

"Do we know what any of the specific charges are?"

"Guillaume de Nogaret has come up with the normal things: disrespect, not believing in Christ, that kisses are exchanged during initiation ceremonies, whatever he believes he can get away with. I am sure the list will change - it will probably be expanded."

"What is it that you want us to achieve?"

"Our only chance of survival is if we have access to our treasury. King Philip IV can arrest us in France, he can steal our land in France, but what he really wants is our wealth to finance the various wars that he has got involved in. We could start again in Spain, Portugal or even England, where we are still respected and revered, but only if we still have control over our money. What you will be required to do is to transport a proportion of the treasury, especially the gold pieces held here in Paris, to your Preceptory in Oxhill and store it there. It is our belief that King Edward would not demand access to it, even if he knew of its existence, which we hope he never does."

"What route would we be required to take? Surely we couldn't return the same way as we came here?"

"No, we have boats in La Rochelle that will take you to Bristol. From there it should be fairly simple to get to Oxhill."

"Do you think that we will have any problems getting to La Rochelle?" Sir Gui asked.

"I hope not. You will have company to cross France as there will be other Brothers taking parts of the treasury to Spain and Portugal by boat. I am hoping there will be safety in numbers and that if you are attacked, you will be able to fight them off."

"When do you think we will leave?" Sir Robert asked.

"That I don't know. Grand Master de Molay is in France at the moment, and he will give the final order. However, I am going to say that you can't afford to be seen in Paris so you will have to stay within the compound. Tomorrow, we will work out how to keep your horses fit, but I'm sure the grooms can take care of that."

The three knights from Oxhill were left in a holding pattern, unable to leave the compound. They started by visiting the armourer to get their swords sharpened and the steel armour rubbed down and cleaned. They also spent time in prayer and meeting the other knights, especially those who would be joining them on their journey to La Rochelle.

Chapter 4
12th October 1307

The morning started like any other morning, but the arrival of a messenger from Grand Master de Molay changed its feeling and pace. The messenger arrived on a horse which was frothing at the mouth and sweat-drenched. He leapt from the saddle and made his way to the Chapter House. He nearly made it before the door was thrown open and Visitor Huges de Pairaud came out, followed by the Preceptor of France, Gerard de Villiers.

He handed the sealed note to the Visitor who accepted it and tore it open. He read it before passing it to the Preceptor who did the same. They both talked to the messenger before turning and retreating through the door. Within half an hour news was spreading around the compound that the Grand Master Jacques de Molay would be arriving that afternoon. He had been invited by King Philip IV to be a pallbearer at the funeral of the King's sister-in-law, Catherine de Courtenay; he would come to the preceptory after the service. The increase in activity around the compound showed how far the news had travelled. Rooms were being cleaned, especially his own set, corridors were swept, and the kitchens were spruced up.

In addition to all of this activity, Gerard de Villiers was busy with a number of knights packing as much of the treasury as he could into crates that had been built over the past weeks to fit the waggons. He had already spent a considerable amount of time deciding what could and could not be taken. It was not so much the value of certain items as their size and weight; the convoy from Paris to La Rochelle would have to move at speed and, if they could not depend on their preceptories across the country to provide fresh horses, weight was a factor. At last, he had made his decisions and sent a sergeant to find all of the knights that would be making the journey.

"As you all know, you will be escorting part of the treasury of Paris across France to La Rochelle where you will split up to sail on different ships. With the Grand Master coming this afternoon, I would suspect that your journey will be starting in the next few days. Hugh de Montlaur, you will be in charge during the journey. You may not be the most senior, but I have decided that your knowledge of the roads, how to bypass towns, and what would make good campsites, makes you the ideal leader. If our information is correct, you will not have the use of preceptories during your journey and should avoid large towns. I accept that you will have to pass through smaller ones where no alternative is acceptable, but please be careful. I can't tell you whether you will meet any official resistance, but six waggons, with you and your grooms riding escort will attract some attention, whether it is official or not. You are to use any force necessary to protect the waggons, I can't stress that enough."

"Can the grooms ride horses that are capable of pulling the waggons? That way we could swap them around?" Hugh asked.

"That's a good idea, I will get the Stable Sergeant to organise it."

The three Oxhill knights met in their dormitory.

"I think we should prepare to leave at a very short notice. I fear that de Molay coming here is not a good sign," Sir Robert said.

"I can't wait. This sounds like proper work, and the chance of a fight as well," Sir Alain replied.

"Sir Alain, I don't wish to hear that sort of retort. We have been given a very important assignment, an assignment that might prove instrumental to the survival of the Order."

"I agree, Sir Robert, but I can't help agreeing with Sir Alain. It is quite exciting."

"Sir Gui, I thought you would have a more reserved

attitude," Robert replied.

"I see the importance, and I am honoured to be given this opportunity to help the Order in this way. I do, however, think that the Visitor and Preceptor paint a very grey picture. A collaboration between us and the Hospitallers would not be such a bad thing. Yes, we would have our differences, but perhaps together we could have influence."

"Sir Gui, we come from different spheres. We can, and have, worked well in the past but joining would be a disaster."

"Sir Robert," Sir Alain asked, "do you think that taking a part of the treasury to Oxhill will put it on the map? I mean, we are a backwater that no one knows about, but my worry is that it will put pressure upon us."

"Sir Alain, very perceptive of you. I think that when we get back, we will have to make sure Oxhill remains a backwater."

"Well, I think I'm as ready as I ever will be," Sir Alain stated.

They had just gone out of the door when the main gates were opened, and a group of knights rode into the main courtyard. There was no doubt who the leader was; at the front of the group rode a large, middle-aged man, his grey hair overlapping the chain mail across his shoulders, and his forked grey beard growing a good six inches below where his chin was. He was wearing a gold-coloured riding cloak with a chain scarf joined at the throat with a large golden clasp. Under the cloak, he wore a surcoat of the same colour decorated with a large red cross and a leather belt at his waist to which his sword and scabbard were attached. He was an imposing figure.

"That's de Molay," Sir Robert whispered to his companions, although this information was not required. He rode to the centre of the yard and looked around, taking in a sight that he had not seen for many a year. Then he saw Sir Robert.

"Sir Robert le Jay, it must be ten years since I saw you last, you look younger without the beard." He dismounted and came across to his old friend. "I'm so glad you were able to join us in Paris. When the Preceptor devised this plan, I said you would be a good man to guard a part of our treasury in England. I don't want to know any details about the preceptory you come from, the least I know the better. How are you?"

"Grand Master, I fear that I appreciate the warmer climates of the Mediterranean more than the cold, wet northern European weather. I am well, I now live a quiet life."

"I'm glad. I take it these two youngsters are with you. I don't want to be introduced, but I will say to them that they are privileged to be riding with you. You were a colossus in Palestine in battle and in clear thought; you two protect him and listen to him, he may not say much but what he says is gold. Sir Robert, there is nothing I would want more than to spend time with you, but I fear it is limited. Now I must go and meet the Preceptor and the Visitor." The two shook hands and embraced before de Molay turned towards the Chapter House.

Inside, the three leaders greeted each other. They had not seen their Grand Master for over a year and were keen to hear first-hand the latest news. For the most part, it was not good. Firstly, he told them that he had been invited to be a pallbearer so that King Philip IV, and more importantly Guillaume de Nogaret, would know his exact location. If the arrests were going to happen, then they would happen tomorrow. This meant that Gerard de Villiers' plans to make safe the treasury would have to be put into action that night.

He was told of their plan; firstly, they would take three barges up the Seine to Asnières-sur-Seine to get them silently past the city walls. From there they would basically head south-west - bypassing Chartres, Tours, and Poitiers - to the coast. The Templars did not have a navy, but they did own several coastal ships and it was these that they would use to distribute the treasury.

By the middle of the afternoon, they had caught up on the news and decided that it was time to give the final briefing to the knights that had been chosen to carry them out. The knights knew the basic plan and also that it was fluid in that Hugh de Montlaur could change their route. There was no timetable, but obviously the quicker that they reached the western port the better.

At eleven o'clock that evening, the troop was mounted up in the courtyard, ten knights, ten grooms, six wagons with their drivers. All the horses' feet were wrapped in bandages to dull the sound of their shoes on the road to the bank of the Seine. Grand Master de Molay, Visitor de Pairaud, and Preceptor de Villiers came out of the Chapter House to wish them well and send them on their way. The main gate was opened and silently the procession walked out and down the hill towards the river. The waggons rolled smoothly and, with the added grease applied to the wheel hubs, quietly. They passed through dark streets, past shuttered houses, most of them reflecting that this may be the last time that they would ride through the streets of Paris.

When they reached the river, three barges were waiting, and they loaded up before punting into the middle of the river where the current began to take effect and carry them north. They soundlessly passed out of the city, continuing their journey to the point where they would disembark and start their journey to the coast.

Chapter 5
Journey to Chartres

That first night, the knights just wanted to get away from Paris as quickly as possible, so they weren't worried about having lookouts to the front and rear; they just wanted to get away. Their first obstacle was the village of Nanterre which they reached in the very early hours of the morning. They had only travelled six kilometres. They stopped outside the village. Hugh de Montlaur had been here many times and, knowing the area, he guided them around it, but this took time. It wasn't that the road surfaces were good, they were muddy and heavily rutted, but once one went off them, crossing fields and trying to keep in the lee of the woods, the pace dropped to a crawl.

By the time they had rejoined the road on the other side of the village, the sky was just showing a weak yellow tinge on the horizon behind them. They were desperate to get to their destination in the Forest of Rouvray. This first day was always going to be the most dangerous for the troop; not only were they still in touching distance of Paris but, if their information was correct, this would be the day that King Philip IV and his senior official Guillaume de Nogaret planned to arrest all of the Templars. The French knights under Hugh's direction had prepared a site for them in the woods, a site in a dip in the land where the waggons could hide. They had gone even further and made camouflaged covers that could be placed over the top of them. They wouldn't bear any close inspection, but from a distance Hugh hoped they would be effective; no one was going to get close enough to inspect them.

They had made their escape. Now, for this first day, they would lay low. Centuries after the events that happened that day it would be recognised that Friday the Thirteenth was unlucky, but that was to be in the future. For now, they were concerned with remaining undetected. Guards were set and changed every four hours, whilst those not on guard rested and the grooms fed the horses and kept them quiet.

The next morning, they were all up for Lauds, a brief service given by Sir Robert, as he was allowed to do when Templars could not receive mass at a church. After the service, and still in darkness, the camouflage covers were packed onto the waggons and the troop broke their fast and headed out.

They had formed up with two knights riding about two furlongs in front of the waggons and, once they had left the camp, there would be two the same distance behind it; one knight was posted about a furlong either side. Effectively, the waggons were surrounded by six knights who could give an early warning to the main troop using rudimentary flag gestures and hand movements. As for the Oxhill knights, Sir Robert was riding with the main group between the two waggons that were heading for Oxhill, Sir Alain was in the point position with Jean de la Roche, a knight of a similar age to himself, but less experienced as he had never been in an actual battle, and Sir Gui was on the left flank. He was feeling pleased to be given such responsibility, but he also knew that it would be a long and probably boring day riding without any possibility of conversation.

As the sun arose above the trees, warming the day and drying the dew on the ground, the troop made good ground. They had been briefed by Hugh de Montlaur that, if possible, they should try to make the village of Fontenay-le-Fleury by that night. He knew of a wood and track just before the village where they could stop.

"Sir Alain, what is it really like to go into battle?"

"Jean, it is the most horrifying experience, it is brutal, it is savage. What I had not been told was that you have no vision of what is going on; when we do tournaments we know where everyone is, it is almost dancing where everyone is playing their part. A battle is unregimented, it is chaos, you can't see, you're scared, and you're hot like you have never been so hot. Then there is the charge and, if I'm honest, that is the time when you really rely on your destrier who will look after you and turn from the next danger."

"Surely it is exciting, chivalrous?"

"Jean, I have only been in one battle, and I can tell you the Scottish are not chivalrous. Dressed in their kilts with their faces painted and slashing their terrifying axes. It is confusion, it is frightening and when it is all over there is just the relief that you have survived. When you have got over that, there is the vista all about; one of death and wounded bodies. The smell, I think that was the worst, and not one I can depict."

"But you would go into battle again?"

"Yes, I would. I would be better prepared before, and I would know what was coming. I have spoken about it to Sir Robert, and he felt the same after the first time, he said that it never gets easier, but winning a battle is far better than losing one and he was at Acre."

"Sir Alain, look," Jean exclaimed, "they are trying to get hold of us, I think something must have happened."

They both turned their horses round and after a moment they saw one of the knights cantering towards them.

"It can't be very serious," Sir Alain said. "They are not galloping."

They cantered back towards the knight and saw it was Raymond de Pontons, one of the elder Paris knights.

"We have had to stop," he said when they met. "One of the waggons has broken a wheel. I don't know how long it is going to take to mend but Hugh said that you two should stay here on either side of the road in case anyone comes down it."

Back at the main troop, it was all go. Three of the grooms had cut down a straight branch from a tree which they had placed under the axle of the waggon and were now trying to lift it. Another groom had started a fire and was heating up a travelling forge. Charcoal had been placed in a metal cage which had been placed over the fire to catch; he was busy using a bellows to get it lit. The three grooms now had levered the waggon wheel off the ground, and another was hammering the wedge out of the axle so that the wheel could be taken off. The issue with it was obvious: a section of the rim had broken, probably from hitting a rut in the road, and needed to be replaced. Once the wheel was off the broken section, it could be removed and the metal rim heated in the brasier, and the kink straightened. By the time that the wheel had been mended and put back on to the waggon they had lost nearly two hours. Hugh de Montlaur was very relieved when they were able to set off again.

By the time they reached Fontenay-le-Fleury, where they had intended to spend the night, it was already nearly dark. They made camp in a wood just outside the village. Hugh had decided to send the clean-shaven Sir Gui to the local inn to see if he could glean any information about the arrest of the Templars.

Sir Gui skirted around the village and entered it as if he were going towards Paris. He tied up his horse outside the busy inn and entered. Looking around the main room of it, he assessed that the customers were split half and half between locals and travellers, the locals sitting together and being generally noisier. No one took any notice of him as he sat down at one end of a table, but a passing maid stopped and took his order. He sat there trying to look thoughtful when he was actually trying to listen to all the conversations. He didn't hear anything before his drink arrived but, halfway through his glass, he heard the word he was mainly listening for: Templar. Without looking at the table he concentrated on the conversation.

"…. heard they were being taken to Paris as quickly as possible."

"Not just them but from all over the country."

"What are they actually accused of doing?" a new voice said.

"Something to do with their initiation ceremony, the mayor

didn't know exactly, but he had orders from high up in Paris to arrest the whole of the Preceptory and to transport them all in manacles to Paris as quick as possible."

"I thought they were immune from arrest, above the Law, and could do what they liked."

"I thought so too. Anyway, they are never going back to Palestine, so what's their use?"

"Money, it's always money. I reckon the King thinks they've got too much, ..."

Sir Gui had heard enough. He finished his drink and made his way out of the inn and back to the camp. When he got back, he discussed what he had heard with the others.

"What I don't understand is how we have not seen any of these waggons transporting our Brothers," Jean de la Roche said.

"I have been keeping off the major routes wherever possible," Hugh de Montlaur said. "I guess we have just been lucky. I think that from now on we are going to have to be even more careful."

Over the next two days, they made their way to Ramboillet and made camp in the Forêt Domanial de Ramboillet. The camouflage boards were brought out again as they were to spend the whole day there to give the horses some rest, as well as themselves. The next morning, guards were sent slightly further out and a charcoal fire lit which would emit less smoke and allow them to hunt for rabbits and cook them. It would be the first hot food that they had had since they had left Rouvray four days before.

Their spirits were up as much as they could be considering the news that so many of their brothers had been arrested and were probably now being questioned by the Inquisitors. They all knew that the term 'questioning' when put with Inquisitors made no sense, it just meant that one would tell the Inquisitor what he wanted to know. Their methods had not changed over the last century and had been expanded with the torture of the Cathars in South-West France in the early part of the previous century; they might not be allowed to break blood, but they had many other heinous methods of inflicting pain that would make anyone say anything.

Their quiet morning was shattered by warning whistles from the guard to the west of the camp. The four knights whose horses were kept saddled rode out to see what was happening whilst the others got ready. The knights, Sir Alain from Oxhill, Jean de la Roche, Stephan Cadell, and Arnold de Caned, rode towards the whistled warning. They were not wearing full body armour, just leather jerkins, but they did have their swords. They dismounted towards the edge of the woods, but still undercover, and went forward on foot. They found the groom at the edge of the wood covered with bracken. He pointed to a group of men, three on horseback and clearly carrying swords along with about twenty men armed with an assortment of agricultural cutting equipment.

The knights knew they couldn't let this group into the woods; not only might they see the waggons, but more importantly they couldn't fight so many in the confined space that the wood offered. They retreated quickly and mounted up before riding back and exited the wood. As soon as they came out of the trees, the group coming up the field stopped. The three that were on horseback drew their swords and they walked on, but the men on foot stayed where they were. Both parties were now walking their horses towards each other until they were about ten paces apart.

"What are you doing?" the obvious leader of the group shouted across the divide.

"Who's asking?" Sir Alain said.

"I'm Écuyer Jean Bircann and you are on my land."

"I apologise, sir. We are camping in the woods on our way to La Rochelle with goods to go to Spain."

"Where are the other men? I was told that there were fourteen men on horses and six waggons, but I only see you four."

"They are in the woods."

"You see, we were told to look out for Templars who might have escaped the arrests, and I think that you look like Templars."

"You are mistaken, we are just traders going to La Rochelle."

"Then you won't mind if I inspect your waggons, and if I'm

satisfied, I'll leave you in peace."

"That will not be possible." The knights all drew their swords and put their spurs into the sides of their horses. They jumped forward straight into a gallop, surprising the other three. Sir Alain went straight for the Écuyer, driving his sword through his chest and killing him immediately. The Écuyer was thrown off the back of his horse and, as Sir Alain withdrew his sword, the tumbling figure was like a Catherine wheel with blood spurting from his chest.

Jean de la Roche and Arnold de Caned attacked the other two, whilst Stephan Cadell went around the back of the three to stop any retreat. The two knights made their attack, but theirs was not as straightforward as Sir Alain's. Jean's first attack was beaten away and he had to turn his horse expertly to have another chance. He was a superior horseman and had a battle-trained horse that stopped and turned by instinct. His opponent was still facing the wrong way when Jean came for the second charge and, this time, he was able to forcibly slash his opponent, cutting him in two. Arnold was involved in a sword fight with the last of the mounted men. Swords clashed, sparks flew, and then his horse reared up and seemed to swivel before kicking his opponent with immense force. Arnold grabbed the mane of the rearing horse as he had been trained to do but the other man had no chance; the kick broke through his rib cage, inflicting massive death-inducing injuries as he disappeared out of the side door.

Within a minute it was all over. Three dead bodies lay on the grass and the men had turned and were running away. There was no point in giving chase, their efforts had to be directed to getting away and putting as much distance between them and Ramboillet. They were just capturing the three horses when the rest of the knights came out of the woods.

"What happened?" Hugh asked as he galloped up to them.

"They thought we were escaping Templars and had been asked to look out for us. Someone reported us entering the wood yesterday. We had no choice but to kill the leaders and I'm afraid that the men with them turned and fled," Sir Alain replied.

"Right, we had better get out of here."

"That was my thought and the reason why we didn't chase the men on foot, but at least we have gained three more horses which will help."

"That will help. Now, let's get going, pack up, and be on the road. We will need to head towards Paris and bypass this village."

Their new awareness affected their speed. They were now travelling on farm lanes and, where possible, undercover. It took them another four days before they reached Chartres, a full two days behind schedule.

Chapter 6
Chartres to Tours

They were glad to have got through Chartres but now they changed their route and headed further south than planned. The first day they hoped to reach Bouville, a hamlet that wouldn't have any administrative leaders present, just a small chateau and a few farmer cottages with their attached barns.

They stopped outside the hamlet on the side of a hill and in the cover of the woods. Hugh and Sir Robert went forward on foot to the edge of the trees. From this advantage, they could look over the sleepy hamlet. The chateau stood out as the largest building, the only house that had two floors and, also the only building made from stone. Still, it was not an attractive one, slightly crudely built with different coloured stones. The door and windows had no finesse. It was surrounded by a yard with a stable block and various other barns or buildings, and a brick wall enclosed the whole property. Smoke was coming from one of the outbuildings suggesting that this was the cookhouse, but apart from that it was quiet. A track led from the gate in the surrounding wall which led to the hamlet, which was a collection of six or seven individual properties, some showing signs of life with smoke erupting through the hole in the roof. As they looked down, a woman left one of the dwellings carrying a bucket which she took into a barn; there was no sign of anyone else. It was this lack of any activity that worried the two Templars.

"It is too quiet," Hugh said.

"Yes, where is everyone else? I would expect more to be happening up at the chateau."

"I agree, let's wait a little longer."

They settled down on the dry leaves to continue their watch, not talking to each other, not because they didn't want to but in some situations there was nothing to say. They saw the sun beginning to set in the west and still it was quiet below. They heard a rustle of leaves behind them and looking around saw Sir Gui approaching.

"You have been so long we thought that you must have gone down there. Is there anything to see?"

"That's the problem. Since we have been here, we have had one woman leave her house and take a bucket to the barn, we have seen nothing from the chateau."

Sir Gui lowered himself to the ground alongside the other two. He looked over the view that had become so familiar to the others.

"Strange, you see that building over there," he said pointing to what the other two considered to be the cookhouse, "that is in the wrong place to have a cookhouse. Who is going to carry food so far to the main house, across the yard? The food would get cold, and one would have more chance of spilling it. No, the cookhouse should be over there," he said, pointing to another building adjacent to the main one.

"You're right, why didn't I think of that? So, what are they using that building for? What else would one need a fire for?"

"I suppose it could be a forge," Sir Robert said.

"No, we would have seen the blacksmith, or at least heard him by now," Hugh answered.

"Brewing," Sir Gui said, twisting his nose and smelling the air. "I thought I could smell something when we got here. I would wager they are brewing something down there, but you would want someone in there looking after the fire."

"We haven't seen anyone, and one could hardly miss someone coming out of that building."

"I don't like it, I think we should stay in the woods tonight, not have any fires and double the guards," Sir Robert said.

"I agree," Hugh said, "it is all too suspicious, and I think we should be ready to ride out at a moment's notice."

The troop spent an uncomfortable night, either on watch or waiting for the order to move out. Many leaned against trees, others lay down under crude blankets. All of them were hungry having only had small amounts of bread and no hot food. They had hoped that the situation in the hamlet would have allowed them to hunt for a couple of rabbits in the woods to be cooked that night. This was now out of the question.

The next morning, just before the first signs of light had begun to show in the eastern sky, not that the troop could see any of this so deep in the woods, they silently began to start their day. The horses were the first to be fed. Without them, the troop was going nowhere. After this, they looked after themselves, taking a bite of rather stale bread and a mug of ale before clearing the site to make sure that no one would be able to know that they had been there. This job of masking their presence was taken further with one of the grooms at the back of the troop using branches to sweep the ground behind them to cover their tracks.

By midmorning, Bouville was well behind them, and they were still travelling through heavy woodland. Although they were not making good speed, Hugh ordered a stop.

"Everyone, we need to break our journey," he said. "Sir Alain and Jean, we will stay here. Can you go and sweep a large circle around where we are? I would like to light a fire, but I don't know who might see the smoke. I want to know that. So go and take a look and we will try and catch some food."

The two Templars rode out, heading downhill until they could see the edge of the wood. They stopped, tied up the horses and went forward on foot. When they got to the edge of the wood, they looked out over fields and could not see any human habitation before the next forest; they were safe on that side. They could see that the hillside they were on extended as far as they could see, so it was only the other side that they were worried about. They crossed in front of the troop, climbing to the top of the ridge. Again they dismounted and walked to the edge of the trees. It was almost the same as the other side, except they could see a few isolated farms, but nothing that would concern them.

When they had set up the camp, they split into two groups, one group, consisting of the two younger Oxhill knights and Stephen Cadell, were to go hunting for rabbits, or whatever they could catch. The three Templars fetched their hunting bows and quivers of arrows and headed out on foot. Without dogs to make the rabbits break cover, they had to rely on their guile and their hunting instinct. They approached the first glade and saw evidence of their foe; sandy holes dug in the ground and droppings. They fell back and split up so that they could come at the glade from three different angles. When they were ready, they crept up to its edge and saw a group of four adult rabbits grazing on the grass to one side, with another two sitting towards the edge as if keeping guard. The snap of a twig at this stage and their quarry would scatter and they would have to move on to the next glade. They were ready, bows strung, and arrows nocked. Sir Alain moved into a kneeling position and brought his bow to the nocking point, taking careful aim at one of the foes. He was just about to release the arrow when one of the guard rabbits slapped the earth with his paw. There was just a moment when everything seemed to stand still and he made his release, but he had not been fast enough, and the rabbits fled in all directions. The three Templars stood up and walked into the glade to collect the arrows that they had spent.

"Bugger," said Stephen. "I thought we had them. Well, we had better find another glade where they are out grazing."

"Yes, I think that the breeze just came up at the wrong time and one of them smelt us. Anyway, they won't be coming out here for a bit," Sir Gui replied.

At the next glade, they changed their tactics with all three of them approaching from the same direction, making sure the breeze was in their faces. Their luck was in and each of them made a hit.

"That's how to do it," Sir Gui said with a broad grin on his face.

"Yes, but three rabbits aren't going to go far between all of us," Stephen replied.

Three more glades and nine more rabbits in their tuck bag and they were ready to return to the camp, very pleased with themselves. When they arrived back, they noticed that a small fire had been prepared in the middle of four trees and a canopy had been erected above it. The idea was to stop the smoke from rising in one plume and to defuse it so that it thinned out, rising through the branches of the four trees. Soon the rabbits had been butchered, the fire lit, and the smell of the herbs, which had been foraged, along with the rabbit was spreading to all areas of the camp making all the Templars feel very hungry.

They all slept soundly that night, not only in the knowledge that they were in a safe location, but all had had a good hot meal and some rest. The next morning, they were again up before the sun had risen and broke camp with the rising sun on their backs and their long shadows in front of them. The late autumn sun and the rest had had a rejuvenating effect on the whole troop, and they made good time towards their next destination, Châteaudun, a town that Hugh knew well because his uncle, who lived in the castle, was a keen supporter of the Templars and would give the troop its first proper rest.

In 1197 the town had been granted a charter by the Count of Blois which gave it autonomy from King Philip. It was also in this period that Hugh's great-great-uncle had built a circular castle keep. They were protected by law and also very thick walls.

Hugh planned to stay here for two days to properly rest the horses and make proper repairs to the waggons to improve upon the running repairs they had made on the road so far, and generally to have a proper break now that they were almost at the halfway stage of their journey. Their host, Count Thibault VI, could not have been more welcoming, but more importantly he seemed to know about what had happened on the 13th and what the feeling was in the locality. He told them of the arrest of all of the Templars at dawn on Friday the 13th from the Paris Preceptory by Guillaume de Nogaret. Grand Master Jacques de

Molay, Gerard de Villiers and Hugues de Pairaud had all been taken to the University of Paris for interrogation. He also knew that the Preceptories in Tours, Blois, and Chartres had all been raided and the Templars arrested and taken to Paris and the properties seized by the Crown.

Although the Count had not painted a pretty picture, it was one that they had expected, but the worrying news was that there were bands of troops actively searching the area for members of the Brotherhood that weren't in the Preceptories when they were raided. These bands were different from the one they had come across at Ramboillet; they were trained soldiers, soldiers who knew how to fight. However, the only good news was that they had visited the castle two days earlier, so the troop would be safe, unless someone had seen their arrival and reported it.

The troop used the two days to get themselves rested and well-fed, knowing now that they would have to be even more careful. They discussed the notion of only travelling at night but rejected it for two reasons: one, they would have to move so slowly, and they risked inevitable issues with the wagons breaking down or getting stuck and two, they could easily wander into one of the brigades of troops without seeing them. They also spent time in prayer, aware that the Vespers service at sunset was the only time that they had regularly been able to fulfil their duty to God.

They had discussed their route with the Count who had provided them with a number of houses that they could call on in the knowledge that they would be welcomed and protected. To ensure this he had written personal letters to their potential hosts. They felt that was as good as they could hope for. It would mean that they would have to reconnoitre each of the proposed locations, but this would be preferable to making camp every night and setting guards.

Their first day took them to Moisy, where they didn't have an invitation to stay. It had been a quiet day where they had travelled under cover of wood for the most part. The only excitement had been when Arnold de Caned, who was riding on the right of the convoy, had spotted a brigade of troops in the valley below them, about two miles away and moving in the opposite direction.

On the third day out from Châteaudun, they had to break the cover of the woods and called in the outriders. They were crossing a field that had not yet been ploughed but, as the ground was soft, it was hard work. All of the grooms were at the wheels of the waggons pushing them forward, up to their calves in mud, just trying to keep the wheels moving.

"Behind, behind," shouted Jean who was at the back of the convoy.

They all turned around and saw a group of about thirty men. Sir Robert quickly counted eleven on horseback. All were carrying shields, and he could see that they all had swords. They weren't wearing any armour, but most of them had chain-mail jerkins. They weren't dressed coherently, and nothing matched, which made him think that they weren't an official force but a group of vigilantes. The Templars rode back to form a line at the rear of the waggons alongside Jean. All had drawn their swords and attached their shields to their left arms. The grooms formed up behind them, ready to come forward and fire rounds of arrows if ordered to do so.

The group of vigilantes also stopped, uncertain as to what to do, uncertain because they had not expected their quarry to be so heavily armed. They had thought that they had come across a small convoy heading towards the coast, probably with goods to export. A nice easy job for them to overwhelm the waggons, steal the goods, and make a quick exit. Now they were faced with ten men - with long swords drawn and shields prepared - who looked as if they knew how to use them; was it worth it?

For their part, the Templars knew what an imposing sight they made. They may not have been dressed in their traditional white surcoats with the red cross, but that insignia was on their shields. One man came forward from the group, a large man with untidy, dirty hair whose chainmail was beginning to rust through lack of care. He was holding a war mallet in his right hand, a menacing weapon that could easily throw one from one's horse if he connected.

"Good afternoon, gentlemen," he said as he still walked forward. "Now, the last thing I thought I would see this afternoon was a band of Templars with waggons. I thought you had all been arrested."

"Stop there if you know what is good for you!" shouted Jean.

"Now, now, don't become unfriendly. I am sure we can work out some sort of compromise here; after all, look how many men I have and how few you have. If I want something, I normally find that I get whatever that is. Now, why don't you tell me what is in all those waggons and if I have no use for it, you can carry on your way. However, if it takes my fancy I will relieve you of your goods, and frog march you to the local constabulary, I fancy I will get quite a good price for you there."

"Sir, you seem to be very sure of yourself, but I'm afraid the contents of the waggons are Templar's matters, not to be bandied about. Now, if you had any sense, I'd suggest you and your men return to the forest and let us be on our way."

"You would, would you? Well, I'm not so sure you are in a position to dictate to me. You see, we have had enough of being told what to do by you lot, we are pleased that our noble King is helping the Pope get rid of you."

"Sir, I do not have the time to debate with you matters that you know nothing about. Now, I suggest that you turn around and go back to your companions."

"The only reason I am going back to my men is to show you that I do not fear you, and then I am coming to get you."

He turned his horse around and started to return to his men. As he did, the Templars made their horses retreat behind the grooms. As soon as they were clear the grooms drew their bows, each aiming at different horsemen opposite. As quickly as they released the arrows, they reached into their quivers and nocked another arrow. This time they aimed at the men on the ground. It was four seconds from the time that they released their first arrow to the time that they released their second. During that time, the vigilante who had engaged them saw all of his horsemen killed along with half of his foot soldiers. He turned around to see the Templars walking their horses forward to cover the grooms.

"What the fuck!" he shouted. "What the fuck was that for?"

All he could see in front of him were ten men with stony, inscrutable faces staring at him, ten men whom he realised were far more brutal than him. He turned in his saddle to see the last of his men running for the cover of the forest and ten horses with their heads down eating grass. *What has just happened?* he thought, as he turned again towards the Templars who had not moved. He was just about to say something when the reality of what had happened hit him. He was beaten, out thought, and humiliated; he turned his horse around and galloped for cover.

Chapter 7
Tours to La Rochelle

Ever since they had had the confrontation with the vigilantes, they knew that they had to move fast to get out of the area before anyone came across the scene. They had been running for four days now, less worried about being observed, but unable to take the stops they had planned with Count Thibault. For the last two days, they had been travelling along the northern bank of the Loire River which meant that they would need to cross over it when they got to Tours. They had decided to split up to cross the bridge, the feeling being that, if the authorities were checking for them, they would be able to slip across individually amongst other waggons.

When they came together to the south of Tours, they were amazed at the ease with which they were able to cross the bridge, pay their toll, and be on their way without any questions being asked. In fact, there had been no security at all. They had one more night camping in the woods on the southern escarpment of the river before trying to make it to Châtellerault, where they had a letter of introduction to Vicomte de Châtellerault. He gave them a warm welcome and assured them that he had heard nothing about their fight although he had heard about a band of bandits who had been robbing travellers in the area they described. His overall feeling was that, if they had broken up the band, the local authorities would be more than happy.

The next morning, after the horses had been fed and let loose in a paddock close to the chateau, the Templars took advantage of the local expertise in sword-making to get their sharpened. They were well-rested by the time they sat down in the main hall of the chateau for a banquet that the Vicomte had arranged in a hurry or, to be precise, he had ordered his staff to arrange.

It was not a large affair if measured by the amount of people attending, but when measured by the quality, and quantity of food and wine, it was superb. He had also laid on entertainment in the form of local dancers and a troubadour to tell them stories from local history. When not being entertained, the conversation around the table was inevitably about the arrest of the Templars and what it would mean to the Brotherhood. The Vicomte was of the opinion that the King had stepped out of line and that the Pope would order their release. Sir Robert wasn't so sure: he believed that the King would say that he was doing the Pope's work for him and would back it up with confessions obtained under torture.

They all awoke the next morning with heavy heads from the previous evening, but they had cleared by the time the grooms had brought in the horses, fed, and groomed. Still, it was mid-morning by the time they pulled out of the courtyard and were on the road to Poitiers.

They were travelling on the old Roman road from Lyons to Saintes that went through Poitiers and had brought economic development to the town. It was a walled town, and they adopted the same tactic as in Tours, splitting up and entering by different gates which were at the same level as the two rivers that ran through the town; once through the gates, they had to climb up to the plateau where the main town was situated. They were hoping to stay in the fortified residence that had been built by Eleanor of Aquitaine just before the last century and was still inhabited by her family.

"Who goes there?" was the question when they knocked on the gate to gain entrance to the walled inhabitancy.

"Hugh de Montlaur with his troop. We have a letter of introduction from Count Thibault."

"You may come in, but your troop will have to wait."

"Henry, is that you behind the grill? The last time I saw you, you were beating me around the head, teaching me how to fight with a sword. I can recognise you by your voice, now let me in and I will show you how far I have progressed."

"Hugh de Montlaur, is that really you?"

"Yes, old man, it is me. Now, please open these gates and let us in."

Hugh could hear the old man cross to the wheel that would raise the gate. He could hear him strain against it, pushing it around, and slowly the gate started to rise. He dismounted and gave the reigns to Sir Robert in order to duck under it and help his old tutor.

"Let me give you a hand," he said, taking the windlass, and began turning it with ease until the gate had risen enough for the troop to ride through. He tied the windlass and turned to embrace his old tutor.

"Marcus, you still look as fit as ever. I bet you could still run down a hare."

"I think my days of doing that, sir, are over. You are looking well, if a bit thin. Now, let's be getting these horses in here and into the stables."

Marcus showed the grooms the stables and the Templars dismounted from their horses. Hugh led them towards the front door which was flung open and a girl in her late twenties ran towards him almost knocking him over, tears streaming down her face.

"Hugh, why didn't you warn me you were coming? Oh, it is so good to see you! Are you well? Why are you here?"

"Marion, stop the questions, I can only answer one at a time," he laughed as he swung her around and placed her back on her feet so that she was facing the Templars who didn't know whether to laugh or cry. "Men, meet my sister, Marion. Don't worry, she does stop talking, but I'm told only in church. Now, Marion, where is the Vicomte?"

"He has gone to La Rochelle; he got a message last night that some very important people were heading there, and he went to meet them."

"Who were these people?" he asked with a worried look on his brow.

"Brother, how would I know? He only told me what I have told you, and he certainly didn't mention your coming to stay. How long are you here for?"

"Did he go alone?"

"No, he took four men with him and a waggon. I didn't see them leave."

"You said he got a message. Who brought the message?"

"Marcus might know. I didn't see him, but he left with the Vicomte."

"Marcus," he shouted, "can I have a word?"

"Marcus," he said as the man approached across the yard from the stables, "the messenger who came for the Vicomte, did you know him?"

"Yes, sir, it was Simon de Pontóns. It was his second visit. He also came after the Grand Master landed at La Rochelle. He was with him in Cyprus."

"Simon came here?"

"Yes, sir. He couldn't go to the Cour de la Commanderie in La Rochelle as it had been taken over by the King's army after the arrest of Geoffroy de Gonneville."

"So, he came here knowing that the Vicomte couldn't be arrested."

"I assume so, sir."

"Then it is quite likely that he has gone to meet us. When did they leave?"

"It would have been after Terce," Marcus said.

So, they had left about mid-morning, giving them a five-hour lead, Hugh thought.

"Sir Robert, I suggest that Sir Gui and Sir Alain ride after them. They have a five-hour advantage, but I'm sure they will spend the night at Niort and if they have a waggon, they will not be travelling very fast. With fresh horses from here, we can catch them. I need to know if they are trying to meet us and why."

"I agree, it is the waggon that worries me. What was in the waggon?" he directed the question to Marcus.

"There were four large boxes, each the size of a coffin."

"Do you know what was in these boxes?"

"No, sir."

"Hugh, do you think that it is possible that Geoffroy de Gonneville managed to get the treasury from La Rochelle hidden here before he was arrested, and the Vicomte now sees an opportunity to get it shipped abroad?"

"It is possible, but I don't understand how he would know about us. We didn't even know until we set off from Paris. And he seems close on our heels."

"I agree, it's as if we have had a shadow following us. I think that the two Oxhill Templars should try and catch up with them. They will not be known around here and at the moment don't look like Templars."

"Marcus, can you tack up the two fastest horses you have?"

"Yes, sir."

The two Templars were on the road in the minimum of time but were not travelling at full speed at first; these were new horses to them, and both wanted to get acquainted with them. Even when not going at their fastest, they knew they were catching their prey as they were travelling with a waggon. Once they felt their confidence in the horses grow, they quickened the pace and felt the exhilaration of riding fast; they stopped for the night at an inn in Niort but were on the road again early the next morning.

They caught up with them mid-morning. They had come out of a wooded area and saw six horsemen and a waggon about a mile in front of them. As they rode up, they recognised Simon de Pontóns who they had met in Paris.

"Simon," panted an out-of-breath Sir Gui. "Is the Vicomte travelling to La Rochelle to meet up with us?"

"Yes, but where are the rest of you?"

"They are at Poitiers and sent us on to catch up with you."

A large grey-haired and bearded man rode up, by the look of

his magnificent horse it must be the Vicomte. "What is it Simon, who are these men?" he asked.

"Sir, these are two of the Templars we were trying to meet at La Rochelle."

"But they are coming from the direction of Poitiers."

"Yes, sir," Sir Gui said. "We got diverted further south than we intended, and Hugh de Montlaur suggested that we stop in Poitiers."

"Hugh is at Poitiers?"

"Yes, sir."

"So, who are you two?"

"My name is Sir Gui de la Granville, and this is Sir Alain Heath."

"You must be two of the Templars from England. Well, we will return with you. The waggon and the men will carry on to La Rochelle and stay at my compound there."

They turned around and started their return journey to Poitiers. The Vicomte was eager not to be seen going back through Niort and showed the other three a way around it. He also didn't want to take the road, so they journeyed over fields in a far straighter line. There was still light in the day when they rode into his hometown and up the hill to his house. The horses were exhausted as they had been pushed hard on the return journey, and the grooms took them to be washed off before a feed and rest. The Vicomte was keen to speak to the whole of the Templar group and had not told the two English knights why he was so keen to meet them in La Rochelle. When he had changed out of his riding clothes and was standing with his back to a large fire in the main hall, he gathered them around him.

"Men, as you know I am not a member of the knights Templar, but this family has always had links to the organisation and has supported it financially and also supplied fighting men for its use over the centuries. In more recent times I have become a confidant of Geoffroy de Gonneville. He was of the opinion that the most treasured pieces should not remain at the Cour de la Commanderie in La Rochelle and asked if I would look after them. This was just after Simon and the Grand Master visited here and I fear that he had been warned in advance of King Philip's intentions. Gerard de Villiers sent me a message, probably on the day of his arrest or just before, to tell me that a convoy was heading for La Rochelle; by the time I got that, Geoffroy had been arrested, so I worked out how you would get there from Paris and how long it would take. Unfortunately, none of my calculations included your coming through Poitiers, but can you take my waggon to wherever your waggons are going?"

"Of course, we can, but the question is where it should go. When we get to La Rochelle we are going in different directions," Hugh said.

"Given that you have three knights from Oxhill, I assume that one ship is bound for England. Most of the goods were given to the Brotherhood by Elenor of Aquitaine and her husband King Henry of England. I think it should return there."

"Sir, I would agree with you, and it would be an honour to transfer the goods and look after them until it is safe to return them," Sir Robert said.

"Thank you, Sir Robert, hopefully, you will not have to look after them for long, and Pope Clement will come to his senses and stop all of this nonsense."

The next morning, the troop set off on the last leg of their journey to La Rochelle but now with the added company of the Vicomte and Simon de Pontóns; both felt that they could help in the unlikely event of the Templars being captured and questioned. Hugh and the Vicomte were able to navigate them across country for the whole of the journey which took nearly three days, but it was worthwhile as they came across no one. The Vicomte insisted that they make use of his compound in the port whilst arrangements could be made for three ships to be loaded and set sail. Hugh was very relieved by this invitation as it had been a worry how they would hide the waggons before boarding the ships. As soon as he could get away, he rode down to the harbour and found the three Captains sitting in one of the harbour side inns.

The ships that the Templars used were not owned by them but rented to them. The captains could take other contracts if they were not needed by the Brotherhood. The three captains that Hugh found were as delighted to see him as he was to see them. During the time of the arrests in La Rochelle, they had set to sea fearful that they would be caught up in the commotion that ensued. Hugh bought a jug of wine and sat down with the three captains.

"How fast can you all set to sea?" was his first question.

"It depends on where you want to go and what you want to take onboard," Jacques the eldest of the three said.

"One boat to Lisbon, one to Coruna and one to Bristol."

"OK, the ones to Lisbon and Coruna can go together without an escort, they can drop off what you want at Coruna and then sail down to Lisbon. The Bristol ship will need an escort, we can't have single ships sailing alone."

"I accept that. Have you got four ships here ready to sail?"

"We could sail on the tide the day after tomorrow."

Chapter 8
A Stormy Return

The three Oxhill Templars were standing on the quay beside the two ships that would take them to Bristol, talking to Captain Jean-Paul Masson, who would be in charge of both of them, and his son, who would captain the second ship.

"See how heavy those waggons are, they can't be loaded on the same ship," the father said.

"How can you tell their weight?" Sir Alain asked.

"Experience, young man, see how the horses are straining and the waggons are squatted down on their springs. I need to know these things 'cos if I load too much on a boat it will be my last journey."

"I think that's a good idea," Sir Robert interjected quickly, seeing that the captain didn't like to be questioned. "If anything went wrong, we would only lose half of our goods."

"That be right sir, I think it would be prudent to divide the horses as well."

"Should we not be getting on with the loading, Captain?" Sir Robert asked.

"Not yet, sir, the ships are not at the proper height, but we can start to unload the waggons. I reckon by the time we have done that we will be able to get them on and then start to carry on the boxes. I want all of them loaded by Nones. High tide is two hours after that, and I don't want to be walking uphill with them. We will set sail after Prime and hopefully make St Nazaire by tomorrow nightfall."

"Will you be docking there tomorrow?"

"No, sir, I won't be putting in there, but there is a cove where we can get some cover for the night."

The three knights stood back and looked at the ships. Only Sir Robert could be considered experienced travelling by sea. For the two younger ones it held trepidations.

"Can these things really cross the Celtic Sea?" Sir Alain asked.

"Oh yes, don't forget that the Romans traded all along the south coast and up the west coast of England. They didn't just cross at the Narrows."

Sir Alain continued to stare at the two hulks, each about sixty-five feet long with a beam of just over twenty feet. At the stern there was a raised platform which he assumed was where the captain stood with a thick wooden pole sticking up at an angle that would be attached to the rudder. By the size of it, two men must be required to steer the ship. It had two masts, the forward of the two being larger, both attached to a boom going up to form what he could only imagine as two large triangles of sail. Currently, no sails were attached, and the masts and booms looked like a baffling combination of wood and rope.

The loading of the ships was completed under the watchful eyes of both the Captains Masson. They shouted orders to those rolling the waggons down the planks between the ship and the quay. It was a delicate balance between pulling from the front to go forward and pulling from the back to act as a brake. When they were aboard, and the wheels tied firmly to the decking, the hard part started; carrying the heavy boxes from the quay and loading them back onto the waggons. Lastly, the grooms led the horses over the planks, and, for the first time, the managerial shouting stopped in case it frightened the animals.

The next morning, they set sail after Prime which all the Templars attended before saying their goodbyes. Over the weeks that they had been travelling from Paris, the knights had grown close as a unit and in all probability, they would never see one another again. The six ships slipped away from the quay and sorted themselves out when they had cleared the sea bar, four of them sailing south and the other two turning north. With the wind bearing from the southwest, the sails were lowered and filled immediately, speeding them north at a brisk pace. Both ships were sailing together, turning at the same time. The older Captain Masson was on the western side and slightly ahead so as not to take the wind from his son. They were still able to shout across to one another and, as the sun began to set in the western sky, the father got his son's attention, pointing to a cove ahead on their starboard side.

The Templars could see why he had chosen the cove; cliffs rose out of the sea all around it with no beach, meaning that they were safe from the land. Once they had weighed anchor, they could move their canons to the port beam to protect them from any attack from the sea. As it was, they had a quiet night. The crews changed watch regularly, with the beginning and ending sounded by the ringing of a bell as the only distraction and the gentle sway of the sea giving the ships a slight roll.

The next day was a mirror image of the previous, the wind in the same direction and the same strength, speeding them north, but their course had slightly changed to follow the coast of Brittany in a north-westerly direction, meaning that they had to tack more and their speed toward their destination was reduced. Again, the Captain knew of a cove, but what he didn't know was that a patrol covering the coastline had spotted them putting into it and had ridden to Brest to warn the local constabulary of their presence.

Unaware of the danger they were facing, they put to sea the next day in very different conditions. The wind was fresher and to the west. They could see the dark clouds of a weather front bearing down on them. They were heading for it when they passed the island that marked the westernmost point of France, but, having passed it, they changed their heading to a more northerly one.

Young Captain Masson noticed them first and gave the notice to his father. Rounding the southern point of the island and heading in their direction were three ships, all flying indistinguishable flags on the top of their masts. His father looked back and, whilst he couldn't clearly see the type of ships that were trailing them or whether they were a danger, from their bow wave he could tell they were moving faster. He looked forward and to the port to see where the weather front was at that moment. It looked as if it would be on top of them within half an hour; he then looked aft to see that the three ships were catching him. He signalled to his son that they should run towards the weather front and immediately turned in a more north-westerly direction. He was busy calculating whether he could run for cover, or whether he would be outrun.

"Captain, we seem to have changed our course toward the storm. Why?" Sir Robert asked the captain.

"Because of those three buggers," he replied, pointing behind them. "I don't know who they are, but if I change direction, they do. They are flying some bloody flag I don't recognise, and lastly the bastards are catching us."

"Do you think we could get lost in the fog on that front?"

"Sir, please let me get on with saving our lives."

Now that Sir Robert was aware of the issue, he tried to put his logical brain into gear. He went to the front of the ship and measured the distance between them and the front; he did this by looking down and slowly bringing his head up until he could see where the fog started while counting: fifty-three counts. Then he returned to the aft and did the same process towards the three ships: sixty-four. He knew it was an inexact science but, to him, it was better than just looking and reckoning. He returned to the bow and repeated the process: forty-two counts. The stern: fifty-two. Yes, they were catching up, but not quickly enough, he reckoned.

Suddenly there was a massive report and both Captain Masson and Sir Robert looked behind them. They saw a ball of smoke swivel and rise from one of the boats following them. Both waited anxiously. The cannonball landed at least two hundred yards behind them and bounced a couple of times before sinking.

"That was nowhere near," Sir Robert said.

"They will get closer when the barrel warms up. And they are catching us, I think we will be in range in about fifteen minutes." He looked up at the weather front which was approaching them. "It's going to be touch and go to see if we can get ourselves lost before that."

There was another report from one of the pursuant ships, again the cannonball fell well short but slightly closer.

"Funny that, both of those shots were from the same ship," the Captain commented to no one in particular.

The race was on; every time the French fired, approximately every four minutes, the captain would slightly alter his course. The cannonballs were getting closer, but the aim was becoming more erratic, some going left, some right, as his ship wasn't where the French gunner aimed. They could now see the rolling fog on the forward edge of the front and the captain made one more change of course. Just as he did, a cannonball careered into the sea between the two ships, soaking the decks with its splash. They were all looking aft when the fog enveloped them and in a space of thirty seconds they couldn't see the French ships.

"Jean," the captain called to his son, "turn twenty degrees to port on my word and keep within sight at all times. Now."

Both ships changed direction in unison as they heard the report from behind them. They didn't see the cannonball land but heard the splash well to their starboard. Now the two ships were tacking to port and starboard at regular intervals, the chasing boats were still firing, but they couldn't hear where they landed, and slowly the retorts became quieter.

Soon the waves increased in size and the wind speed increased. The ships were riding the waves, climbing to their top before plunging down the other side. Both Captains lowered their rear sails completely and reduced the foresail. Sometimes they lost sight of each other as they crested a wave only to regain sight as they went into the trough. The horses were becoming frightened and straining at their lead ropes. The grooms were in the same state but tried to calm them down and stop them from kicking out.

The storm was ferocious but luckily it was not a deep one and, as suddenly as they had entered it, they broke through the other side into blue skies and calmer winds. The waves were still high as it would take some time for them to settle down.

Captain Masson called over to his son, "Well done, now we have to hope that the French turned tail before that and went home. So, keep a lookout in case they didn't. Have you taken any damage?"

"Don't know yet, but I don't think so. Do you think we are west of the Lizard?"

"Maybe, I kept a log of the changes in direction, and I reckon if we now head twenty degrees north of the wind, we will see land before long."

Two hours later there was a shout from the bow of the younger Captain Masson that land was in sight. Both Captains went to their ship's bow, and they could make out a faint line on the horizon; both changed direction towards it and slowly more details became apparent.

"What do you reckon, Dad?"

"I reckon we are looking at Mount's Bay, with Lizard Point on the right and Land's End on the left."

"If we are, you are a lucky bugger, 'cos I don't think anyone could calculate those tacks we made," the son laughed.

"What are we looking at?" asked Sir Robert, joining the captain.

"Sir Robert, you are looking at England, or at least Cornwall," he described the scene before them. "Are we allowed to put into port in England?"

"I don't know, I would doubt King Edward to have followed the same path as the French King."

"I would like to put into Mousehole, which is over there and has a protected harbour, spend the night there and inspect the ships tomorrow morning. Then we can carry on round the coast to Bristol."

"That would seem to make sense, but if that is Mousehole, then that must be Penzance," he said pointing to a larger village along the coast. "Wouldn't it be better to stop there?"

"I wanted to see how the land lies in the smaller port first. Mousehole is just a fishing village, but Penzance has an administration."

"Very well."

It was another two hours before they rounded the spit that protected Mousehole and were able to drop anchor in the bay. The two captains went ashore in a small skiff to see if it was safe. The Templars had mixed feelings; they were delighted to be back in England, even if they weren't quite on English soil yet, but they were apprehensive not to know what sort of reception they would get if it became apparent who they were. They waited anxiously to see the skiff returning, discussing various outcomes, and it was with relief when, at last, they saw the two men bending their backs into the oars as the little boat seemed to skim across the water's surface towards them.

"It seems as if you are in the clear," Captain Masson shouted up as he came alongside. "I went into a couple of inns, and no one knows anything about Templars being arrested. One said they saw some in Penzance about a week ago."

"That's good news. Do you think it would be safe for us to go ashore?"

"Sir Robert, I think it would be as safe as the last time you put your feet on English soil. I'll tie the skiff up here and if you need it, I'll get a couple of the men to row you across."

"Thank you. Sir Gui and Sir Alain, it's been a long time, but today I'll buy both of you a wine or a beer, or whatever they have," Sir Robert proclaimed to the astonishment of the other two.

Chapter 9
The Last Leg

They had arrived in Bristol the day before in the early afternoon. The autumn sunshine welcomed them and all three disembarked as soon as they could, leaving the grooms to transfer the two waggons and the rest of the horses onto the dockside. They were keen to visit the Preceptory in the Redcliffe area of the city, just to ride by it at first to see who was manning the gates. If it was still in Templar hands then they could approach but, if not, they would have to change their plans. The Preceptory and accompanying church stood on land that had been given to them in 1125 by Robert, the First Earl of Gloucester, only five years after they were founded.

"Look," Sir Alain said, pointing to the gates which were still fifty yards away, "those are brothers on guard, aren't they?" He was pointing to four men standing guard in front of the gates dressed in a brown robe with the bodice covered in chain mail, the traditional mode for a brother.

"You're right. Will, they wouldn't be guarding it for anyone else. I believe we will be all right," Sir Robert proclaimed. They rode up to the gates.

"Brothers, we are three knights attached to Oxhill who have been abroad and have just returned to England, please let us through."

"Sir Robert, it is a pleasure, and I'm glad you have returned but we were expecting a waggon as well."

"What do you mean, you were expecting?"

"We have been looking out for three knights for the past

week; Grand Master de la More sent a message to look out for them saying that they would not look like knights, clean shaven and dressed in normal clothes with a waggon."

"Well, that would be us, then. Now that I know it is safe here, we will return to the docks and bring the grooms and waggons up. What's your name, Brother?"

"I'm Brother Matthew. I've got another three hours on guard here, but I will inform the Commander that you are in Bristol."

It was another hour before the three knights led their two waggons to the gates to be welcomed by Brother Matthew who opened them, and the small troop entered. The horses were unhitched from the waggons, and they were manually pushed into a barn whilst the grooms looked after the horses. The three knights walked towards the front door of the Preceptory and were about to enter when there was a shout from the far side of the yard in front of the church.

"Sir Robert, we have been expecting you," Sir Charles said as he walked away from the church. He was a big man with long flowing white hair and a full white beard. He may have been older than Sir Robert, but he looked very fit for his age. "We thought you would be here a week ago."

"Sir Charles, it hasn't always gone our way, but we made it."

"Did I see two waggons? We were told you would only have one."

"That's a tale for later."

The two men had spent many years together in Palestine, in good times and bad, they were together at the end and shared the feeling of letting others down but also the hurt of being let down by others. They came together and embraced, each of them wrapping their arm around the other, glad to come together in more peaceful times.

"Come, my friend, introduce me to your two young compatriots."

Introductions done, the four went into the Preceptory and into the main hall to stand in front of the fire.

"Tell me," Sir Charles asked, "what was it like in Paris? Did you see the arrests?"

"No, I believe we left during the night before. If that is true, it doesn't say much for de Norgaret's organisation. We rode out of the front gate, down to the river and were away."

"What, you mean he hadn't even put guards on patrol?"

"I met him once," Sir Gui said. "I was part of a delegation that had to go to the Palace for a hearing with the King. He was an utter bore, an arrogant, supercilious little man who thought everyone owed him."

"The trouble is that he has King Philip's ear and has promised him money and freedom from debt. That is music to His Majesty's ears," Sir Robert said.

"What did the Grand Master say? I take it you met him?"

"Oh, yes, he rode in on the day we left. Jacques was worried; he knew he had been tricked by going to the funeral, but he still had utter faith that the Pope could control King Philip. I think that he thought of our journey as being an insurance policy, an insurance policy that he could reverse very soon."

"A funeral, you say? Whose funeral?"

"I forget, you probably don't know all that went on in Paris in the days before we left, in the same way we don't really know what happened after it." Sir Robert then fully briefed his friend on all that he knew of the political turmoil that was the forerunner to their departure.

That night the three Templars relaxed in peace for the first time since they had left Paris. They felt at home being in familiar surroundings, within a military timetable where the hours were counted by the church bells sounding the services. It was also a relief to be on home soil for the two younger ones and to know that what was going on in France was not happening in England.

It was four days later when the Oxhill Templars set off again from Bristol. The time had been spent in religious contemplation and reflection, but now they were ready to set out on the final leg of their journey. Their plan was to follow the River Avon up to Bath and then journey up the old Roman road, the Fosse Way, until it passed very close to Shipston-upon-Stour. From there it was only a two-hour ride to Oxhill and home.

They arrived back at their Preceptory late on a dark November afternoon over three months after their excursion had started. Sir Gui and Sir Alain, although glad to have returned, regarded the time away as an adventure, but also had gained recognition within their Brotherhood. Sir Robert had been honoured to be asked to perform the task and it had offered him a chance to renew old acquaintances, perhaps for the final time.

Chapter 10
1308 and Finality

The status quo for the Templars in England lasted until January 1308 when, on the eighth day, King Edward II ordered the arrest of all members. It was not something that he wanted to do, and he still didn't believe them guilty of the crimes laid against them, but Pope Clement V persuaded him to act.

In Oxhill it was as if they had never been away. Sir Guillaume de Stowe was keen that the inspections of the farms and the collection of rents must be resumed. He had not been well in the months that the others had been away. Sir Gui and Sir Alain had been busy in the time leading up to Christmas but even they had had to stop as 1307 turned into 1308 because of winter storms sweeping across the country from the North. The boxes that they had brought from France had been taken off the waggons and placed at the back of one of the barns. They hadn't been opened.

At the beginning of the third week of January, all four knights were in the main hall. Sir Guillaume was sitting in a chair close to the fire, a frail man who was worried that he would not see the trees turn green in the spring. Sir Robert was sat at the table with sheets of parchment in front of him and a quill in his hand, writing the story of their journey. Sir Gui and Sir Alain were restive, they would sit down, stand up and walk around, and sit down again.

"Have you two got nothing to do? You're up, you're down, but you never sit still!" Sir Guillaume said crossly.

"I feel like one of those bears who can only move as far as

the rope lets him. I hate winter and the enforced imprisonment," Sir Alain replied.

"Well, why don't you both go and help the grooms? I'm sure they will be able to give you both some manual labour to do."

"I'm not that bored," Sir Gui replied.

"Well, take the horses out or something. I'm sure the snow won't ball in their feet as it is melting. At the moment, you are both acting like young children. Sir Robert and I need some peace."

Suddenly, there was a furious knocking at the door.

"Am I never going to get any peace? Well, one of you see who it is."

They opened the door to find Sir Henry de Faverham, the knight who had brought the original message from Sir William de la More, the Master of the Knight Templar's, which had started their adventure. He virtually fell in through the door with exhaustion.

"Sir Guillaume, I have a message from Sir William," he panted as he proffered a message. The ageing Templar took it, unfolded a parchment sheet and began reading the contents. The more he read, the more worried he looked. He slumped down in his chair and tears of sadness could be seen in his eyes as he lowered the note.

"Brothers, this is a note from Sir William. He has been informed that Pope Clement V has interceded on behalf of King Philip IV of France and King Edward is about to declare that the knights Templar should be arrested and charged with heresy. He is not sure when this will be declared, but he is certain it is within days, not weeks, so it might even have already happened. He is adamant that the contents of the boxes should be buried so that they are not captured by either the Church or the Hospitallers. He goes on to say that the two treasures should be kept separate, buried in different places. He gives two more pieces of advice; he doesn't think that the King believes there will be much acceptance or belief in evidence that is obtained through torture and that those charged will have to repent, admit to giving absolution without the authority to do so, and show that they wish to be accepted back into the Church."

"What does this mean for us?" Sir Alain asked.

"Firstly, and most importantly, the contents of those boxes must be buried. I suggest you think of individual places for each box. Secondly, that Sir Robert and I must accept that we are going to be arrested and put on trial, a show trial. But you and Sir Gui should think of your future."

"Does this mean we must become fugitives?" asked Sir Gui.

"No, you must never do that, you are a part of an ancient order that is sacrosanct to the workings of the Pope. He has given us rights and freedoms to carry out his Holy orders, and whilst one can sometimes question his actions, they are the Word of the Lord. That cannot be questioned."

"But where do we go, sir?"

"Firstly, you carry out the orders of the Grand Master and hide the Paris treasury that you were asked to oversee in Poitiers. Think of six different places around here where you can bury the boxes. They must be pinpointed between visible points of nature, points that will never change. Triangulation points between hills, below the crests of hills, but never in valleys. Then you must bury a strong box containing the details of where they are located."

"Sir, I will see that it is done," Sir Gui answered.

"Sir, may I ask a question?" Sir Alain ventured. "If we bury the boxes, and bury directions to their locations, who will know where to look for them?"

"Sir Alain, for once you are being very perceptive. If we are all arrested and asked the question, we all know that we will give the location away under torture by the inquisitors. Sir William is not certain that this will happen, but this is what he says Pope Clement V has said to our King. "*We hear that you forbid torture as contrary to the laws of your land; but no state can override Cannon Law, Our Law. Therefore, I command you at once to submit these men to torture…Withdraw your prohibition and we grant you remission of sins.*" He goes on to say that the King will not allow this to happen under the legislation laid out in the

Magna Carta although the Pope wants Templars to be detained and shipped to Ponthieu for questioning."

"I can't see King Edward agreeing to that," Sir Robert gave his opinion.

"I agree with you, Sir Robert, as I said earlier, I think that King Edward will want to keep control of the situation. Arrest us, don't torture us, and give us an easy path back into the community. Of course, we don't know what's going to happen in France. There have not been any trials yet, and we don't know who is going to conduct them. They cannot be under the command of King Philip's judiciary and the trial should be in front of the Pope's Cardinals. Back to the matter in hand. Unless anyone has a better idea, a letter should be left with Father Michael with instructions that it is not to be opened unless in the presence of the Master."

"Sir Guillaume," Sir Robert said, "is that wise? I worry that there may be a conflict of interests. What would happen if instructions from the Pope filtered down to his Archbishop to instruct him to give up the letter? Where would his loyalties lie? I would suggest they would lie with the Church."

"A very good point. The new young Lord of the Manor, Sir William de Periton, what do we know about him?"

"I have spent some time with him since we have been back. I've been doing some sword training with him. I would say that he has matured in the short time that we were away. It is just small things such as asking to accompany us on our farm inspections to see how we do it. He has introduced a forum where disputes can be aired in front of him, but he is not the judge. I know they are only small things, but I have noticed a change," Sir Gui informed them.

"That is good to hear, do you think that he could be trusted?"

"Yes, sir, I do."

"In that case, I will leave the hiding of the boxes to you two and Sir Robert and I will talk to Sir William and if he concurs with your beliefs we will draft a letter for him to look after them."

That afternoon the two younger knights were out riding to

areas that they had discussed earlier, looking for places to bury the boxes. They first rode down to Tysoe and climbed up the hill on the far side of the village to where the white horse had been carved into the side of it. This was not a considered site but the vista from the top highlighted some of the potential sites. Over the next few days, they started to crudely map the sites, noting triangulation points, and testing the soil at the potential places of interest.

The whole exercise took two weeks to find the places they wanted and another week to take the boxes, one at a time, to their graves. At each location, they dug a hole, lined it with wooden slates and placed metal sheets on the inside made for them by their blacksmith, placed the box in its grave and backfilled. Lastly, they buried the strong box that held the clues to all the locations.

Chapter 11
The Present Time

Over the past few weeks, we seemed to have had a party going on every weekend, based around the archaeologists who had stayed up in Warwickshire after their week's work in Tysoe and were helping Andy in our field. The field had taken on a whole new dimension since their test pits had unearthed a second-century mosaic floor in the middle of it. The County Archaeologist, Michael Bain, had declared that it was a scene of great National Importance, and that further action should be taken, i.e., they should do a proper dig. Like everything else in this country, to start a dig of this importance comes with the need of a big budget to finance it. Money doesn't grow on trees, as the saying goes, but that didn't help me. Whilst the two words 'National Importance' hung over the field, I could not farm it. They still didn't know the boundaries of what they had, which meant that I could not plough it, I couldn't graze it, I couldn't use it.

"What's with the long face?" Andy said as I walked into the kitchen and took off my shoes.

"Well, for one, unless you have brought some beers with you, the one you are drinking is the last in the house. Secondly, it looks as if I'm going to be one field down for a few years to come. And lastly, I can't decide if I should have a shower before you buy me a drink in The Peacock."

"I would have a shower first and a change of clothing or Kevin will ban you from entering. Here, take this," he said, getting up from his chair, opening the fridge and handing me a beer.

"You are forgiven. Give me five minutes and don't forget your wallet." I put my head around the living room door to see the two boys going head-to-head on some PlayStation game. I said, "Hi" and, not expecting a reply, carried on upstairs.

We walked down to the pub, discussing the normal rubbish, knowing that when we sat down more important things were afoot. I went through the arch into the beer garden to find a healthy Friday evening crowd of mostly villagers enjoying the evening sunshine.

I sat down at one of the last free tables, reached into my shirt pocket, and pulled out a rather battered packet of cigarettes, battered because I didn't really smoke except down here and I hadn't been for a week.

"God, it's busy out here," Andy said as he placed two pints on the table, "there's no one inside except the Major. I thought I was going to be caught."

"You're becoming quite a local. If you're not careful they will try and get you onto the Church Council."

"No way, I'd run a mile if anyone suggested that. Did you get a letter from Mike this week?"

"Yes, that is what led to my sarcastic comment earlier. I'm sorry."

"No need, it seems that you have a very bountiful field. I'm not sure what he said to you, but they have finished analysing that box we found under one of your dead patches."

"No, he certainly didn't mention that; pray tell."

"The metal sides that surrounded the box date back to the fourteenth century and it is likely that they were made from shields. Templar shields."

"Templar, do you mean Crusades and all of that?"

"Yes, but that's not all of it. Inside the box was a parchment letter, or riddle, or whatever and it is this that has taken longer to decipher. It is written in French, which is not unusual for that time, and seems to give clues about where other boxes are hidden."

"Sorry, Andy, you're saying that there is a document in there which gives clues to other boxes. What, some sort of Middle Ages treasure hunt?"

"Yes, but that is not all. There are some names in the document that have got all number of medieval experts jumping up and down with excitement. Have you heard of Guillaume de la More?"

"No."

"He was the big chief of the Templars in England when King Edward II arrested all of them. He died in the Tower of London."

"OK, so?"

"There are two other names mentioned. Gerard de Villiers and Geoffroy de Gonneville. Do they mean anything?"

"No."

"What do you know about the downfall of the Templars?"

"Nothing. Should I?"

"A nice, trivial fact is that they were arrested on Friday, October 13th, 1307, which is where some people say we get the bad luck day of Friday the thirteenth."

Andy then gave me a history lesson that lasted the rest of the original pint and the next one.

"What the experts are excited about is that they think that these clues may be to the location of treasures that were spirited out of Paris on the night before Jacques de Molay and the rest of the Templars were arrested."

"Wow, do you know I think that is more exciting than the Roman villa? Can they work out the clues?"

"They don't know, but what we have now is a bunch of intellectuals going on an Easter Egg hunt."

"Is it worth anything to me?"

"No, you might have the control document, but technically that belongs to the landlord, and any treasure found will undoubtedly belong to either France or the Government."

PART 4
ROMAN BRITAIN CIRCA 230AD

Chapter 1
Fighting for My Life and Reputation

"This is my testament, and I swear on all that I hold beloved that it is truthful.

I am Antonius Bassius. I was the Legate of the third Legion, sent to rule Britannia Prima, the province to the west of this island with its capital at Corinium Dobunnorum[1], I held this post for five years and I believe that I oversaw the growth of the region to levels that it had not seen before. I secured the territory from the Welsh to the west, and I oversaw the logistical improvements that linked the region to others to the north and east. I grew the taxes due to the Senate. I served five years in my Emperor's service at the highest station within his Empire.

I have returned here to Rome because there are people here in this forum who accuse me of stealing money from the Empire of Rome. Stealing? How low do they think I have dropped, and why do they accuse me of this crime? I have never been accepted by some in the Senate due to a relation who died some one hundred and fifty years ago. Yes, I share his name and I understand your questioning of him, but I would put it to you that the emperor of the day was equally as guilty as my relation. I'm afraid greed is a vice."

I was standing in front of the Senate in Rome, the highest court, fighting for my life and my reputation. Fighting against people who I had thought to be my peers, fighting against

---

1. Corinium Dobunnorum was the Romano-British settlement at Cirencester

stigma, fighting against lies, fighting against petty hate. I had come here from my home in Britain of my own will to try and settle the outrageous charges against me; charges that I had used state revenue for my fulfilment, that I had led a revolt against the empire at its far-flung edges. Charges of corruption, abuse of power and, worst of all, of treason against Rome.

"Senators, if I am guilty of even a part of what I am charged with, why would I come here? Why would I travel from my villa in Britain, why would I leave the community I live in to come here? Surely it would have been easier to stay at home, to ignore the baying of voices from Rome. No, no, I could not do that. That would be like turning one's back to an enemy, running away, showing a weakness, admitting to a wrong when there is none. I come here to inform you, to enlighten you, to bring you truths from the edges of our empire; truths that you might not like to hear, truths about the power given by Rome and its abuse by her Legates."

I was just getting going on a speech that I had started composing in a far-off land, under a hill where cattle roamed, which I had named Oxhill.

"Senators, I understand that it is easy to believe whatever you are told by the people you have put in charge of an area of this great Empire located far away from Rome. Why would such a person exaggerate their achievements? Where is the need? You give us immense power to rule over the land we have conquered, a power that is exercised in your name, but in truth, we are not questioned, no one comes to hear how we rule, and not one of you has been to any of the forts I have built to guard your interests or seen the dangers that are faced by our soldiers and the improvements that have been made by teaching our modern ways. You accept the taxes that we send you, you accept the metals needed for the army and the silver to make coins, and you accept them in such quantity that I understand you have upset the governor of Hispania[2] who thinks that you are taking money from his coffers. But you live in ignorance of real life.

____

2. Hispania is the Roman name for modern day Spain

Then a man comes to you, a lesser man in rank than me, who tells you that the Legates in Britain are conspiring against you, of cheating you of your taxes, of planning to create a separate state independent of Rome. He brings you no proof, he just brings stories, stories that our great playwrights would find embarrassing. Yet you believe him, welcome him with open arms and reward him. Roman law, Jus Civile, is meant to guard against this."

I was interrupted by a Senator who I didn't recognise, an elderly man, waving that he needed to speak.

"Legate Antonius, you make a fine speech, an impassioned one, and the fact that I am the first to interrupt you shows that you have caught our attention. I was worried when the Legionnaire Crassus came forward and made the allegations, but as you say I am ignorant of such matters, and perhaps we acted hastily. His allegations were frightening in their manner, giving details, and naming very convincing names; indeed, you were mentioned at the forefront of the list. I put it to this Senate that we recall Crassus and question him again along with Legate Antonio."

The Senator sat down, and an uproar started with some thirty Senators trying to speak at the same time. The two Consuls sitting on either side of Emperor Severus Alexander rose to their feet, trying to restore order, but it wasn't until the emperor stood with both hands aloft that a sense of order descended.

"Senator Marcus Augustus," the emperor spoke, "as ever, you speak sense when talking about Justice, and this Senate always welcomes your intervention. I agree that we should recall Legionnaire Crassus and question him in front of the esteemed Legate from Britain." He didn't sit down but nodded to his two Consuls and strode out of the Curia.

I was left standing, running what had happened over the last few minutes through my mind. I was oblivious to what was going on around me until I was tapped on the shoulder and looked around to see the elderly Senator standing before me.

"Sir," he started, "thank you for coming forward and defending yourself. For a soldier, you are quite an orator, I must say."

"Senator, I think that the thanks should come from me to you, but can you explain what just happened? I cannot read the Emperor."

"Read the Emperor? No one has been able to read him since he inherited the role. I have issues with two of the words that he used: my 'intervention' and his description of you as 'esteemed'. On the face of it they could both be described as complimentary but, equally, they could be construed as sarcastic. I hope not."

"Senator, I would like to speak to you further before Crassus comes back here. I am not used to the politics of this place. I am a straight-talking person who doesn't understand it. Will you help me through the hearing?"

"That depends on the answer to my next question and whether I believe you."

"And I suppose that question is, am I telling the truth?"

"Yes, are you?"

"Before I answer that, let me explain why I have come to Rome to defend myself. One of my forefathers was a man called Casellius Bassus, a Carthaginian, who tried to persuade Emperor Nero Claudius Caesar that he had found columns of gold."

"I remember the story, but what has this to do with you?"

"Well, to tell the truth, as far as I know there was some truth in the story. He did find some gold and melted it down into rough ingots which he gave to his brother for safekeeping and then he led the emperor's troops on a merry chase around his land. Those ingots have been passed down through the family and are now in my possession. But he never found the columns he described to the emperor."

"The original ingots from 64AD?"

"You do know your history, yes. I took charge of them on my father's death when I was a young man doing my best to advance through the army. I was not a Legate when I went to Britain, I was a Legionnaire posted to Hadrian's Wall to keep out the

Caledonians. Over the years, I was promoted and, with each job, the risks got less, and the power increased. Ultimately, the last time I was in Rome I was appointed Legate of Prima Britannia, the most westerly region of the island."

"You still have the ingots?"

"Yes, they are held in a safe place at my villa, a place only I know. That is the truth. I don't know exactly what Crassus has said, but it pains me to say that I trusted him when he was a Legionnaire under my command; he seemed loyal, he was a very good commander of men, he was astute, intelligent."

"If he had come before you with a complaint when you were a Legate, would you have believed him?"

That was a hard question. Five years earlier, before I retired to farm the land, I would have said Yes. Now, I had my concerns. I had invited this man into my villa in Corinium and introduced him to my wife and children. I had trusted him, and I liked him.

"Yes, I would have."

"Then we had better make your defence watertight."

Those words were just what I wanted to hear. It had taken me three months to travel from Oxhill to Rome, a journey I had spent plagued with doubt as I knew I was going to have to stand up in front of the emperor in a setting that was so far removed from what I was used to. I was not a politician, I was a regional governor, and I didn't know my way around the political scene in Rome.

I shook his hand and told him the name of the taverna I was staying at, saying that I would welcome a visit.

Marcus Augusta did not come single-handed; over the next few days, I was to meet several Senators who also felt that Roman justice had not dealt me an even hand and were prepared to offer me their support. This help was not just support but details of what Crassus had said to the Senate, words I had not heard. He claimed I had held meetings with the other two Legates to discuss forming a British republic, splitting away from Rome, and setting up a force in Britain that could invade Gaul[3].

---

3. Gaul in the Roman name for much that is now France.

Apparently, we had talked of stopping the export of metals from Britain to Rome and keeping the wealth for ourselves, cutting off this valued revenue to the Imperial coffers.

With these Senators, whom I now call friends, we prepared statements, or rather I told them my side of the story and they put it into legal language that would be accepted by the Senate. When I questioned some of the wording, they would retort that I couldn't phrase something that way, or no, you can't say that. It all seemed to take an age and I realised that this was why it took so long for decisions to be taken by the Senate. It was a relief when I received notification that they would hear my case the following week; I could now count backwards from that date and tick off what I needed to do and know.

On the morning of the hearing, Marcus Augusta visited the taverna and we had one last rehearsal of my opening statement as we ate a light lunch before setting off for the Curia. It seemed busier than the last time I was there, but Marcus Augusta explained that there was considerable interest in the proceedings and that the senators were keen to express their vote.

I was shown to a chair on the floor of the Curia. The Emperor's throne was above me to my left along with two chairs for his Consuls. To my right were the banked seats of the Senators, enough seats to hold five hundred of them; although there were more in office, it was unusual for all of them to attend at any one point. I felt intimidated as if I was in the Colosseum and only here to be humiliated for their entertainment. Suddenly there was the sound of trumpets heralding the arrival of the emperor. The Senators sorted themselves out and stood waiting for his arrival. I also stood, as I had been told to.

"Senators, we are here this afternoon in unusual circumstances," he started. "Legate Antonius has been accused of nothing less than treason and, under normal circumstances, he would be here manacled in chains, but he has never had a trial even though this august forum announced that they believed the word of Legionnaire Crassus and his accusations. Legate Antonius has shown the same courage we have heard tell of in the stories of his many battles, by coming here from Britain. He has said that what we have been told is not the truth. This afternoon we will hear from both sides and then decide on which side the truth lies. I see we have Legate Antonius here, but where is Legionnaire Crassus?"

A muttering started going around the forum, and then a soldier approached the Consul on the Emperor's right and began to give him a message.

"It would appear that Legionnaire Crassus hasn't come to the Senate today; guards were sent to his lodgings earlier and it seems that he is no longer residing there. He is still a serving officer in my army, and as such will be given every opportunity to explain his absence. I am sure there is a logical answer but, until we hear it, this sitting is postponed."

Ye Gods, the guy hadn't turned up! He'd fled because he didn't want to face me! How could the emperor now say that he still had to hear what this Crassus had to say? I was frustrated, and annoyed. I had prepared for today for nothing. Crassus had never been a coward, I could at least give him that, so why was he running away now?

A crowd gathered around me, congratulating me, on what I was not sure; I didn't say a word, then Marcus Augustus pushed his way through and embraced me.

"I think you have won; the emperor never likes people who don't turn up before the Senate."

"Marcus Augustus, what have I won? I was never guilty of anything in the first place."

Chapter 2
The Farewell Tour
(5 Years Earlier)

I always knew it was going to happen. The normal length of office for a Legate in charge of one of the regions in Britain was five years, and I was well into my sixth year. However, it still came as a surprise when I got the notice from the Senate in Rome, and thus the emperor, that they thanked me for the job I had done and telling me a new Legate was being dispatched from Rome.

So that was it. I remember going to the bathhouse and sitting in the steam room thinking about what I was going to do. I came to the decision that I was happy in Britain. I had married a local woman, and I wasn't sure I wanted to return to Rome; I wasn't sure what I would do if I did return. I couldn't see myself trying to get elected to the Senate and spending the rest of my time in the Curia, and I couldn't see myself growing grapes and olives. I was also worried about how my wife would fare. I left the bathhouse more organised in my thinking and with a plan. I knew I was going to have to go on a tour of all the forts under my command, not just to say goodbye, but to introduce the new Legate; this tour I would put to good use and find a place that I could live, a place to build a modern villa. I had decided that I preferred the cooler climate of the north. I liked the fact that there were four seasons, that each day could be different and one never knew what it was going to throw at you.

Although I had heard of Legate Titus Decimus, I

didn't know him, but I knew he had a reputation as a robust administrator, a leader of men, and a shrewd tactician in battle. I was looking forward to getting to know him. I was also glad that Rome had listened to my reasoning for not promoting Legionnaire Crassus to the job; I had wanted to hand over to someone from within my command and he would have been the most senior, but there was something that I didn't trust about him, I couldn't put my finger on it. I had spoken to his Tribunes, and whilst they would not say anything against him - I would have been disappointed if they had done so - there were many things that they didn't say about him; no mention of his respect for his men or, more importantly, their respect for him.

Titus Decimus arrived very quietly and with no flamboyance. He had his personal guard of a Century of troops along with several waggons with his belongings, but none of the trumpets and flag waving that I have seen in the past when a new Legate arrives from Rome. I didn't even know he had arrived until he entered the Command Building in Corinium and appeared at my door. He was a massive man, standing as high as a horse's head and as broad as an ox. Dressed in full regalia, he looked impressive.

"Legate Antonius Bassius, I am Legate Titus Decimus, it is good to finally meet you."

"Titus Decimus, welcome to Britain and Corinium, I trust you have had a good journey?"

"It was long, and I think I made the wrong decision when I decided to sail here rather than come overland, but I am here now and looking forward to the challenge."

"I'm glad. Now, will you take a cup of wine, and I will outline the timetable for the takeover."

"That would be most welcome." He took off his helmet and passed it to a servant before lowering himself into a chair.

"As you know, it is normal when a new Legate is appointed for a tour to take place around all of the main forts. It's a chance to meet your commanders and also for me to say "thank you" to them. I have arranged for this to take place at the earliest time possible. I propose that we take a Cohort[4], not for defensive means, but to show your strength from the beginning. There is another reason, there is one Cohort that has a new Signifer[5] and Tesserarius[6] and I want to test them as they have not been on a march."

The first week of the tour took us firstly to Glevum[7], the closest fort. I thought it a good place to start. I rode beside Titus Decimus behind the first rank of soldiers and had a good chance to talk to him. He was very keen to learn about the country, its people, and its traditions. He kept pointing to different buildings and the landscape and he asked questions continually. He received a welcome full of army pageantry and a banquet. He seemed to be at ease when meeting senior officers. He might not have known any of them, but he had learnt what their background was and where they were in their careers. It was the same when he met some of the town's leaders; he seemed interested in what they did and what they thought. Before he even started, he had in abundance the skills that hadn't come my way until I was in my second year.

The next day, we set out to visit Isca Silurum[8] on the north of the Sabrina[9] estuary. This was the biggest military town within the region, based here to form a barrier against the Celts to the west, and the headquarters of the II Augusta Legion. We stayed here for two days whilst he was taken further west to see battle sites to learn how they had been fought differently from many, more like a series of skirmishes than a proper set battle. He discussed all of this with me on our return journey, suggesting that Isca Silurum should be the capital of the region. I reminded him that it was at the extreme border and that Corinium was

---

4. A Cohort was a military unit of a Roman legion, consisting of about 480 men it would be the equivalent of a modern battalion.
5. The standard bearer for a Cohort.
6. A watch commander in the roman army, in charge of getting the nightly watchwords from the commander.
7. Glevum was the Roman name for Gloucester.
8. Isca Silurum was the Roman name for New Port.
9. Sabrina was the Roman name for the Seven estuary.

more convenient being based on the Fosse Way which linked the northern and southern extremes of the province.

We returned to Corinium for one night before setting off south down the Fosse Way stopping at Lindinis[10] and completing our southern journey at Isca Dumnoniorum[11]. I couldn't believe his energy. He was first up in the morning, sometimes surprising the servants who were not ready for him, and last to bed, he always wanted another glass of wine, always inquisitive, always polite, but I noticed that he didn't take fools gladly and that he learned at a cracking pace. Today, he asked a Centurian why there was a gap in the guards around the camp. He obviously got an answer that he didn't like and gave him an earful.

The tour continued eastwards to Durnovaria[12] and then headed north up Portway[13] to Sorviodunum[14] and Calleva[15] before turning northwest to complete the southern circle and arriving back at Corinium. I must admit, I was tired by the time I walked in through the door to my villa. It had been two weeks of riding, being entertained, and riding again. I embraced my wife with relief, sat down, and I think I was asleep before she had the chance to bring me a glass of wine.

For the next part of the tour, we were heading up the Fosse Way to Venonis[16], the most northern town in the region. This was the part of the trip that I was really looking forward to. Parts of Britain had been enclosed by roads but were not occupied. It was uncharted land, land where I could create my own empire.

On the second day of the march, I spotted a hill on the right-hand side of the road that stood proudly above the countryside. It was what I had been looking for all morning.

"Centurian," I called, facing backwards to the Centuriae that

---

10. Lindinis was the Roman name for Ilchester.
11. Isca Dumnoniorum was the Roman name for Exeter.
12. Durnovaria was the Roman name for Dorchester.
13. A Roman road that ran from Silchester to Wymouth.
14. Sorviodunum was the Roman name for Salisbury.
15. Calleva was the Roman name for Silchester.
16. Venosis was the Roman name for High Cross, Leicestershire.

was just behind me. He ran forward to walk beside my horse. "I would like to go to the top of that hill to see the view it provides. I would like to take ten men with me, we should only be a couple of hours and I will make sure that we catch up."

"Yes, sir"

"Why do you want to go up there?" asked Titus Decimus.

"It is merely a whim at the moment, but I have been thinking that I might stay over in Britain rather than return to Rome. I am looking for some land that I could farm that is close to the Fosse Way. This sort of area would be ideal. I just want to see what I can see from up there."

"Would you mind if I came along? All I have seen so far is the view from the road. I would like to see what the interior looks like."

"Be my guest."

The land between the road and the hill was flat pastureland, well grassed with a few sheep idly grazing. In the distance, I could see a collection of the low rustic wattle and daub huts that the natives lived in. The hill was forested on all sides by a collection of oak and beach trees. As we got closer, I could see that the forest floor was not overgrown apart from a few bushes and thick with leaf mould from years of the deciduous trees dropping their leaves in autumn. We dismounted and gave our reins to two of the soldiers. I had seen from afar that the wooded area did not go to the top of the hill, but it was still a steep climb through it before we broke out the other side. Again, it was a grassed area, a thick clumpy grass that came above my knees, and there were trails criss-crossing the hill, presumably made by animals. It was hard work and I sent three soldiers ahead to do the bulk of flattening the growth.

When we crested the hill, it felt as if we were standing on the clouds looking down on the earth. We looked down over a flat valley and across to a ridge that seemed to grow out of it. I couldn't see a river, although there might have been one snaking through the trees below us.

"That is some view," Titus Decimus said.

"Yes, can you see those animals with the horns grazing down there?"

"Yes. By the size of them, they look like oxen."

"They are indeed, and healthy ones at that. I shall name this hill Oxhill. Yes, I like that. This is just what I am looking for."

"You can't be serious, it's just forest. You can't farm that."

"Vision, that's what you need. The trees can be cleared, not all of them, but enough to start with for a temporary villa whilst the main one is built, and whilst that is going on I can start clearing the land to farm. There is no reason that the soil will not be as good as on the other side, and if the natives can farm it, I'm sure a Roman can."

"Antonius, you could go home and buy a farm, settle down, let the slaves do the hard work, drink wine, eat good food; why do you want all of this hassle?"

"That is precisely the reason. I don't want to just sit there, drink wine, eat too much and count my money; I would die within a year of boredom."

"OK, so some questions: one, have you ever built a villa? Two, where are you going to get the labour? Three, what are you going to farm? Four, when you have built your villa, and created your farm, what are you going to do then? Drink wine, eat food and die within a year?"

"You sound very sceptical. Between here and that ridge, this whole valley will become my empire; I will build villages, build roads between them, and get farmers in to farm the land and pay me rent. This will be my land and when I'm finished, I will leave a legacy to my son."

"How will you start?"

"I'm keen on using new forms. Have you heard of people drawing out the land that they see? It's called a "mappa". I will use this to annotate all that is before me, mark where the trees are, the river if there is one - and I'm sure there is - and, as things change, my mappa will reflect that change."

"I have heard of these things, but only for military purposes to record a battle."

"I envisage this being a battle, not against another army but against the landscape."

I remained standing there, looking down on the valley, not really making plans but painting an imaginary picture in my mind: a now, a starting view, and how I saw it ending.

To be honest, I don't remember much about the journey back. From the top of the hill, we took a view over the land; we could see where we had come from but there seemed a far quicker route cutting the triangle to somewhere close to where we were meant to camp that night.

We spent two days in Venonis[17] before heading back down the Fosse Way, two days that were long in my memory, two days of local commanders fawning over their new Legate, two days before we could return down the road and I could climb that hill again. I had grown to respect Titus Decimus and to like him. There was no doubt he was very capable, but what I liked the most was that he asked questions that would provoke one into telling him more than one might want to give.

Yes, I revisited Oxhill on the way back down south. I went on my own. When I got to the top of the hill, I sat down on the grass and just drank in the vista, the beauty, the symmetry, and the dream. I rode down the other side to the tree line and entered the forest. I was worried about getting lost and tried to stay in a straight line. When I got to the level ground, the trees were spread further apart. It was dark, almost moody and I suddenly saw a patch of sunlight. A glade, a chance for the sunlight to reach the forest floor, a floor turned green with grass; I tied up my horse and walked into the light. A stream ran through the middle of the glade. It was the final part of the puzzle, and I walked over to look down into the water, which was crystal clear and running fast over its sandy bottom. Bending down, I scooped up a handful of water and drank it. I didn't wait there any longer but made my way back up the hill through the trees, tying a ribbon to the last one so I would know where to enter the next time.

---

17. Venonis is the Roman name for High Cross, Leicestershire.

Chapter 3
The Planning

The handover was going very smoothly. We had decided on a date it would actually happen and sent an envoy to Rome advising them of the timings. There had to be a ceremony, an official physical handover, so that the people would know that it had happened. It was a rather stupid rule, but the reasoning behind it was that if the populace did not see it, they would not know who their Legate was. The fact was that it took place in the Forum in Corinium with an exclusive guest list and none of the peasants in the region would know either party or care.

The garrison here had been transferred many, many years ago and Corinium was now a regional capital, the second largest town in Britain, so the ceremony was not a military one but a legal one. That did not stop people from dressing in their best clothes, or even ordering new outfits. It was, after all, a celebration. The Forum had been tidied up for the occasion, buildings around its perimeter had been freshly painted, its cobbled surface had been washed down and tables and chairs had been laid out. A dais had been erected at the northern end with one long table where we would sit. The actual ceremony was very short. I would say a few words, hand over a scroll, and Titus Decimus would reply.

"Citizens of Corinium, I am pleased to have been appointed your Legate, your representative in Rome, your voice to the highest administrative body: the Senate of Rome. It is not a role I take lightly; it is a role that will ask questions of me, I want to answer those questions, I want to represent you, and I want to hear your issues, however petty you think they might be. I have sat in the Senate, I have debated issues there, but now my job is to listen; listen, reflect, and judge.

My first command regards your former Legate. It would appear that you have treated him so well that he wants to stay in Britain. I give him a parcel of land from the Fosse Way to the hill we both climbed which he has named Oxhill. His land will stretch as far as one day's ride on either side of the valley, but no further than the ridge at the end of the valley. He now knows his boundaries. Within this area he wants to build a farming community, a co-operative of small villages working together to first clear the land and then farm it. They will grow the wheat that we need, raise sheep and cattle to clothe and feed us. I have come to know him since I arrived and have seen this place. It will not be easy, but I know he will not rest until his dream is fulfilled.

That, for me, is the easy part. Now I must turn to the harder ones, and I don't yet know what they are. I inherit a peaceful region, a region rich in resources, a region that has no barriers to growing its wealth, a region that Rome is proud of. I will endeavour to ensure that it stays this way."

So that was it, I had been given my land. There was never any question that I wouldn't get the land, but his generous gift was going to save me time and energy. I now had the deeds signed by Rome.

My first job was to employ an overseer to look after the labour force and supervise what I wanted to be done. He had to be someone that I respected, that I could trust and someone I knew would get a job done. There was a Legionnaire who was leaving the army. He was British and had been given Roman citizenship; he was known to be a good leader of men, came from a farming background and had a practical, problem-solving mind. I would have to speak to Titus Decimus before approaching him, but I didn't see a problem as he was already leaving the army.

I went to meet him at his base in Isca Silurum. Firstly, I saw his tribune, showing him a scroll from Titus Decimus that allowed me to talk to him and offer him a job after he had left the army.

"Legate Antonius, you couldn't have picked a better man. We are going to miss him when he goes," Tribute Felix said as we sat at a table in the tavern. "What exactly are your plans for him?"

"I want to offer him the job of overseer, first as I have my new villa built, and then, once that has been achieved, as I start clearing land. I also want him to teach me how to farm."

"That's a long-term project, how much land do you have?"

"Too much to start with, it is as you say. I plan to start my own farm first and then turn to clearing the land and encouraging other farmers to rent land off me."

"Whilst you sit back and count the money," he laughed.

"That will be some years away but yes, I can dream."

"I wish you luck and hopefully I will be able to visit you when the villa is built."

"You have an open invitation."

The next day I went to see Legionnaire Lucius. We met up in the same tavern where I had seen his commanding officer. I had never met him before. I had seen him on parade leading his troops, but I had never spoken to him.

"Legionnaire Lucius, as you have probably heard I have decided to remain in Britain and have been given some land. I plan to build a villa and clear some of the land to farm. After that is achieved, I plan to clear parcels of land and encourage farmers to rent it. If this is successful, I can then go further and set up villages within the valley to house the support that the farmers will require. There's a settlement on the Fosse Way which lies within the boundaries of the land I have been given. I would expand it to become the market town for all the farms."

"Legate, what would you require from me?"

"Lucius, although we have not met, I have been following your career as this plan matured in my brain. I have been impressed by your handling of men; you handle them fairly, but with authority. I know your background and want to tap into it. If you take me up on my offer, your first role would be to select a workforce and oversee them to create a track to the site of the villa and then to build a site for the workforce. That's the preparation. After that, I would like you to clear the land for the villa and oversee its building."

"Before saying yes or no, I would like to see the site and ask what reimbursement I would receive?"

"I would pay you one and a half the salary you get as a legionnaire for the first stage of the project. When it comes to building the villa and clearing the land for a farm, I will give you twice the salary that a legionnaire gets. After that, I would offer you a parcel of land for you to farm, land that you would own."

"That seems very generous, but I cannot give you an answer until I have seen the land."

"I respect that, and I can't remove you from your duties until you are free from them. When you are finished, which I believe is at the end of this year, come and see me in Corinium and we will go and visit the area. In the meantime, I will meet with the native British who live in the area and whose land we will need to cross. What I would like you to think about is the labour we will need to clear a track to the proposed site. It is fairly flat, as we will be circumnavigating the hill from where I first saw the valley."

"I'm afraid any estimate of the workforce needed will be very vague until I see the sight."

"That I appreciate."

So, I had met the man that I wanted to manage the first part of my project. I was happy with my choice, but until the new year I would not know if we would be working together. I returned to my villa in Corinium and carried on my plans. This included going to see some of the modern villas that had been built in recent years. I wanted to talk to their owners, find out the issues that they had had with the construction, where they had procured the stone to build them, who had designed the villas, and how many slaves they had needed to build them. A lot of questions but luckily, I was in a situation where I was welcomed into their villas, and they helped answer them.

I was sitting in the room where I worked on my plans early in the new year, writing some notes and looking at my first attempt at a map of the proposed site. It was very basic, very crude and had been drawn from memory, against all the instructions I had been given in map drawing. I was interrupted by my wife coming to tell me I had a visitor.

"Lucius," I exclaimed when I saw the Legionnaire standing in the hallway, "come in, you must be cold, come in. Let me introduce my wife, Valentina. Like you she is British by birth. My darling, this is Lucius who I hope is going to help with our dream. Now, come through to my work room, the heat will be welcome, but I hope it doesn't send you to sleep after your journey."

I couldn't get him to sit down, he wanted to see the maps I had drawn, to discuss the initial track, to know how I had got on with the locals. His enthusiasm was infectious; I just hoped I could keep it going until we arrived at the site.

We set off early the next morning. It was going to be a good day's ride to get there before darkness set in. I had booked us rooms in the local taverna. Having stayed there before, I knew it was not luxurious, it was a staging post on the Fosse Way, a place to have some basic food and put your head down for the night, but we both had spent nights in less comfort. I stopped at the three hovels on the side of the road out of courtesy but also so that they would know Lucius. As we crossed their meagre holdings, I could tell that Lucius was looking at the hill and the thickness of the trees, doing mental arithmetic as we came closer to where I wanted to enter the wood. Firstly, we went to the glade, but the light was fading so we climbed to the top of the hill. I pointed out the ridge we could just see in the distance which I hoped could be quarried for stone to build the villa. I explained that I had been over there and looked at a site where there had been a landslip which had exposed the rock underneath, a beautiful reddish-brown sandstone.

"How far away is it?" he asked.

"It is difficult to say. It took me about two hours to get there, but once we have cleared a track, I think that will come down to about an hour for a waggon."

"I would like to see it tomorrow if that's possible."

"Of course, but we had better be going now before it gets too dark."

We set off early the next morning at first light and went to the top of the hill first. It was the earliest I had ever been up there and the winter morning light spreading over the tops of the trees made for a spectacular view. The ridge on the other side of the valley, one of my boundary points, seemed even more of a defining line.

"That stream that runs through the glade, where does it go to out there?"

"I haven't followed it, but I think it flows up the left over there," I said pointing to an area that wasn't wooded. "I think it goes through that area, but I assume it is wet, boggy ground."

"Did you have to cross a stream or river when you went to the ridge?"

"No."

"That's good, Legate Antonius, you seem to have got a good bit of land."

"I hope so and, as we have both left the army, I think you can drop the Legate."

"Right, there are several things I want to do today so that I can make a judgement on how many slaves will be required and how long it will take. I assume that you are keen to get the first lot of trees cleared before the spring so we can have a long summer to carry out the first phase of the build."

"That's what I was thinking."

We walked back down to the glade discussing certain details and when we got there, I left him to his work whilst I followed the stream to see exactly where it went. We met back in the glade. Sitting on a fallen tree, we ate the bread and cheese I had bought at the taverna.

"I have marked the trees that need to be felled to make the track from the Fosse Way and roughly measured the distance to be about 5 mille passus[18]. I haven't counted the trees but let's say about one hundred. With a team of twenty men, I think

---

18.   1 mille passus = 0.919 miles.

we should be able to fell twenty trees a day. We will also need a support team of, say, five to look after the camp. The digging up of the roots and laying some sort of surface will take almost as long. If I remember correctly, you wanted some sort of palisade around the villa. Well, we will have the wood for that. Are you thinking about a defensive barrier or just a boundary fence to keep livestock out?"

"Halfway between I think, for defence. I don't want someone to jump over it, but I also don't want the villa to look like a fort. I suppose we will have to burn the trees that we don't need?"

"Yes, Antonius, you are not going to need wood ever again in your life."

"So, you are going to make a track from the Fosse Way to the glade. I assume you are going to make a camp there, what is the next section?"

"Then we break out, we start making the track to the quarry which will require another gang, but you will need two experienced stonemasons, one to run the quarry and one to build the villa, and they will come with their own gangs."

"I have spoken to several people who have recently built or expanded their villas near Corinium, and one name comes up time and time again: Felix Aedificator."

"Felix? I know him, he is a good man."

We spent another two days at the site, Lucius measuring, counting, and calculating, whilst I walked and rode discovering new areas of the land.

Chapter 4
It's All Coming Together (One Year On)

I was now spending more time in Oxhill. Not all of my time, but as the foundations became walls, the walls became rooms, and the trees we were bringing down became the rafters, I could see the villa beginning to materialise. Lucius had been very clever in organising the various areas. There was a team to clear the trees under the command of a carpenter who decided which trees would be used for the different jobs: rafters, wall templates, and the rugged outer trunks for the cordon. The builders couldn't work without the kiln workers to make the lime, which was integral to the making of the concrete which was needed to make the foundations and to fill the walls. The stonemasons and quarry workers couldn't work without the road builders who had built a road between the site and the ridge, which I had named Rubrum Lapis Jugum[19], not very original but it seemed to stick.

It had been an early start that morning. The previous night had been our last night in Corinium, and we were travelling with the waggons taking all of our possessions to Oxhill to move into our villa. I was thankful for Titus Decimus's offer to provide an escort for the journey as there had been several incidents recently of bandits attacking travellers on the Fosse Way and I thought our five waggons would be seen as an easy target. It was a slow journey and on some of the hills we had to double up the horses on the waggons, but we made it before it got too dark. Valentina

---

19.   Translates as Red Stone Ridge.

hadn't yet seen the new road that Lucius had had built from the Fosse Way to the villa. It was not of the quality of a main road, but it was much better than a muddy track. Lucius was standing on the veranda of the villa, and I could see that he had got the servants to have the lights lit inside which gave out a warm heat that flooded out of the windows. It was too late to start unpacking the waggons, which could well wait for the morning.

I took great pride in showing Valentina the changes to the villa since she had last seen it. It was not finished - the walls needed to be smoothed and the mosaics had not been laid on the floor - but it was watertight, it was warm, and it was ours. She was determined to organise the decorating of the villa, and secretly I was happy for her input. She had already shown me designs that she had drawn for the walls with scenes of forests, birds flying over hills, of sheep grazing in fields and wheat swaying in the breeze.

Lucius took me for a tour of what had been happening with the land clearing. Already the landscape had changed and we now had more than enough wood to complete the building work, but I was keen to have a stock leftover in case I wanted to extend the villa. What I had thought to be flat land when I first saw it was in fact full of small humps and hollows that added to the beauty by giving it definition. The first small area to be cleared had been ploughed and sown with grass although there were no sheep yet. We had divided the land into square blocks equalling ten heredium[20], and as we went over the property, I could see the different stages that they were in. The nearest plots had been cleared and sown but further out some still had trees. Elsewhere, the tree stumps had not been pulled out yet and in some fires were burning the cut-down trees.

"Lucius, do you realise that you have been here for more than one year now?" I asked as we walked up the small incline towards the villa.

"Yes, I only wish you had come to me five years earlier. I wasn't sure when you first asked me if I would like it, but it has

---

20.   One heredium = 1.24 acres.

been the best year of my life."

"Have you considered the offer I made of a farm?"

"Yes, I have, but I am not quite sure where I would like to live. There is some nice land further down the brook where I thought I might build a house. I can't see that I will have the time for a while yet with all the other work."

"Well, you keep thinking about it; I will not break my side of the bargain."

"Thank you."

We had reached the villa, and he took me to the back of it where we were planning to build the bathhouse. At this stage, the foundations had been dug out so I could see the outline. Near the brook, a smoking heap of a clamp kiln was doing its job, breaking down limestone which would then be mixed with sand and water to make the concrete destined to be poured into trenches so we could build on a solid flat surface.

"I'll be glad when you have finished with that kiln, the smell is something I won't miss."

"Oh, it's not too bad after a time, I think I'm used to it now."

"One thing I was thinking about the other day, could we extend the roof out over the pathway? I saw one villa near Corinium where they had built a covered colonnade to link the back of the house; it just meant that you didn't get wet getting there."

"I don't see a problem and the columns wouldn't need to be very thick as there is very little load."

"That's what I hoped you would say."

It had been two months since I had been to Oxhill and Lucius took me down the road that had been built across the valley to Rubrum Lapis Jugum to see the quarry where we had carved out the rock to build the villa and also provide ancillary products, like the sand for the concrete. The land on either side of the road had been cleared in the same ten heredium sections, allowing people enough land to build a house and start a farm.

"Antonius, can I propose something that may be against your thoughts?"

"Carry on."

"A lot of the slaves who have worked on clearing the land, or digging out the stone, like it here. They have asked if they could be considered as farmers?"

"What, they want to take on a plot of land?"

"Yes."

"But what would they do with it, how would they buy sheep or seed to plant?"

"That is the issue. They see this as a route out of slavery, a chance."

"I have paid for them; how would they pay me back?"

"I have done some figures. If you would start them off and fund a flock of sustainable sheep between a group of them, they would pay you a larger rent until they had paid off the debt."

"I don't know. What is in it for me?"

"Nothing in the short term. It will cost you money, but in the long term you will have a dedicated workforce who can say "I earned this", a workforce that will help you clear the land that stretches for a days' ride in either direction, a workforce that will be loyal to you, fight for you if need be, a workforce that wants to farm your land."

Chapter 5
Invaders (Another Year On)

It was coming up to the second anniversary of the first tree to be felled on the Oxhill property and I was sitting with Lucius in my study, discussing plans for the future and also reminiscing about the journey we had been on.

In the last year, the first few farms that we cleared were beginning to be utilised. Small stone buildings were being built on them for the farmer and his family, the land was cultivated and grazed by sheep. The first fifty sheep I had acquired in Corinium and had driven down the Fosse Way, forty-eight ewes and two rams. The ewes had been covered and in the spring my flock was extended by forty-one lambs. It was these that I had used to introduce Lucius's plan to encourage people to take up the farms, including some slaves. My cattle herd was small, but growing as more pasture was cleared and we were considering buying more. During the last year, we moved the tented campsite from near the villa to a location further down the brook and built several houses to home the workers and slaves in, this had been added to by building two shops with living accommodation. This was all in the area where Lucius wanted to build his house, but it didn't compromise his plans. I was worried that it would, but he assured me it wouldn't. I was hoping that this would be the start of a village I would call Oxhill. It would serve the local farms and become a hub of social life.

"I know you are probably bored of it, but I think next year we must have another push on land clearing," I started. "If we start cutting back from the new road it should be a bit easier there as it is less wooded."

"I agree, I think that we should build another road from the new one to the ridge, see if we can start a new quarry there. Then it would be easier to build farmhouses and other buildings."

"Good idea, if we can get those up and running, I think we could push on with starting a market. I must speak to the Legate about that."

A few days later I unexpectantly got my chance. I was in my study when I started to hear an increase in noise outside. I got up and walked out to the veranda to be met with the sight of a century of troops marching down from the Fosse Way with the Legate and a centurion riding out in front.

"Titus Decimus," I said as he dismounted in the yard at the front of the villa, "what a surprise!"

"Antonius, I was on my way to the site where we are going to build a small fortress and couldn't not drop by. How is it going?"

"Very well. Would you like a glass of wine?"

"Yes, Centurion, get the men to fall out, I won't be long, and they could probably do with a rest."

He came into the villa and insisted on being shown around much to Valentina's distress as he would be the first person of importance to see her decorations. He stood there in the living room looking at the decorations on the wall, whilst she stood behind me clutching nervously at my tunic. He said nothing, then took a sip of his wine before turning round with a big smile on his face.

"Valentina, you must be very proud of them, they are beautiful," he said. "You really have got an eye; I will suggest others come here to see them." She left us with a beaming smile on her face.

"Antonius, the other reason I came here is that there have been several instances of a group of bandits raiding farms, killing all that they find and stealing the livestock. As far as I know, they haven't got this far up the Fosse Way yet, but with winter approaching they might see your sheep and cattle as easy food. This is why I am building a small fortress. The troops I have with me will be posted there to act as a deterrent."

"That's very worrying, has this happened at well-defended villas?"

"Yes, they seem to be well-armed and ruthless. What are your defences like here? I see you have got a barricade around the property; how secure is it?"

"I was hoping never to find out. Lucius built it with the house. I didn't want it so high, but he persuaded me that it might be needed to keep out more than cattle."

"I fear he may be right; do you want me to leave a contumerium[21] ? It might make you feel safer."

"It also might show that we have got something to steal. No, I don't think so at the moment. How far have they come up the Fosse Way?"

"The last attack was on a villa on the other side of Bourton."

"That close? It is the small farmers that I am worried about, there is no way they can defend themselves."

"Could you use the hill as a lookout post? If I remember, from up there you would be able to spot a large group of people coming well before they got here."

"That's a good idea. If I had a brazier up there and another on the ridge they could be used to warn people."

"Well, hopefully, I've given you enough time to prepare. Now I must go before the soldiers get restless and loose concentration. It has been good to see you, friend, and I am sorry that I have brought you such bad news. I promise that I will come for a longer visit next time and let you show me around."

"I would like that and thank you for the warning."

I was a worried man when I found my wife relaxing in the bedroom, and she was a worried woman after I had told her of the warning. It wasn't about our situation; it was the farmers who concerned us. How would they protect themselves? I sent a servant to ask Lucius to come up to the villa. I put my worries to him and told him I had refused soldiers to be on-site. I also told him my thoughts about using the hill and the ridge as lookouts.

---

21.   8 soldiers, plus 1 officer.

"I think we can do better than that," he replied. "If they are coming up the Fosse Way, how are they going to get onto your property? They would either come down the road to here or they would come over the hill. The fortifications around the villa and the farm buildings will be enough to stop them from getting in here. I propose that we build a small fort on top of the hill. It will serve two purposes, both to protect the route and also to give shelter to those on lookout up there. I will check, but the fortress will probably be able to see it as well."

"How big are you suggesting?"

"Small. We have enough wood to easily build something that is, say, twenty passuses across, and have a platform running around the top."

"How quickly could that be built?"

"In a few days if we transferred all the labour to it."

"Then get it done."

We chucked everything at it. First, we cleared a path up the hill so that we could get materials up there. Then we dug the holes which would take the posts for the walls. Next, the carpenters built the walls themselves, and a walkway that went around the top with a platform for the brazier to be mounted upon. I climbed up to see the view that they would have. I could see the Fosse Way as expected and I had a view down the road for two mille passus until the road dipped down a hill. It was enough to give people a warning and to act as a deterrent to any raiders coming over the hill.

We arranged a rota with five men in the tower during all daylight hours. For days they saw nothing. The weather took a turn with snow falling for a week and northern winds blowing. The land became a winter wonderland, the trees looked stark with the snow sticking to the branches in the lee of the wind and the land softened.

I was awoken by the sound of the horn being blown from the top of the hill. It was a warning signal for the villa. I got up quickly. The servants were running around in a panic, but I didn't have time to calm them. I needed to know what had been seen and to make sure our fortifications were secure. I was helping to close the two big gates through which the road to the Fosse Way ran when one of the lookouts came running out of the woods that led to the hill.

"Sir, we can see a large group coming down the road, and the brazier has been lit."

"How many did you see?"

"There were waggons, and men on horses and men on foot."

"Man, how many men did you see?"

"About fifty men, sir."

"Thank you. Now get yourself a hot drink from the villa and return to your post."

"Yes, sir."

I needed to get word to Lucius so that he could get word to the soldiers at the barracks. I found one of the slaves and gave him instructions, stressing the importance of speed. I couldn't do much more, except wait and wonder.

I climbed up to the ramparts and stood above the main gate, joining the five workers that were already up there.

"Please don't show your bows, keep them out of view. I don't want to provoke a reaction," I warned them. As ever, it was the waiting that I found difficult. I pulled my winter cape closer around me, trying to stop shivering. And then I heard a new noise. There was a scrape, a squeak, and then I heard the noise that can only be made by horses' hooves on the hard surface of the road. I held up my hand to keep the men quiet.

"Can you hear that?" I asked.

"Yes, sir, it sounds like several horses coming down the road with waggons."

The sounds got louder and then we saw them coming around the corner. There were four horsemen at the front riding side-by-side, followed by men walking behind. I looked at them as they approached with a military eye. They were a bedraggled bunch; I definitely wouldn't have said they marched. The horsemen were not wearing any armour, but they had swords strapped to their sides. The men on foot were not dressed any better and didn't seem to be armed. I counted them quickly: twenty and then some more horsemen and finally four waggons with some women and children. I stood still and waited for them to reach us, but they stopped, and a single horseman came forward at a trot, reining in to stop below me in front of the closed gate.

"Good morning, sir," he said in a strong local accent. "My men and I are looking for a place to camp and some food to eat which we would pay for with our labour."

"I'm afraid we are not looking for any labour at the moment."

"Can we at least camp and ask if you have any spare food, if only for the women and children?"

"No, we have little enough food ourselves."

"Sir, I see only yourself and five men. Look behind me. I have asked politely, but I think you will agree I have the force to take what I want."

"I think that you should turn round and carry on up the Fosse Way. We have heard about your exploits at other farms and have prepared for your arrival here. I can assure you that we won't just open the gates and let you in."

"If you have already heard that when we want something we get it, you are either brave or stupid to try and stand against us."

I was desperate to try and keep him talking, giving Lucius time to ride for help.

"I know if I give you food, you will just come back for more. If I let you camp, I will be a prisoner in my villa. And if I thought I would get any work done by you, or your men, I would have to get it done again by men I trust. So, I suggest that you turn around and go back to the road."

"I don't see that you are in a situation to suggest anything. Now, I will give you one more opportunity to open these gates and to save your villa and your life before I burn them down."

I knew that, from a military point of view, I was in a strong position. My five bowmen, each with thirty arrows that could be fired every thirty seconds, would devastate the force in front of me. I just needed them to turn around, so, I silently gave the signal and the men picked up their bows and nocked an arrow.

"Don't provoke me, sir, I don't want to have to do this with force."

"Just turn around then and leave my farm and my farmers in peace." Two of the bowmen drew and released their arrows. One took out one of the horses with a clean hit to the heart and the other killed its rider squarely through his.

"You haven't heard the last from me," he said as he turned his horse around and cantered back to his men, who slowly turned and walked away. I let out a long, low sigh, but stayed standing there with a mixture of relief and shock that he had turned back.

I stayed up there for most of the morning in case he returned but sent one of the bowmen up the hill to tell the lookouts about the soldiers coming from the barracks and also to make sure the bandits had left the property. I hoped that the two would meet on the road.

I was still standing there when I heard the familiar thumping sound of men marching down the road and saw the soldiers coming down it towards the villa. They stopped in front of the gate and their officer came to the fore.

"Legate, we heard that you had some visitors."

"Yes, didn't you see them on the road?"

"No, the road was empty."

I was explaining what had happened when Lucius came galloping up from his property, jumped the stream, and came to a breathless stop.

"They must have missed the soldiers. They have torched two barns on the road to the ridge, come quickly before they do any more damage."

I looked around towards the ridge and saw the plumes of smoke rising above the trees. The officer had already ordered the soldiers into a quick march, and they set off at almost a run towards the danger. I shouted to one of the slaves to get my horse ready as I climbed down the ladder and ran towards the house to collect my sword. When I got back, the horse was ready, and we rode off in pursuit of the soldiers.

We caught up with them just as the soldiers were forming into mobile units. The front six soldiers held their shields in front of them, the next row had them covering their heads. They were stationed on the road to the ridge, facing one of the barns that had been set alight. The leader of the bandits stood with his followers between them and the barn. A few had their swords drawn, but most were just carrying farming implements, either those they had brought with them or more likely stolen from the barns. They were trying to look and sound aggressive, shouting insults at the soldiers and the farmers, who were standing to one side. The leader suddenly noticed me and pointed at me, shouting.

"This is all his fault, if he had not been so aggressive this morning none of this would have happened."

I was determined not to look at him. Instead, I looked at the officer who had moved around to be in front of the troops.

"On the authority of the Legate Titus Decimus, I demand that you put down your weapons and surrender."

"Surrender only to be slaughtered, you mean. Men, we have done nothing wrong. It is not wrong to want to feed your families."

"Troops, draw swords."

"No, officer, stop. We don't have any grief with you. We just want some food."

"Troop, arrest anyone with a sword." The Troop started forward in silence, a silence that was broken by the sound of metal falling on stone. The leader turned round to see the cause and then realised he was the only one still carrying a sword.

"Aaaaaaah," he shouted and raised his weapon before charging towards the soldiers, swinging it in circles above his head before crashing it down onto their shields. The Troop stopped as their attacker continued to try and battle through them. Then suddenly the shields parted slightly in the middle, for a second, and a sword was thrust through the gap and into his stomach. As soon as he was hit, the shields lifted slightly, and another sword scythed his legs cutting him down at the knees. He dropped like a stone, blood spurting out of his stomach and the cuts in his legs. He cried out once before the Troop marched forward, trampling over him and leaving him dead behind them.

"Halt!" The officer shouted just before they got to the bandits who were scurrying backwards. "Troops, arrest all of these people, tie them up, but make sure that they can walk."

"Lucius," I shouted, "let's get some water moving to douse these flames. Form a line of people with buckets from the pond."

"Yes, Antonius."

I left the Officer and soldiers to do whatever needed to be done to the bandits. I didn't want anything to do with them, they disgusted me. Instead, I started to organise another bucket line to the second barn. Luckily, they had decided to burn down two of the wooden, temporary, barns and hadn't tried to burn the roofs off the stone-built ones. I didn't think we would be able to save them so after an hour I called off the exercise as being a waste of time, effort, and water. It was only when I was walking around the back of the barns that I discovered the callous butchery that had taken place. The dead carcasses of four cattle lay in the mud. Their throats had been cut and an amateurish attempt made to butcher the meat which had left the site like the worst slaughterhouse.

I went to find Lucius to tell him what I had found. He saw my face and took over moving the carcasses to the barn which we used for slaughtering our animals. I mounted my horse and started the ride home with a heavy heart and a brain that was overloading.

Chapter 6
Squaring the Circle

I was desperately worried about how vulnerable we were to any roving gang of bandits. We might have got away with it this time and only lost two wooden barns and some livestock, but it could have been a different story. From my time as Legate, I knew how dangerous these gangs of bandits were and how difficult it was to stop them. They weren't visible until they struck, they were mobile, and lived deep in the forests. Whilst their preferred target was normally waggons on roads, it now seemed that they had grown sufficiently in confidence to attack a farm.

When I had returned home the day before, Valentina was visibly shocked and in tears; I had tried to calm her down but all she could see was another attack.

"You don't know these people," she had said to me. "It is all right for you, when you were Legate you had the protection of the army, you were sitting in a secure villa. We are out in the open here. You may build a wooden wall around the villa, but you can't build a wall around the whole estate. These men are vermin, they are hungry, and that makes them dangerous."

"I know," I started to say.

"You don't know, you have no idea how lucky we were today. If we hadn't been warned, those gates would have been open, they would have ridden in here, slaughtered all the males and raped all the women before selling them into slavery. I'm not worried about what we have in the villa, I'm worried about our lives; and don't say "I know," because you don't."

"My darling, I appreciate that we have had a stressful day,

but let's not overreact."

"Overreact? I'm not overreacting, I can assure you. I'm worried, I'm scared and, quite frankly, I wouldn't mind being back in Corinium."

"Let me speak to Lucius in the morning. I can see the big picture, but he is better at seeing the smaller one, the local picture."

"The "local picture" is that we are not safe here."

"My darling, please, let's not get hysterical, I'll talk to Lucius."

To say that the atmosphere for the rest of that day was the same as the weather outside would be an understatement.

"Lucius, what other measures can we take?" I asked the next morning as we were in my office. "We can't patrol the perimeter the whole time."

"No, and the perimeter will increase the more land we clear. I think the lookout on the hill works well, and we should set up more on the high points of your land."

"That's all well and good, but who is going to man them?"

"The farmers; it will be part of their payment to you for their land to provide a few hours a week on their local lookout. After all, it is in their interest not to have another day like yesterday."

"That's a good idea. At the moment, we would only need probably one further down the ridge and we could see each of them."

"The other thing that must happen is that the gate should always be closed. And we must set up better communication between here and the top of the hill."

"The trumpet worked well yesterday."

"Yes, but it still meant that a man had to come down here to tell you what the problem was."

"Point taken. I remember when you were in Isca Silurum you had some sort of system for written messages, what was it exactly?"

"Very basic, I think you would call it, but it could be adapted. It was a pot attached to a rope so that it slid down. Very good for one-way messaging but not very good if you need to send a reply."

"But we don't need to. I can go up there if I need to tell them something."

"I suppose so, let me think about it. I also think that you should build a new defensive wall all around the property, a stone one."

"I don't know, I've lived in forts for so much of my life I don't want to make my home one."

"I think I know someone who might think differently."

"Good point. Let's draw up some plans and make it the summer project."

"One last thing. You told me way back that you had some boxes that you had to keep safe. I assume they are in the villa, but would it be a good idea to create a safe place on the villa farm to hide them?"

"I was thinking the same, I just don't like burying them. How are the farmers?"

"Considering what they have been through, I would say they are relieved and impressed that the soldiers turned up so quickly; even if they did lose a couple of barns, they didn't lose any lives."

"That's right, a couple of calves which I can make up, but yes, we are still here."

The raid, or attempted raid as I saw it, changed many things around the villa: the gates were permanently closed, there were always guards on the walkway above them, and the two lookouts were also manned. Spring also returned to my relationship with Valentina, who approved of the new wall and Lucius's other suggestions.

Several weeks later, I was just about to go on a visit to some of my tenant farmers when the trumpet sounded from the top of the hill. I immediately went to the gate and climbed up to the walkway. Looking out, I could see nothing, and nor could the two soldiers on guard. Then a man came crashing out of the trees, running from the tower.

"Sir, some soldiers are coming down the Fosse Way."

"From which direction?"

"Coming up over the hill from Bourton."

"Get them to signal again if they turn down our road."

"Yes, sir," he replied, turning to run back up the hill. I wasn't worried about soldiers, but it made me think that maybe we could devise different trumpet signals to tell us whether we were dealing with trouble or friendly troops.

I climbed down and was just going into one of the barns when the trumpet sounded again. We had visitors.

"Sir, it's the Legate," came a call from the walkway above.

"Open the gate," I ordered and went to welcome him. I stood in the middle of the entrance to our villa, recognising my friend riding at the front of a Century of troops.

"Good morning, my friend," he called out as he trotted up to me. "I hear that you had some visitors yesterday." He stopped in front of me.

"Come in and get warm, then I will tell you all about it."

We were settled in the living room where the under-floor heating was just about winning the battle against the cold.

"I saw the new tower from the road, did it help?"

"Yes, but we must get a better system of communicating with it than a runner dashing down the hill. I have asked Lucius to try and think of something."

"Could you try some sort of pulley and rope system? The lookout could warn you by trumpet signal, and then send you down a more detailed message in a jar which they could then reel back up again with your response."

"We were thinking of something along those lines," I lied as we had only been talking about a message going one way.

"Well, you will be glad to hear that the lot of them spent an uncomfortable night in a corral in Corinium and I am glad that the leader has been taken out. Stupid idiot, what did he think he was doing?"

"I don't know, I can only think that he thought that death was a better option than being captured."

"You may be right. So, what are your plans now you have had

a lucky escape?"

We discussed the various plans as two military leaders would discuss the plans for an operation, posing questions to each other, answering questions, and raising others. In the end, he agreed that a stronger wall was needed but thought that it should totally surround the property, including the land where the torrent ran.

We talked on and it was obvious that he was in no hurry to leave. We were relaxed, discussing various matters both political and economic, when he dropped his real reason for the visit.

"Do you remember Legionnaire Crassus from when you were Legate?" Words that didn't frighten me to start with.

"Yes, he was someone I had considered as the person who could have replaced me as Legate; he was a good officer, I thought, but when I asked around, it appeared that I may have got the wrong impression about him."

"I don't know how much you know about him, but I will fill you in. Crassus comes from a wealthy family, holders of vast estates around Rome, and a politically active family. It is rumoured that his grandfather nearly became the emperor in a political coup that only failed when two of his Generals realised he was not going to give them the power they sought. Somehow, he kept his life and his land, but he was politically ruined. His father was tainted and, although he kept his seat in the Senate, he did not have its respect. Crassus is the second son, so he inherits nothing which is why he is in the army."

"I didn't know all of this, but what has it got to do with me?"

"Crassus has gone to the Senate with a story that you and two other Legates planned to make Brittania an independent state, an island that is easy to defend. Rather than giving Rome your taxes, you would charge them for the provision of silver and whatever you could export to them."

"What! How would that work? Brittania can't survive without Rome and Romans living here. The people who inhabit these shores are basically heathens who would go back to living in mud huts if that happened. They would not survive without Rome."

"I know that. Unfortunately, he has convinced the Senate otherwise, and they have sent a message that you are to be questioned. Not by me, but by the Senate."

"This is crazy. Are you here to arrest me?"

"No. Well, probably I am, if I interpret orders that way. I would suggest that you go to Rome and speak to the Senate; they don't know what is going on most of the time. Tell them what it is like being a Legate in the most far-removed province, tell them what Rome has brought to it, tell them of the success of Roman rule, and ask them where the evidence is. You have stayed here, you have prospered here, you have paid Rome what is due to Rome. Go and answer them.

Chapter 7
The Present Time

Do I really have time for this? I thought as I brushed the soap onto my face before scraping it off with a safety razor. I was going to have to wear a suit today, look business-like, wear a jacket and tie, all the things that I hated to do when put in the context of my job, and livelihood. Today I was going to have to go to Oxford to find out if I was going to lose a field to archaeology. Well, that's exaggerating, but at least *part* of a field.

Professor Michael Bain would publish his report on the findings. The findings were that they had found a perfectly preserved Roman villa floor plan, along with a bathhouse, in one of my fields. There were rooms with second-century mosaic floors and a complete hypocaust heating system that hadn't collapsed. It was said to be a major discovery, historically significant, a site that should be preserved for the nation. I knew that I couldn't argue against that as I had started the whole process off, but I didn't know the consequences then.

I drove Sandy's Audi to Oxford, revelling in the comfort compared with being behind the wheel of my pickup or a tractor. I loved the silence, followed by the raw deep throb of the engine as I changed up gears on the back roads taking me from Oxhill to Tysoe, across the hill to Hook Norton and into Banbury, picking up the main road to my destination. All the time I was thinking of what the outcome might be. Andy Eames had said that I should not be worried, but I was a farmer, not a keeper of a national relic.

I parked where I was told to and walked over to the building.

It felt like I was entering another era; the building had been built in the time of Henry VIII and was wooden panelled, stone-floored, cold, and uninviting. A table had been set up by the door and it seemed I would have to register to enter.

"Geoff, how come you are early? That's a first!" Andy welcomed me before I even got to the desk.

"Ewes have taught me to be on time. That, and you buying a beer, which I hope comes soon. How are you?"

"Nervous. I know we are technically on different sides, but we are still friends, aren't we?"

"Look, whatever comes out of this, we are bigger than that. Our friendship may not go back to Roman times, but you are a friend."

"Thanks."

We both walked into the meeting room, a room that ranged from the Tudor glory of its walls and ceiling to a clashing modern glass table with eight computers and chairs arranged around it. The four seats opposite the main door were already taken. Professor Michael Bain was sitting in one of the end seats. I didn't know the three other people, but they were busy reading and generally looking occupied.

"Good afternoon, Andy and Geoff, please take a seat," Michael said before beginning to outline the archaeological treasures that had been discovered in my field. He went on.

"We have not done a full, forensic dig of the site, or even surveyed the wider area. It is assumed that this is not just an isolated villa, it must have had a supporting network such as a farm with associated farm buildings. This could be one of the most important discoveries of second-century Roman remains to have been uncovered for several years. I'm afraid that, as with everything else, funding has raised its ugly head. As an Archaeologist, I would dig up any site that showed the excellent potential that this one does, but I don't have the money to do it. So, what I am suggesting is that the parts we have dug so far that have yielded results - the villa, and the bathhouse - should be documented, protected, and then backfilled with topsoil. Then the field should be returned to Geoff Knight who does, after all, farm it. However, we would stipulate that he does not plough the field in case future archaeological finds are damaged."

"Can I ask a question?" I wasn't sure if I should have put my hand up and waited to be asked what I wanted to say. "That field has, to my knowledge, been ploughed annually for at least the last fifty years and yet you say that, by continuing to plough, I risk damaging any future finds. I admit that the area that has been dug, and where we know there is a villa and bathhouse, should not be ploughed as the structure of the soil has changed, but the rest of the field?" I left it hanging.

A fair amount of huffing and puffing came from across the table before Michael asked a question, "Geoff, I hear you. How much would it affect your farm if that field was used as pastureland?"

"I would probably have to put extra drainage in at the bottom. The field is the furthest from the farm, which is not ideal."

"We can't tell you what you can do, we can only appeal to you, and tell you what could happen."

"Could you tell me what sort of money is required for a dig of this magnitude?"

"A full cost analysis has not been done, but it is safe to say it would be a six-figure sum."

"If I gave you a five-year commitment to keep it as pastureland and allow you to carry on doing any survey work, at the end of that period, if there are other areas of interest, then we can look again, you at your budgets and I at how it has affected my income. Does that sound fair?"

PART 5

THE FIRST ENGLISH CIVIL WAR, 1642

Chapter 1
The Tower of London

It was the seventh of January, a cold and dank day that brought pleasure to no one. The steward entered the grand hall in the North Tower of the White Tower at the start of his duties; a large fire burned in the furthest part of the hall and in front of it he could see two high wing-backed chairs with the smoke of two pipes forming their individual clouds that joined halfway between their sources and the ceiling. It had been a tumultuous four weeks, it was his job to service the Lieutenant of the Tower of London, a job he had carried out since he had been appointed by Sir William Balfour in 1630. He had seen it as a privilege to keep the Lieutenant's accommodation within the Tower a place of comfort, a place where he could relax away from the political, military, and complex trading that was involved in the job. That had all changed when Sir Thomas Lunsford was appointed to take the position of the previous incumbent, a job he would keep for five days. Now he had a new Lieutenant to serve; Sir John Byron, an arch-supporter of King Charles I, a former MP and, as he was learning, a man who didn't take fools gladly.

A table stood between the two chairs on which stood two wine cups and a jug, as he walked down the room, he could hear the murmur of their two voices talking quietly. He knew that they had heard him approach as Sir John gave a cough, and they stopped their discussion.

"Another jug of wine, please"

"Yes, sir." He picked up the empty jug and retreated and as he moved away, he heard them return to their discussion.

"All in all, I'm quite glad to see the back of 1641," Sir John said.

"I'm sure you are," Captain Charles Drinkwater replied. "What has amazed me is the lack of respect that Parliament has shown to the King."

"I know, and it's that lack of respect that has emboldened the population. They would never have behaved like they have had Parliament had come in line with his wishes and paid for his Scottish excursion. We would never have had the riots in the streets, Strafford would still be alive, and the bishops would still be in place."

"You don't really think the King would reintroduce Catholicism, do you?"

"No, and don't confuse all of this with religious belief. This is all about who rules the country, the King, or Parliament. Believe you me, if the King goes to York - and I think he will - we will be on a downhill ride towards civil war."

"It won't come to that. Surely, they will back down. Anyway, who is going to fight whom? Neither side has an army to speak of."

"Oh, don't worry about that; cities, towns and even villages, will make their minds up about who they support. There will be few trained soldiers fighting, it might even be shepherds against shepherds, shopkeepers against shopkeepers, each slugging it out on some unknown field. Prince Rupert will bring his cavalry over and at least they will have some knowledge of how to fight."

"You seem very depressed about the future."

"Charles, how can anyone seem optimistic about the future? As I see it, this country is about to be plunged into an abyss that is totally avoidable, an abyss that will raise questions that should not be raised. I believe in Parliament, an institution that should question the divine right to rule. That was what the Magna Carta was all about - a balance of authority. I think that Pym and the others have tried to tip the balance. What we really need is a single figure, a royal figurehead to look up to, a person almost above the law yet beholden to it."

"The King is not above question; he has made some bad mistakes even in the last few weeks. How he thought it was a good idea to appoint Lunsford – a convicted murderer! - to your job, only to have to remove him four days later, I don't know. And then that ridiculous appearance he made, charging into the hallowed halls of Parliament. It doesn't make any sense, and it certainly doesn't show great wisdom or leadership."

"You're right, but I'm afraid that my heart and my brain say that this country needs a monarchy, a balance of power. Who would question Parliament and the decisions it makes without the monarchy and the House of Lords?"

"Where do you go from here?"

"I don't know. I expect the King to go to York and I will go with him."

The steward entered the room at a pace that ensured the two stopped talking and turned to see what was interrupting them.

"Sir, this has just been delivered from St James's Palace," he said, handing Sir John a letter bound by a large red seal. Sir John tore it open and read its contents.

"Well, Charles, I think we are just about to discover what the future holds for us. We are both invited to an audience with the King. We'll take a carriage with outriders to make sure we are not stopped. We must leave immediately."

Darkness had descended over London; a mist had formed over the River Thames as the temperature dropped below freezing and this mist now rolled up over the riverbanks, engulfing the road which followed the water's westward course and upon which they were travelling. Shortly after passing Parliament, they turned north through parkland until they arrived at St James's Palace. Sir John noticed that it was more heavily fortified than was normal. The guards were more numerous, carried more arms and were supported by soldiers on horses. They were accompanied through to the forecourt and taken up to the King's quarters on the first floor of the Palace where they were shown into a room the likes of which Captain Drinkwater had never seen before in his life. The walls were painted a shade of light blue with intricate gold patterns, heavy architraves, again decorated with gold, and the ceiling decorated with scrolls in the form of branches and leaves. It appeared as if there was no one else in the room but then a voice welcomed them from the far end behind a highchair.

"Gentlemen, please would you join me." They walked down the room, almost to the far end before turning and bowing to the King.

"Yes, yes, yes," King Charles said, "now we have things to discuss, and we don't have much time. Sir John, you might be wondering why I appointed you to the Tower. Parliament will make your position untenable. They will fight every decision you make but don't worry, I knew they would. I only ask you to stay there for a month or so whilst I move the Court to York. When I give you word, you can resign. I will then want you to join me there. Although it is the last thing that I want, I fear that I will not be allowed to reign freely as is my prerogative. I cannot reign with one hand tied behind my back with Parliament cord. There will be some sort of confrontation, I just hope that it will be short and, if possible, bloodless."

"Yes, Your Majesty."

"Sir John, I will not have a problem bringing together an army, but I do have a problem finding experienced officers to lead them. Prince Rupert will come over from France and bring his cavalry. I would like you to lead another regiment of cavalry after you have resigned from the Tower."

"I would be honoured, sir."

"My plans are very fluid. At the moment, they will need to be reactive as I will have to act in whatever way they force me to act. Sir John, I need you to do two things: first, to make yourself an absolute nuisance to Parliament, starting by asking for a meeting with Pym and the rest of them every day. They are obliged to listen to you and answer your questions. I want them distracted. Secondly, I want you to start to raise money for my campaign quietly. There must be traders in London who will support me, they can't all be stupid enough to support Parliament when it is ruining their profits. Captain Drinkwater, I asked you here as I have nothing but good reports about you, I want you to take over Sir John's planning and preparation for his trip to York and set up a cavalry regiment."

"Yes, sir."

"Tell me, could you count on any of the London Bands?"

"I'm sure we could recruit from them secretly, but we couldn't count on them per se."

"That's what I thought. Recruit who you can, but make sure you are taking the cream and leaving them with the whey. Well, that is all for tonight, gentlemen. Thank you for coming here and we shall speak soon."

They were dismissed and five minutes later were back inside their carriage making the return journey to the Tower of London.

"That went quite well, I think, don't you?" Sir John asked.

"Yes, the King seems very pragmatic and resigned."

"Yes, I thought he was quite chipper. I think I will enjoy the next few weeks making a nuisance of myself. That is the easy part. I'm not sure how much revenue I will be able to bring in, though. I fear you have the harder job, acting secretly to steal the cream of the London Bands without being found out."

"I can only do what I can do, but where I have had difficult orders to carry out before, I have never been given them by the King himself. It makes it feel even more important."

"That's why he did it. He wants to make sure that he gets the soldiers and Parliament are left with the shopkeepers."

"It may not be that easy."

"Charles, you can only do what you can do. Don't worry, I'm sure history won't say that King Charles lost his kingdom because Captain Charles Drinkwater couldn't recruit some of the London Bands."

"You are enjoying this, aren't you?"

"Yes, I feel more certain that this country will descend into civil war than I did before. I'm sure that I can profit from that. I see a good time ahead."

As it was, Sir John Byron wore down Parliament in a matter

of six weeks and, in the middle of February, he resigned from his post a few hours before he was removed from it. It gave him the moral high ground to claim that Parliament had stopped him from performing the job that the King had asked him to do. Charles had also been busy spreading the notion that real soldiers should join the King if it came to a confrontation; after all, the monarchy understood the army. What did Parliament know about fighting battles?

After he had resigned, Sir John was free to join the King in York, free to openly support him, and was rewarded by the King who gave him the command of the Royalists' First Regiment of Horse.

Chapter 2
The Route to Oxford

The spring and summer of 1642 could well be described like no other two seasons in the history of England. For the first time since the country had had an elected Parliament, that institution and the Monarchy were charging towards civil war. Neither side would give political ground, while both sides were recruiting, armouring, and selling propaganda for their cause.

In April, the King fancied getting his hands on the large arsenal held in Kingstone upon Hull but was challenged by the Parliamentary governor and retreated to York. He returned in July when he heard that the governor would hand the town over if he could do so whilst keeping his honour. The King marched south again with some four thousand men only to find that Parliament had reinforced the town, so he laid siege to it, but not very effectively as Parliament had control of the Navy.

Parliament's preparation was twofold. At the beginning of June, it published its Nineteen Propositions outlining how it would limit the King's powers. At the same time it was recruiting and preparing its army. It knew that the time for talking was over. The King was never going to accept its Propositions, a view that was confirmed when the King issued a Commission of Array. This law had last been used by Queen Elizabeth I and had never been repealed. It was a wider call to arms that he sent to county and city leaders that he thought would support him.

The final act happened on the 22nd of August in Nottingham when the King raised the Royal Standard, which was in effect a declaration of war with Parliament.

Sir John Byron was sitting at the breakfast table in the house that had been appropriated for him in York. The food had been cleared and just a jug of ale and his cup remained. He was concerned, not for the outcome of the conflict, or that he had chosen the right side, no, he was concerned about his own finances. Yes, the king was paying the wages for his regiment, but he was looking for more. He saw that this conflict, which he believed would be over after the first battle, probably before the end of the year, would supply him with an opportunity to make a fortune.

There was a knock at the front door, and he could hear one of the servants scurrying down the hall passageway to answer it. There was a brief conversation, he heard the front door bang shut, and then there was a knock at his door.

"Sir, there is a Royal Messenger here who would like to speak to you."

"Well, send him in, Betty, we can't keep a Royal Messenger waiting," he replied before the man entered. "Yes, how can I be of assistance?"

"Sir, I have a request that you join the King in his quarters. He would like to give you instructions."

"Just give me five minutes to get properly dressed."

It took just four before he was downstairs in full uniform with his sword attached to his waist, although he knew he would have to remove it well before his appointment. His horse had been saddled and was waiting for him to make the short journey.

"Good morning, Sir John. I trust you have had breakfast?"

"Yes, Your Majesty."

"Good, then we can talk. I can never have a proper conversation until I have had breakfast. Tomorrow, I'm going to travel down to Nottingham to raise the Royal Standard. It has to be done from there as it is central, and I can move around. Having done that, I am probably going to Shrewsbury. I want you to go to Oxford. Oxford is loyal to me, and the colleges have donated silver and money that will be used to pay the troops' wages for the rest of the year. If this conflict should become prolonged, Oxford will be my seat of Court."

"Yes, Your Majesty."

"You will take a hundred and fifty dragoons to act as support for the convoy and take the waggons to meet me in Shrewsbury. If I hear of any movement of Parliamentary troops, I will send support, probably in the form of Prince Rupert, who is itching for a bit of action."

The conversation went on for another fifteen minutes with the King telling Sir John his thoughts on many matters, not least his plans for Parliament when he was victorious. When he was done, he dismissed him, and Sir John left to start the preparations for his journey south to Oxford. His first thought was that this could be his chance to secure his wealth, but this was a thought for later; for now, he had to get ready. He returned to the house and ordered his travelling box to be brought up to his bedroom. He then instructed a maid what to pack. He would wear his uniform on the journey, but he would need some others for Oxford. He certainly wasn't going to miss the chance of having a good time there.

When he was ready, he sent a runner to find Captain Drinkwater with instructions he was to come to the house. He asked for wine to be served in the front room and settled down in a leather-backed chair with his notebook and quill nestled on the writing slope on his lap. He was a man of lists and whilst he waited for the captain to arrive, he started his planning in list form: supplies, where to stay, support staff, and waggons needed. He stopped there as he heard a knock at the door and the familiar voice of his Captain being welcomed into the house.

"Charles, come in, I have arranged for some wine."

"Thank you, sir."

"I had an audience with the King today and he has asked me to go to Oxford where the colleges have donated items that he wants to be taken to Shrewsbury. More importantly, he has agreed your promotion to Major, so you will be in charge of the dragoons we will take with us. Major, can I pour you a glass of wine?"

"Sir, I'm honoured, when are we going to leave?"

"I had originally thought that we should leave tomorrow, but the King is going down to Nottingham the day after and I think it would be prudent to march with him there and then carry on independently to Oxford."

"Sir, we both know that the Royal train moves at a snail's pace, often depending on when the King can be bothered to get out of his, or his mistress's bed. It could take forever."

"Charles, I think that you should moderate your language. His Majesty is totally preoccupied with the welfare of his kingdom and has no time for carnal thoughts."

"I'm sorry, sir, I didn't mean to disrespect the King."

"I know, but I reason that if we travel with the King to Nottingham we will not be seen as an independent force, and when we get there, we can slip away and not be noticed."

"How secret are we meant to be?"

"Charles, you know troops are moving around the country from both sides. No one wants a conflict at the moment. We will be another regiment marching, positioning themselves, going somewhere, but no one knows why, or where."

"But what happens if we meet a band of Parliamentary troops?"

"We will avoid them. The area between Nottingham and Oxford is mainly supportive of the King, we should be safe."

They didn't leave for another two days. They were meant to leave on each of those days, but on the first the King was not feeling well and on the second, although the whole convoy was mounted and ready to go, the King didn't appear until mid-afternoon and then decided that it was too late in the day to start. Even on the third day, it was nearly lunchtime before they set off. The frustration was not sitting well with Major Charles Drinkwater.

"This is what I was worried about," he said to Sir John Byron as they rode down Micklegate behind the King's empty carriage. The King was on horseback in front of it, waving to the crowds that lined the street shouting their acclamation.

"Don't worry, Charles, we're not on any timetable. Relax, enjoy the ride, it might be the last time you will be able to have time to look at the countryside without trying to see the enemy."

It was a very slow journey. Every time they stopped for a meal, or at the end of the day, it seemed to take an eternity to start again. Every morning, they had to wait for the King to get ready and have breakfast. Every time they stopped during the day there was something that stopped them from starting. On one occasion, the livestock got loose, a wagon wheel broke, and the wheelwright couldn't be found until someone looked underneath another one to find him asleep, snoring, and drunk. The King also wanted to stop at every town to take in the perceived love of his subjects. This did not always turn out the way that he wanted, especially when they travelled through an area that supported Parliament. It wasn't just the shouts, which the King wouldn't have heard because of the cheering of his own soldiers, it was the eggs thrown from the side of the road which were harder to hide from him. Very soon he agreed to pass through a town that might not support him in his carriage.

The journey from York to Nottingham should have taken four days but after six they had only completed half of the journey. Supplies were getting short, and they would need to get them from the local community. Of course, the King was unaware of any of this, and his table was never short of food or wine.

On the tenth day, they rode over the hill and looked down on the town of Nottingham and the River Trent flowing through it.

"I never thought I would be so glad to see the Trent and Nottingham," Sir John said to Charles.

"Well, we would have been here almost a week ago if you had listened to me."

"Charles, I will have none of that. You must remember who your patron is, and not get above yourself. I decided to make the first part of our journey with the King for reasons that you do not know or would not understand. Now, I hope I won't have to speak to you again about this."

They spent another three days in Nottingham. The King had notified Sir John that he wanted to speak to him before he set off to Oxford, but the invitation never arrived. On the third day of waiting, Sir John took matters into his own hands and camped out at the castle keep where the King was staying. Even he was now getting impatient. At last, around mid-morning, he was given an audience during which the king stressed the importance of getting to Oxford with haste.

"Sir John, you have seen the love, even devotion, my subjects have shown to me on the way down here. This country wants a king, needs a king, and God has divinely anointed me to rule this country."

"I agree, Your Majesty, but you must recognise the reason you have come to Nottingham."

"Sir John, don't confuse my loyal subjects with those men at Westminster." He couldn't even say "Parliament." "My loyal subjects know what's mine is rightfully mine, and those idiots are trying to steal it. Well, we will show them. Now, you are off to Oxford. I want you to be very diplomatic, very humble, and quite hard with them at the same time; those Deans of the Colleges can be cunning, and I don't want them to forget their Royal Patronage. I expect them to give generously to the cause. Remind them that Oxford is likely to be where I will locate my Royal Court and stress the benefits that will bring to the city and their colleges."

"Yes, Your Majesty. Do you have a figure in mind?"

"No, and I only say that because they are so secretive about their wealth. People have been giving them all kinds of silver plates for centuries as bribes to get their sons an education. I doubt they even know how much they have."

It was with these words ringing in his ears that he rejoined his troop and hastily rode out of the city. It was roughly one hundred and twenty-five miles between the two cities, normally a four-day journey, but he wanted to push the pace and see if they could do it in under three days. He wanted to test the soldiers, knowing that speed was going to be a prerequisite in the coming months. Also, in these late summer days they could make use of the extra daylight, knowing the horses could rest when they got to Oxford.

They rode late into the evening on the first day, a beautifully warm and sunny August day, which meant that when they stopped, they wouldn't have to put up tents as they could sleep in the open, just hobble and feed the horses and themselves, wake early and be on their way again. By the second night, they had reached the village of Oxhill and chose the field between that village and the next hamlet, Whatcote, to spend the night. Sir John was pleased with his choice. The field offered a good stream running down one side where the horses could be watered, cover in the form of a wooded hill, and good grazing. He made a note of it in his diary for if he was ever coming this way again.

It was lunchtime the next day when they rode up to Oxford Castle on the western side of the city, a sorry shadow of its former self as it was in the process of being strengthened and in parts rebuilt. It had been bought by Christ Church a few years earlier and leased to families but was now being used as the King's Army headquarters.

Letters were given by Sir John to the commanding officer who, upon realising he was looking at a document signed by the King himself, could not do enough to ingratiate himself to his visitors. Two floors were given as sleeping quarters for the men who were not quite so impressed when they realised that a crack in its walls was wide enough almost to climb through. Thank God it's summer, was the main feeling. Imagine if it were December and there was snow blowing in! Sir John and Major Charles had accommodation that was much more civilised, with mats on the floor, solid beds with covers, and servants at their beck and call.

"We haven't had a chance to make a plan for the colleges yet," Sir John said as he sat back in a comfortable chair with a glass of wine in his hand. "Do you think that we should visit them in a particular order? I'm assuming that they will not give us their fortunes readily, but they will shimmy around the subject saying that they don't have anything to give. The letters from the King should be a kick up their arses."

"I think we should start with Christ Church, as we are staying on their land. If they have got enough money to buy this, they have plenty more to donate."

"Good point, so let's start there tomorrow. Who is the Dean?

"One Samuel Fell. Didn't the King also say that he would like to use Christ Church as his headquarters and his Court?"

"Yes, he did, so if he goes there and sees the silver plate that should have been given to us, he will not be pleased."

"Let's start with him. Leave it a couple of days and hit the rest. News will have got around and if Christ Church has given generously, the rest will too."

"Good plan, Charles. Now, can we organise some more wine?"

Over the next three weeks, they made their way around the major colleges of Oxford. In all cases they were greeted with reverence upon supplying the letter personally addressed to the Dean. They were wined and dined and fawned upon, lied to regarding the finances of the college, and apologised to when, a few days later, they discovered that they did indeed have the funds to supply to the King. There were days when they would return to the castle, their sides hurting with laughter at how an indignant Dean would become a grovelling giver of his college's treasure.

By the end of the first week of September, they had completed their rounds of all the colleges and institutions in the city and had collected enough to fill fifteen large wagons. It was with these, and an enlarged guard of one hundred and fifty dragoons, that Sir John Byron left Oxford on September 10th on his way to Shrewsbury.

Chapter 3
Powick Bridge

Sir John Byron's convoy of one hundred and fifty Dragoons and fifteen waggons of silver treasure and money collected from the Colleges of Oxford was a slow-moving, cumbersome beast that could only move at the fastest pace of the slowest waggon. They were moving slower than the King's march from York to Nottingham, but this time it did not frustrate either Sir John or Major Drinkwater, as both knew they were starting early in the day and going as quick as they could. It was for all the usual reasons that they were slow: the waggons, purchased in Oxford, were not the best and kept breaking down, and after a hot summer, the ruts in the roads were caked hard so that a broken axle or wheel were common occurrences.

They were making their way west, through Kidlington and towards Chipping Norton, always on the lookout for Parliamentary forces but not expecting to see them.

"We must be attracting attention, this slow, slug moving across the country," Major Drinkwater proclaimed to Sir John.

"I'm sure we are, but we can't go any faster, the King knows the route we are taking, so I'm hoping that if he hears anything he will send a messenger."

"It is just that I feel rather vulnerable, like a sitting duck."

"Don't worry you are not the only one."

The next day, they were going over one of the higher parts of the Cotswolds on their way to Broadway when the shout was given that a rider was fast approaching from the rear. The convoy stopped. A lone rider was hardly going to give them an issue and it might be a messenger from the King. Indeed, it was.

"Essex left London on 9th September heading for Northampton with an army of 12 Regiments of Foot, 6 of Horse, 1 Dragoon and his own Lifeguard Regiment. Believe he knows of contents you carry."

"Shit," John exclaimed, "I was hoping that they would continue to argue about how to build an army and not make it treasonable. Well, Charles, it looks likely that we might not be invisible." He handed the message over and the Major read it.

"I knew that the Committee of Safety were fairly bullish, but I didn't think they would leave London."

This Committee had been set up in July. It consisted of five members of the House of Lords and ten from the Commons and sat as the voice of Parliament. Their biggest issue at this time was that they didn't know how to proceed against the King's Raising of the Flag in Nottingham, which was a declaration of war against them. How does one fight the King and not commit treason? It was a moral, ecclesiastical, legal, and real question that was being asked, and their answer seemed to be to blame everyone except the King for the issues they were facing. Sir John Byron knew that Robert Devereau, the 3rd Earl of Essex, had had an interesting relationship with the Monarchy. His mother had been the only daughter of Sir Frances Walsingham, Queen Elizabeth's spymaster, and his father had been executed by the same Queen for leading a rebellion against her, for which he lost his head. For some reason, King James restored his title upon his coronation. Essex was aged thirteen. Later, he served as Lieutenant-General of King Charles's army in the Scottish Bishop's War of 1639, only not to be contracted for the Second War, and this pushed him into the arms of the Parliamentarians.

"Well, they are on the move now. If he is going to Northampton, he is not coming in our direction. We push on. I'll send this messenger back to the King so at least he knows we have received it."

They carried on through Broadway and onto Evesham without hearing any news. They were welcomed at every stop but had to question if the support they received was because the local populous was supportive of the King, or the fact that the convoy was protected by one hundred and fifty well dressed and armed Dragoons. They were on their last day's ride towards Worcester when the next message arrived.

"BE AWARE, Colonel John Brown sent ahead of Essex army to intercept you before Worcester. Have sent Prince Rupert ahead to reinforce you. Make Worcester at all costs."

They entered the city on the nineteenth of September and were welcomed with acclaim. They rode into the castle with relief, but with trepidation. Would the Parliamentarian troops actually attack a King's castle?

Major Drinkwater organised the waggons and set a guard around them, a guard that would not only protect them but also stop any prying eyes from discovering what they held. Having made sure that everything was to his liking, he went through the process of checking the other Dragoons and that the stabling was sufficient as he needed the horses to be well rested in case they had to leave in a hurry.

"Colonel John Brown approaching Worcester, Prince Rupert believed to be very close. Do not, repeat, do not surrender convoy."

In the afternoon of the twenty-second of September, there was a sudden commotion from the soldiers who were on the city walls. Both Sir John and Major Drinkwater ran up the steps to see what was happening. They looked over the meadow and down the River Severn and could see troops marching towards them.

"Are they Parliamentary troops?" Sir John asked.

"They must be as Prince Rupert's only got cavalry."

"Do they think that we will just open the gates and let them in? Where's your commander?" he asked one of the soldiers.

"He's been sent for, sir, and should be here very soon. Do you think they will attack us?"

"Soldier, you are safer here than out there. No, I don't think that they will attack, they know this is a royal town and to attack it would be an act of treason."

Colonel Brewster, who was in charge of the city's defences,

came up the steps to join them. A man in his late fifties with a bulbous red nose and, below it, a thick moustache and full beard, giving him the look of a fierce fighting man, which he was not. His military rank had been given to him as a favour from the King. He had never seen battle and was scared at the thought of it.

"Sir John, what should we do?" he asked.

"Do? We should do nothing until we know what their plans are."

As he was saying this, the troops stopped some three hundred yards away and three horsemen came through the ranks towards the walls at a walking pace. All were dressed in fairly primitive body armour, although they were wearing metal helmets and had swords attached to their sides. They stopped just below the walls where the men stood.

"Is one of you Colonel Brewster?" the man in the middle asked.

"Yes, that is me."

"Sir, I am Colonel John Brown, in command of a regiment of Parliamentary Foot and Cavalry. I have been ordered here by my Commanding Officer, the Earl of Essex, and request that you open the gates to the city and allow my troops entrance."

"What do I say to him?"

"Tell him that you can't do that and that it would be an act of treason to do so."

"Colonel Brown," he shouted down, "I'm afraid I can't do that."

"Who is the man giving you advice, is it Sir John Byron?"

"Correct, sir," Sir John shouted down. "I have advised Colonel Brewster that if he opens the gates, he will be complicit in an act of treason, acting against a direct instruction from the King."

"Sir John, we mean no harm to the people of the City of Worcester, but you are stopping me from carrying out my orders. I don't see the King here so it would not be treasonous."

"That, sir, would be for a Court of Law to decide, and, until they have decided, these gates are not going to be opened to you."

"Sir, you may have cause to regret your words and actions," the Colonel said before he turned his horse and retreated to his troops.

"Well said, sir." Colonel Brewster said.

"It will only be well said if he now turns around and goes away, which I think is highly unlikely."

In this Sir John Byron was partly wrong. Colonel John Brown did retreat from the city, but he took up a position near Powick Bridge thinking that Sir John would cross there and follow the west bank of the River Seven to Shrewsbury.

The following day, the regiment of Parliamentary troops could not be seen from the walls of the city and normality returned. Bakers baked their bread, farmers from the local area, not aware of what had happened the day before, were allowed into the city to sell their goods and the troops on top of the walls relaxed.

For Colonel John Brown the previous day had been one of utmost disappointment and frustration. He believed that he had got to Worcester before Sir John Byron's convoy and would have easy access to the city. He knew that, if Sir John had not been there, the weak Brewster would have opened the gates and let his troops in and then he could have had the upper hand and captured the convoy of treasure. Now he was stuck on the wrong side of a bridge from where he wanted to be, and he knew he couldn't besiege the city or take it outright. At lunchtime, his frustration got the better of him and he called Colonel Sandy for a conference.

"Sandy, I'm not just going to sit here and wait for them to make me look an idiot. I want you to take the cavalry across the bridge and occupy Wick Field. Then they will be able to see us and won't just carry on as if we weren't here."

"I agree, sir, it is crazy that they can have a market today as if nothing has happened."

"Yes, Sandy, they hide behind this barrier that whatever we do is treason, but that's bollocks, we represent the democratic view of the Land and should be respected. The King and the Monarchy have had their time of everyone bowing down to them and doing whatever they want."

"I agree, sir."

"So, go over there and make camp. Make sure that they can see you, charge up and down, just make a nuisance of yourselves."

"Yes, sir"

Prince Rupert had arrived in Wick Field the previous evening and had quietly set up camp. He had sent out scouts who had reported back that Colonel John Brown's force was camped on the far side of the bridge. He realised the reason for them camping there, but for some reason, some inexplicable motive, he suspected that they might cross the bridge and was waiting for them.

Colonel Sandy and his cavalry crossed the bridge, the horses' hooves clattering on the wooden surface, and headed down the lane that was lined by hedges on both sides towards Wick Field. They were relaxed, talking to each other, laughing and unaware that they were being watched from the other side of the hedge. When the back of the cavalry troop was level with the guards, the order was given to open fire. Thirty muskets acted with one enormous bang, smoke erupted from the thirty barrels in one line and delivered carnage to the back quarter of the cavalry troop. Silence followed by terror cut through them. At the front of the troop, the soldiers turned round in their saddles to see that they had lost many men, and their horses were galloping through them in panic. This emotion was picked up by their horses and some bolted uncontrollably. Suddenly, the whole troop was at the gallop but not knowing where it was going. They entered the field to find Prince Rupert's cavalry lined up, swords drawn waiting for them. The rabble Parliamentary troops slowly got control of their horses but were not in any formation and Prince Rupert gave the order to charge, giving their opposition no option but to turn and retreat out of the field and back down the road towards the bridge.

Colonel Brown heard the initial retort and sent muskets

across the bridge in case cover was needed for any retreat. His cavalry came out of the field at the gallop and headed towards the bridge past their dead comrades. When they had passed their troops, the muskets laid down covering fire to stop Prince Rupert from following them and then retreated across the bridge. The retreating cavalry was now totally out of control, galloped through their camp and kept on going. They kept on going down the River Severn to Upton and onwards toward Pershore where they met up with Essex's Lifeguards. Both forces believed that Prince Rupert was pursuing them separately. Colonel Brown hurriedly broke camp and followed his retreating cavalry.

"That was fun, nothing like a plan that works," Prince Rupert said to one of his officers as they rode back to their camp.

"Yes, sir, and we lost no men and only have one wounded musket soldier with a burnt face. The stupid bugger hadn't cleaned his barrel properly."

"Put him on a charge and make an example of him. We can't start losing men from their own laziness."

"Yes, sir."

With Colonel John Brown's force in tatters, Sir John left the city that night heading north towards Shrewsbury to finally deliver his treasure to the King.

The Earl of Essex, furious with what he considered incompetence by Colonel John Brown, moved north from Pershore and entered Worcester with no resistance.

Chapter 4
Plans to Return to Oxhill

In early October, both the armies of King Charles and the Earl of Essex were in western England. King Charles was at Shrewsbury and the Earl of Essex at Worcester, forty miles apart. It is fair to say neither was where they wanted to be, which was in London, the relatively undefended capital city. The Earl of Essex had convinced himself that the King would try and get there by coming down the River Severn and had sent an advance force to Bewdley, to provide a warning. On the tenth of October, Prince Rupert led a detachment from Shrewsbury to Stourbridge confirming to the Earl that he was right. However, the King did march towards London but on a more northern route towards Kenilworth, which he reached before the Earl realised his mistake. On the nineteenth of October, he left Worcester to chase the King.

Sir John Byron and Major Charles Drinkwater were still in charge of the waggons of treasure collected from the colleges of Oxford and were marching with the King. There was a different atmosphere about this march; far more intent, it moved quicker and marched for longer each day.

"This is more like it. You do realise that if we carry on like this we will nearly be back at Oxford," the Major said as they rode side by side in front of the waggons.

"I thought that when the King told me about the route he was taking. You couldn't write it, could you?"

"No, as a professional soldier, it seems to me to be a shambles. The only professional bit of soldiering has been by

Prince Rupert at Powick. It was sensible to send out scouts, he made good use of the Dragoons in the hedgerow and scared the shit out of the cavalry. He didn't lose any men and showed that idiot Brown who was boss. If that is how they are going to fight a proper battle it will all be over by Christmas."

"I know Prince Rupert is a bit of a party animal, but I think his experience in war, of leading cavalry charges and leading men, will be invaluable."

"I agree, sir."

"Do you think they will catch us up, Charles?"

"They should do, as they are travelling lighter than us, but you never know. Essex is meant to have experience from Continental wars, though I haven't seen it yet."

"He was in the First Bishop's War, but he wasn't considered by the King for the second instalment; it pissed him off no end."

They were entering Leamington Spa when a messenger came down the line to inform both of them that the King requested the pleasure of their company for dinner that night when they stopped in the town. They spruced themselves up and rode to where the King was staying in the hostelry. Having made themselves known to a King's lifeguard captain who was standing guard outside the front of the establishment, they were shown into a reception room that had been quickly dressed for the King, which meant that covers had been put over the chairs, the floor had been swept, and candles had been lit. The King was sitting in a large, high-backed chair with a cup of wine in his hand and the flames from the fire highlighting his face. He looked relaxed, smiling at those around him, his generals and also Prince Rupert whose voice could be heard above all others.

"Sir John, come and join us and have a cup of wine," he said. "Thank you for coming over, I wanted to have a private word with both of you after dinner, so if you stay, it would be appreciated."

"Of course, Your Majesty," Sir John answered.

"Good. Now relax, have some wine, and I'm sure I don't need to introduce you to anyone here."

They were dismissed and retreated to speak to others whom Sir John knew. Charles felt a bit out of his league among the current company of leading Royalists, but relaxed as he was made welcome. The conversations were only about the upcoming war that no one could see a resolution to; there were simply too many armed men in both armies chasing each other around the country and, whilst neither the King nor the Parliamentarians wanted war, they couldn't see a way to avoid it.

At the end of dinner, they were called through for their audience with the King and found that they were not alone. Prince Rupert was lounging on a sofa and talking to Charles Gerard and Basil Feilding, the 2nd Earl of Denbigh, both senior generals within the Royalist army.

"John, Major Drinkwater, please come in. Rupert, rather than slumping on that sofa, can you offer my guests some wine?" They walked towards the stout table that the King was sitting at, reading some papers, stopped and bowed before him.

"Take a seat, John. I know that you think I have had you chasing around the country with a convoy of waggons until you are nearly back to square one, and I apologise for it, but I needed a good man to look after them. Now, I need that good man to do what he has been trained to do; lead men in what might be the definitive battle between us and Parliament."

"Thank you, sir."

"As you know, we are marching for London and trying to get there before Essex, who is somewhere behind us. I fear that at some stage we will have to turn and confront him, and what's more, I fear that we are close to that stage."

"Do you know his exact location?"

"No, but some of my quartermasters have come across some of his looking for billets in the same village, so they are close. Major, I also don't want to lose your expertise in escorting the convoy, I want you with me."

"Yes, sir, thank you, sir."

"So, tomorrow morning, I want both of you to slip away with the waggons and go cross country as if you were making for

Oxford, a journey you have done before. Camp up as on your last trip, but split up your force, half will go with the convoy but you two and the rest of the Dragoons are to make for Banbury where you will rejoin us."

"Sir," Sir John spoke out, "won't that leave the convoy vulnerable to attack?"

"It may well, but I'm hoping that if anyone is looking, they will see your full force and not be bothered. Also, I am trusting that I'm a bigger fish than you."

"I see, sir."

"You were telling me before that you had found a good place to camp. Remind me where it was."

"A village called Oxhill, sir."

"Oxhill, you say. Basil," he called out across the room, "you remember that man who came to offer allegiance, Blackford was it?"

"Yes, sir, Daniel Blackford from Oxhill."

"I knew I had heard of Oxhill before. John, this man came to us offering help but didn't have much more than words, no troops to speak of, but he might come in useful to you. Look him up whilst you're there."

"I will do, sir."

They left a short time after this conversation, glad that they would at last get rid of the waggons and have the opportunity to do some proper soldiering. There was something else that they needed to discuss in greater detail that night, something that had smouldered between them for most of the time that they had been playing chaperone to the King's treasure.

"Charles, I know that we have spoken about this before, but time is running out."

"Yes, I know, sir. Another thing I know is that for us to succeed the last person we want to meet is Daniel Blackford; he could scupper everything and be a right pain in the arse."

Sir John Byron chuckled before he replied, "I know, he sounds like a right loser going to the King to offer allegiance when all he has to offer is words."

"Still, it is going to be tricky to pass so close to the village and for him not to notice."

"Well, we will have to play that as we find it. I'm sure he will visit but we can use a certain amount of royal hush, hush, can't say anything, secret business, you know what I mean. I'm more worried about what - or which - chests we are talking about."

"Don't worry, I have reorganised some of them and have my eyes on two. Thankfully, we are probably the only two people who have any idea what is in those chests."

"Look, as much as I respect the King and loathe what the Parliamentarians are trying to do, I am looking at this as war bounty. God, it has been going on since men decided to fight each other. To the victors, the spoils. I'm not letting these spoils go begging."

"I agree, sir, it is probably my only chance to get ahead and provide for my family."

"Charles, you haven't got a family to provide for."

"OK, not at the moment, but at some stage I will."

This conversation seemed to bring the two men even closer. They both knew what they wanted, how to get it, and the consequences if they were found out.

Chapter 5
Oxhill in October 1642

It was a crisp October morning when Daniel Blackford came downstairs and said good morning to the servants who were preparing the family breakfast. He walked through to the back room of the house where the dogs slept, opened the door, and received his morning welcome from the two lurchers he kept for hunting but had become domesticated. They both jumped up to try and show their affection to him, also knowing that his entrance meant that they would be fed and let out. He had picked up the leftover food from the previous night's dinner, which the servants knew to place in a bucket and separated it into two plates. He stood back and watched them demolish an amount of food - which would take him at least fifteen minutes - in a matter of seconds. It was only then that he opened the back door and let them run outside.

Following them, he stretched his arms, pushed back his shoulders, and looked down over the meadow where the two dogs were chasing each other, both playfully acting, running, turning, chasing, and having their morning exercise. Down further over the garden lawn to the river where a mist had formed hovering above the water, an ethereal blanket between contrasting temperatures that he knew would dissipate as the sun came up. The dew soaked into his shoes as he shuffled over the grass and the dogs came bounding over to him, having seen his movement and anticipating further exercise, putting their paws on his chest to encourage him.

"Down, boys, not now. It's Sunday and I have to get ready to go to church. Go on, here's a treat, now run along and get some exercise," he said as he pulled two pieces of stale bread from his trouser pocket and offered it to them. They bounded away and he turned back to the house, Oxhill Manor. It was a sturdy Elizabethan building, not classically designed, but built of the local stone, an orangey brown sandstone that had been quarried from the hills above Tysoe, as had many of the local buildings, but it had grandeur in its proportions; the tall chimneys and the finely designed windows gave it a regal look. It was what it was and was not trying to be anything else. Perfect.

Going back inside with a smile of happiness on his face he was confronted by his wife, Mary, who was starting to heap food onto her plate in the dining room.

"I swear to God that you pay more attention to those dogs than you do the whole family put together. What have they got that we don't?"

"Good morning, darling. As I have told you time and time again, they are just my toys. Like good toys, they give me pleasure, listen to me, and don't answer back."

"And I suppose you would like us to act in the same way?"

"My darling Mary, it's Sunday morning and I think we should temper our language, especially before we go to church. Now, are the boys going to join us for breakfast?"

He was met with a stony face of silence, a silence that epitomised the feeling within his family and the whole village: was this a Royalist one or a Parliamentary one? It was the question on everyone's lips.

The whole family went up the hill to St Lawrence Church in the family coach pulled by two horses and parked it outside before entering and taking their places in the front pew on the right of the aisle. Rector Daniel Smarte, now in his sixties, was a man who was worried about the state of the Nation and more importantly to him the state of the Church within that State. He had heard rumours that the King would like to revert to Catholicism and that his wife had consecrated a Catholic chapel within the Royal Palace in London. The thought appalled him.

How could a country have its king and queen following different beliefs, a parliament that was at odds with its monarchy, and a populace being asked to decide whose side they were on? He had been worried by his sermon ever since he had sat down in his study to write it; up until now, he had made a point of avoiding all references to the current political upheaval, knowing that Daniel Blackford was firmly behind the King, but suspecting that his wife might fall on the side of Parliament, not that she would ever say anything contrary to her husband's thoughts. The rest of the village was a mixed bunch, some following one side or the other, but most not having a point of view; feeding their families was more important.

"This morning, I feel it is my duty as your Rector to talk about things that are outside the Scriptures but will impact all of us. I feel that, as a Rector, like many that have gone before me, it is partly our job to inform you of affairs going on outside our community that are not strictly pastoral. In our church, we have wonderful stained-glass windows depicting God's actions as we would read in the Bible. We have these windows to tell us about these events in case we cannot read them. I'm not going to create another window and try and build it as a story, I'm going to try to put both sides of the debate that this country finds itself in, not to influence but to inform. Today we find ourselves in an area where it appears that two armies consisting of thousands of men are chasing each other around our fields. My friend the Rector of St Peters in Kineton told me, only yesterday, that he was visited by quartermasters for both armies. Both armies trying to stay in Kineton."

Rector Daniel Smarte continued for another fifteen minutes, trying to outline the differences between what the monarchy and parliament wanted from each other. He had his notes, he had his thoughts, and he believed that he should try to explain things but the more he talked the more he became confused, confused with his own thoughts.

"Well said, Rector," Daniel Blackford said as he got to the church porch, "a very good summary, I look forward to discussing it further with you over lunch. One o'clock as normal."

In the eighteen years that he had been the Oxhill rector he had always been invited for lunch by the Blackford's. He looked on it as an honour although he realised that sometimes it was an excuse for Daniel Blackford to question what he said in his sermon, or to criticise some part of the service. This he could take as he sat around their dining table, his glass refilled with wine and his plate overflowing with food.

He returned to the vicarage after the service and asked for refreshments to be brought to his study. This was one room where he felt at peace, a room where he could pace from one side to the other in front of the blazing log fire, a place where he could sit at his desk and look down the garden at his apple trees, a place he could write his weekly sermons based on scriptures that inspired him. Today it was a pacing day. Maisy, the maid, had delivered a jug of wine and his favourite goblet which he was holding, swirling around and pacing. He came to a stop in front of the fire and stretched his back and his backside in front of the heat, wondering what reaction he was going to get from his sermon.

His thoughts were interrupted by the sound of horses and waggons coming up through the village, a great many of both. He went to the front door to see Sir John Byron's convoy pass his front door, turn right to pass the church, and then go up Green Lane towards Whatcote. He could see the symmetry of the Dragoons riding three abreast in front of and behind the fifteen waggons, their officers dressed for parade behind the advanced troops, but in advance of the waggons, their uniforms shining with both inspiration and cruelty. From his front gate, he watched them pass, with just a nod of acknowledgement from the officer in the middle who was dressed in better armour and whose horse was of a different quality to those who rode beside him.

He hurried back into the house and straight through to the back door, out into the yard where a young lad had his horse tethered to a ring on the outside of the stable and was grooming him.

"Don't worry about that, Jim, get him tacked up as soon as you can. I need to get down to the Blackford's now."

"Yes, sir," he said before running off and coming back carrying a saddle and bridle.

In a short space of time, he was cantering down the village street, a gait that his size made uncomfortable and his lack of balance made precarious, but he made it down the hill to the house, rode into the yard and tumbled out of the saddle and literally threw the reins to a shocked stable lad.

"Rector," Daniel Blackford said as he came out of the kitchen door, having wondered who had been coming down his drive in such haste, "that was quite some entrance, you look as if you have seen a ghost."

"Did you see them?"

"Who?"

"The troops and waggons, they came through the village and went up Green Lane."

"Whose troops?"

"The king's, I think. All the soldiers were in the same uniform, and they had a dozen waggons, maybe more."

"Going up Green Lane, you say."

"Yes, where do you think they are going?"

"How should I know, but I do know that we can move quicker than them, so let's follow them."

"Do you think that's wise?"

"Come on, Rector, what are they going to do to the Lord of the Manor and a country Rector? String us up as traitors? We won't tell them which side we are on until they tell us which army they belong to."

"I'm not sure. I didn't feel safe coming here at the speed I did. I don't think I'm made to canter a horse."

"But you could canter a horse and cart. You take the cart and the boys and I will ride. What could be better on a sunny Sunday morning than chasing an army?"

Before long, Rector Daniel Smarte was flicking the reins down the neck of the horse pulling the two-seater buggy to encourage him into a canter and to keep up with the three horses that were pulling away from him up Beech Lane. Where he had felt nothing but fright on his way down, now he felt excitement and a thrill as they climbed up the lane and turned left towards the church.

When they got up onto Whatcote Road, they slowed their pace and soon were rewarded by the sight of the last few waggons waiting in the road to turn right into the field. They rode up to the back of the convoy and, as the Rector could not pass in his buggy, they stopped and waited.

"Good afternoon, gentlemen," said one of two officers who rode up to speak to them, "I'm sorry to delay you but we just need to get the last of these waggons into the field."

"I was just wondering what you were doing. I observed you coming through the village. You see, this is my field."

"I was going to introduce myself to Mr Daniel Blackford to ask him who owned the field when we had got everything off the road."

"I can then save you the time as I am Daniel Blackford."

"Mr Blackford, I was given your name by the King, who asked me to present myself to you. I am Sir John Byron, and this is Major Drinkwater."

"The King, you say? Well, that answers my next question: how long do you plan to stay in the field?"

"We will have left by first light tomorrow."

"The King is close by, Sir John?"

"I'm afraid I don't know his exact location."

"You're not riding to meet him?"

"Sir, you will have to respect that I cannot tell you what my orders are."

"Of course, stupid of me to ask. As he may have told you, I offered him any help that I could give. I did not expect it to be lending some of his troops my field to stay in. Sir John, Major, would you do me the honour of joining my family for lunch?"

"We would be delighted to, Mr Blackford."

An hour later, the two officers of the King were sitting

around the dining table in Oxhill Manor enjoying a Sunday lunch and drinking Daniel Blackford's wine. The discussion around the table was probably the same as those around many a table that day; when would the two forces meet in battle and what would the outcome be?

Chapter 6
The Battle of Edgehill

On Wednesday the 22nd of October 1642, the Earl of Essex was sitting in the back room of the Halfway Tavern in Kineton, his senior commanders around him. A roaring log fire was heating the room from the inglenook fireplace, logs lining the recess to heat them for the night ahead. He was a worried man. So far, since he had left London and tried to snare King Charles into a conflict where he held the upper hand, he had failed. Now he was here in Kineton, looking on the levels looking up at a ridge called Edgehill. He knew that the King was on the top of the ridge looking down on him.

"Christ, how did we let him get up that ridge, why didn't we face him here on the flat?"

"Sir, we weren't close enough to stop him. He has even turned around and come back to face us knowing he has a height advantage and will be looking down on us."

"Ballard, I know that; if I go outside, I can see his camp some three hundred feet above us. What I want to know is how did we let him have that advantage? Well, we can't do much about it now, we will have to entice them down. Has anyone seen Hamden's regiments; how come they have fallen so far behind?"

"Sir, they were in the rearguard to protect the artillery, which is always the slowest in a march."

"Ballard, I don't want excuses, I want Hamden's regiments and the artillery."

On the top of the ridge, King Charles's foot soldiers were camped around the village of Radway. If they had looked out northwest down over Red Horse Field, they would have seen Kineton and the Parliamentary army camped on the levels. They were a relaxed army, a confident army, not only due to the relevant positions of the two of them, but also because they felt they were the stronger force. King Charles and his generals were further away at Arlescote, enjoying a night in camp. They were confident that the position they were in was to their advantage.

"Men," he addressed his generals and commanders, "we are on the precipice of what could be the one, and only, conflict within this dispute. I hope it is, as the last thing I want is for Englishmen to fight Englishmen, but I have been pushed into this intolerable situation by the traitors who claim to represent the people. Tomorrow, we will face the army that Parliament has gathered under the Earl of Essex, a man my family reprieved and returned to title after his father had been convicted of treason against the Monarchy, a man who now rewards my family by pitting an army against me.

So, tomorrow we will defeat their army, but we will do it by capturing the Earl and not by the unnecessary slaughter of Englishmen.

Gentlemen, I give you a toast: to victory, to the capture of the traitor, the Earl of Essex, and peace within this country."

The next morning, in the Royalist camp it was as if there was nothing out of the ordinary going to happen on that Thursday the 23rd of October 1642. The King was reluctant to leave his bed, and his commanders were not prepared to provoke his temper by suggesting otherwise but his army was lined up on the top of the ridge in front of the village of Radway, overlooking Red Horse Field. Eventually, he rose, demanding food and drink before getting dressed for the day as commander of his forces. It was two o'clock before he joined his troops to survey what lay in front of him. He looked out from the heights to see the Parliamentary army laid out on the other side of the field with the village of Kineton behind them. Both armies were of equal strength, about fourteen and a half thousand men each, although the King had a slight advantage in cavalry numbers. He looked down on eight regiments of infantry creating a front line, with another four behind, their cavalry amassed at either side of them. *How very traditional*, he thought and then, looking at the formation of his own troops, he realised that it was very similar. He rode down the hill until he was in front of his infantry and then rode along the line, stopping to speak to commanders he recognised, giving words of encouragement to the troops. When he came to the end of the line, he continued until he reached Kineton Road where Prince Rupert was at the front of his cavalry.

"Rupert, I think that we are in a very strong position and the men know it. I have never sensed such confidence in an army before. Have a good afternoon's hunting."

He started the climb back up to the top of the ridge where his own guard was positioned. He had just arrived when the first rounds of artillery were fired from the Parliamentary ranks and return fire came from his own. Both bursts of fire were ineffective and fell short of their intended targets.

The King ordered Prince Rupert to advance Ramsey's cavalry who were demoralised by Sir Fortescue's horse troop's defection to the King the previous evening. Ramsey fired one volley at the advance before he turned and fled the field of battle, riding back to London claiming that there had been a complete defeat. The Royalist cavalry on the left wing advanced against Bedford's cavalry opposite them who turned and ran, chased by the Royalists. So, within a very short time, the Parliamentary cavalry had fled the battlefield with their Royalist counterparts chasing them uncontrollably, leaving the field bereft of cavalry.

In the centre, the Parliamentary foot soldiers advanced and slowly pushed their opposition back, nearly capturing the royal princes, Charles and James. It was close fighting with inexperienced men on both sides slashing, pushing, punching, poking, their terror being their saviour as they had never been trained to kill. It was also a scene of confusion, where no orders were given, or couldn't be delivered, and no one knew the position of their troops; the Parliamentary brigade under Balfour was shot at by their own troops when they were coming back into formation..

As the light began to fade, the Parliamentary troops did break through and captured the Banner Royal. Still, this effort coincided with the return of the Royalist Cavalry who managed to recapture it. This was their last effort before they withdrew, too tired to carry on. In the fading light the armies separated to their original positions but stayed on the battlefield both that night and for most of the following day. As for a result, it was pretty inconclusive. The King's army still controlled the road to London to which they headed, but the battle had knocked the confidence out of the foot soldiers who had suddenly learnt about the horrors of battle. The Earl of Essex retreated to Warwick but with a much-reduced army as it was scattered across the fields of South Warwickshire.

That Friday night, Sir John Byron and his regiment were camped on the banks of the Cherwell River outside the village of Adderbury. For most of them, it was the first battle that they had encountered and when they made camp that night there was a general feeling of relief that they had survived it. Having moved up to cover Prince Rupert when he chased his opponents off, they had had an afternoon of observing the brutality that was going on around them and only got involved in the fighting towards the end of the day when riding to stop the King from being captured.

"Shit, Charles, I never want to go through that again," Sir John said to Major Drinkwater as they both sat in front of a campfire enjoying the first proper meal since they had dined with the King before the battle.

"As a learning curve, it was pretty vertical. I never thought that Prince Rupert would chase them so far and then come back and withdraw. What an utter idiot."

"I agree, but I would be careful what you say. Prince Rupert has got the King's ear and doesn't like anyone to criticise him."

"Oh, I know. Sir, what's going to happen to Oxhill?"

"I don't know, it seems we are moving away from it."

"Do you think this will go on?"

"This civil war? I think we can definitely call it that now. Yes, I'm sure it will. If we had been disciplined and decisive we could have broken Essex and put the whole argument to bed, but he will regroup and come back, of that I'm sure."

"So, it is possible that we will come back this way?"

"Yes. Whilst Prince Rupert might want to lead a cavalry charge through the streets of Westminster, I don't think the King will allow it. He is canny enough to know that public support is vital and, if he loses it, he will lose his army who will fade away back to their homes to feed their families. I think he will go to London to make sure that he looks strong and then retire to Oxford to see this out."

"If we are in Oxford, could we go to Oxhill and back to Oxford?"

"I'm not sure that what belongs to Oxford should ever return to it."

Chapter 7
The Present Day

I had given a commitment to the archaeologists not to plough the field and I didn't really want to use it to graze cattle, it was too remote from the farm to be practicable. So, I was left with the question of what to do with it. The answer came over a pint of Hooky down at The Peacock, speaking to Dom Trethewey who had originally suggested sowing rape seed in the field, which had started this whole business.

"How much of your hay do you buy in?" he asked.

"Nearly eighty per cent, some of that I cut and bail myself, but I still have to pay for it. Why?"

"I was thinking about your field. Rape seed is out 'cos you can't plough, but you could make it a hay meadow."

"Hay, I hadn't thought about that. How much would that cost, do you think?"

"You use Brian Mansfield, don't you?"

"Yes."

"Well, I'm sure he would give you a good price." He was talking about the Grain Merchant we both used. "It will depend on what mixture you use."

The conversation went on for some time, the advantages of bermudagrass over orchardgrass and what legume to use. Two more pints of Hooky were pulled by Kevin as we discussed the options and I left to walk home with thoughts of clover and birdsfoot going through my head.

"I was speaking to Dom down at the Peacock," I said to Sandy over dinner that night.

"Oh, and what crazy idea has he now put into your head?"

"Harsh, if I may say, no, we got talking about hay…" I told her the idea.

"But won't that mean that you will have to build another barn to store it?" Forever the practical accountant.

"No, I don't think so, we shouldn't be storing any more, we will just be buying less."

"Let me put it through the PC and see what it comes up with."

"Thanks."

PART 6
VIKING TIMES

Chapter 1
Life in Ribe

My earliest memories are of sitting on my grandfather's knee at the back of our hall in front of the fire, listening to stories. I was named after him: Torsten. And, because we shared this, I felt closer to him. Whilst I had his knee, my older brother, Harold, had to sit on the rugs that were scattered on the hard earth which made up the interior. When I say hall, it wasn't really a hall, we couldn't afford one of those, and only the village elder lived in a proper one. Ours was a hut, but to me as a young child it was a hall. My Grandfather was known as Torsten the Terrible because of a tale that when he was a young man, he had gone fishing and netted so many fish that he sank the boat, a terrible mistake. The name had stuck with him for another fifty years, even if the story had been lost. He would say it was because he was such a frightening warrior.

He had been one of the first to have sailed from Ribe, our village on the west coast of what we Danes call Denmark. He sailed on one of the seven ships west to where it had been reported was a land that held treasure, good farming land, and an abundance of good slaves to be captured. The first summer that he made the trip he was one of the soldiers and rowers to have braved the rough seas, the winds, and the storms to land on the coast of Northumberland. There they raided a town called Dun Holm[22]. He told of how they burnt down the wooden walls around it and walked in with very little resistance. He was amazed by the buildings in the centre of the town. They were

____

22. Dun Holm the Saxon name for Durham.

built of stone, with two floors, one above the other, a concept that he had never thought of, but they were not being used. Moss grew on the outside walls and the inside ones, the roofs had holes in them letting in more water, the floors were made from small stones that made a design and then underneath the floors was a gap, for what reason he didn't know. He told stories of how stupid they were only to have one God. How could that work? One God to do everything? He must have been swamped, but he was well paid as their temples were full of treasure, gold, and silver, decorated with rare stones. He hadn't had to row on the return journey as they had captured slaves to do that job.

He told me that it was from that first trip that he was able to build a boat of his own from his share in the treasure, his first skeid, and how proud he was when it was launched for the first time. He took it on a short trip, the slaves rowing it out from the coast until he could order the oars pulled in and the sail set for the first time. He told of how the boat, the Gullbringa, rode the waves, settled on top of them, surfing the white frothing mass before diving down the far side, of the exhilaration that made him laugh as he stood at the helm steering her into the next one. The next year he was one of a fleet under a Drakkar, a dragon ship, which returned to Northumberland, raided and pillaged but returned to Ribe with fewer Danes as some had decided to stay and make a living farming the lush fields close to the coast.

I was now in the same situation. My older brother, Harold, was to be given half of my parent's farm which he would farm alongside him. He would inherit the other half on their death; that left nothing for me. It was an age-old problem and one that no one had solved apart from going on raids, stealing land, and settling. I was going to set off in a large force, but we were going to go much further south. Previous raids had identified an area called East Anglia that was rich in treasure with land that was flat and fertile. In past years, raids on this land had been typically short smash-and-grab ones where we would land close to our target, usually a house of their God, take what we wanted in treasure and slaves and leave. This time we were going to land with an army, move inland to draw out their King and defeat him in battle; it sounded so easy when I was told the plan, what could I lose by going along?

My parents, Harold, and to a lesser extent, my wife, Helga, supported me. They promised me that they would look after Helga and support her whilst I was away, knowing that it was either this, immigration, or both of us working for another Lord and being forever at his beck and call. We are a proud family, a farming family, and a family of warriors. Helga knew of the issues when she married me, and I did not hide them. She knew I would have to go on raids and fight in battles and that she would be alone and would never know if I was alive or dead until I walked back through the door. None of that made this evening any easier.

I had spent the day walking around Ribe, going to places that I hadn't been since I was a child, walking up the hills where I had herded cattle to the stone shelters we had built to protect us from the winds that would blow, the early snow in autumn, or the late snow in spring. I visited the campsites we used to build in the forests, remembering the summer nights that Harold and I had spent there with our friends playing out scenes of raiding parties. I walked down to the shore and walked on the sandy beach where we also played as children and where I had learnt to ride a horse as my father thought the landings would be safer on the sand.

I returned to the small hut that I had built for Helga and myself before we got married located behind my parents' larger one. Even before I got to the entrance, I could smell the contents of the pot that was sitting on the fire in the middle of the hut, steam and smoke escaping through the roof and out of the entrance.

"Something smells good," I called out.

"Your mother gave us some deer for your last meal," she said as she came out shaking her head to loosen her hair that she had recently washed. Normally it would be tied in two long golden pigtails. She smiled at me, but I could see that she had been crying by the redness of her eyes. Up to this moment, she had been very brave about my leaving, knowing that it was the only solution, but as the time for departure drew nearer, her fears grew. She came up to me, putting her arms around my neck, drawing my head down to her level, and kissed me, then took my hand and led me into the hut.

The whole village was celebrating that evening. Thirty males would be sailing the next morning. We had all had our last meals at home and met in the centre of the village where a large fire had been lit and beer was being distributed from barrels. Music was playing and it didn't take long for the dancing to start. All of my friends were there, some soon to become shipmates, others who had been on raids before. As the beer was drunk, the talking got louder, along with the claims of what we would achieve, how much treasure we would capture and how many horses it would buy. We drank late into the night and only the captains of the ships reminding us of what lay ahead and what was expected of us in the morning broke up the party.

I was woken early the next morning by the sound of Helga's tears and when she realised that I was awake she pulled me frantically to her, wrapping her arms around me for our last intimate moments together.

The seven ships from Ribe were all ready to leave when I arrived down at the harbour, riding the slight swell, their anchor ropes taut to keep them apart. A crowd had gathered on the beach. Some were men who had not boarded their ship yet, some were parents and wives, and some were there just to see the ships leave. They were a silent crowd and I walked through them to the shore's edge before wading out to my ship. I had asked Helga and my parents not to come down; we had said our goodbyes.

The atmosphere on my ship was lighter than on the shore. We were impatient to cast off, put out our oars and be on our way to meet up with the other ships that made up King Sigfred's force. We rowed out to the area where all the other ships were congregating, some sixty or seventy ships in all. It was a magnificent sight, the masts bobbing on the increased swell like a forest of trees and the shouts of the men welcoming their friends. We were a confident army heading off to make our fortunes and capture land.

Chapter 2
Sailing Forth

That first day on board seemed to go on forever, waiting in the catchment area for the last few ships to join us. Being still at sea is always the worst; you are sitting on a bench, holding onto your oar, three of you in a line then a walkway and then another three. You have to row both ways to keep the ship still. The swell is unpredictable and you feel the bow of the ship starting to rise up and you are rowing forward, but suddenly the oars come out of the water and, with no resistance, you are catapulted backwards, scrabbling on the floor, desperate not to lose the oar. You make it back onto the bench and then the ship is plunging down the other side and you have to row in the opposite direction.

"Shit," Olav who was sitting on my right said, "I have never known going nowhere to be so painful."

"Why are we waiting, can't they catch up?" I asked.

"Don't ask me, what do you think I am, a Captain?"

"He's worried if we have started without them, they will just go home," Megs offered, being on Olav's right and making up our three.

"No, he's worried about starting out. This could be the beginning of a storm," Toke said from the bench in front of us.

"Rubbish," Olav said. "This is normal for the North Sea, if we get going it will be easier."

There were shouts from the ships around us as if the same conversation were being had on others. Suddenly the call of the horn came, a harrowing sound that rose above the sound of the gulls that hovered above us and the swell that was turning white to become waves.

"Right, lads," our Captain shouted, "that's our call. On mine, let's go forward to new lands. Let's have a safe voyage there."

We were now pulling up the swells, pulling over them and pulling down them until the ship's crew set the sail and the wind took over from our exertions, the captain ordered the oars to be pulled in, and we were off under sail.

All three of us collapsed over the oar, trying to catch our breath, relax our legs, and thank Njord, our god of the wind and the sea, that we were relieved from rowing. Drinking water was given out to all of us and then the captain came down to the walkway.

"Men, well done," he shouted. "I have been on raids for the last six years and the first day is always the worst. We are now under sail and hopefully your duties are done until we get to the coast of East Anglia. I suggest that both sides pull in their oars and relax, eat, and sleep. It might get a bit rough tonight, but nothing to worry about, our ships are built for these seas. Just a word of warning; don't puke on the man in front of you, it doesn't go down well." Laughter greeted his last comment.

So, we settled down for the first night of the crossing, most of us leaning forward to relax over the two wooden poles that were the oars from both sides of the ship. It was not comfortable. I had spent the night before in the arms of my Helga, under the covers of blankets made of wool. Now I had the company of Olav who seemed to fart every two minutes and his apology was only met with another one.

During the night, the waves increased in size and clouds obscured the stars, taking away the captains' tools for navigation. The wind increased in strength to the point where orders were shouted to all the boats to take down their sails and ride out the inclement weather. For us, it was a night in hell being tossed around not knowing what the next movement of the ship was going to be. We could see the lights from those around us, but they didn't tell if that ship was rising or falling. Just as there was a hint of light in the East, it got worse and started raining, raining as I had never seen it rain before. The raindrops, which were the size of pebbles, were soon making puddles in the bottom of the ship and buckets were given out to start bailing. This was my job being the closest to the central aisle, but I couldn't stand to do it, I had to sit on the bench and reach down, scoop as much water as I could into the bucket and pass it down to Megs to throw it overboard. This process was repeated for the next two hours as the light got better, and my back became more painful, unaccustomed to the angle at which it was being asked to work. I felt I was in a losing battle as I was able to fill the bucket with more water than the last time and it was made worse when we were caught by a wave on the port side which cascaded over it. Suddenly I was not scooping but just filling my bucket from the water that was up to my knees. More buckets were handed down to us and, in desperation, we bailed, passed along, threw over the side, passed back and repeated.

Only our god Njord knows how long this went on for but gradually the rain eased, and the wind lost its edge, but the waves didn't lose their momentum. The water level fell from my knee to my calf and from my calf to my ankle and it was only then that I could take a break, lean back against the oars behind me, and rest. I had never known such exhaustion, every muscle in my body was screaming, I couldn't get enough air into my lungs, and the pain, it was like nothing I had experienced before.

"Sailors," our captain addressed us, "thank you, you saved us; without you, we would have been swimming in the sea. I have never seen an effort like it. Unfortunately, it seems that for two ships their bailers were not up to your standard, or they did not pay enough attention to Njord. The storm is now behind us, we will be hoisting the sails soon and hopefully, we will make land after another three days."

"Thank fuck for that," Olav said, "cos I know I couldn't take another night like it."

"I'm with you on that, every muscle is complaining and quite a few I didn't know I had."

It wasn't until the afternoon that the seas became calmer and the swell regular, allowing us time to sleep and to dry out our clothes. We settled into a routine based on when we could eat and get some exercise. What we never knew was when we were going to be needed to row.

It was on the third afternoon that we first saw some gulls circling above us, welcoming us with their screeching calls that were so familiar. At the time we were slightly becalmed, and the captain had called for the oars to be used. I never would have thought it, but it was a relief to be rowing again, and we were a team now, all timed to row together, all the strokes the same short ones that we had been taught. With our backs to the direction that we were rowing, we had nothing to concentrate on, but we heard the cries of "Land!" come from the ships further forward. Never had I been so glad to hear such a simple word.

Getting closer, we felt the breeze in our faces as the onshore wind picked up and we shipped our oars, and the sail was once again raised. I remember turning round to stare over the bow. At first, I couldn't see anything, but Olav pointed out a dark line on the horizon. The closer we got, the more detail we could see; the dark line became more defined and then we could see the yellow of a sandy beach contrasting with the green of the land. I don't know how far out we were when we were put into a holding formation. Two ships broke off the front end of this formation and rowed north.

"Don't worry, men, it will not be long now," the captain called out, "we have sent two ships north as they have been here before and know the coastline."

"Thank Njord for that, for a moment I thought no one knew where the hell we were," Olav stated in his usual gruff manner.

"I will just be pleased when we run these ships up a sandy beach, and I can walk on dry land," I replied.

"You and me both," Megs agreed. We all stood there watching the two ships sail away from us until they became a dot in the distance; then suddenly there seemed to be a wisp of smoke rising from them.

"Do you see that?" I said to no one in particular.

"Yes, I think that's the sign, but I don't know which one," Olav started saying before the captain shouted out.

"Wrong way, damn. Men, they have gone north, but now think they should've gone south."

"Blimey, they only had two options, you'd think they could have got that right." I had almost had enough of Olav's negative thoughts, but I kept my mouth shut and just watched the ships turn around and get larger in my sight. They didn't get as far south before we could see another puff of smoke from one of the ships and cheers went up from the others as well as from our captain. What the difference between the two signals was I had no idea, but there was a renewed sense of urgency amongst the crews, and we were all ordered back to our oars.

Firstly, we rowed closer to the coast and then turned to row parallel to it. Luckily, being on the right of the ship I could see the coastline; it seemed fairly flat, very green with some woods, but not the forests that we were used to at home, the beach was sandy in some places although there were areas of stones. We seemed to be turning into an estuary and before long I could see land on both sides. The left side seemed to have steeper banks, but I hadn't seen any human activity on either side. I thought of the thin area of land between the sea and the higher ground in Ribe and how well-populated it was but here there was nothing. They must have vast amounts of land not to use what looked like fertile farming land.

We carried on up the estuary for some time until our captain told us to stop rowing and keep the ship on point. I looked around and saw that some of the ships were very close to the banks and men were swimming to land, banging mooring stakes into the ground or tying the thick ropes to trees where they could. As soon as they were secure, there was a mad rush to unload the ship, depositing first men and then those making a chain to pass trunks of goods from hand to hand to the shore; lastly, the horses were encouraged into the water and swam, or walked to the shore. When the first ships had unloaded, they were untied and rowed back into the river and another fleet of ships came forward to repeat the process. This went on for some time until it was our turn to move forward slowly, a man on the bow calling out how deep the water was. Suddenly, on a shout from the bow, we got the order to back row, and men jumped overboard to secure us.

"Right, men, I'm sure you have seen how it is done. The tide is going out at the moment, and I don't want to get stuck here. Over you go, let's get her unloaded."

I jumped over the side, landing in the water, which came up to my waist, and started to wade towards the bow, then further towards the shore until I was the next man in the chain. It was a non-stop process; turn left, take whatever that man had, turn right, and pass it on. Not all the boxes and trunks were heavy, but boy, oh, boy, some were. I could feel my feet sinking into the soft sand under the water, making me lose my balance and stumble, then get my footing again and carry on.

"Last one!" I heard those words shouted from the bow of our ship and knew I was, at last, going to get my feet and legs out of this water. When I had passed the last box on, I stood there, bent over with my hands on my knees, dragging in mouthfuls of air, exhausted.

"Here, have some beer and pass it on," the man on my left said. I didn't know who he was, tall and lanky with blond hair and a scar across his left cheek running from his eye to his earlobe.

"Thanks," I took the bag and drank heavily before passing it on to Olav on my right. "I'm Torsten, I don't think I know you."

"Ah, Torsten, I've heard about you, you've got a brother, Harold, you call him," I didn't know how to take this, it was just that with his looks I couldn't tell if he was being friendly, or whether Harold had caused the scar.

"Don't worry, he didn't do this, but I could tell you were thinking he might have," he said, bursting out laughing. "I had a beer with him before we left, and he asked me to look out for you. My name's Odin and this is the result of a battle for Reading on my last raid. Now, come on, let's get out of the water before we grow fins."

We waded ashore and I remembered Harold asking to look out for Odin, saying that I couldn't miss him, but not mentioning why. When I had got to the top of the bank I turned round and offered him my hand to pull himself up.

"Right," he said when we were both safely ashore, "first things first, how's your hunting? Plenty of rabbits here I should imagine. Get your bow and let's get some meat, I'm famished." With that he set off up the slight incline, wading through the bracken until he stopped and looked back at us. "Come on, it's every man for himself when it comes to catching food. The first ships will have got any rabbits close to the river, we're going to have to go much further, and bring your mate as long as he can stop farting, scare the rabbits that would."

We followed him making fresh tracks through the bracken until we came to one that was obviously used by animals from the prints on the soft earth. We followed this until the slope flattened out and the ground gave way to shorn pasture, thick and luscious.

"Look, we might be in luck," I said, pointing to droppings scattered around.

"Shush," Odin whispered, "I think they will have heard us. From now on, no talking, and move quietly."

I removed the short hunting bow from my back, took out an arrow and nocked it before following him. For such a big man he moved very quietly but it must have been about one hundred paces before he stopped and turned with his finger to his lips. We stopped and watched as he drew his bow back. I could not see what he had seen. He released the arrow, and I heard the thud and then the cry of alarm. That was no rabbit, I thought. I crept up to where he was standing.

"I think that will do for this evening," he said pointing ahead.

"Wow!" I exclaimed as I saw a medium-sized deer still in its death throes, with an arrow in its neck. "You would never have got that close to him back home. Are they not scared of men?"

"They are still learning, I guess," he laughed and drew out his knife. Walking up to our dinner, he finished off the job of putting the creature out of its misery. "That will make a bonny meal for the three of us, and the skin might make me a new shirt. Ah, I love East Anglia."

Later that evening, the three of us were sitting around a fire, steaks from the deer cooking in the ashes, beer - which we had swopped for some of the meat - in our hands. The day had been a learning curve, a steep curve, and it seemed that Odin wasn't finished yet.

"Come on, we've got to get some bedding. Olav, you stay here and look after that meat, don't let anyone near it, these bastards would steal it in a second. Come on young Torsten, you are going to sleep on a bed of bracken for the first time, and I swear you will never get a more comfortable bed until you get back to your Helga."

I will never know if Odin had purposefully placed himself to my left when we were unloading the ship, or if it was luck. Olav and I had found our leader, our teacher, our mentor.

Chapter 3
Battle of Ipswich

It was as if we had sailed across the sea and then stopped. For the next week nothing happened, or should I say nothing happened as far as I was concerned. I had to rely on Odin for what to expect and he kept telling me we hadn't stopped. Guthrum, our leader, wanted to secure a base here on the shores of the River Orwell. He would then march west, and the first objective was to capture the town of Ipswich.

"How do you know all this?" I asked him one evening as we sat in front of a fire cooking three rabbits I had killed that afternoon.

"I listen, my friend, but listening is not enough, it's who you listen to that matters. Now, yesterday there was a council where Guthrum called all of our leaders together to hear what the scouts had to say. You probably didn't see them return, but I did."

"How did you see that? I was with you all day."

"That's 'cos I know what to look for."

I was determined to pay more attention the next day, but to what? I looked at the big tent that Guthrum had erected for himself, and I kept looking at it, seeing who came and went, not that I knew any of them until I saw the captain of our ship enter. That was interesting.

"Why would our captain be going to see Guthrum, Odin?"

"Getting orders probably. He's not just a sea captain, he's a great warrior. I should think he'll be in charge of our shield wall."

There was even more excitement that afternoon when some of our men arrived back to camp herding about thirty horses.

Guthrum came out to inspect them and suddenly jumped onto the back of one of them. It was obviously unbroken as it threw its head up, gave a terrific whinny, and bucked him off. He tried again, but this time he didn't try to put his legs over it; instead, he draped his entire body over the horse's back. Again, the horse wasn't happy, but Guthrum hung on and slowly it quietened down. He climbed off it and went round to the horse's head to make a fuss of it. It was still throwing its head but, with the quiet words and the affection, it settled down. Now he tried again, first just putting his body over its back, and then slowly moving to get his legs astride it. By the smile on his face, he was very pleased with himself, sitting up there with the horse slowly getting used to having a weight on its back. He didn't stay mounted for long and, when he was back on the ground, he called for a rope harness to be brought to him. Talking soothingly to the horse the whole time, he slowly got it to take the rope bit in its mouth and the noseband with the reins attached. Then he used the reins to lead him around until it was used to them. The breaking of the horse went on all afternoon until he was able to steer it left and right with his legs and the use of the reins. He could trot and canter the animal, but stopping it was a problem.

That night around the fires, all the talk was about the horses. They weren't all unbroken, and all seemed to be fit and well-fed. I was not surprised at that, given the amount of lush pasture that was around. It seemed that now we had the horses, Guthrum was prepared to march on Ipswich. When we would do this was up for offers; some said it would be in the next few days, others said he would want another week to train and get accustomed to the horses.

As it was, we marched five days later. We were told the night before to get ourselves ready, not that picking up one's sword and shield took very long. In good humour, we set off, walking across the fields in groups that were made up of friends, following the group in front and generally being guided by the scouts, now on horseback, who had been to the town before. We kept the river on our left, walking inland over flat pastures, but not seeing any animals or farms. It was as if we were the only people who lived in this country.

The first I saw of Ipswich was the smoke from fires within the town rising into the blue sky. The whole town had the river as one side and fortifications around its perimeter, made of earth. They were not very high and, to my eyes, not very secure.

We surrounded the whole town in one big half-ring of men, four deep, making a deafening noise. We shouted and banged our swords on our shields, all designed to scare the town's inhabitants into running away, but they had nowhere to run to. Some men appeared on top of the earthworks looking out at us and soon it was filled with men on top trying the same as us. We walked forward, closing the gaps between us, then stopped about one hundred paces from the bottom of the earthworks.

"Now, young Torsten," Odin said to me, "this is going to be easy, so don't worry, just do what I tell you and tonight you'll be drinking their beer and humping their women."

"But we can't just climb up there and kill them," I replied. In truth, up to now this whole trip had been a bit of fun, but now it was dawning on me that those people on the top of the earthworks were not going just to run away, they were going to fight, they were going to try and kill me.

"Now, we will be ordered to form up into arrow shapes. The men on the outside will hold their shields outwards and those on the inside will hold theirs above the men in front. That way, we should be safe from arrows. And then we walk up the hill, hacking at anything you see move, but be careful about them trying to hack at your legs."

"How do we win?"

"We win because we are stronger than they are. Our arrows of men will punch holes in their static lines. Once that is done, we can break out and chase them into the town and slaughter them."

"You make it sound so easy, but their swords are as sharp as ours, they could easily kill us."

"Oh yes, some will die, some will die because they have fear in their blood that makes them panic, then they make a mistake. You, you're not like that. I saw that when we were in the storm; you put fear aside and kept on doing what was needed to be done. You'll be all right."

"Right, men," the call came from somewhere, but I didn't know where, "form up in groups of twenty-one, and create an arrow. I know this will be new for some of you and I am relying on the old hands to help our battle virgins, tell them what to do."

"You stay beside me on the inside, less dangerous there, but make sure you cover my head with that shield."

We were in the third row of our arrow, and I had Odin on my right with Olaf on my left. We closed up as close as we could. I lifted my shield over Odin's head and tried to look around to see if I was doing all right. One of our commanders came up on horseback to inspect us.

"Men, I want you to close up more; if I tap your shield, it means that I can see through, and if I can see through, an arrow can get through." I could hear the horse around us but didn't feel a tap on my shield, although I heard some on others.

"Good, you are now straight, just walk straight, and don't stop. Good luck."

We started shuffling forward, taking half-steps, I couldn't see where I was going, I was just trying to walk straight and keep my fears down. I was terrified, I felt as if I was walking into death, and I couldn't get out of the way. Suddenly, I heard the sound of bows releasing arrows and heard the hard thud of them landing on shields. Then I felt one land on mine and the force of it made my elbow give.

"Keep that bloody shield up," Odin shouted at me.

We had now reached the bottom of the earthworks and started to inch upwards. More arrows rained down on us and, between the shouts to direct us to move forward, I started to hear the cries and screams as some arrows penetrated our formations. Suddenly there was one from just behind me, followed by a push in my back. The whole formation lost its structure and became vulnerable.

"New man in," came the call from behind and we stopped, reformed, and carried on.

We were climbing now, climbing up the steep side of the earthwork and Odin was telling me to change the angle of my shield. Their arrows were continually being shot at us and I felt them land on my shield. Some stuck to it and some bounced off, falling to the ground to be stamped on and broken by the men behind me.

I had been concentrating so hard I hadn't realised that we were almost at the top until I heard the East Anglian shouts directly in front of me as if they were shouting at me; then I heard the sound of sword on shield.

I don't know why I noticed it, but the smell changed. Suddenly I could smell blood, I could smell sweat, fear, adrenalin, and death. It was a toxic mixture that would live with me until the day I died and would mean only one thing. Battle.

We stopped at the top as we came against the defensive line. They had the height advantage, but we pushed against it, we pushed, we shouted. They pushed, they shouted, they slashed at our shields. Some broke and the head under it was then targeted, the skull split open if another shield did not protect it. Blood made the ground wet, and muddy. We were walking over bodies. I didn't know if they were ours or theirs, they were just bodies.

Suddenly, there was a release of pressure and we pushed forward. A cry came from our front men that they were through, the second row added to this, and then I realised my shield was not getting a beating; we were through them.

"Keep going, men, don't stop until we are totally through them."

We were now on the top of the earthworks, a flat area. We couldn't go further, and Odin told me to take down my shield.

"Now the killing will start," he said, with a face made of grim determination.

"How do I know if they are the enemy?"

"If they look scared and are running away, kill them."

We broke out of the formations and saw the enemy running

away down the other side of the earthworks. With a scream, we launched ourselves after them. Some turned and kneeled down, hoping for clemency. They just made it easier for us to slash at them and kill them. I had never taken a man's life before but at that time I didn't think anything of it, it was the release.

We had got to the town now and were hunting for more men to kill, hunting through the hovels that they called homes. We weren't worried about the women at this stage, which would come later. The blood lust was with us, and it needed feeding. We were herding them towards the river from all sides and, at last, we came to an open space by the river, a natural corral. Some of them put up a defence but they were outnumbered and afraid. We were merciless.

The killing stopped when the lust left us, which was pretty soon after their resistance folded. There seemed no point in killing any more. Now the second phase started; the looting. Firstly, we went to the house of their God and the people who lived there tried to stop us from coming into it. They were saying that they hadn't got anything of value and that it was a sacred place.

"It's hardly sacred. It didn't save you and you always lie," Odin shouted at them, then advanced, holding his sword high. I followed. They kneeled down in the mud, putting their hands together in front of their chests and chanting some sort of song. Odin just pushed them over and walked into this house, a house like I had never seen before. It was built of stone blocks. They were not just rocks but had been cut into regular shapes that fitted together. It must have been three times the height of a man and there were round pillars, again made of stone, to hold up the roof, which was covered in slate tiles.

I could only stand there and stare at this building. It seemed so sturdy, solid. How did they build it, how did they lift those straight stones so high, and why? I was still standing there looking at it when Odin shouted at me.

"Scamp, you will have plenty of time to stare at these... whatever they are. Come on, it's time to get rich." He marched up to a gap in the stone that was filled with wood and kicked it in the middle, the wooden patch split in half, folding back to create an opening. I followed him through it into a cavern of open space lit by holes in the stone to let light in. There was another row of strange round pillars running down the centre of this strange building.

"Come on, they usually bury it at the far end by that table. Start poking your sword in the earth until you find a soft piece."

I raised my sword and brought it down on the floor. It hit stone, sending vibrations through my hands, up my arms, and into my shoulders. My sword bounced out of control, clattering on the floor.

"Oh, I didn't tell you they put stone on the floor as well," Odin said behind his laughter.

It was Odin who found the soft floor and we started digging, firstly with our swords to loosen the soil but then with our hands, scraping it away. Just below the surface, we came across a box, made of wood with metal bars going across the top. We dug down from all four sides and eventually freed it from its prison. Together, taking one end each, we heaved it, with some difficulty, out of its hole.

"Poke about in there, Scamp, see if there is anything else."

I poked around, but my sword didn't hit anything. Looking back at Odin I saw he had hacked off the lock and was opening the lid. I rushed over to see what was inside. He had placed the box in a patch of sunlight on the floor. A golden light radiated out of it, shining up and almost increasing the light in the building. He leaned forward and pulled out a golden plate the likes of I had never seen before. It would have measured from my wrist to my elbow, and golden like I had always imagined gold would look. Circular, with a bowl in the middle, it was the most beautiful object I had ever seen, decorated with hammered dimples to form a pattern on its flat sides. I had heard of these bowls before and had dismissed the teller of the story as to their beauty. He hadn't exaggerated; this was pure magnificence.

"That will make a few arm rings when it is melted down,"

Olav said as he held the plate. "Yes, Ipswich has paid for itself."

"You can't melt that down, it's beautiful."

"Scamp, beauty is not bounty. Get a life! This plate is mine and yours. It is the first of many that will buy us a ship, and we will be the captains and not the rowers."

He then battered the plate in half, and then in quarters until it was small enough to fit in his bag.

"Now for the fun, let's get some."

Chapter 4
The Aftermath of Ipswich

It was three days after we had taken Ipswich by force, slaughtered most of the town's men, raped most of their women, and looted all of the buildings of substance for treasure. What had we gained, what had we learnt, were we better off than before? We would leave here, we would march on, and what would we leave behind? Empty buildings, another empty town, the women would march with us as they had no choice but to become our bed warmers or starve.

"Is it always like this after we have raided a town?" I asked Odin as we sat around a fire near the edge of the river in what would have been the centre of the town. Three women were to the left of us preparing our meal over another fire. The meat that was cooking had been caught by them, butchered by them, but none of it would be eaten by them.

"What did you expect?"

"I don't know, it seemed so wasteful, so stupid."

"What, are you going soft? We beat them, we killed them, and we raped their women. That's what we do; what were you expecting?"

"I don't know, but something more. Let's say that we capture half of the men we killed, made them slaves, rowers of our ships, and indoctrinated them with the Viking. Wouldn't we have gained something?"

"Yes, we would have gained a whole heap of other problems; feeding them, guarding them, and making sure that they knew which end of an oar to hold. Look, mate, plunder is the reason most of us are here, pure and simple."

"You make them out to be stupid but look at some of the buildings. We could never have thought of those ideas."

"That's my point: they are stupid! Why build them and let them fall down? On my last raid, I was in a place called York, and you should see the buildings there, they were far more impressive, but falling down. I was told that they had been invaded by another race that had built them and then left. So, you see they are used to getting invaded, they are weak and stupid."

I sat back on the stool and leaned against the wall. I'd come to look up to Odin in the short time that I had known him, but I couldn't agree with him on this point. The locals must have learnt something from these people who had built this building. I wanted to know more but didn't know who to ask.

The next day, I was sitting on the same stool, sharpening my sword, and pondering my thoughts of the day before when I noticed the captain of the ship walking towards me.

"You're Torsten, aren't you?"

"Yes, sir."

"I've been keeping an eye on you, especially since the storm. My name is Birger. I am Guthrum's son. My father wants me to lead part of this army and I am looking for men to lead Arrows, to be in charge of the twenty-one men, to be at the back of them, directing them, encouraging them. You would get a horse in payment and a larger piece of the treasure we capture. Are you interested?

"Yes, sir."

"Was the battle your first one?"

"Yes."

"What were your thoughts?"

Sometimes I wonder why I can't keep my big mouth shut, but I told Birger my thoughts. I criticised the discipline of his father's army after the battle had been won, and I criticised the butchery of men that we could have used as slaves.

"Interesting, and probably correct, but the first battle of a campaign is always like that, and anyway we aren't sailing anywhere, we are to march to York."

"York, is that far?"

"Many days' march and many battles, so you'll be glad of the horse. I asked Odin about you, and he said you were a good man. He also said that you thought too much. Now I know what he means. Would Odin fight for you, would you have him in your twenty-one?"

"Yes, Birger, I would. He's a good soldier, but I'm not sure he would be a good leader of men."

"Why do you say that?"

"He would always want to be in the first wave, at the head of the Arrow. Men will follow him but that is different from leading them."

"I agree, and I think I have made a good choice in you. Now, go and get your twenty-one and bring them to me to see how well you have chosen."

What just happened there? I thought to myself, reflecting on the conversation. I had just got myself out of the dreaded Arrow and was now going to lead one. Well, I wasn't, unless I got myself a twenty-one.

"Odin, thank you for putting a good word in for me with Birger."

"Well, he originally asked me to lead one, but that's not for me, and I can't ride a horse, so I put you forward. You might not thank me when you are sitting on the horse at the back of the Arrow 'cos you're an easy target. I'd get myself a metal hat and some basic armour if I were you. So, who have you asked so far?"

"No one, you're the first. I was going to ask Olav and Megs but, after that, I don't really know too many."

"OK, I thought as much. I had a word with a few of the boys who were with me on the last raid; that's fifteen plus the three of us, so you only need three more. Now, who impressed you in our Arrow, can you think of anyone?"

"Odin, I can't thank you enough. Let me think… how about Bjorn, Loki, and Frode?"

"Loki, which one was he?"

"He was on the other side of you. Big guy, thick beard."

"Big guy, thick beard, by the God Njord, you are going to have to improve your powers of speech; that could describe nearly everyone in this army, but I know who you mean. Yes, I would say they would do well. Now, what are you going to offer them?"

"I don't know, what did you offer your friends?"

"Wealth and women. What every good warrior wants. Now go and see if they will join you 'cos I can't wait to see you on a horse."

I went in search of the three, knowing that if I found one the likelihood was that they would be together. I found them out hunting on the other side of the earthworks and made my approach. Odin had been correct. When they learnt who was already in my team, they were impressed and more than happy to join. I had my Arrow.

I stood in front of them for the first time that afternoon. I looked at them, all big men, some showing the rewards of battle in scars, one missing an eye, another an ear. I told them what I knew: that we were going to York, that we would be fighting, and capturing every town on the way there. That we would find treasure and women a plenty. That the better we fought, the more rings we would earn. I told them that from now on we were a brotherhood, that we would look out for each other, that we would fight for each other, and when I had finished, they cheered me, each of them coming up to me and slapping me on the back to show I could count on him.

I marched at the head of them as we all went over to the corral where the horses were kept. Birger saw me coming and came forward to greet me, clasping my arm and slapping my back.

"So, young Torsten, you have chosen your men, and I see you have chosen well," he said as he nodded a welcome to some he knew. "Now, we had better sort you out a horse, one to carry you to York."

He climbed over the fence and started to walk amongst the

horses. I couldn't tell if he was looking for a particular one or just one that he thought he could afford to give away. He eventually picked a bay-coloured mare with two white socks and a white star on her forehead and led her back towards me.

"This one is for you. I rode her this morning, and whoever broke her did a good job. She might not be the fastest, but she will look after you. Come on, take her, see if I have chosen well." He handed me the rope reins and I walked her around in a circle, patting her neck and getting her used to me. Then I jumped up on her back and got my legs astride her. She tossed her head and started a crablike walk until I managed to settle her. Then, squeezing her sides with my knees and flicking the reins, we were away at a trot. She soon extended her stride to a canter, and I turned her left and right. When I was comfortable, I eased her to a stop on the other side of the corral. I was talking to her, I don't know what I said, just rubbish talk but getting her used to my voice. When I felt her relax, I trotted her over to Birger and my men.

"Well, what do you think?"

"I think she's perfect, Birger, thank you."

"You can keep her down here with the others but you and only you should ride her from now on. Get her to love you and she will look after you."

"That won't be difficult. Can I ask you another favour? I realise that I will be at the back of the Arrow, but I haven't got any armour, not even a helmet, where can I get one?"

"At our first battle, you steal one from someone you kill, even better if he's got chainmail on; steal that as well, and if his shield looks better than yours you steal that. I don't want to see you badly dressed after the first fight, I want your men to look up to you and say our Arrow leader is the best dressed and has more armour than any in the army. Now, we will be leaving here in a few days and marching towards a town called Thetford where we think that the King of East Anglia is holding out. We want to beat him and then we can take all of his land. Stay with me, Torsten, and you will get your wish, you will become wealthy, you will have your own farm."

I walked over to my men, feeling ten feet tall.

"You never told me you could ride a horse," Odin said with a smile on his face.

"You never asked. Isn't she beautiful? I'm going to call her Helga, that way I am only loving one name, it will make it easier if I talk in my sleep," I laughed.

"Do you know when we are leaving?"

"Birger said we would be leaving in a few days, heading for somewhere called Thetford where he thinks the King of East Anglia is hiding. I don't know all the details yet, but I think we will have a big battle against him and take his kingdom."

Chapter 5
A New Learning Circle

The next morning, I got all the men together again and, with the help of Odin, we sorted out who would be the eleven on the outside of the Arrow and then where everyone would stand on the inside. I sat on Helga, partly to get her used to the men, but also because when I was on her back, I could look down on the top of the formation to see if there were any gaps and move men around to get the best combination, playing to their strengths. Birger came over to see what we were doing. He had never seen men put into particular positions in the formation.

"Young Torsten, you have some funny ideas. Men just form one Arrow; they won't remember which position to stand."

"We'll practise until it becomes second nature. It will make them a team."

"Team," he laughed. "I'm glad you are making use of the horse at least. Can you come to the Hall in the middle of the town this afternoon? The local King is coming to offer a treaty and I think you will find it interesting."

"I'll be there, thank you, Birger."

I couldn't believe it; I had gone from nothing and being called Scamp to being asked to join in Treaty talks. I don't know what Birger saw in me, but I wasn't going to change anything.

"What did the captain want?" Odin asked. He tilted his head back when I told him and laughed. "I'm twice as glad I didn't take him up now. I was part of some talks when we were here last, and it was the most boring thing I've ever been part of, all this sitting around and talking in two languages. Well, I'm glad for you, you certainly have made a friend with the captain, keep on the right side of him and you'll do well."

"Don't worry, I intend to. As I see it, it will be good for all of us. We'll get better positions in battle and he will use us first when going to sack rich places."

"By the way, the men think it is a good idea that you have placed them carefully in the formation, I think you are getting them behind you, and that's important."

"Thank you."

Early that afternoon I walked down to the centre of the town, to the house where they worshipped their God. To my mind, it was a magnificent building, built of stone, with high ceilings and windows that let in the light. Compared to anything we built, the Romans were so advanced. I was amazed. I was standing outside the building looking up when I noticed Birger waving to me to come and join him.

"Come, let's go in. I don't expect much will happen this afternoon. Edmund seems very arrogant, he doesn't seem to think we are very strong, he thinks that he can easily beat us in battle. My father is playing the silent game, drinking beer, eating meat, and listening."

We walked into the cavernous interior. Men crowded all around the walls, talking, and drinking, whilst, in the middle of the room, there stood a large throne upon which Guthrum sat. He had a large jar of beer balanced on the arm of the throne and was sitting there looking bored. Opposite him sat a man I had never seen before, in a much smaller chair. Around both leaders stood their advisors and in the middle, the man who was obviously translating the conversation. Edmund, for that's who I assumed the other person to be, was getting quite animated and at one stage got out of his chair.

"The King is wondering why he is the only one speaking, and that doesn't sound reasonable," the translator said to Guthrum.

Guthrum burped loudly and shifted his position on the throne. "Reasonable?" he said. "I have not heard anything reasonable from him since he came to my town. All I have heard is the demands he makes of me, telling me what I can do and what I can't. Oh, and that I must jump in a river and proclaim my loyalty to this God of his."

The translator turned and spoke to Edmund. This is stupid, I thought and whispered to Birger.

"The most powerful man in this room is the translator. That's crazy."

"What do you mean?" he said gruffly as if I had insulted his father.

"Your father doesn't know if the translator is correct. How does he know whether he has translated what Edmund said faithfully, and, in turn, how does he know whether he has translated what he himself has said."

"What, the translator could be making up everything?"

"Who knows, your father needs someone on his side who speaks the language."

"But we don't have anyone."

"There must be someone here who could teach it to a person your father trusts."

Birger left my side and went over to his father, leaned over to talk into his ear, then pointed to me, and indicated that I should come over.

"Are you saying that the translator is incorrectly translating?" Guthrum said to me.

"No, sire, I'm suggesting that none of us knows."

He burst out laughing and slapped me on the back. "That's about the most sensible thing I have heard all afternoon. You will be my translator, learn the language." He then pointed to the translator and said to him, "Tell your master that I am bored of listening to his demands. I am here, I have a strong army, and I will take what I want. Tell him I think he is weak, tell him I don't believe that one God can look after everything, tell him that I will take what land I need and, if he has a problem with that, he should come onto a battlefield, and we will see who is strongest."

"Sire, I cannot translate that to my Lord, he will not like it!"

"Man, you are here to translate what I say to him. If he doesn't like it, you are here to translate his answer. You are not a peacekeeper, you're a translator."

He then turned to his master and, in what I perceived to be a slightly higher octave, gave a translation. The reaction was immediate. Edmund rose from his seat, pointed to Guthrum, shouted some words, and marched out of the building. Everyone in the hall fell silent and then the translator followed and all of Edmund's men followed him. The silence in the hall was broken by Guthrum laughing. It was a laugh that seemed to start in his belly and travelled north through his body until it erupted out of his mouth, accompanied by a shaking of his shoulders and a slamming of his hands on the arms of his throne, knocking the pot of ale on to the floor and breaking it. Slowly, the outbreak died down and he spoke.

"That was worth all of the poxy whores in this country. By God, he is going to pay for coming in here and trying to make an idiot out of me. Son, who is this man who is going to be my translator?"

"Father, he is Torsten and a leader of one of my formations."

"Torsten, Torsten you say? Do you have a relation by the same name, who would be older than me, from Ribe?"

"Yes, sir, my grandfather."

"Well, well, you're Torsten's grandson. Men, this fellow's grandfather was a great warrior, a man who stood in a battle wall with my father, a man who taught me how to fight, a man of courage, a man to be respected. Torsten, I'm awarding you two of my bands, bands that I have worn, bands that I have been awarded by my betters."

He took two bands off his right wrist and motioned me forward. I knelt in front of his throne because I didn't know what to do.

"No," he said, "I don't want you kneeling to me. Stand! That's better. Now, if you have a thought, I want to know it. So, how are you going to learn their language?"

"Sir, I think that the most intelligent persons that I have

seen over here are the people who live in the houses of their one God. There are a few here that weren't slaughtered. These men write their own runes onto what looks like very thin cattle skin. These are the men who could teach me their language and what their characters mean."

"My son is going to lose a leader, but you are more useful to me as someone learning how they speak. Go and find a man who already speaks our way and get him to teach you their ways."

I was dismissed.

"Men," I was addressing my formation later that evening, standing next to Birger, "it seems that I have lost my position of command. It must have been the shortest command in Danish history- here today, gone tomorrow. However, I leave you as a unit, a team, and I know Birger will keep you together. I believe that what we practised today is the way forward, and I think I have persuaded Birger the same. Good luck, good fighting, and may the rewards of battle come your way!"

The next morning, I was down where the men we had captured and not slaughtered were being kept in what I assumed to have been a cattle yard. There were several what they called priests, distinguished by the brown robes that they wore, who I assembled in one corner, facing me.

"I want to know if any of you speak my language?" All of their heads remained bowed. "I want to learn from you, I want to speak your language, I want to know about your God." One of them raised his head slightly. "You, did you understand what I said?"

"Yes, sir, I understood."

"What is your name?"

"Harold."

"That's the same name as my brother. Would you be interested in teaching me your language?"

"Your language is the same as mine."

"You are a Dane?"

"Yes, I was captured after the first raid on the Island of Lindisfarne. Well, it was not a raid, but my ship got detached from the fleet and we smashed into the rocks. I managed to get ashore, but the rest didn't make it. I was taken in by the monks, cared for, fed, and taught."

"Taught, taught to speak their language?"

"Yes, and their religion, and how to write, how to pray, to be merciful, to forgive, to love."

"You will teach me the same."

"No, I can't. It is not like sailing a boat or shooting an arrow, it is a feeling, and unless you have that feeling you will not learn."

"What is this feeling?"

"A feeling for our God, that he is the one true God, the maker of heaven and earth. That he sent his son to earth to show us redemption and that he died, crucified on a cross."

"He didn't do a very good job, then."

"It was a message to us, a message that we believe in, the message that we follow."

"Tell me these stories, tell me in their language so that I can learn it. Teach me."

"Why, why do you want to learn their language?"

"So that we aren't cheated. To know what their leaders are saying without some interpreter deciding what the leader has said."

"I will try, but it is not going to be easy. I will try by teaching you the word of the Lord."

I took Harold out of the compound, and we went to the hall where all of this had started that afternoon. As soon as he walked in through the front door, he fell to his knees and made the sign of a cross on his chest, bowed his head, and seemed to be speaking words silently to himself. He then got up and walked the length of the room to a table at the far end and again fell to his knees, but this time fell forward so that his forehead was on the ground with his arms in front, his hands together, as he mumbled feverishly.

I observed him and let him be. Eventually, he got up and walked towards me. It was not until that point that I noticed how broad and tall he was. It was as if he had grown since we had entered this hall, his demeanour had changed, he seemed more confident, more assertive.

"We will start tomorrow. Tonight, I will stay here and pray."

"Then I will stay here with you."

Chapter 6
Winter in London

Harold started by reading to me the book of their God. At first, he would translate it into Danish and then the words in English. It was hard work, and to begin with, I thought I was getting nowhere, but slowly I started to recognise some of the words. The more I stuck at it, the more words I learnt. Harold then took the exercise further and during our time together he would only speak to me in English and would only answer questions if they were asked in English. The more time I spent with him, the more I respected him and understood why he had converted to their God.

I was in the great hall that Harold called a church when there was a commotion outside. It was Guthrum, returning victorious from defeating Edmund at a place called Thetford. The men crowded into the square and I desperately hunted for my men. I saw Odin first and headed over to him.

"Odin," I shouted to get his attention, "how did you get on?"

"Scamp, oh, what a battle you missed! We smashed them, we didn't lose a man, and only Bjorn, the stupid idiot, got a cut, well, it was a scratch really. He stuck out his leg and someone slashed it. We were the first through and you can see the treasure we have brought back. There is a whole waggon of it." I had never heard him say so many words in one go.

"So, the formation worked?"

"Nothing got through, the shields were full of arrows. Then we broke through and attacked them from behind. They were kids back there, kids that shouldn't have been on a battlefield.

They fled, oh, how they fled, running back to their town, but we were all over them."

"And there was gold in the town?"

"Gold, beer, and women. What two days we had!"

There was a celebration that night, a feast from the food they had brought back cooked on fires around the square. Birger invited me to eat inside the hall I had spent all my time in whilst they had been away. A table had been set at one end with two more laid out along the length of it. It was a feast, a feast of meat and beer, of laughter, of song, of stories of bravery and stories of depraved celebrations.

After the army had returned, there were a couple of weeks when nothing happened. Work on the ships was always going on, but Guthrum seemed quite happy to hunt and enjoy his victory. It seemed that we would be wintering in Ipswich. Until a Viking ship sailing up the River Orwell changed all of our plans.

The main Viking army had marched south after their summer campaign and was wintering at a place called Reading. We would be joining them the following summer, but Guthrum decided that we would winter in London, a town on a large river that had been extensively rebuilt by the Romans and provided a better defensive position than we had here. Once this decision had been made, there was a rush to get the ships ready. Within five days, we were sailing down the River Orwell on the ebb current.

When we got to the estuary, we followed the coast, heading south. The land was flat and looked marshy, there were few areas of inhabitation, just small fishing villages. Then we were turning to the west and could see land on both sides of the ship as we entered a wide estuary on a flood current that meant that we could take the sail down and only half row, letting the current do the hard work. Slowly the banks came closer to us, and we could only sail two abreast. Then buildings appeared, and the banks on the north side of the river were made of stone. Harold had told me about a structure that went from one bank to the other, a structure that you could ride a horse across, march men across, a structure made of stone. Here it was just in front of me, many arches spanning the river their stone uprights disappearing below the water, then the uprights curved over on the underside, but were flat on the top. These arches were joined at the top forming what would have been a solid road over the river except the two centre arches had collapsed. I looked at it in wonder thinking that where we would have poured earth and stone from the banks to make a ford at low tide, they had built a road in the air.

Everything seemed very foreign to me. One could moor the ships directly to the land, even at low tide and the buildings were like nothing I had seen before. I was overwhelmed by the stench of the streets and the mud and dirt. Mainly it was the people, there were people everywhere, people and animals.

"Right, Scamp, we had better find somewhere to stay. Come on, one of these buildings must be empty."

We found a large warehouse building where all twenty-one of my men could comfortably sleep, and I could stable Helga. It wasn't much apart from a roof over our heads, but it kept the rain out and the warmth of the fire in. Additionally, it was by the river, so we were close to the boat, but more importantly, we had some fresh air coming in from that side. This was to be my base for the winter until we could safely sail further up the river and meet up with the rest of the army.

London was a fascinating place and I loved walking around it, seeing the buildings. The amphitheatre, which I was told in ancient times was used as a place of entertainment, where men fought in the middle, and people watched them, sitting on the steps that went way up to the sky. There were cages where animals could be kept, and it was said that men fought them too. Why? Then there were the other buildings, so big, tall columns holding up their roofs which would have been higher than I could throw a spear.

It was a wondrous place, but a lonely one. I missed my wife, I missed her company, I missed her in my bed. Most of my twenty-one had sought this sort of company and, by the depth of winter, nearly forty people were living in our building.

Living, eating, sleeping, shitting, not caring about anyone else but themselves. I had to get out, I couldn't take it any longer.

One day towards the end of winter, I took my beloved horse, Helga, out and headed north. I didn't know where I was going, but I didn't care. The days were getting longer, and slowly, in mid-afternoon I could feel the heat of the sun on my back. Soon we were free of the town and in fields and open land. Helga seemed to feel the same as I did. She pulled at the reins, tossing her head, and wanting a run. I let her have her head and she almost bolted away, going from a gentle trot into a full gallop. I lifted myself up in the saddle and gripped her mane, my hands pushing her forward, my legs encouraging her. We came to a hedge, and I drove her forward. She saw a stride, took off far too early but had the bravery to stretch out her front legs and we flew. The exhilaration, the feeling of freedom, the feeling of speed and the feeling of being at one with a horse was immense; I thought of pulling her up, but no, it was too much fun, and we galloped on until we were stopped by a coppice in front of us and we both stopped and caught our breath.

I jumped off her and tied her to a tree, then looked around at the landscape I had arrived in. We were on the top of a hill with a coppice around us. From here, I could look down over London, I could see the estuary and where it became a river. I could see our ships tied up, and the smoke rising from the fires from the buildings, a cloud hovering above the town. It was as if I could look down and see it, but also look above to see the sun shining down on the misery below.

I stood there looking at the view below me, wondering why people would live in such a small space, would live in such squalor, and would accept that was the norm. It was a major turning point in my life. I wanted to use the obvious advantages of the building the Romans had built, their foresight, their ingenuity, their practicability, and their sheer genius.

That winter, it wasn't the cold that got to me, but the rain. It never seemed to stop raining, which meant that the building we were all living in got wet and stayed wet. The roads were a quagmire and I had given up walking around the town. Helga was my transport; it was easier to groom the mud off her than off me. There was a two-week period after one of their religious celebrations when we got the weather we were more used to; a cold, icy spell pushed in, with winds coming from the east, froze the river solid. For three days we were able to walk over the river and play on it. We played a team game called Knattleikr, where a stone was hit with sticks of wood with the object to get the stone between two posts. That was all the rules, so it became a fight on the ice, people being hit with the sticks, being tripped, the stone flying around and also skipping off the ice. It was brutal, it was fun, and it allowed us to let off steam.

As the days got longer, eventually one could feel the sun when it came out. Then the talks began. Guthrum called all of the leaders together to decide when we would leave and sail up the river. Winter in London had ended, and we were leaving.

Chapter 7
A Visit from Birger

So much had changed in the last six years; I had gone from being the boy who had landed in East Anglia, through being trusted by Guthrum and friends with his son, Birger, to being a warrior. I now spoke West Saxon and Mercian and was respected by both sides, but I was still a Dane at heart, and would always be. I had been given land to live on and to farm. I had brought my wife, Helga, over from Ribe to live here. We had a family, we had a house, we had a farm and buried on that farm was the treasure that I had won in battle or been given.

My farm was in the northern part of Wessex, close to the borders of Mercia and also close to the border with the territory that Guthrum had already captured and ruled under Danelaw. It was an area that was called Oxhill by the locals. Why it was called this had been lost to time but I had always thought that it had been named by the Romans. In the shadow of the hill from which the place took its name, they had built the house that we lived in. I am sure that it would have looked far better then than it did now, but I was trying to learn from them. I had found the building in ruins, put on a new straw roof and cleaned the stones that the walls were made from, but I could not fathom the mixture that they had used to hold the stones together. Over the time since they had left, the land had changed. Trees had grown up, but I had cleared some of the land and found old walls and tracks made of stone, tracks that ran in straight lines and would have been wide enough for ten men to walk along side-by-side. It wasn't a big farm because at first we had had to clear the land to farm it, but it grew each year. We now had land to graze sheep and cattle plus land to grow crops and we could live well off it; we were settled, and we were happy.

All of this was about to change. I didn't see it coming at first as it started with the noise of three horses crashing through the woods behind me. Birger, Olav, and Odin emerged.

"Torsten, how goes it?" Birger asked as he reined in his horse.

"My friends, what a surprise, and what brings you into enemy territory?"

"Don't worry, we're not raiding, we came to see you. We came to see where your true loyalty lies; with us or with Alfred, whom we understand you both know and advise."

"I wouldn't say I advise him. I don't think anyone advises him; he is the most arrogant, self-centred person I have ever met."

"He's upset you, has he?"

"No, he hasn't upset me, but you have to understand the man. He is complex, he is a warrior who thinks nothing of hacking a man to death on a battlefield, he is a brilliant thinker, a strategist who could outthink me, you, and even your father. Yet he has a weakness, a weakness that is so apparent it is there in front of you the whole time. His religion."

All three dismounted. Birgen dropped the reins of his horse over its head and went to sit on a tree trunk that I had chopped down earlier while the horse put its head down and started grazing on the sparse grass. Olav and Odin came over to slap me on the back in welcome.

"Do you think we could use his religion to get at him?"

"No, I can't see how. He's like two different people; when he is reading his god's book or talking to him in his church, he's always apologising for things he has done. Then he will walk out and do something stupid like rape a woman or get drunk and have to go back and spend time apologising again."

"This religion, I hear that he demands all of his leaders and soldiers follow it. Has he asked you?"

"Yes, many a time."

"Guthrum has an idea. He thinks that Alfred is vulnerable during their religious festivals and that, if we attacked him during one, he could be beaten."

"Yes, Guthrum may be right."

"He was wondering if you could help us?"

"It depends on what you want me to do."

"We need someone to tell us what is going on in Alfred's camp. To give us information, when it would be a good time to attack, and when it wouldn't."

"You want me to travel to Chippenham, to live with them, to spy on them?"

"Yes, that's what he would like."

"Come up to the house and we can discuss it better up there."

We walked up to the house, all of us catching up on what had happened; fights, and battles for them, whilst mine were mainly battles against nature. When we got up to the house, they couldn't get their heads around where I was living. They had seen houses like mine in London, but they had never thought of using them. They couldn't see the point of mending something so old when one could build a new hall in the traditional way.

I knew I had changed. I thought differently from before. I admired what the Romans had built and thought of them as being far more advanced than we were. That is why, when I found this stone-built house with its defensive wall around stone-built sheds where they would have kept their animals, I thought I should use it. It was warmer than our houses and, after I had fixed the roof, dryer. I liked the decorated floors that I found under the muck and mud, the separate rooms, and not having the smoke from the cooking fire everywhere. I liked the hard work it took to clear the land, raise the stock, plant the crops. I liked being a farmer, a husband, and a father.

Now I was being asked to sacrifice all of that, to give all of that up and to put myself back in danger.

We discussed it all afternoon, drinking beer that I had brewed and eating food that Helga had cooked. My loyalty was questioned, my loyalty to Guthrum, to my family, and my beliefs. I knew what I should do, I should tell them to go away and leave me alone, but I could also see how I could help them, and how by helping them I could make my land more secure.

I was going back to Alfred.

Chapter 8
Battle of Chippenham

I travelled down to Chippenham with just the horse I rode on and another carrying my goods and shackles. Unfortunately, I was not riding Helga, the mare that Guthrum had given me way back when we first landed in East Anglia; she had sadly passed. I was mounted on a gelding I had taken after battle some five years earlier. I was travelling light through the mid-winter months, sleeping between my two horses to give me warmth, and making the journey as quick as possible.

I arrived at the gates of Chippenham and was stopped.

"What is your business?" The guard of the northern gate asked as he stood in front of me, barring my way.

"My business is between King Alfred and myself. It is not your business."

"I am sorry, but everything coming into this town is my business."

"If I wait here, could you send a messenger to the King that Thorsten is here to see him?" I dismounted and stood at the side of the road, not knowing how long I would have to wait. I walked over to some stalls set up beside the road selling food. I wasn't hungry, but I wanted to practise my West Saxon as I knew I would be speaking it all the time I was here.

It was not long before I saw three of Alfred's personal guards coming down the road towards the North gate. One of them I recognised as Werian, who was close to Alfred and often stood guard at his tent.

"Torsten, is it really you? I thought you had settled down to the farming life further north."

"I had, but I have some news for Alfred; I assume he is here."

"Yes, he is here for Epiphany and will be staying here for the whole festival. Come with us, he was not sure you were the right Torsten."

I lead my two horses through the gate and walked with them through the lower part of the town until we started to climb up towards the church where he had his camp. The town's population had grown since I was last here and was even bigger as the King was here with all of his court. His fyrd[23] had been dispersed, as was normal between military campaigns. The Lords and their men who made up his army, dispersed back to their farms when not fighting, only to come together again when called.

We arrived at the church and the accompanying dwellings around it, of which one was Alfred's house. For a King, it was not much of a palace, but I was glad to see that he had tried to use some of the stones that the Romans had used to build their houses. He had obviously come across the same problem I had; where to find the lime to bind the stones together. My two horses were taken away from me to be stabled, watered and fed, whilst I was taken to his palace. I had always held Alfred in high regard. He was an intelligent man, a man who could read and write, who had taught me the values of that art, but in other ways he had not learnt from the past. The palace may have been large, yes, but it was drafty, it was smoky from the fire, it was dirty from the number of dogs running around and the mud brought in by people. The floors were covered with straw, but that straw was not changed very often.

"Torsten," he greeted me, coming forward to lock arms and then pushing me back to look at me. "I think farming suits you more than fighting; you look well."

"I am, Sire."

"Have you come to celebrate the Epiphany with us? You

---

23. A description of an early Anglo Saxon army that was mobilised from freemen.

could get baptised as we celebrate Our Lord Jesus's baptism, which would be very fitting, wouldn't it? Oh, it is good to see you again, it must be three years since the last time. I heard that you have brought your wife over and are doing things with these Roman buildings. We have so much to catch up on."

This was typical of Alfred, babbling on with unconnected sentences, rolling one topic into another.

"Now, come and have some wine and we can talk," he said, putting his arm behind me and guiding me towards the fire. "Tell me some good news, tell me that Guthrum has decided that East Anglia is big enough for him and he wants no part of Wessex. Tell me that he and Ubba want no more of our island and then we can push them back towards the sea that they came from and recapture our lands."

"No, Sire, I cannot tell you that, I wish that I could. I come to tell you that Guthrum and Ubba plan an attack on Wessex, to capture you and to take your land."

"No, they would not do that, we have a treaty, a treaty that both Guthrum and I signed."

"Sire, I have warned you in the past, Guthrum doesn't believe in written treaties, he believes in treaties made of gold. He believes that if you pay him to leave a town, he will leave it until he has spent that gold and then he will recapture it. It is a spiral that is central to our culture."

"No, he would not break a treaty!"

"Sire, he would, and I am here to warn you that he is planning to enter Wessex this spring and to engage you in battle."

"Where are you getting this information, and more importantly why are you telling me? You are a Dane, you look like a Dane, and you wear the Dane rings, why are you coming to me telling this?"

"I am telling you this because I don't want to get caught up in fights and battles, I am telling you this because I want a peaceful life, a life where I can farm my land and raise my family."

"That is very convenient for you, but do I believe you? Guthrum has always said, once a Dane, always a Dane, why are you different?"

"Because I want peace; because I don't care who is the king of my kingdom. Whoever is king doesn't make my lambs fatter, he doesn't make my crops produce more, he doesn't put food on my table."

"So, you come to me to tell me of an invasion into Wessex. Why, it wouldn't affect you who was king, it wouldn't affect your crops. So, why are you here?"

"To warn you, to give you time to get your fyrd out."

"No, there is another reason. Your land is close to the Danelaw border, it is too risky. Why are you telling me this? That's the question I must answer. My spies tell me he is preparing an army, so I don't doubt the accuracy, it's *your* motive that worries me."

"My motive is simple. I want peace for my family. Can't you understand that?"

"Torsten, words are cheap, especially from a Dane. You can stay here tonight, but I want you to leave tomorrow. Go back to your family, your sheep, and your crops, carry on being a farmer and don't get involved in matters that you don't understand. Now, you will pray with me, and then we eat together for the last time."

The next morning, I rode out of the North Gate, making sure I was the first man through as I wanted to get home. I had my information, and I wanted to get away. I rode my horses hard but, whenever I reached high ground, I checked that I wasn't being followed. It would not have surprised me if Alfred had sent Werian to check that I was going home.

It was in the middle of the afternoon that I met the Viking army marching towards Chippenham and found Guthrum.

"He is in Chippenham without an army, he has his personal guards, but that is all."

"Where is his army?"

"It has dispersed, sent back to their farms. They will only be recalled when they are needed."

"So, he doesn't know I am marching towards him?"

"No, he has spies in your camp, so be aware. You're only a

day's march from where he is, make sure that no one rides on ahead."

"Anyone who tries will be flushed out and killed. Thorsten you have done well, you will be rewarded. You will join us to see him routed and killed, and then Wessex will be ours."

"Is that wise? If I am seen, he will know I have deceived him and never trust me again."

"Don't worry about that, he will be dead, and Wessex will be mine."

I rode with them the next day, but I kept at the back. Birger found me in the middle of the day, wondering why I was not more prominent.

"You don't understand him," I said. "You will sack the town, kill off his guards and capture plenty of treasure, but I bet you this arm ring you will not capture him."

"Why, how will he escape?"

"He will find a way; he will have prepared a secret way out."

"You know the trouble with you is that you have too much respect for your enemies."

"No, I know Alfred."

"OK, how will he get out?"

"That I don't know, but he will, and he will head for the wetlands in Somerset."

Birger laughed and put the heels of his boots into the side of his horse, galloping off.

That night, the Viking army surrounded the town of Chippenham. They were quiet, stealthy, and determined that at first light they would storm it.

The attack was simple because the town was not expecting it and there were no defenders. There were four gates that were meant to control the entrance and exit to Chippenham, four gates that had not been very well maintained, and there were four men on each gate. What chance did they have? The gates were easily broken down and three thousand marauding Danes poured through and headed straight for the large church in the middle of the town. There they found Alfred's guards protecting both the church and some of the dwellings around it. There were only a hundred or so of them. Even though they defended stoutly, they couldn't stop the invaders who broke into all the houses looking for the Wessex King. He was not found. They found where they assumed he had been staying from my description, but he had disappeared. When Guthrum discovered that his quarry had flown, he went into a monumental rage that even the discovery of the King's treasure could not diminish.

It was two days later that Guthrum sent for me. His rage had been sated but he still was cross that he hadn't been able to capture Alfred.

"Where has he gone?" he asked without even welcoming me.

"It would be a guess, but I suspect that he has gone into hiding on the Somerset Levels."

"What are these Levels?"

"They are a large area of marshland where a man can get lost, and it would be almost impossible to find him."

"Could you find him?"

"Maybe. I could go to areas that I know he has been to in the past, but I would need to go alone. He would never trust me if I came with any Danes."

"What do you think he will do?"

"I should think that he has some men with him. He will lie low for a time and then he will send out messengers to his senior Lords. He will call up his troops and then I think that he will come looking for you."

"Well, you had better be my early warning system."

Three days later, I left Chippenham, or what was left of it, and headed south-west with my two horses as company. I was travelling light and making for the abbey at Glastonbury to begin my search.

It took me four days to get down to Glastonbury. For my first night, I put my horses into the stables of a tavern and had dinner and listened. My compatriots were a mixture of locals, pilgrims heading to the abbey, and some fleeing the Danes that they assumed would be coming after them. I was listening for any word of or mention of Alfred. I kept to myself, kept my head down, but I heard nothing.

The following day, I rode down onto the Levels. The landscape was as strange this time as it had been before. The tracks I followed were wet and seemed to move. They were only wide enough for one horse. With the reeds arching above my head and to both sides, obscuring any view of where I was going, I could see neither where I was going nor what surrounded me; it was only by the sun that I knew I was heading in the right direction.

I was heading to Athelney, a place in the middle of the wetland that I had visited before, where I suspected Alfred would go. It was easily defended as it had two hills that rose out of the reeds and Alfred had talked of building a fort on one of them. I just hoped that I could find it again and that, if he was there, he would trust me.

It took me a week to find Athelney, a week of walking backwards and forwards across the wetlands leading my two horses, a week of trudging through the mud and thinking of what I was going to say to Alfred and wondering what his reaction was going to be. After all of that time, his reaction was not what I expected when I eventually arrived there.

"My dear Torsten, you have been the main source of entertainment for all of my men for the last five days." These were the words that he greeted me with a laugh and a smile on his face. "We have never seen a man go backwards and forwards, forwards and backwards, so many times, making the noise of an army; you even passed within five rods of here twice. I take it you are looking for me, and my only question is, why?"

"Yes, Sire, I was looking for you. I have come to offer my services."

"Do you really think I need the services of a Dane?"

"I don't consider myself a Dane anymore, not after what happened at Chippenham. I have come to you to convert to your God, to be baptised, and to pray with you."

"Well, well, well, I was not expecting that. You have always thought my religion was single-minded and stupid. 'Naive' was the word you used. Now you want to convert. You see, Torsten, I don't know if I can trust you. You came to me to warn me about the attack on Chippenham, and I gave you short order, but did you know that it was coming the next day? I don't know. Anyway, you are here now rather than marching around the wetlands destroying my defences. Come on up to the fort and we can discuss this further."

We walked up the slope to the fort that he was making. He was leading my pack horse himself, all friendly and welcoming. The fort - you couldn't really call it that when I arrived - was a series of huts to house the twenty-five or so soldiers who were there; it had no fortifications around it, it had no defences apart from altitude.

As the weeks turned into months and the winter turned into spring, the fort gained its fortifications and Alfred then turned his attention to recruiting his army. Messengers were sent to all the Lords to turn up at Egbert's Stone with their men three weeks after Easter.

Chapter 9
The Battle of Edington

We got to the meeting place, Egbert's Stone, to the south of the wetlands, to wait for the army to assemble. It was a nervous wait for Alfred. He stayed in his tent, prayed, and didn't eat; he wouldn't even see me. I knew that he doubted that anyone would turn up, it was always a problem. On the second day, the first few men drifted in, and Alfred came out to welcome them, for the first time since we had arrived, with a smile on his face.

The next day, the numbers started to arrive in a stream and the field that we were in began to resemble an army camp, with groups of comrades meeting up for the first time in over a year, lighting cooking fires and building light shelters. Alfred was greeting each Lord on their arrival as if they were old friends, and I suppose they were, but I only knew a few of them. He called for dinner in the field that night for all. There were no tables set, the men stood with a plate in one hand and a tankard of ale in the other. The atmosphere was one of determination to regain their land, to beat Guthrum, whom they felt had cheated them and acted in a cowardly way in his attack on Chippenham.

I woke the next morning with a sore head, a stiff body, and an appetite like no other. The last was satisfied by freshly baked bread and beer before I went in search of Alfred. I found him with a number of the Lords, instructing them of his plans.

"Ah, Torsten, I'm glad you could join us, it would seem you have not got used to Wessex beer yet. Everyone, this is my friendly Dane who sought me out after Chippenham. If he had marched around the reeds looking for me anymore, making the tracks wider and scaring the birds, my hiding hole would have become apparent to everyone. I have known him for many a year. He has translated for me and against me. Harold of Lindisfarne taught him; he is trusted and has converted."

"My Sire, are you sure that's wise to have a Dane in our camp?"

"Lord Edgar, this man, who I trust with my life, has had the opportunity to leave the wetlands every day that he has been there; he could have left and returned with the Dane army at any time, but he didn't."

"Is he prepared to join us on a wall?"

"That's not a question for me, but I wouldn't hold it against him if he didn't."

"If he is here but is not going to fight for us, he could be a traitor."

"My Lords," I started, "I am here for peace, I went to Chippenham to warn the King of an imminent attack, but it was not believed, and I was sent away. I saw what happened there, you didn't, when the King wasn't found. If he had been, he would no longer be here. I followed a hunch. I am your King's man, but not your King's soldier. I will not fight in a shield wall against my countrymen. I will not do that not because I am a coward, but because they are my friends, my countrymen. Lastly, you are fighting for your land, your country, your King. My land is many days' ride north of here, where I have a farm, a wife and a family in a village called Oxhill. I want to return there with the knowledge that I can live a peaceful life."

"Gentlemen, I think you will agree that Torsten has a right to be here, to march with us and does not have to stand in the wall to prove that," Alfred announced and was answered by many nodding heads.

Over the next week, the rest of the army arrived until Alfred had command of a force of about six hundred men ready and eager to fight to get their country back. I could tell from talking to the men that they were confident but, more importantly, they felt that they had been wronged, and wanted to right it.

We marched towards Chippenham, knowing that Guthrum would already know that Alfred had called for his army to convene; he may have even known the location of the meet had his spies been good enough, but, failing that, he would definitely know that we would eventually come to him.

We came across them at a place called Edington, with both sides facing each other on flat land that even this early in the summer was dry and firm. There wouldn't be time for a battle on the day the two armies met as it was late in the afternoon, but both sides lined up and shouted abuse at the other. It always made me laugh when this happened; I was about the only one who could understand the insults from both sides. As darkness fell, the shouting subsided and thoughts turned to the empty feeling in all of our stomachs. Both armies drifted away to eat, sleep, and prepare for the battle in the morning.

Alfred had asked me many times about the arrow formation that the Danes used, why they used it, its purpose and how to defend against it. It was the last part I was not sure about; if they were well-formed, arrows would always be effective, but the most vulnerable part was the legs, as it was for any shield wall. The problem was that if one bent down to try and cut at the legs the attacker was compromised because his back was exposed. We had discussed this at length, and there was an obvious answer, but we both doubted that it would work in the heat of a shield wall battle. During our time at Egbert's Stone, Alfred had sounded out the Lords and put my solution to them, but it had not gone down well. In their minds it was fairly simple; one pushed against the enemy, stabbing, shouting, and slashing if one had the room to wield one's sword. The stronger army pushed the weaker one back until they broke through. End of battle. My idea of the second row in the wall covering those in front with their shields whilst the front row slashed at the legs of the wall was considered revolutionary.

"Well, Torsten, it looks as if we are equally matched, don't you think?" Alfred asked me later that night.

"Yes, but I think their insults are better."

"If it is only their insults, then we will beat them."

The next morning the sun rose in a clear blue sky that dried the dew from the grass and began to heat up the day. Although both armies had retreated the night before, they reformed quickly, and the shouting started all over again. Alfred's men formed a battle line that was six deep in front of a line of archers and I could see the Danes were the same, apart from where they had formed two arrows.

Slowly, the two lines moved forward and the archers from both sides started to fire their arrows. At that range they were ineffective, more of a nuisance than deadly. Then the lines of men clashed together; there was an audible clash as the shields came together, and the shouting increased in intensity. Men were pushing men, trying to hit or stab the man opposite but there was not enough room to swing one's arms. If a man fell down, he was kicked and trampled on before being replaced by the man behind him. And all the time arrows were falling on the melee.

I had never intended to get involved with the battle, but I got drawn in, drawn in when I saw that my countrymen were just about to break through the Wessex line. I ran over, drawing my sword, and entered the fray. I slashed at the Dane as he broke through thinking that he had broken the wall. He defended himself with his shield and then tried to stab me, but I blocked him with mine. Others were pushing him forward and I knew we could not let him breach the line. I called others to help and slowly we pushed him back, but now I was involved and in the middle of a fight.

It was every man for himself, swinging, bludgeoning, defending. I remember being hit on the head and feeling blood running down my face. I didn't feel pain - I was too occupied trying to stay alive - but there was a loud shout from my right, and I could see men moving forward. The man in front of me started to retreat, still swinging his sword, trying to kill me, but going backwards. My eyesight was becoming bleary, and I failed to block one of his strokes, taking the blow on my left arm. Screaming, I moved forward, knowing that if I didn't kill him now, I would be killed. I thought I saw him slightly turn as if to run away and I stabbed at his neck, feeling the blade sink in. I saw the blood spurt out. He dropped his shield, and I was able to finish him off with a stab to the heart.

Exhausted, I sank to the ground, letting those behind me pass and chase the Danes who were now in full retreat, the retreat of a beaten army.

I woke up lying on a pallet filled with fresh bracken, soft and aromatic. My head felt as if it was going to burst and I tried to move my left arm but couldn't.

"The hero awakes." I moved my head towards the voice and made out Harold kneeling and praying at the side of the tent.

"What happened?"

"Don't you remember?"

"No, who won the battle?"

"King Alfred has won back his territory."

"Where am I, and why can't I feel my left arm?"

"You have not been well. You were knocked unconscious in the battle and also suffered a wound to your left arm that got infected. I'm afraid I had to amputate it to stop the infection from spreading."

I looked down at my arm which was heavily bandaged. There was nothing below the elbow but I could feel my fingers, I could clench my fist, I could feel it, but I couldn't see my hand.

"Now, you must rest, you are very weak. I will go and get you some food."

I lay back, and my whole head felt as if it was going to explode. I tried to remember the battle, but nothing would come. The last thing I could remember was talking to Alfred, but that must have been before the fighting began. I shut my eyes.

I could hear voices talking quietly and opened my eyes, Harold was talking to Alfred at the foot of the pallet, but I couldn't make out what they were saying.

"Torsten, you are awake. No, don't try and get up," Alfred said. "You must rest and get better, or I will have to make a very lonely journey to Oxhill."

Harold came around with a bowl, steam wafting from it.

"Come, have a few spoonfuls, it will do you good." He fed me a small mouthful. It tasted rotten, and I tried to cough it up. "No, it will do you good."

I must have fallen asleep again as when I awoke, I could see the sun shining through the material of the tent.

"Good morning, how are you feeling?"

"Shit. Can you tell me what I have missed? I can't remember anything."

"King Alfred won the battle. The Danes turned and fled. Guthrum was captured and I'm afraid Birger was killed in the battle. There was a big treaty conference between King Alfred and Guthrum, and I had to translate for both. At first, Guthrum seemed to think he could still stay in Wessex, but King Alfred would have none of it. He told him that he was nothing, he was beaten, he had to leave and go back to East Anglia and never invade Wessex again. That wasn't all. King Alfred then demanded that Guthrum convert to the Christian faith and be baptised, pray with him, and wear a cross around his neck. Of course, it will mean nothing to him, but he was humiliated."

"Has he left Wessex?"

"Yes, with the tail firmly between his legs."

"That's it, then. It is finally over. Harold, can you get me back to Helga and Oxhill?"

"Not for some time, friend. You are too weak to travel, you must rest and gain strength."

I laid back and closed my eyes.

Chapter 10
Helga Gets a Visit

Alfred, in his normal bipolar mood, was both ecstatic about beating Guthrum and regaining his kingdom and sad about the friends and countrymen lost in the battle. He was particularly sad about the death of Torsten whom he had grown to love over that spring. He had been a person who had sought him out, a person who had converted to his religion, and a person who, in his mind, had very strong beliefs. He had sat with him when he had the time after the battle, prayed for him, and spoken to him. He had never wanted him to get involved in the battle and had understood why he didn't want to, but he would always be grateful that he had since his actions had saved the day. If the Danes had broken through, it could have gone the other way as a line broken never regains its hold. He could have lost.

He was also finding solstice in the quiet, godly ways of the Dane Harold, who had been saved on the island of Lindisfarne by the monks and converted to the true God. It was he who had taught Torsten to speak the Anglo-Saxon dialects. Even now, after Torsten's death, he sought out Harold to pray with him and to talk with him.

"Harold, you must go north to Oxhill to tell Helga and to comfort her," he said one evening after he had spent the day arguing the details of his surrender with Guthrum.

"I think that we should both go, united in God, united in grief, and united in the will to comfort her. She will be facing a hard life bringing up her children on that farm. She will need help farming the land, and she will need to know that although her husband sacrificed his life, she doesn't need to do the same for her family."

They couldn't leave for another two weeks due to Alfred's commitments, and it was a small group that made the visit to Oxhill, consisting of the two of them and ten soldiers to act as guards for the King. Harold was the only one who had been there before and he noticed changes as soon as he rode in through the gate; the courtyard was dirtier, cows that should have been in the field were in the yard, chickens were roaming free, and it generally had the look of being run down.

Helga appeared at the door with her two children clutching at her legs. She looked dishevelled, dirty, and, to Harold's eyes, had lost weight. As soon as she saw him and not Torsten, she let out a cry of anguish and fell onto the doorstep. Harold was the first to react, dismounting and running over to her. He scooped her up and carried her into the house. Alfred followed them in to find Harold trying to console the children. Helga was sitting on the ground, inconsolable.

"You, you're to blame for this, I can tell by your look," she shouted at Alfred, not knowing who he was. "He should have been here looking after us and the farm. Why didn't you let him go? It wasn't his fight."

"Hush, hush Helga, King Alfred is not to blame. He didn't want Torsten to fight. Now, where can I get some food for the children?"

"King Alfred, what was he doing fighting for you? I thought he was fighting for Guthrum," she wailed.

"That's for another time," Alfred said. "I will go and look for some eggs and get one of the men to resurrect the fire."

"Now, now Helga, it is a time to stay strong for the children," Harold said, putting his arm around her shoulder. Then he beckoned the two children over, "Boys, your mother has had a shock and is upset, she will need you both to be strong and to help her."

"Is our father coming back?" the oldest asked.

"No, I'm afraid he won't be coming back."

"He won't be coming back because of these men," she said out of the side of her mouth, leaving her children no doubt where she thought the blame lay.

Harold moved away from the group, leaving them to their grief. He went outside and found Alfred chasing chickens, looking for eggs.

"She doesn't mean it; she is in shock. She will calm down and then we can explain what happened."

"Yes, I know. Where have these buggers hidden their eggs?" he asked no one as he hunted around. The soldiers came to help him and, as Harold walked back into the house, there was a cheer as a find was made.

Even in the short time he had been out of the house, her tears had died down and she was quietly talking to her boys. "Come and pray with us, Brother Harold, see if your God can answer some of our questions."

He knelt with them and was silent, but when Helga looked at him she could see his mouth talking silent words. He stopped and looked at her.

"Lord, please look down on this family and help them in their time of sorrow, help them to make decisions, help them to find themselves again, help them to live and grow."

"Thank you."

Later that evening the house looked cleaner and smelled of cooking, thanks to Harold making up games for the boys that involved sweeping and cleaning, washing, and drying. Some chickens had been caught and slaughtered, flour had been found, and bread was baking. This job had not been given to Alfred!

It was not until the next morning that they were able to sit Helga down and tell her the full story. She was still in grief but was able to listen to them, understand what they were saying, and even ask questions. Harold offered to stay with her until she got her feet under the table again, to help her with the farm and to see if she was able to carry on living there. Alfred and his guards were keen to get going as soon as possible. Having fought to get his country back, he had many plans that he wanted to put into place and felt that he was wasting his time there.

Over the next few weeks, Harold worked tirelessly on the farm and also got to know some of the neighbouring farmers in the community that was named Oxhill. It appeared that Torsten was liked and respected, but people were weary of his Danish background and hadn't warmed to Helga who only spoke a few words of their tongue. Slowly, he got the farmyard tidied up and the cattle back into the fields and eating the summer grass, but it was too late to start planting any of the other fields.

"Harold, what are my chances of surviving here in Oxhill?" Helga asked one evening.

"It is not going to be easy. For the next year, you will have to buy all of your food as none has been planted. It will be hard work for you, physical hard work."

"I don't know if I want to do that without Torsten. I might be better back in Ribe with my family."

"I can't help you with that decision."

"No, you can't."

"Did Torsten leave you any plunder?"

"Yes, but I don't know where he hid it, it could be anywhere."

"He didn't tell you?"

"No, he always said that I shouldn't worry about it."

He stayed there all summer helping her to sell the stock, mainly to local farmers, and to pack up her belongings before escorting her and the family back across East Anglia to Ipswich.

EPILOGUE

The Present Time
Church Farm, Oxhill

I was sitting in the kitchen with my wife, Sandy, notepads, and pencils at the ready; we were going through plans for our fifteenth wedding anniversary, crossing off things we had completed and seeing what was left to do. The idea was to have a barbecue in the garden. We were getting The Peacock to organise it (ticked off) and getting a marque to seat the fifty people (ticked off). Invites were sent, and the seating plan done (both ticked). The drink to be ordered was highlighted with my name against it, and flowers were also highlighted with Sandy's name. The entertainment was not marked with anything, and we had to decide on that tonight or we weren't going to get anything booked in time. Decorations for the marque (ticked off), crockery, cutlery and glassware were blank and not allocated. Sandy, being the accountant she was, was entering all of the items into a spreadsheet.

"So, entertainment. I'm not keen on that folk group from Banbury, I thought they were a bit naff," I put forward.

"Yes, but they were good, and we have a big range of ages coming."

"What about, what was his name? Barry was it? From Kineton, the guitarist?"

"Not if we are dancing in the evening. You can't have a strummer who sings a bit if people are dancing."

"People dance to Ed Sheeran, not that we could afford him."

"Geoff, this is our anniversary, not Glastonbury. I know we haven't spoken to him, but do you remember that DJ from Kanen and Tom's wedding last summer? He was good, and I have his card somewhere."

"I'm not sure about a DJ, you know I like live music. What about that band from Stratford that did all the 80s and 90s music?"

"The Travellers, yes, they were OK, but a bit expensive."

We eventually finished the planning session and were pleasantly surprised that there was not that much we still had to do. Things were moving from one side of the spreadsheet to the other. The one thing that we couldn't organise was the weather, but we were used to that and knew how to make contingency plans.

The day arrived and the weather gods decided to play ball which meant that Greg and I could get all the livestock taken care of early with the help of our youngest, Sean, scampering around in his dumper truck. The marque had been erected the day before, leaving that morning's job of filling it with tables and chairs that had been stored in one of the barns. Another job for Sean after he had thoroughly washed the dumper. The two large barbecues also turned up early and had to be lit as soon as they arrived so that the two lambs could be put on the rotisserie. Things were definitely taking shape. Sandy had decorated the marque before the caterers arrived to dress the tables and we even had time to have some lunch sitting at a table outside of it.

People started to arrive mid-afternoon, and Micky was kept busy directing traffic in the Home Field making sure the cars were correctly parked. I don't know where the time went. One minute I was greeting people and the next we were sitting down and eating. Three hours had disappeared, and it was nearly time for me to stand up and thank everyone for coming.

It wasn't until later in the evening that I got to have a quiet drink with Andy.

"Thank you for today, you must be delighted with the way it has gone."

"Yes, but that's more down to Sandy than me, I just did what I was told."

"That lamb was spectacular. I assume they were yours?"

"Yes, you should have seen the paperwork that it took. It is OK to butcher a lamb and eat it, but it can only be eaten by the farmer's immediate family if they are living on the farm. So, it had to be slaughtered and butchered off site, then the department had to sign it off before I could store it in their deep freeze, and it had to be signed off when it was unfrozen. Never again."

"That sounds crazy. Talking about farms, did those barren spots go away after they were dug?"

"Yes and no. They all went apart from one."

"Let me guess, the one nearest the wood and the farthest from the road."

"Yes, why did you say it would be that one?"

"I don't think we ever dug it. We got so tied up with digging the villa that I think we forgot about it. I was thinking about it a couple of weeks ago."

"It was never dug but it had all the surveys done on it and showed up nothing."

"Oh yes, it was surveyed very early on and showed nothing."

"You know what I'm going to say, Andy, don't you?"

"No, you're not thinking of getting your spade out are you?"

I don't know if it was due to the alcohol I had had that afternoon, or secretly I had always felt slightly cheated that the only thing that had been found was the floor map of a Roman villa. I had always thought there was more in the field. I had dreamt of finding something more than the World War II ammunition box.

"You're not doing anything tomorrow, are you? We could always take the tractor with the digger arm up there. It wouldn't take long."

"You are kidding, aren't you?"

"No, we are only digging a hole, just a hole." He looked at me to see how serious I was and burst out laughing.

"Just a hole."

The next day, after we had cleared up the garden and with slightly heavy heads, I drove the tractor up to the field while

Andy, along with Sean, followed me up in the van. I opened the gate and drove through, bumping across what had been a field of rape and around the area that was fenced off but contained the villa.

"Should I just scrape away the surface first?" I asked Andy.

"Yes, I'm not going to be too particular, unless we come across something. Scrape away the first six inches, and let's have a look."

I positioned the tractor, put down the stabilisers and started to move the digging arm with the levers, first extending it until the bucket was at the far side of the barren area, then going down and bringing it back towards me. I was not as good with the digger arm as those who used it every day, but I considered myself competent. Again, the arm went out and I pulled it back, bringing about three inches of topsoil. I cleared a square that was about three yards on each side and Andy stepped into it to have a look.

"Nothing, take it down a foot and I will have another look," he called up.

We went down another foot, and then another, but still nothing. We went down five feet and still nothing, but Andy did spend more time and was scraping the surface with his trowel.

"Can you see something?" I called out.

"No, but the colour of the soil is changing slightly. Just go down six inches this time."

I was on my third go when I felt a slight resistance and a noise.

"Stop, stop," Andy shouted and jumped in. He started to scrape away the soil where the digger had stopped. Then he stopped and vertically used his trowel, and I could clearly hear him hit something.

"There is something down here and it's metal."

I climbed down from the tractor and into the hole. I knew I would not be allowed near whatever we had found, I might be good with a digger, but the archaeologists thought me reckless with a trowel. Slowly he started to clear away the soil.

"That's weird, it's a metal object, but it seems to be covered in sacking." He carried on clearing the top and sat back on his haunches, "Have you got a tape measure?"

"Yes, in the cab." I jumped out, collected it from the toolbox, and tossed it to Andy.

"It's a B167, what the hell is one of those doing buried here?"

"A B167, what the hell is that?"

"It's a metal ammunition box used by the US Army in the Second World War."

"Not another one."

"No, this is different, these were used for mortars whereas the other one was for bullets. If I'm right, these should be nine inches across, twenty-one and a half inches long and nine inches deep."

"How do you know that?"

"I've worked on World War Two sites before."

"And you think there is only one of them?"

"Yes, I can feel the edge. Geoff, get me the spade from the van and I will try and dig this out."

Andy very carefully dug around the box, exposing more and more of it. Slowly, the hinges appeared on one side and the latches on the other.

"Can't we open it now? If it's empty it will save us digging it all out."

"Not a bad idea. Do you want to do the deed?"

I couldn't wait. I cleared the sacking off the top and tried to pull the clasps open, but they wouldn't move. I picked up the trowel and wedged it underneath. Suddenly, it gave, and I moved on to the other. I looked over to Andy and then to Sean before I tried to open the lid. It wouldn't budge so I pulled a can of WD40 from my belt pouch, spraying the hinges. I tried again and there was movement and a creaky groan as it let me get my fingers under the rim. I went down, putting both of my hands under the rim, bent my knees, pushed up with my legs and pulled with my arms. Suddenly, it all gave way. I fell backwards, still holding the lid.

I got up to see Andy and Sean bent over, looking into the box. I joined them. There was what appeared to be a letter on top of more sacking. Andy picked it up and put it to one side. I pulled back the sacking.

It was as if a torch was shining in my eyes. All I could see was gold. Gold ingots. I reached in and touched it. It was cold, yet it seemed to radiate heat. I pulled one out. It was heavier than I expected.

"Gold. It is gold, isn't it?" I said, in a daze.

"It looks like it, but where has it come from?" I could hear the tremble in Andy's voice.

"I don't know, I don't care. It is gold buried on my land. Gold."

Andy picked up the letter and started to read it whilst I pulled out the ingots and piled them on the grass, counting as I went. Twenty-eight.

Andy read the letter.

My Dear Cousin Marco,

If you are reading this, then you have found your escape from poverty. I couldn't have believed that when I came to Oxhill I would find my cousin, a captive, a prisoner of war, made to work on a farm run by an idiot who thought he was so clever.

You are the clever one. We did it, we found the gold.

When you get back to Italy, write to me and I will fly over to see you and bring my brother. This family will be stronger together than apart. Together, with the gold, we can build something, all of the cousins together.

I can see it now, a family business, a business in Italy as well as in the USA, a pizza business with shops on the corner of every street, in every city throughout the world. Caruso will be the place to go, the place to eat, the place to hang out.

I'm so sorry I can't celebrate your find with you but I needed to get my gold home and working for me, I just hope you do the same. Marco, I really appreciated the time we were allowed to spend together. It has been a greater gift than the gold to have found you and been able talk to you about our fathers, our mothers, and our memories.

So long, arrivederci,
Pete.

Main Characters

Present Time

Church Farm

Geoff Knight	In my mid-40s, I am the lucky man to be the tenant farmer of Church Farm in Oxhill, a six hundred acre farm that combines both arable and pastoral. I have been here for two years, and I am forever learning. My farming life started at Cirencester Agricultural Collage, now known as the Royal Agricultural University, and progressed through working on various farms in South Warwickshire. Now having my own farm, I am keen to know everything about it, its history, how it works, and why it works.
Sandy Knight	My wife and the strength behind our family. We met when I was farming close to Oxhill, and she was doing her accountancy exams. Still an accountant, she brings an order to the farm planning that I never could. A great wife and mum to our two children.

Michael (Micky) Knight	Our oldest son. Aged 12 and a sportsman rather than a farmer. He is never happier than when he has got a ball in his hand and is either kicking it or hitting it.
Sean Knight	Two years younger than his older brother, Sean couldn't be more different. I think he will become a petrolhead and a farmer. He is never happier than when he is driving the dumper truck around the farm and looking after the animals.
Greg Peebles	He came with the farm; he has worked on it since he left school. Probably ten years older than me, he brings experience and a wealth of knowledge on stockmanship. A rugby man who played for Stratford RFC, Micky looks up to him as a mentor in an area where I can't compete.
Sam McNally	The previous leaseholder of Church Farm, now retired to the South Coast.

Oxhill Village

Kevin Coleman	Aged 23, lives with his parents in the village and works at The Peacock. He is doing a catering course at Banbury and Bicester College.

| Major John Harker | Aged 87, a retired Army Major who moved to the village just before the Second World War as a teenager. A big supporter of village life. |
| Dom Trethewey | Aged 47, farms between Whatcote and Idlicote. Has acted as some kind of mentor to Geoff and is contracted to harvest his rape seed crop. |

Archaeologists

Andy Eames	Aged 45, an archaeologist friend from college of Geoff's. Also, his Best Man and Godfather to Michael.
Professor Paul Gil	Aged 50, a university lecturer in archaeology, in charge of collating and interpreting the geophysical survey results.
Max Nokes	Aged 32, works with Paul Gil, and does the geophysical surveys.
Dave Fallon	Aged 48, a professional archaeologist who specialises in interpreting soil layers and also heads up the field walking team.
Charlotte Cummins	Aged 35, not a professional archaeologist but part of the Tysoe team. Is going out with Max Nokes. Her interests are local history, in particular the English Civil War.
Jonathan Ellingworth	Aged 20, the youngest in the team. Is studying archaeology under Paul Gil at Oxford.

| Brian Mansfield | Aged 21, also studying archaeology under Paul Gil. |

World War II

Americans

| Major Pete Caruso | Aged 28, born in New York of Italian extraction, joined the USAAC in 1935 and flew as a fighter pilot. He was shot down when serving in Pearl Harbour in 1941. He had a superb war record flying the De Havilland DH.98 Mosquito in 93-night raids until being moved on to flying the Fairchild 24 in clandestine flights dropping agents behind enemy lines after the Normandy landings. |

| Captain Antonio Caruso | Aged 26, Pete's younger brother, joined the Army after Pearl Harbour and, after basic training, progressed through the ranks in the Transportation Corp to his current rank. He landed in the second wave during the Normandy Landings before being transferred to Lyon. |

| Airman Tommy Hughes | Aged 25, a mechanic for the USAAF, based at Barford St. John, but was in charge of Major Pete Caruso's plane when it was at Oxhill. |

| Technical Sergeant Teddy Frost | Aged 32, the USAAC was his life after he joined up in 1931, aged 18. He went on to specialise in radio communication. |

| Colonel John Polman | Aged 35, a career airman and friend of Pete's, but also his CO. |

Private Alun Witty (Funny Boy)	Aged 28, a driver in the Transport Unit under Captain Antonio Caruso. Landed in Normandy with him.
Private Julian McLeary (Jules)	Aged 31, a driver in the Transport Unit under Captain Antonio Caruso. Landed in Normandy with him.
Private Donald Murdoch (McD)	Aged 29, a driver in the Transport Unit under Captain Antonio Caruso. Landed in Normandy with him.
Private Roger Anderson (Rog)	Aged 32, a member of the Transport Unit under Captain Antonio Caruso. Landed in Normandy with him.
First Officer Richard Cashmore (Money)	Aged 33, second in command within the Transport Unit. A medic. Landed in Normandy with the Company.
Private James Bohan (Jake)	Aged 21, a member of the Transport Unit under Captain Antonio Caruso. Landed in Normandy with him.
Private Peter Clugston (Pete)	Aged 25, a member of the Transport Unit under Captain Antonio Caruso. Landed in Normandy with him.
Private Steve Prosser (Pro)	Aged 19, the youngest member of the company. He joined it in Paris having transferred from an infantry regiment where he was renowned as a point man.

Italians

Major Marco Caruso	Aged 35, a career Army Officer in the Italian Army. Captured in the first Battle of Alamein in July 1942 and interned at Ettington POW Camp, worked as a 'Co-operator' after the Italian surrender in May 1945 in Oxhill.

Oxhill Village

Mrs Charlotte Holland	Aged 44, widowed in 1940 when her husband was killed during the retreat to Dunkirk. A keen horsewoman who hunted before the war, she then went to work for the War Office.
Frank Brooks	Aged 42, a former merchant sailor, invalided out after being torpedoed in 1943, living with his sister and helping her run The Peacock.
Deborah Hare	Aged 30, married to Kevin, who was on Active service in Northern France. Debs was born in the village and lived there all of her life. At the time of this story, she was running the pub on her own after her husband received his call-up, but was finding it hard.

Bill Ward	Aged 64, he took over the village store after his father died in 1921. The only time he spent out of the village was when he volunteered to fight in WW I, where he served in the trenches in Northern France. Didn't spend too much time in the shop – spent more time tending his smallholding, growing vegetables.
Kathy Ward	Aged 60, ran the village store. Both Kathy and her husband were Oxhill through and throughs. She was at the centre of it, the provider of news about what's going on.
Tom McNally	Aged 25, took over farming Church Farm from his father in 1939 when he died suddenly. Was exempted from military service.
Clare McNally	Aged 23, a keen rider and looked up to Charlotte Holland as a mentor and friend.
David Hatch	Aged 62, he farmed Brooklands Farm using Italian POWs to pick his crop of apples.

Civil Servants

Adrian Steel	Attached to the War Office, he was invalided out of the Army having been wounded in the retreat from the beachhead at Dunkirk.
Dermot Dunne	Attached to the Foreign Office.
Frederic Marland	Attached to the Foreign Office.

The Templars

Historical Characters

Jacques de Molay	The 23rd and last Grand Master of the Knights Templar, he led the order from 1292 until it was dissolved by an order from Pope Clement V in 1312. He died, burnt at the stake, in March 1314 under the orders of King Philip IV of France.
King Philip IV of France	Born in 1268, he was King of France between 1285 and 1314. Known as Philip the Fair, he was a warrior king who was influential in European affairs but could not afford all the wars he started and was in debt to the Templars.
Guillaume de Nogaret	Born in 1260, he was a senior councillor, or civil servant, to King Philip IV, remembered for two things that became connected. The conflict between Pope Boniface VIII and the French King in which the King and Nogaret were excommunicated but with the death of the Pope they gained absolution from Pope Benedict XI and on his death, they were behind the appointment of Pope Clement V, a French man, and the move of the Papacy to Avignon. He was instrumental in the imprisonment of all Knights Templars on Friday, October 13, 1307. Died April 13, 1313.

Gerard de Villiers	One of many of the de Villiers family to have joined the Knights Templars, he rose to become Preceptor of France, a role he held when the arrests of October 13th, 1307, took place. He is rumoured to have escaped Paris on the previous night with some of the Paris Treasury in hay carts and headed for Switzerland.
Hugues de Pairaud	Held the role of Visitor of the Temple in 1307, he was found guilty and sentenced to life imprisonment on March 18th, 1314. he was spared being burnt at the stake due to accepting his sentence in silence.
Geoffroy de Gonneville	Born c 1260, he was Preceptor of Aquitaine and Poitou. He was arrested on October 13th, 1307, and, according to some theories, burnt at the stake along with Jacques de Molay in March 1314.
Sir Guillaume de la More	The Master of the Knights Templar of England, he was arrested on January 10th, 1308, and held in the Tower of London until his trial in October 1309. He died in the Tower on December 20th, 1312, having never confessed to the charges held against him.
William de Periton	Lord of the Manor of Oxhill between 1306 and 1344.

Oxhill

Sir Guillaume de Stowe	Born in 1242, he was the Templar Commander of the Oxhill Preceptory, he had fought alongside Jacques de Molay at the fall of Acre in 1291. An old man, he spent most of his time in prayer.
Sir Robert le Jay	Born in 1250, he was the younger brother of Sir Brian le Jay, a former Knights Templar Grand Master of England who was killed in the Battle of Falkirk in 1298.
Sir Alain Heath	Born in 1277, he was knighted before the Battle of Falkirk in 1298. He would have liked to be part of another crusade to free Palestine from the Mamluk rule.
Sir Gui de la Granville	Born in 1277, he was knighted before the Battle of Falkirk in 1298. A more pragmatic Templar who believed that the movement would change.
Sergeant Simon Amblard	Born in 1285, a sergeant at the Oxhill Preceptory.

London

Sir Henry de Faverham	He was used by Guillaume de la More, Preceptor of England, to take messages to Oxhill on two occasions.

Paris

Hugh de Montlaur	Attached to the Paris Preceptory, he was originally from Poitiers. He was made the leader of the group of Templars that fled Paris on the night before the arrests.
Jean de la Roche	Attached to the Paris Preceptory, he was a young and inexperienced Templar.
Arnold de Caned	Attached to the Paris Preceptory, a more experienced Templar who had been to Palestine.
Stephen Cadell	Attached to the Paris Preceptory. A native of Carcassonne, he lead the ships going to Spain.
Simon de Pontóns	Travelled with Jacques de Molay from Cyprus to France.

Roman Times

Historical

Emperor Severus Alexander	Roman Emperor from 222AD to 235AD, succeeded his cousin aged 13 to become the youngest emperor in Roman history. His mother influenced him to improve the morals of the people, and he was keen for his soldiers' welfare, giving them the right to name anyone as their successor.

Oxhill

| Legate Antonius Bassius | I was once the Legate of the Third Region of Brittania, now retired. My successor granted me a substantial estate based around a hillock that I named Oxhill. It is here that I buried my legacy; gold discovered by my ancient relation in Carthaginia. |

| Valentina Bassius | My wife and my love. I first met her in Corinium, a local girl but a girl that had talent in art, in drawing, in design. For her it was a great change to move to Oxhill and away from her roots, but her designs made the villa. |

| Legionnaire Lucius | Lucius became my right-hand man, the man I could depend on, the man who got things done. I had hired him when he was leaving the army and he could have taken the land offer to him. He was a soldier who had risen up through the ranks, a local who had taken the oath to fight for Rome, an officer and just my best friend. |

Corinium

| Legate Titus Decimus | Bassius' successor as the Legate of the Third Region. By reputation a good commander and a good administrator. Showed Bassius the land at Oxhill. |

Legionnaire Crassus	A senior Legionnaire from Corinium whom Bassius had considered recommending to Rome as his successor, but never trusted him. The man who took unjust and incorrect accusations about Bassius to Rome.

The English Civil War

Historical

King Charles I	The King of England from 27th March 1625 until his execution on 30th January 1649. He quarrelled with Parliament throughout his reign as they sought to cut back on his royal prerogative, which resulted in his entering Parliament on 4th January 1642 to arrest five Members charged with high treason, only to find that "the birds have flown". The Battle of Edgehill, 23rd October 1642, was the first pitched battle of the civil war. He was captured after defeat at the Battle of Naseby on 14th June 1645 and convicted of high treason at his trial which started in January 1649. He was executed at the end of that month.

Sir John Byron, 1st Baron Byron	Born in 1600, he became an MP for the town of Nottingham and later for the county. In December 1641, King Charles I made him Lieutenant of the Tower of London, but he resigned in 1642 at the behest of the House of Commons. He fought at Powick Bridge and commanded his own regiment of horse at the Battle of Edgehill. He took only a small part in the second English Civil War and was one of the seven persons barred by Parliament from all pardons in 1648. He died abroad in attendance on the Royal Family.
Robert Devereaux, 3rd Earl of Essex	Born on 11th January 1591, a parliamentarian and soldier. He became the first Captain-General and Chief Commander of the Parliamentarian Army but couldn't score a decisive blow against King Charles I. Eventually overshadowed by Oliver Cromwell and Thomas Fairfax. He died in 1646 - without an heir - while hunting in Windsor Forest.
Prince Rupert of the Rhine	Born on 17 December 1619. He had a varied military career but was one of the few who had military experience prior to the English Civil War, fighting alongside the Dutch in the Eight Years War and against the Holy Roman Emperor in Germany. Aged 23 he was given command of the Royalist Cavalry until the siege of Bristol in September 1645, after which he was banished from England only to return as a senior Naval Officer. He died in London from a bout of pleurisy in November 1682.

Fictional

Major Charles
Drinkwater

Born at the turn of the century, he was the second son of a merchant sea captain. His elder brother inherited the family business. He joined King Charles I's army and gained experience fighting with the Dutch in the Eight Years War, where he met Sir John Byron. Their relationship was cemented while Sir John was Lieutenant of the Tower of London who had dealings with his father. He was promoted by King Charles I to Major prior to the Battle of Edgehill.

The Vikings – Great Heathen Army

Historical

King Alfred

Also known as Alfred the Great, he was born in 849. Became King of the West Saxons in 871 and, in 886 King of the Anglo Saxons until he died in 899. The early part of his reign was dominated by fighting the Viking invasion and it is thought that he paid them in silver to leave. During the Great Heathen Army invasion of 877, he was defeated at Chippenham but defeated Guthrum at the Battle of Edington and as part of the Treaty of Wedmore the Viking left Wessex. He was known as an administrator who brought in a tax system to help fund his army and the Burghal system to defend his kingdom. He died on 26th October 899.

Guthrum

Born about 835, he was one of the leaders of the Great Heathen Army. He first conquered East Anglia, and later Mercia. In 878 he made a surprise attack on King Alfred at Chippenham, defeating him and driving him to hide in the wetlands of Somerset. He was subsequently defeated at the Battle of Edington and was forced to convert and be baptised and, more importantly, to retreat to East Anglia. He is thought to have died in 890.

Fictional

Torsten

I am sorry but I don't know, in your years, when I was born, except to say that it was two years after my brother. Those two years meant I had no future in Ribe as my brother would inherit the farm. I joined Guthrum's ships that sailed to East Anglia, Ipswich and became friendly with his son Birger. He made me learn their language and I helped Guthrum in his subsequent negotiations; I fought, looted, and received my share of silver from treaties. I became interested in Roman buildings because they were so superior to ours and found a villa in Oxhill which I made home and was where I buried my treasure.

Helga

My wife, my love, my confidante. She joined me at Oxhill, and we had two sons. She was the loveliest woman you could meet, but it was best not to get on the wrong side of her as she would fight her side of an argument.

Birger   The son of Guthrum. I suppose he was a bit older than me and took me under his wing. He was a warrior and took after his father, but I think he was more intelligent and prepared to take on new ideas and thoughts.

Olav   Olav was with me from the start and sat to my right on the rowing bench when we left Ribe. He was with me when I set up my first arrow of men.

Megs   Likewise, Megs was with me from the start.

Odin   He was older than me and had sailed with my brother, knew the ropes, and became a mentor to me when we first landed.

Harold   A Dane who was shipwrecked off the island of Lindisfarne and taken in by the monks. He learned their language, converted to their faith, and later became attached to the church in Ipswich. It was Harold who taught me so much, not just the language, but faith, belief, and humility. It was because of him that I became the man I did.